tiger's destiny

COLLEEN HOUCK

HODDER

First published in Great Britain in 2012 by Hodder & Stoughton
An Hachette UK company
First published in America in 2012 by Sterling Publishing Co., Inc.

1

A CIP catalogue record for this title is available from the British Library

Paperback ISBN 978 1 444 75752 1
eBook ISBN 978 1 444 75754 5

Printed and bound by CPI Group (UK) Ltd, Croydon, CR0 4YY

Hodder & Stoughton policy is to use papers that are natural, renewable
and recyclable products and made from wood grown in sustainable
forests. The logging and manufacturing processes are expected to
conform to the environmental regulations of the country of origin.

Hodder & Stoughton Ltd
338 Euston Road
London NW1 3BH

www.hodder.co.uk

. . . . ling
. . . . and
. . . . al.'
ush

'Epic, grand adventure rolled into a sweeping love story . . .'
Sophie Jordan, author of *Firelight*

'Every now and again there comes a book that makes me wish I could read things more slowly so that I could savour every page . . . within a couple of chapters I felt like I had fallen inside the book, I was so swept up in the story . . . Houck weaves mythology into the plot seamlessly.'

junipersjungle.com

'An epic love triangle that kept me eagerly turning the pages!'
Alexandra Monir, author of *Timeless*

'WOW! This book. *Tiger's Curse* by Colleen Houck is so entirely wonderful – filled with so much emotion, great characters, action, adventure.'

flutteringbutterflies.com

'If you are a fan of Stephenie Meyer or Amy Plum, you will love Colleen Houck!'

thepewterwolf.blogspot.com

'I was caught up, hypnotized. I read this novel in a matter of hours and can't wait for the next one.'

bookgirlsbooknookblog.blogspot.com

The Tiger Saga

Tiger's Curse
Tiger's Quest
Tiger's Voyage

About the author

Formerly a student at the University of Arizona, Colleen Houck has worked as a nationally certified American Sign Language interpreter for seventeen years. Her first book, *Tiger's Curse* has already received literary praise and digital success. Her self-published eBook claimed the no.1 spot on Kindle's children's bestseller list for seven weeks. *Tiger's Destiny* is her fourth book in the epic fantasy-romance series. She lives in Salem, Oregon, with her husband and a white stuffed tiger.

For my brother Jared and his wife, Suki,
who provide fan support, tech support
battle-scene support, moral support,
and, most important,
keeping-it-fun support

contents

tiger's destiny

rising phoenix

By Colleen Houck

Does Rising Phoenix know his fate?
He's born, grows strong, and learns to fly.
He builds a nest and seeks a mate,
He sleeps and thirsts and hunts the sky.

Does he know his future blazes?
A quelling flame will take his life?
When purging heat the pyre raises,
Consuming all his earthly strife?

Does stinging dread seep through his breast?
Does he regret past choices made?
Does heartbreak stir his feather'd crest?
Does he perceive the price he's paid?

Exquisite once, his body burns
As he cries out in pain and fear.
Charred and black his feathers turn,
Conceding life, he sheds a tear.

From death so dire, another soul
Emerges new to take his place.
With destiny and purpose whole
A glorious dawn begins apace!

Does Rising Phoenix thank his sire
For embers black that gave him birth?
Does he too know his fate is fire?
Can he enjoy his time on Earth?

space and time

All at once, they were lost, swirling through the inky black whirlwind of time. Seconds passed. Eons passed. Molecules shifted and stirred. Then, a light pierced the cosmic dust and just as suddenly, a wave of understanding washed over him.

Through trial and error, he had learned how to control the vortex and skip through the years. If he ran too fast, he entered an unknown future. If he stepped back in haste, the world ceased to exist. Time required a delicate hand, an exacting touch. At first he bounced roughly through millennia, like a smooth stone skipping on a lake. But soon he moved in a dance with the cosmos, practicing the steps that would take him to the places he needed to see.

He scanned the centuries as if they were books in a library. When he was finished, he knew his place in the universe and how to best serve those he loved.

Sensing she was ready, he smiled and squeezed her hand. Then he gathered her close and shifted them between the stars, moving them to the beginning of the end and the end that would lead to a beginning.

pursued

ocking on the waves of the ocean, I dreamt I was swimming with a great dragon who winked at me. As he moved past me with a flick of his tail, my body jostled. I moaned and struggled as rough hands wrenched my limbs. The drone of an engine replaced the sound of the waves, and my dreams shifted. Suddenly, I was in a forest and I could clearly hear the steady thunder of tiger paws against jungle leaves running toward me.

Nightmares began after that. Sharks in the water, pirates on the *Deschen*, being captured by Lokesh's men.

A voice whispered urgently in the distance, *Wake up, Kelsey.*

Dizzily, I cracked open my eyes. I was lying on a four poster bed. *It was all just a terrible dream*, I thought gratefully.

The setting sun poured its waning light through the window above the bed. The window had thick glass and bars running across it, preventing anyone from getting in . . . or out.

"No!" I shouted to the empty room. It wasn't a dream at all. I tried to remember everything. I had gone on three quests to free Ren and his brother, Kishan, from the Tiger's Curse. We only had one more gift to find for the goddess Durga in order to break the spell. We were on a ship, and there had been a battle with Lokesh. That much I knew. Then three tiny pricks (tranquilizer darts?), a motorboat . . . placing Fanindra and the amulet into the water, and then blackness.

I was locked in a strange bedroom, a prisoner in a cage. I raced to the door and pulled uselessly at the knob. Focusing my inner energy, I lifted my arm to blast the lock open but nothing happened. Confused, my hand flew to my throat to touch the goddess Durga's Black Pearl Necklace.

How did I lose my fire power? Where am I? Where are my tigers, Ren and Kishan? Did Fanindra find them? What happened to Mr. Kadam and Nilima? Are they on their way to rescue me? How am I going to get out of here?

I tried to take stock of the situation. I had the Pearl Necklace, and the Divine Scarf was still threaded through the belt loops of my jeans, but Durga's bow and arrows and the Golden Fruit of India were nowhere in sight. Stifling a bitter laugh, I realized that I could make all the water and fabric I wanted with all that remained of Durga's gifts, as if that was going to help me.

I casually felt between my fingers for the small tracking device Mr. Kadam had painfully implanted. It was still there, which meant there was a chance the cavalry could come rushing in to save me. It was a small chance, but it was all I had.

My head hurt, and my mouth felt like it was full of cotton. I tried to swallow and ended up coughing, which made me feel even worse.

Get a grip, Kelsey Hayes! I thought and forced myself to try to make sense of my surroundings. Through the window, there were trees and snow, and I was at least three stories up. I thought I could make out some mountains but there was no way to figure out where I was being held.

My stomach heaved and I lunged for the bathroom. After rinsing out my mouth, I stared at my reflection. A crumpled, haggard, frightened woman looked back at me. *What happened to the girl from Oregon?*

Just then, a silky voice broke through my thoughts. I froze. It was my captor, Lokesh.

"Please dress for an early dinner, my dear. As you can see, there is no escape, and I have confiscated your weapons. It's time we meet again. I have a proposal to make to you, Kelsey Hayes. I believe that it is time for you to embrace your destiny."

My insides lurched again as I contemplated what kind of destiny Lokesh had in mind for me. I couldn't see any cameras or speakers in the room, but I knew I was being watched. Strangely, I felt detached from my situation. The cold fear I'd experienced when facing Lokesh in each vision had been replaced with shaky determination.

I considered my options. First, I needed to get out of this room and map out possible escape routes. This predicament could only end in one of four ways: I'd escape on my own (possible); Ren and Kishan would rescue me; I'd die (definitely not my first choice); or I'd end up being the kept woman of a psychopath, which didn't sound like much fun either. I also needed to recover the Fruit and my bow and arrows. Durga had warned me that if her weapons fell into the wrong hands the results would be devastating. I bit my lip and hoped I wouldn't have to choose between saving myself or the weapons.

If getting out of this room means having dinner with the devil, so be it. For now I'll play his game, but if I'm going to go down, I'm going to go down fighting.

Instinctually, I knew that playing a damsel in distress wouldn't work. To beat Lokesh at his own game, I'd have to become something I wasn't—a woman who was strong, beautiful, powerful, and self-assured.

After perusing the closet and finding only a form-fitting sheath with a plunging neckline, I decided to take a calculated risk. I asked the Scarf to create me new clothes in the quietest way possible and instructed it not to do any of its kaleidoscope color changes.

Pulling the new outfit from the closet, I marveled at its detail. The Scarf had created a glamorous *lehenga* in gold and cobalt blue. The short-sleeved jacquard top cinched my waist, and the tight, long-skirted *lehenga* hugged my curves. Wearing Ren's and Kishan's colors gave me a dose of much-needed courage, and I thought the fancy dress would help me act the part I intended to play. The Scarf had even made me a pair of sapphire-like dangling earrings from a lightweight fabric.

Just as I finished dressing, a tall, lean, and dangerous-looking servant opened my bedroom door. I begged him to let me go, but he shook his head and replied something unintelligible in Hindi. I stuffed the Scarf up my sleeve, tried to recall the few Hindi words I knew, and repeated my plea for help, "*Trahi!*" But the man just led me down a hall lined with more barred windows, thick carpeting, and paneled walls.

Next, we walked through a series of locked doors, each guarded by a sentry. As another door slammed shut and locked behind me, I had the sudden recollection that this was how Ren's cage at the circus had been set up—doors within doors to protect the humans from the tiger. I quickly made a mental note: *Escaping on my own will be difficult if not impossible. But, on the plus side, Lokesh believes that he needs a high level of security to contain me. Maybe there's a way to use that against him somehow.*

The last door opened into a dining room where a table had been set for two. The servant pulled out a chair and gestured that I should sit before he quietly left the room. I toyed with my butter knife as I waited. My stomach twisted with nerves, and I wondered how I'd be able to face Lokesh alone. On our previous quests to break the Tiger's Curse, I'd battled a Kraken and a megashark. But somehow those beasts didn't seem quite as dangerous as the evil I was now up against, the monster that had turned my two Indian princes into tigers more than three centuries ago.

"How nice of you to accept my invitation to dinner," Lokesh said, suddenly appearing in the seat across from me.

He looked different from the last time I saw him. Younger. Though I still recognized the black malice swirling behind his black eyes, I was able to pull myself together. Lokesh picked up my hand and kissed it roughly.

"It's not like I was given a choice," I replied.

"Yes." He smiled and squeezed my hand just a bit too hard. "I didn't give you a choice of clothing either," he continued, "and yet, here you are, dressed in a different garment. Might I inquire as to where you obtained it?"

In one smooth motion, I covered my knife with my dinner napkin, scooped it onto my lap, and slid the utensil carefully into my pocket. Hoping he hadn't noticed, I remarked derisively, "When you tell me where *your* power comes from, I'll be happy to show you how to create a wardrobe from the air." A new surge of courage ran through me now that I finally had a weapon of sorts.

To my surprise, Lokesh laughed. "How delightful it is to be around a woman with spirit. I think I shall be tolerant of you, *for now*. But don't test my patience."

His smile turned into a leer. Up close, Lokesh looked more Asian than Indian. His dark hair was cut short, parted on the side, and smoothed to the nape of his neck—quite unlike Ren, whose hair always fell into his blue eyes.

The sorcerer moved with tight control, keeping his shoulders and back stiff. He was more muscular and handsome than before, even striking. But I knew the madman lurked beneath, and his features still carried an undercurrent of darkness.

Food was brought and our plates were quickly filled with spicy Indian selections. The servants were efficient and utterly silent. I picked at my meal, struggling to find my appetite.

"Did you use sorcery to look younger?" I asked cautiously.

His black eyes darkened but then he smiled. "Yes, do you find me handsome? Does it make you more comfortable to see me closer to your own age?"

Strangely, it did.

I shrugged. "I'd be uncomfortable no matter how you looked. Why do you care anyway? I'm surprised you don't have me chained in the basement preparing to drive screws through my thumbs."

A crackle of blue light caught my attention, and I looked up. But if it had been there before, it was gone now. Lokesh frowned and rubbed his fingers.

"Would you prefer to be chained in the basement?" Lokesh asked casually, teasing in a disturbingly lecherous way.

"No, I'm just curious. Why am I getting the special treatment?"

"You get the *special treatment* because you are special, Kelsey. As you demonstrated tonight, you have powers of your own, and I'd prefer not to stifle them." He clucked with disappointment. "It would seem that you don't understand me at all. I'm sure my cause has been misrepresented. Now that you have the chance to get to know me better, I think you'll find that I am not a difficult man to please."

I leaned forward, seeing an opportunity to challenge him. "Somehow, I doubt Ren would agree with that assessment."

Lokesh dropped his fork with a clatter and then smoothly covered his rage. "The *prince* rebelled at every opportunity. That is why he was treated so . . . harshly. I hope that *your* response to me will be different."

I cleared my throat and answered, "I suppose that all depends upon what it is that you want from me."

Lokesh took a sip from his goblet while eyeing me shrewdly over its edge. "What I want, my dear, is the opportunity to show you what a man of power truly is. It would be a mistake to continue to ally yourself with the tigers. They have no real power, not like you or I. In fact, the amulet cursed them. It was never meant for them. I am the one destined to unite the pieces. I am the one the Damon Amulet calls to."

I dabbed my lips with my napkin, stalling, as a crazy plan started to come together. *If it's a powerful opponent he wants, I'll give him one. Time to put my one drama class to good use. Act One: Dinner with a mysterious girl with superhuman powers, a bad attitude, and nerves of steel. It's showtime. . . .*

"As you probably know, I no longer have a piece of the amulet. If you were hoping to *flatter* me out of my piece, you will be sorely disappointed."

"Yes, your precious tigers must have it. Perhaps they will bring it with them when they try to rescue you."

Startled, I paused, but only for a split second. "And what makes you think they're coming?"

"Come now, my dear Kelsey. I've seen how they look at you. You've captivated them even more effectively than my daughter Yesubai did. You are not as beautiful as Yesubai, but there is daring and defiance in your eyes. I suspect the only reason that Dhiren survived my interrogation techniques is because he wanted to return to you. Both princelings are crippled by their love for you. It makes them weak and stupid."

Here goes nothing. I gave Lokesh a simpering smile. "Perhaps you will fall into the same trap they did," I threatened.

"Are you saying that you *tricked* the princes into falling for you? For if you did, my estimation of you has risen."

While terrifying at first, the playacting actually strengthened my spirit. My fear melted down to a little nub in the pit of my stomach, becoming just small enough to ignore. I licked my lips in a deliberately slow attempt to distract him.

"A smart woman uses all the tools at her disposal to obtain what she desires."

Lokesh narrowed his eyes, meeting my verbal volley. "And what is it that you desire, Kelsey?"

Channeling a brazen Scarlett O'Hara, I laughed throatily. "Surely you don't expect me to give away all my secrets during our first meeting.

I'm not that naive. But . . . if you wish to put our cards on the table now, tell me. What do you want from me?"

"Ally yourself with me instead of the tigers."

"How?" I asked, trying desperately not to shudder at the thought.

Suddenly, I felt a tingling sensation creep over my skin. It didn't hurt, but it was intimate, invasive. A slight breeze lingered over my bare arms and circled my throat. Invisible fingers slid up my neck and into my hair and then trailed down to my collarbone. Although he hadn't moved a muscle, I was sure Lokesh was to blame. I did my best to ignore it.

The sorcerer leaned forward and chuckled portentously. "My purpose here is twofold: It gives me pleasure to steal you away from the princes. Imagining their distress is gratifying. But the real reason is to combine our powers in every way possible . . . with a son."

"A son," I replied smoothly, despite the fact that my stomach was doing flip-flops. "Why me? I mean, why after all these years? I suppose I'm just shocked that you haven't already found the Bonnie to your Clyde, the Morticia to your Gomez. Wasn't hooking up with Yesubai's mother enough?"

Lokesh hissed, "Yesubai's mother was a simpering idiot. She was beautiful but she cowered before me. She was *not* my equal."

"It probably didn't help that you killed her either."

This time he didn't bother to hide the angry blue crackles at his fingertips.

"Careful," I warned, "If you show me yours, I'll have to show you mine, and we would spoil this lovely conversation we're having."

He closed his eyes and got himself under control.

"Suppose I agree to your proposal, give you an heir, and share my power with you. I want something in return. You once said that if I stayed with you willingly, you would allow the tigers to live. Will you keep your word?"

"Whether or not you agree is immaterial."

Time for Act Two: Mysterious girl shows off her powers. I pulled the Scarf out from my sleeve. Holding it in my palm, I asked it to change colors. It obliged, changing first to red and then to blue when I pressed it to my cheek. Lokesh stared at the Scarf with fascination. I raised an eyebrow, and the Scarf shot threads across the room, creating a large web. Then it shrank back down into a white handkerchief, which I folded and set next to my plate.

"What if I shared this power with you?" I asked nonchalantly.

If he was impressed, it was only for a moment. Lokesh narrowed his eyes, tossed his napkin onto his plate, and approached my side of the table. Roughly, he took my arm to yank me to my feet, smiling when he saw the look of terror on my face.

"I will consider allowing the tigers to live if you do what I ask willingly."

As if to seal the deal, Lokesh stroked my cheek and leaned close to whisper in my ear. "Tell me, Kelsey, what amuses you? What," he breathed heavily, "frightens you?"

When I didn't answer, he chuckled—then yanked me closer and viciously kissed me, biting my lip hard. As he finally let me go, I wiped my bruised lip with a thumb and glared at him.

Lokesh laughed happily. "And still you are defiant. You will give me much pleasure, Kelsey."

"Glad you think so," I spat, now more angry than afraid.

"You see, my dear, I care nothing for the tigers except to get their amulets. If you give me a son and help me gain the power I seek, I will leave the tigers alone. Now that the terms have been settled, I will show you back to your room so you might reflect on your decision. I look forward to getting to know you better," he declared with a leer that made me shiver.

Taking a deep breath, I snatched up the Scarf, gingerly placed one hand on my pocket, and let Lokesh escort me back to my prison.

"We shall talk more of alliances tomorrow, my pet," he whispered breathily in my ear. "And do return the knife you took from the table."

The comment took me by surprise, but I tried to maintain an even expression. Smiling, I took the butter knife from my pocket and pressed the tip lightly against his chest. "You can't blame a girl for trying."

Delighted, he wrapped his fingers around mine and tugged the knife out of my hand, harshly scraping the blade against my palm. Seeing that he drew blood, Lokesh brought my stinging palm to his mouth. I watched vile ecstasy overtake him as he kissed my palm and licked the red droplets from his lips.

At last he let me go with a final threat. "I'll be watching your every move, my dear. I look forward to our . . . exchanges in the future."

The door closed behind me, and I heard the click of a heavy lock, happy for a change to be separated from him by dozens of thick, metal bars.

Curtain falls, I thought and collapsed onto my bed, completely drained, and wondering how on earth I was going to get myself out of this latest mess.

ascension

he next day, Lokesh became even bolder, and I was mentally exhausted from the constant high-stakes verbal dance. I suffered no delusions. Even if he let me live long enough to bear a child, I knew I wouldn't be around to raise it.

I was released from my room throughout the day but never without a guard or Lokesh himself by my side. The place was a fortress, its decorations sparse. There were no pictures, and the minimal furniture was heavy and expensive looking. Most importantly, there didn't seem to be any doors leading outside.

As we walked, he limited himself to bruising squeezes and pinches. Every time Lokesh grabbed my arm or pulled me too close, I closed my eyes, thought of how Lokesh tortured Ren and broke his fingers in the Baiga camp, and told myself I was lucky.

To distract him, I showed off more of my "powers." I made a replica of the amulet with the Scarf, refilled a glass with water with the Pearl Necklace, and produced a magnificent, gold-trimmed coat. Lokesh was gleeful at first, but soon tired of the display. It was clear he was growing impatient.

As we dined that evening, I thought longingly of the Golden Fruit and wished Lokesh hadn't taken it from me. Mr. Kadam's delicious crêpes sprung to mind . . . and to my surprise, a plateful of berried crepes with whipped cream appeared before us.

I scanned the sitting room quickly, looking for possible hiding places. *The Golden Fruit must be close by!*

Lokesh jumped from his seat. "This is another one of your powers?"

"Yes," I replied, looking up to meet his gaze. "I can create any food or drink you wish."

It happened so fast; I was completely unprepared for it. Lokesh slapped me hard across the face and jerked my chin toward him, wrenching my neck painfully in the process.

"You should have told me of this before. Never lie to me again," he threatened.

A tear dropped onto my cheek. I grit my teeth and shook with rage. I thought of all the things I could do to him, but none of them would be lethal. They would only anger him further.

My cheek burned and itched where he'd slapped it, but I refused to rub it or acknowledge the pain. I tried to change the subject, to distract him from his anger. Thinking that a man such as Lokesh would love nothing more than to talk about himself, I relaxed back in my chair, sipped my water, and said, "Tell me about your past. If we are to have a son, I'd like him to know his heritage. I already know he'd be half American."

"A fact I'd prefer to eradicate from my mind."

"Then tell me more about *your* background. Aren't you proud enough of your own history to pass it on?"

His face became mottled red again and he spoke between clenched teeth. "No one will judge me or my progeny and find them lacking."

I raised an eyebrow. "Alright. Then tell me."

Lokesh considered me for a moment and then sat back in his chair and began. "I was born the eldest illegitimate son of the Shu emperor during the time of the Three Kingdoms. My mother was an Indian slave girl who was captured in a caravan in the year 250 CE. She was beautiful so the emperor took her for himself. She died by her own hand a year after my birth."

"An emperor?"

"Yes." Lokesh smiled naughtily. "Our son will have royal blood."

"What was it like? Growing up the son of an emperor, I mean?"

He snorted, "My father, in an uncharacteristic act of human kindness, took me under his wing and taught me what it meant to have power. He said that a truly powerful man listens only to himself because he can trust no other, takes what he wants because no one will hand it to him freely, and uses weapons others fear to wield. I watched his example carefully over the years and learned his lessons very well. He carried a piece of the amulet and taught me of the power it had."

I blinked and lowered my fork, the delicious crêpes forgotten, as Lokesh continued.

"He told me I would only be able to wield its power if he died without a proper heir. From the moment I learned of the amulet's existence, I lusted after it and thought of nothing else.

"When I was just a boy, war came to our empire and for the first time we were on the losing end. Desperate, my father tried some last minute bargaining and offered to take a barbarian leader's teenage daughter as his bride. He hoped that this would save his empire. I was disgusted by this. He'd become weak, fearful. He was not the man who inspired fear in others any longer.

"His barbarian bride bore him a son and as the boy grew, I was dismissed from my father's side. No longer did he confide in me. No longer did I have a claim to the empire. I vowed then that I would take the lives of my half brother and father. I was ten.

"When my brother was seven and I seventeen, I took him out hunting. Dismissing the guards, we rode out following the tracks of a stag.

It was an easy thing to push him from his horse. I rode back and forth over his body using his own horse until he was quite dead. Then I killed his horse, and took his broken body back to my father.

"I told the emperor that the horse had thrown my younger brother and then went wild, trampling him until he was dead. Reassuring him, I said that the beast was now dead by my own hand. The fact that he believed my lies was a testament to how weak he'd become.

"A few months later, I slipped a knife between my father's ribs while he was sleeping and took the amulet. He didn't even wake. When I ascended the throne, I immediately had my father's barbarian wife killed and took the rings of the empire. My father had worn one and the barbarian princess wore the other one, the one he'd given to my half brother upon his birth. It was a symbol that he was to be the next emperor."

Lokesh twisted a ring on his right index finger. "This is the emblem of the Shu Empire and this," he wiggled his pinky finger, "is the ring of the crown prince. The ring my half brother wore."

I swallowed my revulsion and asked, "How long were you the emperor?"

"Not long. My father's weakness had become an excuse for other warlords to constantly try us in battle. I had no interest in ruling from my father's seat of power, and when my armies fled in cowardice, I escaped. By then I was only interested in obtaining the other pieces of the amulet."

"So the amulet has kept you alive all this time?"

"That coupled with some black magic I've learned over the years."

"I see. But how do you—"

Lokesh interrupted, "Enough questions. It's my turn. I wish to see you demonstrate the use of your weapon."

"My weapon?" I queried hesitantly.

"Your golden bow and arrows."

Slowly, I scrunched my napkin between my suddenly sweaty palms. *Durga's bow and arrows were here somewhere too!*

"Alright," I agreed.

He rubbed his jaw and summoned a guard. I counted how long it took the guard to bring in the bow. *Sixty seconds.*

When the weapon was back in my hands, I nocked an arrow—just as Lokesh warned, "Don't even attempt to use them against me. I deflected your arrows before and I can easily do so again."

Figuring that he was probably right, I turned my aim to a statue on the other side of the room and watched the arrow sink into the marble.

"These were a gift from the goddess Durga," I explained. "The arrows magically refill and also disappear from the target so they can't be tracked."

"Interesting." Lokesh indicated the target and asked for a repeat performance.

This time, I tried to imbue the second arrow with lightning power to make the effect more impressive. My hand began to glow but sparked out quickly. *Still no fire power.*

Lokesh stared at my glowing hand, fascinated.

I made up a lie as quickly as possible. "When I shoot an arrow, my hand glows. I believe it is to help me aim better."

"Most interesting. So tell me how you found this," he said as he placed the Golden Fruit down on the table.

I set the bow and arrows aside and told him about the lost city of Kishkindha. I explained that Durga asked us to locate four items, each with magical properties, and, in exchange, the tigers would be men again. I didn't tell the whole truth or go into too much detail, figuring it was better that Lokesh not know everything.

"Why do you care if the men are tigers or not?"

"When I discovered the gifts Durga shared with me, I wanted more," I lied smoothly, playing to Lokesh's thirst for power.

He nodded thoughtfully and rolled the Golden Fruit between his palms. "Perhaps we will finish your quest together and offer Durga her prizes. In exchange we will both gain the power you seek."

I smiled. *This crazy plan just might be working. . . .* "I would be . . . privileged to share her powers with you."

Lokesh summoned a servant to remove the Fruit and the bow and arrows. Impulsively, I instructed the Scarf to attach an invisible thread to the bow and told it to follow the bow to its hiding place. I had it attach the other end to the statue and asked the thread to bury itself in the carpet and blend in.

Taking a risk, I heightened the challenge. "Now that I have shared some of my powers with you, perhaps you will return the fav—"

Before I could finish the sentence, an icy chill swept over me, and I was frozen in place, not able to move, talk, or fight back.

Lokesh touched my cheek, smiled evilly, and came closer.

"You so generously shared some of your talents with me. I thought I should reciprocate."

He ripped the shoulder of my gown and then groaned and trailed bruising kisses from my bare shoulder to my frozen lips. He ran his hands roughly up and down my back and pulled at my hair. I wanted to vomit but couldn't. His warm, spicy breath became all I breathed in.

Panting, he straightened. His eyes gleamed with feral pleasure. Lokesh trailed his fingers lightly over my collarbone and played with the torn fabric by my shoulder. He murmured, "You please me greatly, Kelsey." He pressed a final kiss on my bare shoulder and then backed away, smiling.

"If I wanted to, I could kill you by freezing you in an instant,"

Lokesh gloated. "The only reason you can breathe is because I haven't frozen your lungs or cardiovascular system." He cupped my chin almost lovingly. "There now, wasn't that an effective demonstration?"

Lokesh released me, and I blinked and realized I could move again. My shoulder hurt. I clasped the torn piece of my dress to my shoulder and nodded, swallowing thickly. "Very effective."

"Do you have any other questions?" he asked.

"I'll let you know," I muttered, as I desperately tried to control my shaking limbs. I was hoping to get him to show his hand and figure out an Achilles' heel, but I wasn't prepared for *that*.

While I pulled myself together, Lokesh strode toward the mantle and stoked the fire. The flames crackled and danced. I was grateful that he was at a further distance.

I told him about Durga's other quests without divulging the actual prizes to give myself time to recover from his disturbing assault. He was most interested in the golden dragon's hoard. I told him Mr. Kadam's theory was that these prizes had been stolen from Durga and that she wanted them back.

"How old is your Mr. Kadam? I know he wears the other piece of the amulet," Lokesh said.

"A few years older than Ren and Kishan." Hoping to learn more about the amulet, I pushed on. "How is it that you can look like a young man? Is it the amulet?"

"Partially. Shortly after I'd found the second piece, I realized that my life was prolonged. Though my natural state is to look fifty, I can alter my form to appear to be a young man at will. Often I choose the age that will help me to accomplish my aim."

"I know the amulet has kept Mr. Kadam from aging, but he doesn't have the ability to make himself look younger like you do," I commented, circling back to the amulet.

"He only has one piece of the amulet and his ancestors never wore it."

"What difference does that make?"

"The power is compounded the more pieces you have," Lokesh explained. "The descendants of those who wore amulets live very long lives, even if they'd never worn it."

I need to know more. It's the only way to figure this whole puzzle out.

"Yes, Mr. Kadam mentioned that his children and his children's children lived longer-than-average lives. Do you think that is why Ren and Kishan have lived so long even without wearing the amulet?"

"The amulet cursed them. In defying me, they suffer an eternity of life as beasts."

The curse. I bit my lip and thought back on everything we had learned from our previous quests. *Isn't the amulet protecting Ren and Kishan? I need to know more.*

"Does that expression mean that you still care for the beasts, my dear?"

"It's not that. I just worry that they may return and try to take your amulet pieces," I lied with a look of concern plastered on my face.

"Do not fret. Should they return, we can easily weave a trap for them from your magic threads, and obviously I know more of the power of the amulets than they."

I smiled shyly, laying it on thickly through lying lips. "May I ask how you found the amulet pieces, my . . . liege? I'm sorry if it's forward of me to designate you as such, but you were an emperor, and a man of your stature should be addressed properly."

Smiling, he studied me shrewdly and then said, "I wandered for many years asking scholars, monks, and kings for information about a great battle that united the kingdoms of Asia. During that time, I began studying the black arts and witchcraft. I sought those rumored to be dark wizards and learned whatever they would willingly teach me and extracted whatever they held back. I followed many clues that led only to dead ends. But, one by one, I discovered all five parts of the amulet. Ren and Kishan were the last pieces of the puzzle. Even now it irritates me that they have eluded me this long."

"Why didn't you just kill Ren and Kishan from the start?" I asked.

Lokesh sat back and replied, "The short answer to that very shrewd question is that I wanted to savor the moment. When I first found the royal family, Dhiren was five and Kishan four. Their parents, Rajaram and his wife, Deschen, never wore their amulet pieces in public. They also surrounded themselves and their young princelings with honorable, trustworthy guards who made their palace impossible to infiltrate. I watched the royal family for several months.

"That was when I first became fascinated with Deschen. She participated in every aspect of running the kingdom. She was clever, beautiful, and had an alluring combination of strength and softness. Any fool could see her sons would grow to be the greatest leaders of their time. I found to my surprise that I wanted to reunite the amulet, but I also hungered for Deschen and for strong sons of my own.

"Pretending to be a wealthy merchant in the neighboring kingdom of Bhreenam, I stirred up enough talk to gain a position on the king's council and through thievery, betrayal, and cunning I was appointed commander of his military. I siphoned money from the government, took goods from the common people, and worked to undermine the kingdom. I also sent spies to Rajaram's land.

"During that time, a wealthy merchant offered his daughter in exchange for favorable treatment. She was beautiful—tall, lithe, and young. And she had the most striking violet eyes."

"Yesubai's mother."

He nodded. "Later, when she confessed she was pregnant, I was pleased. I envisioned a strong son like Dhiren but with violet eyes. I coddled her and spoiled her—"

I suppressed a shiver as I wondered what Lokesh's definition of coddling and spoiling might be.

He went on. "—and it was early during her pregnancy when we were married. The night she gave birth to Yesubai, I picked up the child. The baby's eyes were indeed violet, and it took several seconds before I realized it was a girl. I put the child back into its cradle. I was enraged. I had wanted a son and now I had a worthless girl. Without regret or pity, I strangled the life from Yesubai's mother."

I swallowed, thinking about the poor girl and knew that her fate would likely be mine. "What was your wife's name?" I asked softly.

"Yuvakshi." He clicked his tongue. "Now, now. I know what you're thinking. It's been several hundred years since that happened. I promise you that my attitude about women has progressed with the times—at least somewhat. Besides, you are much more valuable to me than my first wife was and I had no control over my temper at the time. If we find out the child you carry is a girl, we'll simply remove it and try again."

I sucked in a breath and tried to turn my grimace into a smile. "Of course, you are right. I'm not worried at all," I choked out. When I noticed the gleam in his eye, I cleared my throat nervously. "So, when did you decide to use Yesubai to gain access to Rajaram's kingdom?"

"How very clever of you, my dear," Lokesh said, still looking at me in a very disturbing way. "Yesubai learned from a young age to obey me without question. She was beautiful, like her mother. By the time she was sixteen, I'd killed off the old king and taken the throne. I began expanding the military and attempted several infiltrations of Rajaram's palace without success. He simply had the stronger military. I turned to diplomacy, which got the Rajaram family to open their arms to me, but every time I visited, one of the boys was missing.

"Yesubai reported that she'd seen the amulet worn by the younger one. In an attempt to bring both brothers to the palace at the same time, I negotiated a marriage between Yesubai and Dhiren, but planned for her to marry whichever brother was more easily influenced. Then I'd kill the other brother and Rajaram, take Deschen for my own, and claim their pieces of the amulet.

"It turned out there was no controlling Dhiren. His brother, Kishan, however, was more susceptible to a pretty face."

I thought about what Kishan had told me of Yesubai. I couldn't visualize her being so cold and deceitful. I decided to give Yesubai the benefit of the doubt. Whatever she had truly felt and done, she didn't deserve the life she got.

"So you really didn't want to kill Ren when he and Kishan changed into tigers?" I asked, trying to make sense of how and why the curse happened.

"No. I wanted to use him. Keep him under my thumb and cause him pain. Drag out his death slowly. I tried to control him through blood magic. I bought a medallion from a priest of the dark arts. Those I'd used it against had become mindless servants, willing to do anything I asked.

"But it didn't seem to affect Dhiren or Kishan. The amulets they wore may have affected the spell and it changed them into tigers instead. It was not I who set the Tiger's Curse into motion. In retrospect, I should have killed Dhiren when I had the chance, but I felt I had already won. Obviously, things didn't go my way."

With a flourish, Lokesh took my hand and put his mouth roughly against it—his version of a caress. His black eyes flashing menacingly, he held my gaze and said the words that made my blood run cold.

"Time's up, my pet. Will you offer yourself to me freely in exchange for the tigers' lives?"

3

shotgun

I swallowed thickly. I'd been planning on "offering myself freely" to someone I truly loved and who loved me. It wasn't too long ago that I had the luxury of choosing whether that someone would be Ren or Kishan. I had chosen Kishan, but none of that mattered now. I was all out of options. If I didn't agree to go through with Lokesh's plans, we would all surely die.

Knowing there was nothing else I could say, I affixed a forced smile to my face. "Yes, I've decided to accept your offer. There's something to be said for a mature man of the world. And your power . . . excites me." Panicked, but trying desperately not to show it, I demurred, "But . . . I have one small request."

Lokesh's eyes glittered impatiently. "And what is that?"

My mind sifted through possible ways to put off his advances when suddenly the answer came to me. I quickly explained, "My parents died when I was young, and I was left alone. I don't want that to happen to our son."

"That will not happen." Lokesh raised my wrist to his mouth and nibbled on it brusquely. "I fully intend to instruct my son in all aspects of my power as you will instruct him in yours. I intend to be a *hands-on* father."

"I'm sure you will be," I reassured him. "But what I'm trying to say is . . . I want him to have your name. I don't want to bring an illegitimate child into the world. You suffered much because of that status, and I will not have my son be usurped. I want you to . . . to . . ." I gulped, not believing I was actually saying the words, "marry me."

Lokesh took a step back and stared. "You wish to be my wife?"

"Surely you didn't expect me to be your concubine? You offered as much to Yesubai's mother. I wish the same. I want our union to be not only one of strategy, but also one that's binding by tradition, if not legally. You can use whatever name you wish but I want to be married before we . . . try to have a child." I lowered my gaze and took his hand, squeezing it lightly.

After a quiet moment he declared, "You are wise to bargain for this. It shows you are thinking of our son and his place in the world. I will do as you wish. We *will* marry and as a gift to you, I will allow you to remain chaste until you come to my marriage bed. Is this satisfactory?"

"Yes, thank you, my . . . husband."

Lokesh smiled like a cat cornering a mouse. "Then I will leave you to create a bridal gown while I arrange the wedding and a feast. I will send a servant to retrieve you tomorrow for our wedding supper. I'd escort you myself but there is much to do and I still do not trust you enough to leave you to your own devices. You understand, of course?"

"Of course," I answered, relieved that I'd bought myself another twenty-four hours to come up with an escape plan.

Kissing me before he left, Lokesh pulled and pushed and bit and shoved as if I was a piece of clay being molded into whatever shape he desired. When he finally drew away, I managed a shy smile, though it hurt.

Patting my shoulder roughly, he said, "By this time tomorrow, you will be my wife. Sleep well, my pet. You'll need your rest."

"Good night," I replied woodenly and returned to the freedom of my empty prison.

I didn't sleep much at all that night. Through closed eyes, I silently prayed that Ren or Kishan, Mr. Kadam, or even Durga would help me. I was running out of time.

During the brief moments I did sleep, I dreamt I was sitting up in bed holding a precious baby boy. It was Kishan's vision in the Grove of Dreams. The baby slept, and I couldn't help but wonder if his eyes were the color of a vibrant ocean or sparkled like a golden desert.

I smoothed his dark hair and kissed his baby-soft forehead. Little fingers wrapped around mine as the baby stirred. When he yawned and blinked, I recoiled in horror. My baby's eyes were pitch black. Slowly his sweet baby expression melted and his lips twisted cruelly. Then I heard the words of a pitiless young boy whisper, "Hello, *Mother*."

I woke up with a scream. Quickly, I composed myself and rolled over, stuffing a pillow under my cheek. Escape was too much to hope for, but death, either Lokesh's or mine, would be my goal. I would not allow him to touch me, let alone consider bearing his child. He was a deadly predator and when a predator wants to devour you, you can run, you can hide, or you can kill him first. I had no choice but to fight for my life.

But how could I kill my captor? All I had for weapons were the Pearl Necklace and the Scarf, which meant I could try to hang him or drown him in his bathtub. That wasn't exactly a foolproof plan. I knew I wouldn't be able to access the bow and arrows, and I had no fire power.

I tossed and turned, considering strategy after strategy until I heard a noise at my window. In the predawn darkness, I looked out on the empty, snow-covered landscape. Then I felt the whisper of material on the ledge. The Scarf had embroidered a message:

Kelsey?
Are you there?
It's Kishan.

Kishan is here! I might still have to kill Lokesh, but I won't have to do it alone! I wondered if Mr. Kadam and Ren were also nearby.

If it weren't for Lokesh's prying eyes, I would have jumped for joy. Instead, I asked the Scarf to stitch a reply and pressed the cloth to the window.

Am okay.

Lokesh marrying me tomorrow night.

Cameras and guards everywhere.

I stifled a sob as the cloth twitched and the Scarf obeyed Kishan's instructions. Flipping it over, I read:

Stall him as long as possible.
We have a plan.
We're coming for you.

I pressed my hands against the glass and nodded. Staring through my window, I watched the woods for the longest time, searching for a flash of black or white.

The next morning, I anxiously rose from my bed and headed to the shower. I was exhausted in every way possible. I'd kept my emotions under such a tight rein; knowing that my imprisonment was almost over, one way or another, overwhelmed me to the point that I couldn't hold them back anymore.

I worried about Ren and Kishan challenging Lokesh. I wondered if I would remain locked in my room while they fought and perhaps died. I thought about what would happen if they failed, and I ended up having to marry a monster.

Standing in a scalding shower, I cried quietly, hoping the steam that shrouded the mirror would also fog up any hidden cameras. Spent, I sank down until I sat back in the tub and let the hot water pummel my body until it turned cold.

Today could be the day I die.

With that morbid thought, I prepared for my wedding.

I took a long time drying and brushing my hair. Spending hours in the sun, hiking the jungles, and swimming in the ocean had bleached my brown hair, which now had champagne-blond highlights. *Mom would have liked it.* I wondered what she would have thought of my upcoming nuptials. It certainly wasn't the wedding I'd envisioned for myself.

I had asked the Scarf to create a wedding dress befitting an ancient Chinese princess. I ignored it as long as I possibly could, but finally slid open the closet. I gasped at the silky red dress, which looked similar to the one the bride had worn at the wedding Li and I attended.

The gown was elaborate, and I was glad it would take me at least twenty minutes to put it on. It was trimmed in beads and elaborate gold stitching. There was a Mandarin style ruff attached to a golden tunic adorned with a large lotus blossom. Strings of beads crossed back and forth over the tunic, and its thick, embellished sleeves draped over my hands while the silky under sleeves extended at least a foot beyond my fingertips. On the thin apron of the tunic's top layer, the Scarf had stitched a gorgeous fiery phoenix.

A long, golden scarf wrapped around my back and draped to the floor. I stepped into red silk slippers embroidered with golden flowers and fastened the pièce de résistance—a magnificent hairpiece with golden feathers and flowers, intricate braids, beads, and ornaments woven throughout.

I turned to gaze at my reflection. I looked like an exotic bird, a phoenix, in fact. Like the great bird, I was beautiful and vibrant, but I was also deadly; and soon, I would be consumed by fire.

I tucked the Scarf into one of my long sleeves, concealing it for later use. After dabbing a flowery perfume on my wrists and behind my ears, I sat down to await my groom.

Too soon, one of Lokesh's servants came to collect me. He ogled my costume with a shocked expression, then quickly ducked his head and stayed as far away from me as he could.

Is he afraid of me? I wish Lokesh felt the same way.

The servant guided me to what looked like a small library and handed me a note and a box on his way out. I heard the click of the lock behind him and then silence.

I let out a pent-up breath and hoped that whatever plan Ren and Kishan had dreamed up would be put into motion before the wedding ceremony. Closing my eyes, I made a wish that we would all make it out alive.

I sat stiffly before opening Lokesh's note, which said that we were to dine before a magistrate performed the ceremony. Tugging the white ribbon off, I opened the gift from my husband-to-be.

It was the biggest diamond I'd ever set eyes on. The stone was round, multifaceted, and pink. Two smaller pink diamonds were set on either side. It might have been my imagination, but the five prongs holding the large diamond into place looked like thick fingers. I imagined Lokesh's own grasp—so strong there would be no hope for escape. I slipped the ring on my middle finger just as the doors opened.

"Ah, there you are, my dear. And what do you think of my gift?"

"It's lovely." I managed to give him a smile.

Something flashed in his black eyes, and he took a sudden step toward me. I stood proudly but inwardly cringed. He grabbed my chin and murmured softly with a repellent smile, "I shall enjoy tearing your pretty dress to pieces tonight. I do hope you'll have enough spirit to make the evening interesting, Kelsey. I wouldn't want to be disappointed."

I jerked my chin away and leveled my eyes on him. "Believe me when I say that *all* my energies will be focused upon you tonight, my liege."

Leering with anticipation, Lokesh took my arm and led me into the ballroom, which sparkled with the light of hundreds of candles and was perfumed by dozens of white flower arrangements. If it had been anyone else's wedding, I might have appreciated the setting more.

We sat at a small, intimate table, and though my face was frozen into a plastic smile, beneath the many layers of sleeves, my hands were clenched into fists.

Lokesh clapped his hands to begin a traditional ten-course Chinese wedding feast, not unlike the one I ate with Li at his cousin's wedding. There was shark's fin soup, stuffed melon, two whole lobsters in garlic-butter sauce, five-spice beef, squab with noodles, roasted suckling pig with fried rice, sautéed prawns with honeyed peas, Peking duck, scallion-and-ginger fish, and pink buns filled with sweet lotus paste.

I tried to stretch out the meal by talking about the symbolism of each course, but Lokesh remained silent. In fact, all he seemed to be in the mood for was scrutinizing me. His dark gaze studied me like a hawk watching a rabbit.

At one point during the meal, I felt an icy touch find my ankle under my layered skirts. Slowly, the biting cold traveled up my bare leg and caressed my thigh. I wasn't sure if he was using his air or his water power or a combination of both, but I kept silent and nibbled at the dinner as best I could.

The minutes ticked by, and still there was no sign of Ren and Kishan. If they didn't make an appearance soon, I'd be Mrs. Lokesh Shu or whatever his last name was. I was on my own. Helpless darkness swelled within me. It overwhelmed me until I felt as heavy as a stone sinking into a muddy river. This was not what I'd envisioned for my future.

Instead of walking down the aisle to a man who looked at me with love and tenderness, I'd be walking toward a villain—someone who'd rather twist my arm than place it on his. Instead of Mr. Kadam taking my arm proudly, soothing my nerves, and giving me to the care of a man he called a son, I had no one. Instead of promises and sweet vows of love, I'd hear bubbly lies roiling with black filth. When the bubbles burst, I'd be covered in layers of corruption.

The feast was finally cleared away, and I couldn't stall the wedding any longer. Lokesh took my hand.

"Are you ready, my dear?" Lokesh asked and, without waiting for my response, called for the magistrate to enter.

Though I wanted to wring my hands and run away, I placed my palm confidently in his and smiled. "Of course."

"Shall we proceed?" asked a smooth, silky voice.

I gasped and whipped around. The magistrate's blue eyes flashed with anger, and his priestly robes whipped behind him as he strode into the center of the room. *Ren!* I thought he was the most beautiful thing I'd ever seen.

Weapons flew through the air. The *chakram* whirled, and darts from the trident sped toward Lokesh, who easily deflected them.

Lokesh gripped my arm and laughed. "Greetings, Dhiren. You must have received your invitation."

"You will wed her over my dead body," Ren threatened.

Lokesh shrugged. "As you wish."

With a twitch of Lokesh's fingers, Ren stopped moving.

Lokesh shifted his eyes nervously around the candlelit ballroom, seeking the black tiger.

Where is Kishan? I need to defrost Ren. Think, Kelsey. Think!

Seeing no other move, I draped my arm around Lokesh's, hoped against hope, and asked, "Did you kill Ren?"

"No, my dear. He's still alive."

"Good," I purred. Determined to act out my part well, I turned to Ren, gave him a pitying glance, and said, "It's really too bad you had to find out this way. But since you're here, you can be a guest at my wedding."

Lokesh smiled and instructed the guards to find the real magistrate. Ren's blue eyes burned into mine.

"Oh dear, how rude of me. Of course, a guest should kiss the bride," I said mockingly before kissing the man who had come to save me, biting his lip until I drew blood. *I'm so sorry!* I thought, wishing Ren could read my mind . . . and then I slapped him square across his beautiful face.

His pupils widened with shock, and I imagined the sting in his heart was much greater than the sting on his cheek. Yanking the Scarf from my sleeve, I dabbed at his bruised lip and tucked it into his collar, clucking disdainfully as Lokesh laughed with glee.

I stayed long enough to see the light go out in Ren's eyes. Turning back to Lokesh, I frowned. "But will he have a good view from all the way over here? I really think he should be moved, don't you? I want him to have a clear picture of the man I chose over him."

Lokesh pinched my cheek, twisting it harshly. "What a devious little vixen you are," he said happily and watched with delight as I used the Scarf to bind Ren's arms to his chest.

As soon as Ren was sufficiently tied up, Lokesh unfroze him. Ren's muscles strained against the Scarf aggressively. I wiggled my fingers lightly against my skirt and shook my head, hoping he would understand my signals. Settling down, Ren relaxed and walked to the side of the make-shift altar.

Lokesh lifted his hands to freeze Ren again, but I cut him off by saying, "That will not be necessary, my love."

I twisted my fingers, and the Scarf wrapped around Ren's legs until he was mummy-wrapped from neck to feet

"You've done a magnificent job, my pet," said Lokesh, "but I think I'll keep his tongue frozen, at least for now. I wouldn't want him spoiling our nuptials after all."

"Wise decision. Shall we begin then? Did you find the magistrate?"

Lokesh clapped his hands, but not a single servant or the magistrate appeared. He shouted once, twice, and rang a bell in frustration. His only answer was an explosive blaze of fire burning from every candle in the room.

Lokesh raised his arms and tried to blow them out with a brisk wind, but the flames only rose higher. Grunting, he waved his hand and doused each candle with water as Ren looked on and smiled.

Sensing that things were afoul, the evil sorcerer took my arm, growled "Come with me!" and yanked me down the hallway to make a quick escape through the kitchen.

Silently, I instructed the Scarf to free Ren and weave him a message.

Try as he might, Lokesh couldn't open the kitchen door. He used lightning but the blue crackle only left scorch marks on the wood. Finally, he ripped the door off its hinges.

I edged back a few feet while Lokesh stared incredulously at a room I'd filled to the top with chocolate cake. I smirked, pleased with myself, and explained, "A girl should be able to enjoy a little chocolate at her wedding, don't you think?"

At my whispered word, the cake burst open and boiling chocolate fudge sauce spilled all over Lokesh. He screamed and turned toward me just as Kishan broke through the side door and ran into the hallway. A dead guard fell at his feet.

"Kishan!" I shouted, so happy I could have cried.

Kishan stopped only to throw me a wink before he raised his palm and sent off bubbles of light that exploded directly in front of Lokesh like a strobe firecracker. He screeched in pain and covered his eyes. Using both hands, Kishan shot several lightning bursts into Lokesh's body.

Before I could give Kishan the biggest tiger hug he'd ever have, Ren joined us in the hall with my bow and arrows and the Golden Fruit. Without skipping a beat, he shot trident darts into Lokesh, who soon began to look like a spear pincushion, and then asked the Scarf to mummy-wrap him.

The Scarf sprang to life in Ren's hands and spun long layers of linen. Tightly, it wove between the spear darts. Lokesh hollered in pain and spat out vehement words in Hindi and Chinese. His legs were bound together, and the Scarf's wrappings twisted around his neck, looped around an awning, and raised his body off the floor. Lokesh twitched and bucked, and I momentarily turned away, not wanting to watch.

Somehow Lokesh managed to wrench his hands free, and his power slid over me immediately. It felt like he was scratching me, ripping my skin with his claws. Groaning, I wrapped my arms around my body, staggering and panting at the pain. Ren dashed to my side to catch me in his arms before I fell.

"I've got you, *iadala*," Ren whispered softly.

Kishan blasted Lokesh again, and the pain began to fade.

Incredibly, Lokesh was still alive but in terrible agony. Kishan lit his mummy-wrap on fire, and then I heard an inhuman scream and smelled burning flesh. With a sudden whoosh of water, Lokesh put out the fire. It was going to take more than just flames to kill the sorcerer.

Ren lifted the Golden Fruit and a coating of oil slid over the water-soaked linens. Kishan lit it on fire again, and Lokesh's body wrenched back and forth.

Recovered enough to move, I yanked on Ren's shirt. "Let's go!" I pressed, unable to witness the scene any longer.

I pushed the boys into the hall, shut the door, and rammed a fire poker through the handle, hoping Lokesh would either burn or hang or both. The house began shaking; his black magic created an earthquake.

It was time to run. I asked the Scarf to create more practical clothes under my wedding dress. The brothers kept me between them as we raced down staircases and through a complicated maze of hallways and busted-open doorways. Blast marks peppered the walls, and my feet crunched over broken, once-hidden cameras. We leapt over dozens of fallen guards. As we pushed ahead, I cast off Lokesh's diamond ring and my Chinese bridal wear piece by piece.

Finally we came to an open window whose bars had been severed cleanly. Kishan leapt outside and landed in the bushes twelve feet below. Ren picked me up and tossed me into Kishan's open arms before joining us. I was dying to talk, to scream, to whoop with joy, but by the time we reached the motorcycles, my heart was practically bursting out of my chest and I was completely out of breath.

But I was free.

With no time for anything more than a brief squeeze of my hand, Ren pulled me onto his bike, and with a rev of engines, the three of us shot off like blazing comets into the night, leaving a trail of discarded red fabric in our wake.

4

reunion

We rode for several hours in silence without stopping. The chilly December wind whipped through my hair, and I wriggled closer to Ren, who had somehow managed to take off his leather jacket and give it to me without slowing down. I gratefully put it on and hugged Ren tightly in thanks.

I had no idea where we were though I suspected based on the road signs we were not in India. When the boys finally pulled over, it was early morning, maybe an hour or two before sunrise. I wearily got off the motorcycle. Ren and Kishan hid their bikes in the brush, and finally, finally, we were able to have a proper reunion.

"I thought I'd never see you again," Kishan said tenderly, wrapping his arms around me and running his hands up and down my back. "Are you okay? Did Lokesh hurt you?"

I shook my head. "Only a little. He gave me a few bruises and kissed me a few times but for the most part he left me alone. I never saw his torture chamber."

It felt good to be back in Kishan's embrace. Safe. For the first time in a long time, I let my guard down completely. I was with my tigers again. I was back where I belonged.

"Good," Kishan grunted, holding onto me as if he'd never let go.

When he finally did, Ren approached me with an indiscernible expression in his eyes. He said nothing, but I could have sworn he was reading my mind. Hesitantly, he touched my cheek and tears welled up in my eyes. Before I could say anything, he pulled me into his arms. Wrapped into that safe haven, feeling the unspoken connection between us and the warmth of his strong body against mine, I finally relaxed, and all the terrifying emotional turmoil spilled out of me in a torrent.

Seeing the state I was in, Kishan lowered his gaze and busied himself setting up a tent while I cried quietly in Ren's arms. My body shook in racking sobs. I clawed Ren's shirt, gathering it in my fist while he murmured softly and stroked my hair. At some point I realized I wasn't supporting my own weight anymore. He picked me up and carried me into the tent.

Ren cradled me against his chest, and Kishan made me some hot tea. I shook my head, too overwhelmed to drink, but Ren insisted. When I'd finished, he whispered some words to Kishan, who changed immediately into the black tiger and stretched out along the cushions. I lay next to him, stroking my black tiger's fur, knowing that the curse still required them to take tiger form for six hours a day.

"Try to sleep, *priyatama*," Ren said, placing his palm lightly against my cheek. Then he changed into his familiar white tiger form and lay on my other side.

For a time, the only noise was me sniffling and Ren's comforting purr. Exhausted, I finally fell asleep with my fist gripping the soft fur at Ren's neck.

I slept for a long time, only partially waking with the movements of the brothers as they tried not to disturb me. They spoke softly in Hindi, and the lovely, musical words helped me relax and fall back to sleep.

When I finally woke, the sun was high in the sky. Though it was cold at night, it had warmed up to around fifty degrees, which in Oregon is like early summer. I sat up grimacing and shoved the helmet hair out of my face.

Kishan ducked into the tent and grinned. "Thought I heard you get up."

"Do we have time for at least a sponge bath before we go?"

"If you're including me in that statement, I'll make the time."

I sighed, stretched, and gave him a half smile. "I've missed your teasing. Hey, where are we anyway?"

"Uzbekistan."

"That doesn't help . . ."

"Central Asia. We're about a thousand miles from home."

"Wow, that's a long way to come on motorcycles," I said and paused before continuing. "Kishan? Do you think he's . . . he's dead?"

"I don't know. Lokesh has lived a long time."

"I hope he's dead."

Kishan studied me thoughtfully. "I hope so too, Kells."

I took his hand. Though my heart still stirred for Ren, I had made my choice: Kishan. *Round pillow, square pillow, they're both still pillows*, I remembered, thinking fondly of Phet.

"Kishan, thank you for coming for me."

His golden eyes gleamed. "Anytime, beautiful."

Kishan left me to clean up, and I asked the Scarf to create a makeshift shower curtain and the Pearl Necklace to create a shower on a section of flat rock not far from the tent. I stuck my hand into the water and was surprised that it felt like a warm tropical rain. I scrubbed the makeup and perfume from my body and imagined I was washing away a thick layer of false skin, sloughing off the girl who would have been the bride of Lokesh.

Refreshed and feeling like myself again, it was time to go home.

When Kishan asked me to ride with him, I glanced at Ren, who would not meet my gaze. I bit my lip and threw my leg over Kishan's bike.

Wanting to get as far away from Lokesh as quickly as possible, we kept up a grueling pace. I got the feeling that the brothers only stopped for me and to refuel.

At a gas station, Kishan filled the bikes while Ren and I picked up a comb and a bottle of sunscreen. As I began working out the tangles in my hair, Ren insisted on rubbing the lotion over my arms, nose, and cheeks.

"How are you?" he asked quietly.

"I'll survive."

"Of that, I have no doubt." Finished with one arm, he moved to my other one. "Lokesh was making you marry him?"

"It was actually my idea. I wanted to . . . stall him as long as possible."

Ren stiffened and his fingers gripped my arm for a moment. He looked me in the eye and asked carefully, "Did he . . . hurt you?"

I put my hand over his. "No, not the way you're thinking."

Ren nodded and cupped my face with his palm. "If you need to talk, I'm here."

"I know. And Ren? I'm sorry about the kiss. I didn't want to hurt you."

"I know why you did it. It hurt worse knowing you were a prisoner and not being able to save you."

"Thank you for rescuing me."

He sighed. "No matter where you are, I will always come for you, *iadala*. There is no need to thank me."

"Still, thank you."

Ren kissed my forehead. "Have I told you lately that you're a very stubborn woman?"

"Not recently," I replied playfully, enjoying our familiar banter and feeling a warm tingle flow throughout my body. "Let's go home. I can't wait to see Mr. Kadam. I have so many things to tell him."

Ren reached out for my hand and pulled me closer, suddenly serious. "Kells, we . . . haven't been able to find him. When Lokesh's pirates ambushed us, he stepped in front of a harpoon meant for Nilima, and they both disappeared. We can't locate them on the GPS. Both of their signals went missing. We saw yours, but not theirs."

"What? That can't be. Let's go then. We need to find them." My mind filled with new worry for Mr. Kadam and Nilima. Nothing would be right until we were all back together.

Ren held out his hand. "Will you ride with me?"

His question hung in the air. I looked over at Kishan, who had just finished filling the tires with air and gave me a merry wave.

Kishan is my boyfriend. I should ride with him, I thought.

"Please," Ren added quietly. "I need to feel you near me."

I lowered my eyes and took his hand. My resolve crumbled. "Alright," I said, climbed on behind him, and wrapped my arms around his waist.

Ren wound his way over to Kishan and announced, "We're riding together on this leg."

I quickly added, "If that's alright with you, Kishan."

Kishan shrugged good naturedly and warned, "Ren rides like a grandpa, but it's fine with me."

To thank him, I kissed him lightly.

Kishan grinned and said, "I might be better off. This way if I ride behind Grandpa, I can admire the view."

Ren grunted and said something brusque in Hindi, but Kishan just laughed and ignored him.

That night Kishan scouted out a place to set up camp and returned excited. I followed him up a rocky hill to a circle of stones around a hollowed out area of packed clay.

"Fill it with water," Kishan suggested. "Voilà! Your very own Jacuzzi."

I laughed and brushed my hand across the Necklace at my throat. The basin quickly filled with a bubbling mineral bath, and Kishan blasted it with fire power. The cold air billowed with steam.

"Enjoy your bath, Kells. Oh, and if you need the water warmed again, I'd be more than happy to oblige."

After my soak it was Ren's and Kishan's turn. Kishan ripped his shirt off. "First one there rides all day with Kells." Ren took off like a shot with Kishan whooping after him.

With only one more day of travel to go, we were all starting to fall back into our normal routines, at least as normal as they could be under the circumstances. Both brothers were careful with me, treating me as delicately as a precious China cup.

Later that moonlit night, when Kishan smiled and leaned over to kiss me, it was warm and brief. Something flashed in his eyes when he pulled away.

I took his hand. "What is it?" I encouraged gently.

"If I do something that reminds you of Lokesh or hurts you in any way, will you tell me?"

"The fact that you're even worried about it is a sign you could never be like him. Don't be afraid to touch me. I won't break."

Kishan nodded, pressed a kiss to my fingers, and lifted the amulet from his chest. "You were smart to send Fanindra to me with this, but you should wear it now."

He fumbled with the chain and fastened the amulet around my neck. I rubbed the smooth stone with my fingers.

"That's how you created those balls of light? With the amulet?"

"Yes. This piece of the amulet is quite a weapon."

"I was wondering how you did that. That never happened to me."

"You probably could do it if you tried. The amulet seems capable of creating any type of flame."

I considered how I'd seen Lokesh use his pieces of the amulet and suddenly stood and took Kishan's hand.

"Where are we going?" he asked.

"I want to blow something up."

Kishan laughed. "You are definitely the girl for me. Let's go."

When we found a large rock, I infused so much energy into the burst that the rock disintegrated. I stared at my hand incredulously. I had no idea I'd become so dependent upon my power and knowing for sure that the amulet was the source was a relief. I could put on and take off the power at my leisure.

Kishan and I practiced drills for the next half hour. He taught me how to create bursts of light so they'd explode right in front of someone's eyes to temporarily blind him, how to snap my fingers to start a fire, and after finding some roadkill to practice upon, how to use the beam to burn the flesh. It wasn't my favorite thing to do, but I knew that if Lokesh was still alive and came after me again, or if I had to face another monster in order to fulfill Durga's fourth prophecy, I would have to be able to use this technique.

When we returned to the tent, Ren was moody and yelled at Kishan for walking off with me and not telling him. "We need to watch over her constantly. We have no idea if Lokesh is still alive, and I don't want to take any chances on losing her again," Ren said sternly then turned around and left.

After he stormed off, Kishan sighed and picked up my hand. "He's right. We have to remain vigilant where you're concerned."

I scooted closer and lay my head on his shoulder. "I'll just make sure one of you is always around."

He put his arm around me. "He shouldn't be that mad anyway. He won the bet. He gets to ride with you all day tomorrow."

I teased, "What happened to doing whatever it takes to win?"

Kishan grunted. "Apparently, he took my advice. He shoved me face-first into a boulder. It broke my nose."

"What?" I gasped. He started laughing. "I don't find anything funny about that," I said.

"I do. Ren's never cheated in his life. He must have been pretty desperate."

"Hmm."

That night, I dreamed of Mr. Kadam. He was standing in front of a movie screen studying various battle scenes that flashed by so fast I couldn't make them out. When I touched his arm, he turned and smiled. There was something different about his eyes. He seemed much older and a little sad.

"What is it?" I asked. "Is something wrong?"

He patted my shoulder. "It's nothing, Miss Kelsey. I'm just a bit weary."

"Where are you? We can't find you."

"I'm much closer than you think. Try to relax your mind and go back to sleep."

"But I am asleep. This is a dream."

Mr. Kadam paused. "Of course it is. Just close your eyes and focus on your breathing. It will take all your strength to face what lies ahead, but for now, rest."

When his voice began to fade, I felt the darkness gently engulf me. I wanted to nod but couldn't. As his presence faded from my mind, I felt a light touch, a gesture of comfort and understanding.

Ren and Kishan were thrilled about my dream the next morning. They believed it was a vision and that the amulet had reconnected us with Mr. Kadam somehow.

When we finally pulled onto the pebbled drive of our Indian jungle mansion, I felt tears fill my eyes. As we stepped into the house, I breathed in the warmth and felt the spirit of the Rajaram family envelop me.

With Kishan and Ren flanking either side, I crossed the threshold and announced, "We're home."

5

putting the pieces together

While Ren and Kishan checked the house for signs of Mr. Kadam, Nilima, or intruders, I reacquainted myself with Fanindra, who had indeed swam through the waves near the shore of Mahabalipuram and found her way to my tigers. My golden pet blinked her jeweled emerald eyes and raised her head under my palm.

"I missed you too. How clever you were to have found the boys." I stroked her head for a moment and then she lay on her top coil and froze.

A look through Mr. Kadam's computer and security system told me that no one had entered the house or tried to contact us during our absence.

"What's our next move?" Kishan wondered aloud. He perched on the arm of the couch and pulled me back against his chest, much to the disappointment of Ren.

As if in response, the air five feet away from us began to shimmer. Specks of light seemed to move, dancing and bouncing like scattered raindrops on a windshield. But then they coalesced toward the center and began to take form. The light became brighter, until two very real bodies materialized.

A familiar, beloved voice called out, "Hello, Miss Kelsey. We have much to talk about."

"Mr. Kadam? Nilima!" I raced around the table and hugged both of them. "You're all right? Where were you? Are you injured?"

Nilima smiled but staggered a bit under my embrace.

"Ren, Kishan, will one of you help Nilima to her room? She's still weak from our journey and needs to sleep," Mr. Kadam said.

Coming immediately to her aid, Ren carried Nilima upstairs to her room, and Mr. Kadam continued, "Miss Kelsey, shall we sit? If you can afford the time, we should speak." He chuckled at a thought he didn't bother to share, which made me wonder what could possibly be in store for us next.

Ren joined us on the couch, and I held Kishan's hand, happy to have my little family reunited and hoping Durga's fourth prophecy would be easier than what we had just gone through.

"Mr. Kadam, please tell us what happened to you," I asked.

He leaned back, stroked his short beard, and briefly paused, as if undecided. "The amulet protected me on the ship. When I saw the harpoon heading toward Nilima, my only thought was to save her. I wrapped my arms around her and the next thing I knew, we were transported to another place."

"Where?" Ren asked.

"I'm not sure it was a 'where,' for we were no longer on Earth."

"What do you mean?" I sputtered, shocked. "Was it like one of Durga's other-worlds, like the City of the Seven Pagodas?"

"No. We traveled to a time beyond time, a place beyond space. It's an experience I fear I will have difficulty in describing. Suffice it to say we are safe and we are home."

I could sense that Mr. Kadam wasn't telling us the whole truth. He was holding something back, but I had no idea what it could be or why.

"I will be very busy in the next few weeks," Mr. Kadam continued. "It is imperative that we begin our journey to find Durga's fourth gift soon.

If we leave too early or too late we will miss our window of opportunity and the success of our endeavor will be jeopardized.

"Above all else, I must impress upon you the need to trust me. I will ask some difficult things of all of you in the near future, and you must heed my direction without question. There are certain things I have been made aware of that I cannot share with you."

Mr. Kadam looked at me kindly. "Your safety and your happiness is and has always been my priority. Please don't question me on this, for I can say no more."

"Will you need help with the research?" I offered.

"Not this time, Miss Kelsey, but thank you."

Something was wrong. Mr. Kadam had never closed himself off from us before. He seemed distracted, uncomfortable. To break the silence, I said, "Perhaps now would be a good time to share what I've learned."

Mr. Kadam nodded for me to begin describing my experiences with Lokesh. I told them about his history, of how he killed his brother and still wore his father's and brother's rings, and about the powers I'd observed him use.

I explained, "He can make wind tunnels and blue static electricity at his fingertips. He freezes not only people but things, which makes me wonder if he has control over ice or water because he doused fire."

"It's a reasonable assumption," Mr. Kadam acknowledged.

"Thanks to Kishan, we now know the amulet I wear is connected to fire, and he's discovered more uses for it in a month than I could have in a year."

My thoughts turned briefly to the golden flame that was a result of Ren's touch, but somehow I knew that the special power didn't come from the amulet or even my henna tattoo. It was something I only felt when Ren and I connected.

Swallowing, I turned to Mr. Kadam, who nodded sagely, but his expression was strange, as if he already knew what I was going to say.

I cleared my throat and said quietly, "Lokesh also used his power to . . . touch me."

Mr. Kadam interrupted. "Perhaps it is too uncomfortable for you to speak of."

"No, I think you all should know. He used invisible fingers of air that could penetrate my clothing and right before we left I felt him scratch my skin from the inside out. He could've probably rearranged my insides."

"If that devil wasn't already dead, I'd strangle him with my bare hands," Kishan spat.

Mr. Kadam sat up, clearly fascinated. "You believe he's dead, then?"

"We hope so," Kishan answered. "We left him hung, speared, and burning."

"Interesting."

Ren leaned forward and pressed his head into his hands. "This is my fault, Kelsey. I should have kept you by my side constantly." He turned to me and took my hands. "Forgive me. I sent you away. If I had kept you by my side Lokesh couldn't have abducted you."

"There is nothing to forgive. Please don't blame yourself. I'm safe because you rescued me."

He raised his head and nodded but said nothing, so I continued to recap what I had learned. "The amulet keeps Lokesh young. He looks about fifty years old, but he's actually much older than all of you. He said he was born around 250 CE. With the combined power of the amulet pieces, he can manipulate his appearance at will."

Mr. Kadam looked off into the distance but said nothing. In fact, it seemed as if his thoughts were somewhere else.

"Lokesh also talked about the night you two became tigers," I added. "You mentioned that the amulet protected you. I have a theory." I turned to Ren and said, "Tell me exactly how Lokesh cursed you and changed you into tigers."

Ren answered, "He took a wooden medallion from around his neck, cut me, dripped my blood onto it, then began chanting. Kishan was affected too. All I remember was the white light, intense pain, and the feeling of my body being reshaped."

"Don't forget the burning," Kishan added. "The amulet burned my skin where it rested."

"Really? The amulet didn't burn me," Ren contradicted.

"Hmm." I drummed my fingers on my knee. "Lokesh said the amulets *punished* you by changing you to tigers, and he confessed that he wasn't trying to do that. He wanted to turn you into zombies or something."

"Why did he use an elaborate and slow blood ritual? Why not freeze us? What did he hope to gain?" Ren asked.

"First, he likes to torture people, especially you two. The amulets were in his grasp. He said he wanted to draw out the process. Enjoy it for as long as he could. He probably hadn't yet figured out how to partially freeze like he does now. Also, he wanted a son-in-law who had the support of the people and who would do as he asked."

"Alright, so Lokesh didn't change us into tigers. What do *you* think happened, Kelsey?" Kishan asked.

"I think the amulet protected you, just like it did with Mr. Kadam."

"Then why didn't it protect Lokesh's father or brother?" Ren asked.

"Well, this may be a little far-fetched, but Lokesh feels it is his destiny to reunite the amulet. What if the Damon Amulet *is* supposed to be put back together again, but it's not *his* destiny but yours?"

Kishan laughed. "You're right. That is far-fetched."

"Think about it," I argued. "It's called the Damon Amulet, and it changed you into tigers. Damon is Durga's tiger, the Durga who sent us on these quests. The Ocean Teacher said that this happened *to* you, as in, for a reason. What if you're supposed to save the amulet?"

Ren rubbed his hands together as he mused, "Perhaps Kelsey's right. If Lokesh didn't curse us, then maybe it *was* the amulet that did it."

I nodded enthusiastically. "We should go back to Lokesh and take the amulet from him."

"No!" Mr. Kadam said definitively, startling us with his sudden outburst. Seeing our dismay, he sat back in his chair, but his fingers dug into the leather. "You cannot go back. There is no time. When the fourth gift is recovered, that is the time to pursue Lokesh."

"But wouldn't it be better to do it now while the boys can still heal?" I suggested.

He shook his head. "This is one of the times I will ask you to trust me."

I nodded glumly and shared a tense moment of eye contact with Ren and Kishan. Mr. Kadam had a very strange expression on his face. He watched the three of us with a mixture of fondness and sadness and he didn't write down any notes. That wasn't like him at all.

"Are you alright, Mr. Kadam?" I asked.

The Indian businessman blinked, and a tear fell down his cheek. He sucked in a quick breath and cleared his throat. "Yes, of course. I'm just so sorry, Miss Kelsey, that you were held prisoner. It would be hard to find a more cruel and vicious man than the one who abducted you. You were very clever in manipulating him, and I applaud your creativity in such a dire situation. Such a brave girl. I'm very proud of you. All of you."

Another tear fell, and he wiped it away. "I believe I could use some rest as well. If you three will excuse me . . ." Mr. Kadam stood and with a dignified mien, walked to his room and closed the door softly behind him.

We had never seen Mr. Kadam look so old, so tired, so . . . world-weary. Ren, Kishan, and I speculated quietly but decided to let him and Nilima sleep as long as they needed to. I checked on both of them from time to time, and though they seemed peaceful, I couldn't shake the feeling that our respite would be short-lived.

When Nilima finally awoke eighteen hours later, she seemed back to her cheery, matter-of-fact self.

"Well, hello, Miss Kelsey. Aren't you a sight for sore eyes," she said, smiling over a bowl of yogurt.

"Nilima," I asked, "what happened to the two of you?"

"I don't really know," she admitted. "One minute we were on the ship, and the next we ended up here. It was magic, I suppose, or maybe Durga helped us."

I smiled and nodded but I wondered how she and Mr. Kadam could have such different memories of the same experience.

While Mr. Kadam still slept, Nilima wasted no time plunging with gusto back into the family business dealings. She spent many hours on the phone and the computer with Ren and Kishan at her side, watching and learning how she ran things.

Unlike Nilima, Mr. Kadam was still somber, contemplative, and mysterious when he awoke. Though he insisted everything was fine, his behavior worried me.

"Mr. Kadam, why are you so closed off from us? What's bothering you? I miss you."

"Nothing, my dear Miss Kelsey."

I looked up, but Mr. Kadam wouldn't make eye contact. "Yes, there *is* something bothering you. Don't you trust me?"

He sighed deeply. "Of course I do. It . . . it's myself I don't trust. There are some things in this world that a person must face on his own." He tilted his head and considered me. "May I be so bold as to ask you a personal question, Miss Kelsey?" When I nodded, he went on. "If you had a child who was learning to walk, would you pick him up and carry him each time he fell or would you encourage him to keep trying?"

"To keep trying, of course."

"And if you saw sharp corners or broken glass in his path, would you clear the way for him?"

"Yes."

"And what if your child was trapped in a house of burning flame? What would you do then?"

Without hesitation, I answered, "I would run in and save him."

"Yes, you would. In spite of the danger to yourself, you would endeavor to protect your precious ones." He smiled. "That is precisely what I needed to hear. You have given me great comfort, Miss Kelsey."

"But I haven't done anything."

"You have done more than you know. You have a heart pure and loving. It is a priceless gift that you have offered to all of us."

"You're my family."

"Yes. We are. Don't worry so over me."

After a pensive moment, I sighed. "Alright," I responded softly.

Impulsively, I wrapped my arms around him. Mr. Kadam gently enfolded me in a warm embrace and pressed his cheek against my forehead. He patted my back, and I felt another teardrop land on my nose.

Clearly, some things were certainly not back to normal, but Kishan did his best to rekindle our romantic flame nonetheless and brought up the idea of a date. First he suggested a romantic dinner by the pool, but we decided on a movie in the theater room instead.

"It's a date," Kishan said, poking his brother with his elbow. "And just to be clear, *you* are not invited. Three's a crowd."

Ren threatened, "Just don't hurt her." With a retaliatory shove, he stormed upstairs.

A few minutes later, we heard the unmistakable sound of something big being smashed against the wall from the direction of Ren's room.

I sighed and wrapped my arms around Kishan's waist. "It's not nice to throw us in his face like that," I said gently.

Kishan pressed his lips against my forehead. "Ren needs to understand that I'm not giving you up."

"He does understand, but that doesn't make it easy. Think about how you would feel."

"I know exactly how he feels. He wants you back, and I don't plan on accommodating his wishes."

"Kishan—"

He cupped my chin and tilted my face to look at him. "You're my girl, aren't you?"

"Yes, but—"

With a questioning look in his golden eyes, Kishan asked softly, "Do you want to go back to him?"

I froze, not knowing what to say. After a moment I shook my head slowly. "I chose you, and I meant it."

He smiled, tilted his head, and said, "I'm not very good with words, and I know you've been through a lot these past few weeks. I told you we can take this slow once before, and I'm saying it again. We haven't really had time to talk since, well, since Ren got his memory back. If you feel hesitant or unsure about me, it's okay. I'm not saying it won't hurt my feelings, because it will, but if you want to start over, back up, or hit reverse, I'll understand."

Once again, I marveled at the kindness and patience of this good man. I really didn't deserve him. I pressed my cheek against Kishan's chest and said with confidence, "I think what I'd like to do is to move *forward* with our relationship."

He grinned. "Just how much forward are you talking about?"

I laughed. "Why don't we just start with a kiss?"

"I think I can manage that."

Kishan's kiss was gentle and sweet. I sighed and wrapped my arms around his neck. I felt thoroughly safe and loved and protected in his arms. Kissing him back and loving him was as easy as slipping into a comfortable pair of sneakers. There was no golden fire. There was no powerful jolt of passion. There was no steel tether that connected us. But there was love.

A happy lifetime could be built on that strong foundation. Kishan would cherish me, and I knew that we would form a bond of our own. Over time, my stubborn heart would soften and would let Kishan possess it completely. I didn't know when, but I hoped it wouldn't be too long for both our sakes.

We broke apart when I heard another crash upstairs.

"Talk to him, Kells," Kishan said intuitively.

With a nod, I headed toward Ren's room. It was time to clear the air. So much had happened since he had regained his memory. I needed him to be at peace with both Kishan and me.

I found Ren sitting at his desk, staring out the window at the pool. Papers and notes were strewn across the floor and a small bookshelf lay in a heap as if it had just folded in on itself. I stooped to gather the pages and realized they were poems.

"What do you want, Kelsey?" he asked in a quiet voice without turning around.

"I'm here to see what all the commotion is about. Were you trying to take down an elk?"

"What I do in my own room is my business."

I sighed. "You make it *our* business when you're that loud."

"*Fine*. The next time that my life is destroyed, I'll try to express my distress in a quieter fashion, far away from your tender sensibilities."

"You do have a gift for exaggeration."

Ren spun around and stared at me incredulously. "The only exaggeration is that you are in possession of tender sensibilities. Obviously that is not the case. A *tender* woman would admit she is wrong. A *tender* woman would listen to her heart. A *tender* woman wouldn't spurn the man she loves. Do you realize I almost lost you forever? Don't you have any idea how that affected me? The thought of Lokesh hurting you was more than I could bear.

"Did you know that I could feel you? Your fear, your terror became mine. I haven't slept in a week and my every agonized wakeful thought was spent wondering if you were hurt and suffering. The hope that I might get you back, to hold you, finally, in my arms and know that you were safe was the only thing that kept me sane."

"Ren—"

He interrupted, "Then you come home and what do you do? You go traipsing back over to Kishan. I'm allowed to offer you comfort but not love. *Kelsey*, how can you still deny what you feel for me?"

"You always wax poetic when you're angry." I picked up a book and ran my hands over the leather cover. "I prayed for you to come. I knew that the two of you would move heaven and earth to find me if you could. I'm not denying that I love you. I've admitted as much to you, in fact."

"Then explain it to me again. How can you love me and choose Kishan?"

"If you don't think I love Kishan, you're mistaken." I sat on Ren's bed and sighed, tossing the book onto the nightstand. "Do you believe he's a good man? That he loves me, will watch over me, protect me, and keep me safe?"

"Yes."

"Then, in your mind, there is nothing wrong with my choice, except that he's not you."

"And there's also the fact that you're not *in love* with him," he said dryly.

"Kishan's good and kind and brave and wonderful, just like his brother. Isn't it enough that he makes me happy?"

"No."

"Then there's nothing more for me to say." I smoothed the stack of poems and left them in a neat pile on his desk.

Ren's eyes burned holes in my back as I quietly left the room.

Downstairs, while Kishan and I watched a James Bond film, I thought only of Ren. He was the person I'd always confessed everything to. He was my friend, and he also knew me well enough to see I was holding back. He knew there was something more to my choice, and like a tenacious hound with a juicy bone, he was not going to let it go. I sighed, snuggled closer to Kishan, and lay my head on his chest.

6

Uaishno deui shrine

The next day we started the long journey to a temple of Durga. The temple Mr. Kadam chose was actually located in Katra, in the Indian state of Jammu and Kashmir. We were going into the Himalayan Mountains and about as far north as you could go and still be in India. Katra was four hundred miles away, not far from the border of Pakistan.

Even with Mr. Kadam driving faster than would be legal in the United States, we were stuck in the car all day. The only breaks we got were a few quick stops for gas. After I was told our destination was Katra, I tried to explain how Spock's "katra" ended up in Dr. McCoy's body in *Star Trek*. Ren had seen *Star Wars* so he kind of understood what I was talking about, but Kishan soon lost interest. When I brought up the time travel episodes, Mr. Kadam seemed particularly keen to know what happened to all the characters in the future if the space-time continuum was disrupted.

Finally, the snow-capped mountains near Katra came into view. I had thought the Himalayas were cold in the summer, but now, in the winter, the air was downright freezing. The worst part was that we'd have to hike up thirteen kilometers to the mountain temple.

"I'm sorry, Miss Kelsey. I promise that we will rest often along the way," Mr. Kadam said.

I shivered. "Fine. Snowy mountain peak temple it is. I'm just glad this is the last quest."

At sundown we asked the Scarf to set up a thick tent with mounds of blankets inside. Mr. Kadam made us hot bowls of stew using the Fruit, and I used the power of the amulet to warm the interior of the tent. Heat waves of energy pumped from my hands as if I were a radiator.

The next morning was cold and bright. After a breakfast of hot cereal, we donned several pairs of wool socks, spiked hiking boots, and layers of cold-weather clothes, topping off the layers with down jackets. Ren kept creating extra things for me to put on. Unsatisfied with my scarf, he made a thicker one and wrapped it three times around my neck. Then he added a ski hat that covered my whole head except my face and put another hat with ear protectors on top of that. When he started criticizing my gloves, I pushed him away and told him to go bother someone else.

"You're not in Antarctica, Kells," Kishan commented as the four of us started the hike to Durga's temple.

"Bug off. Ren's being overprotective. It wasn't my idea."

Kishan grinned. "Here. At least I can carry your backpack for you. Looks like you're packing double your weight in clothes anyway."

I shoved my bag at him and marched off toward the mountain in a huff. "Come on. Let's get this over with."

Kishan laughed uproariously, and the four of us hiked toward Durga's temple.

Mr. Kadam caught up with me quickly, followed by Kishan and Ren, who took up the rear after staying behind to break camp.

On the way to the temple, Mr. Kadam walked by my side and kept me distracted by talking about the area and its shrine.

"Would you like to hear the story of the temple?"

"Yes," I said. I slipped on an icy patch of ground, and Kishan was next to me in an instant, his hand under my elbow to lend me his support.

Mr. Kadam inhaled the brisk mountain air and let it out with a sigh. "Around seven hundred years ago, a demon called Bhairon Nath chased Durga, or Mata Vaishno Devi as she was called then, into these hills. When Bhairon Nath found her hiding in a cave, she cut off his head with a trident. It is said that the large boulders near the mouth of the cave are the petrified remains of his body."

"I have a question. Why do Hindu gods and goddesses have so many names and forms? Why can't Durga just be Durga?"

"Each form is called an avatar, a reincarnated form of the goddess. In one life she may be called Durga; in another she may be Parvati, for example. The concept of reincarnation varies from religion to religion. Some believe a person is reincarnated because he needs to continue to learn, and he only stops reincarnating when he has gleaned from his human life that which he needs to know to ascend to the next level of existence.

"In Buddhism, reincarnation is seen not so much as the same spirit inhabiting a new body, but it's more that the old spirit gives rise to a new one, like a dying flame igniting a new candle. The candles are different but the flame comes from those who have gone before."

"But aren't gods and goddesses already enlightened?"

"Ah, in India our gods and goddesses are not perfect."

"It's still confusing."

"Yes." He smiled. "Many also believe that the goddess calls to her devotees from this very temple and that they will drop whatever they are doing to make a pilgrimage here."

"That's interesting. Do you feel a calling to be here?" I teased.

He looked up at the looming mountain trail ahead of us. "Yes. In a way," he replied softly.

We continued hiking for several hours on a well-worn path that angled up the mountain.

Mr. Kadam's spirits seemed to lift a bit the closer we got to the temple. He was more distracted than usual, but he smiled often, and we talked of many things. I hadn't realized just how much I had missed him until then.

The last part of our journey was a series of icy carved steps that led up to the cave. Though we'd been equipped with ice-climbing boots, I was glad to be able to lean onto Ren and Kishan for support.

We stopped briefly to catch our breath at the mouth of the cave and then moved through to the end of the one-hundred meter structure to the stone temple beyond the cave. The temple's conical structure was similar to the Shore Temple. Its layers of thin stone were carved and notched, almost like a rock-climbing wall in a gym. The exterior was gray at the top and more sepia-colored near the doorway. The four of us stepped inside and began searching for the statue of Durga.

Though the outside of the temple was drab, the interior was bathed in color. Near an alcove on a dais stood the goddess we'd been seeking. This time the goddess was not carved of stone or even bronze but was made of wax.

Durga's face and arms were painted an alabaster tint, and she wore a gown of heavy jeweled fabrics and garlands of silk roses, jasmine, and gardenias around her neck. Her hair, under a headpiece adorned with jewels, looked real. A ruby *bindi* rested between her arched brows and her golden nose ring and earrings gleamed with semiprecious stones. Behind her, the alcove was painted as red as her lips.

"She's beautiful," I whispered.

Kishan studied the statue for a moment and then answered, "She is."

"So this is it," I said calmly. "Mr. Kadam, are you sure we're in the right place?"

Mr. Kadam smiled strangely. "Trust me. We are in the right place."

"Okay, let's give this a try."

I asked Kishan for my backpack, and he helped me lay all of our offerings to Durga at the feet of the statue. Mr. Kadam had instructed us to bring a box of long matches, several fat candles, a few pieces of wood, some charcoal, a couple firecrackers, a lighter, and a string of very hot chilies. When it was time for me to brush the bells on my anklet, I discovered I couldn't reach them. My many layers of clothes prevented me from bending over.

Kishan laughed heartily at my dilemma. Ren just growled softly, knelt at my ankle, and brushed his fingers across the bells. Then he stood and we joined hands.

Ren began our plea to Durga. "Today we seek your help on this, our last task. We have come to complete your fourth and final challenge and ask for your blessing that the path ahead may be smooth and our feet sure and steady."

I added, "Please help us to have the wisdom and the skill to make it safely through this last part of our travels."

When it was Kishan's turn, he said, "And when all is said and done and we lay your four gifts at your feet, we ask for an opportunity for a new life in return."

After a few seconds of silence, Kishan nudged Mr. Kadam, who had been staring absently at the floor.

"Oh, yes. I ask you to please watch over and protect my charges so that what is destined to be will come to pass."

I turned and stared quizzically at Mr. Kadam, who merely shrugged his shoulders while Ren and Kishan changed into tigers.

What happened next scared me to death. The candles and matches burst into flame, the firecrackers exploded, and fire quickly spread around the dais and began licking the walls behind the Durga statue. From there, the blaze spread wall to wall, and we were soon encased in a box of fire.

Anything flammable was quickly consumed, but the four stone walls didn't burn for long. Instead, the fire danced across the floor, burning moss and dust particles between the flat stones. In a snap, we were engulfed in a pillar of fire. Ren and Kishan turned back into men and tucked me between them, our backs to the encroaching circle.

I screamed when the tail of Ren's shirt caught on fire, but Kishan quickly slapped the fire out. Smoke filled the room, and I buried my face into Ren's shirt to stifle my coughs. Though a cold breeze blew through the room, it was still hot, hot enough that the wax effigy began to melt before our eyes. Her jeweled headdress turned into a pool of rainbow tears that slowly dripped down her beautiful face.

On the wall behind the figure, a handprint glowed red in the hot stone. Ren insisted on touching it first and burned himself. I asked the Pearl Necklace to cool it down and soon a curtain of cold water descended from the ceiling to meet the hot stone. At first, the water hissed and steamed, but within a few minutes, it slid over the stone smoothly and pooled on the temple floor.

I stepped forward, placed my hand into the hollowed-out print, and focused my energy. The henna design surfaced, and prickly heat tickled my palm.

Durga's melted figure began to glow. Her hair burst into flame and stood out from her head like a fiery mane. Wax dripped off the figure to form a large puddle near her bare feet, leaving behind a beautiful woman who radiated the warmth of ten suns. Her skin was honey-caramel and her gown sunset-orange. She only had two arms, one adorned with a simple golden band, though the wax figure had boasted eight. With her eyes closed, she took a deep breath and smoothed her hands over her black, silky hair. The flames disappeared. The only jewelry she wore was the armband and a golden belt at her waist.

The goddess smiled at the four of us, and I heard the sound of tinkling bells as she spoke.

"It is good to see you all again." Pointing to the floor, she laughed. "As you can see, your offerings have been accepted." Durga waved her hand in a big arc, and the sooty walls and lumps of burned material disappeared.

A light squeeze on my arm reminded me that Fanindra was eager to see her mistress. Approaching the dais, I slid the jeweled cuff off my arm and handed her to Durga. The snake immediately animated, raised her head, and wrapped around Durga's arm several times.

The goddess stroked Fanindra until Kishan cleared his throat. Without looking at him she sighed and censured, "You must learn to be patient where women and goddesses are concerned, my ebony one."

Kishan quickly apologized, "Forgive me, Goddess," and bowed chivalrously.

The ghost of a smile appeared on her face. "Learn to love the moment you are in. Treasure your experiences, for precious moments too quickly pass you by, and if you are always rushing toward the future, or pining for the past, you will forget to enjoy and appreciate the present."

"I will endeavor to treasure every word that passes from your lips, my goddess." Kishan raised his head, and Durga leaned forward to touch his cheek. "If only you were always so . . . devoted," she said.

Ren took my hand in consolation while my boyfriend made goo-goo eyes at the gorgeous goddess.

When Durga finally looked at me, her expression changed from wistful to gracious.

"Kelsey, my daughter. Have you fared well?"

"Umm, mostly. A giant shark took a bite out of my leg but other than that, I've been good."

"A giant . . . shark?" She seemed confused, and her eyes darted toward Mr. Kadam.

Something strange is going on.

"Yes. A shark. But we got the Pearl Necklace for you. See?"

I showed her the Necklace, which she studied with a smile.

"Yes, I am glad. This gift will be very much needed in your next quest." Durga's eyes drifted to my face, and she took my hands with motherly concern. "Your hardest days lay ahead, my precious one."

"You must help her," she addressed Ren. "Shore her up. A cleansing comes—a burning of the heart and soul. When the three of you emerge from this you will be stronger, but there will be times when you may be tempted to ask for the burden to be lifted from your shoulders.

"Kelsey will need both of you in the days ahead. Think not of yourselves or of your dreams, but focus on what you need to do to save her and on what you must do to save the rest of us. We are *all* depending on you."

"The tigers get to be men full time after we find the next prize, right?" I asked.

Durga answered thoughtfully, "The form of the tiger was given to them for a purpose and soon that purpose will be realized. When this fourth task is completed, they will have the opportunity to separate themselves from the tiger. Come and take your last weapons."

From her belt, the goddess drew a golden sword and, in one quick motion, split the blade into two weapons. With a flash of her arms, she spun the swords in each hand, twirling the weapons until both blades rested at Ren's and Kishan's throats. Her eyes gleamed with delight.

Ren demurred, and the goddess tossed him a sword, which he accepted gracefully. But she kept the tip of the other pressed against Kishan's throat. His eyes tightened slightly, and I wondered if he was going to challenge the goddess.

Durga grinned at Kishan and twirled the sword again, but he anticipated her actions and avoided the blade. They did a deadly dance together, and Durga seemed delighted by his prowess. After a moment, she cornered Kishan, who froze, this time with the blade aimed at his heart.

I sucked in a breath while she teased, "Not to worry, my dear Kelsey, for the black tiger's heart is very hard to pierce."

Kishan glared at the beautiful goddess in fighting stance. Her orange gown was slit from hem to mid-thigh, and I couldn't help but notice her taut and lovely long leg.

She might not be perfect, but her legs sure are. Even when I was practicing wushu regularly in Oregon, my legs never looked that good.

A scowling Kishan appeared to be noticing the same thing. His gaze traveled from her bare leg up her face, and when she raised a mocking eyebrow, he glowered at her.

I put my hand on his arm. "Kishan, she's just demonstrating how to use the sword. Relax."

He did, but the goddess grinned as if she could read his mind. He batted the blade away from his chest before sullenly taking the sword. The goddess straightened and removed two brooches from her golden belt. Taking a step down from the dais, she pinned one on Ren's clothing and the other on Kishan's. Kishan stood immobile, nodded hesitantly, and watched her every move as the goddess demonstrated how to use the seemingly innocuous pins.

Durga covered Kishan's brooch with her palm and spoke. "Armor and shield."

Immediately the brooch grew and golden metal shot out in every direction, encasing Kishan's body. Soon, he was wearing a suit of armor and was holding his sword and a shield.

Durga pressed the brooch again and whispered, "*Bruucha*, brooch." The suit of armor shrank back down until it was only a gleaming decoration once more. "Perhaps it would be better for the time being for you to remain in these . . ." she said in a low, sultry voice, running her hand over Kishan's broad shoulder, "modern clothes. I have a weakness for handsome men dressed in battle gear."

Kishan's expression changed to one of surprise.

What was going on? Durga had never flirted with Kishan this . . . blatantly before. It was as if we were watching a badly acted soap opera.

"These brooches were created especially for the two of you," Durga continued. She stared into Kishan's eyes; the heat between them was palpable. "Do you like my gift, ebony one?" she asked softly.

Kishan sucked in a breath, stepped forward, and took her hand in his. "I think you are . . . I mean, I think it is . . . incredible. Thank you, Goddess," he said and kissed her fingers.

"Hmm," she smiled appreciatively. "You are welcome."

Ren growled softly, and Mr. Kadam finally broke the tension.

"*Perhaps*, we had best begin our journey. Unless you have more to tell us . . . Goddess?"

Durga immediately took a step away from Kishan, who looked at her like she was a tasty morsel he wanted to devour. She returned his gaze, and the looks that passed between them were steamy enough to melt the stone floor.

Durga glanced at Mr. Kadam and nodded her head. "I have said all that is necessary. Until we meet again, my friends."

Her features began to solidify and desperately, I asked, "When will we meet again?"

Durga smiled and winked at me. Then flames rose around her body, obscuring our view, and when the fire diminished, she was an eight-armed statue once again. I stepped up to the dais and held out my arm for Fanindra, who stretched out and wrapped herself around my upper arm, settling into her normal position.

As I turned back, I jerked, shocked to hear an angry voice echoing in the quiet temple.

"*That* was entirely inappropriate!" Ren spat at his brother and punched him in the face.

7

destiny

Kishan rubbed his jaw and glared at Ren.

"If I ever see you treat Kelsey that way again, I'll do a hell of a lot more than just knock some sense into you. I highly encourage you to apologize. Do I make myself clear, little brother?" Ren's tirade continued.

Kishan's eyes widened, and then he nodded meekly.

"Good. We'll wait for you outside, Kelsey," Ren said and left, with Mr. Kadam trailing in his wake.

"He's right. I apologize. I don't know what I was thinking. I'm sorry, Kells." Kishan wrapped his arms around me. "You're still my girl, aren't you?"

I nodded against his chest, and he took my hand and led me outside.

"You can be mad at me if you want. Go insanely jealous and beat me down. I deserve it."

The odd thing was . . . I wasn't jealous. I was more curious than angry. Making a mental note to discuss it with Mr. Kadam later, I hurried along the path and was shocked to see that all the ice and snow around the temple had melted.

Going down the mountain path was much easier than going up, but both brothers insisted on holding my arms as we descended, just in case I slipped. By the time we passed Katra, I was dead tired and not sure I could make it the last mile.

Mr. Kadam, who was usually so accommodating, insisted that we keep going and even suggested that one of the boys carry me. I sighed and trudged on slowly until Kishan picked me up and cradled me in his arms. I was asleep by the time we finally arrived back at camp.

While I rested my sore feet by the fire, I was able to sneak in a private conversation with Mr. Kadam.

"Mr. Kadam, I . . . well, I just wanted to know what you thought about Durga and Kishan. I'm not sure how I feel about what happened in the temple. You saw it too, didn't you?"

"Yes. I . . . yes, I noticed."

"Should I be concerned? About Kishan, I mean?" I squirmed under Mr. Kadam's gaze. "The old myths talk about gods falling in love with mortals and even having children with them. Do you think Durga has a thing for Kishan? I'm not sure how I'm supposed to feel about that."

Mr. Kadam looked up at the starry night sky and then smiled at me. Gently, he said, "How *do* you feel?"

"I feel . . . like I should be really upset, but I'm not, and that bothers me a little. I trust Kishan. I believe he loves me."

"You're right about trusting him. Kishan wouldn't be with a goddess when he has you. He loves you."

"I know he does, but Ren was so upset."

Mr. Kadam sighed. "Ren . . . loves you, too. He confronts anything that threatens those he loves. He has always given of himself, even to the point of setting aside his own desires, to make sure that others have the things they need. In war, he would rather ride to the front lines and place himself in harm's way before allowing his men to die."

Yep. Sounds like Ren. I nodded. "I've seen this first-hand. He broke up with me because he couldn't save me when I almost drowned. He sacrificed himself so Kishan could get me away from Lokesh's henchmen. He constantly pushes me away to save my life."

Sagely, Mr. Kadam inclined his head. "Ren will always jump to your defense. That is how he shows his love for you, Miss Kelsey."

What if that's not the kind of love I need? I thought.

Mr. Kadam continued. "Kishan was the opposite in battle. The win was more important to him than how he won. He would also protect those he loved and would also ride to the front lines, but his purpose was to challenge himself, to lead the other warriors and to inspire them.

"Both Ren and Kishan have changed much over the years. They have matured, becoming better men than they once were. Kishan has become more outwardly focused. He no longer tries to win at any cost, and he has learned that a victory for his team can also be a victory for himself, even if he doesn't wield the sword.

"Ren's dreams have turned inward. Once, he faced armies, fought for his people, and sought peace for his country, but now he yearns for a soul mate. He wants a family of his own and someone to love." Mr. Kadam steepled his fingers, pausing to listen to the crackling of the burning wood. "Both men love you in their own manner, in the fullest way they are capable of. I believe the goddess Durga holds a certain fascination for Kishan, because he recognizes a kindred spirit. She is much the way that he used to be.

"Durga is a warrior in her own right, and she challenged him by holding the sword at his throat. The old Kishan would have immediately risen to that dare, but your hand on his arm held him back. I would not see this as a cause to doubt Kishan's affection for you."

"Thanks." I smiled.

Mr. Kadam squeezed my fingers, just as the brothers approached.

Kishan sat down near the fire and pulled me into his arms. "Time for our bedtime story. What Greek god are we going to hear about tonight?"

I stroked his arm and smirked, teasing him. "I think tonight I'll tell you about Zeus's many affairs with mortal women and how his wife, Hera, punished them all."

Ren snickered while Kishan winced. But he sat still, determined to get back into my good graces and said sweetly, "I will endeavor to treasure every word that passes from *your* lips, my goddess."

I elbowed him, but he only chuckled.

"And don't you forget it, my friend."

Quietly, he whispered, "I won't, love," and kissed my ear.

Ren stopped laughing and grumbled, "Get on with the story."

During my often embellished verbal chastisement about unfaithful men, Mr. Kadam retrieved his Samurai sword from its velvet case and polished it in the firelight.

The wooden logs had turned to glowing coals by the time my story neared its end. Mr. Kadam stared into the flames quietly, his sword resting on his lap. I finished with, "And that's what happens when spouses cheat," when we heard a familiar, twisted voice.

"I must say, your choice of bedtime stories proved most prophetic this evening. You are a woman of many gifts, my dear."

My heart slammed into my throat, and I clutched Kishan's arm. Thanks to Ren and Kishan, I had learned how to remain calm when confronting dangerous creatures, and I was proud of my ability to fight back without flinching. The only exception to the rule had just stepped into the light of the fire and stared at me hungrily.

Lokesh had found us.

Ren and Kishan immediately bound to their feet and grabbed their weapons. Mr. Kadam reached out to touch the three of us—and then all movement stopped. I felt my body lurch. I was being sucked into something from the inside out. My molecules were being squeezed tightly together, and my guts were rotating toward a vacuum. Suddenly, my body felt as if it was being compressed like a data file, pushing me toward a drain with a suction so strong, I couldn't fight it. In a second, I was spinning in a black void. Then a tiny light penetrated the darkness.

With a disturbing pop, I materialized next to Kishan behind a line of thick shrubbery, about twenty-five feet from our campfire. Mr. Kadam smiled and removed his hand from my shoulder.

"What . . . what just happened? How did we get here?" I asked, disoriented.

Mr. Kadam replied, "I moved us through space. There isn't much time to explain." He squeezed Ren's shoulder; then put his other hand on Kishan's. "My princes, my sons, you have trusted me since you were young, and I ask you to trust me again. You must do something for me, and you must obey my exact instructions. Will you do this?"

Ren and Kishan nodded. Mr. Kadam continued, "Do not, under any circumstances, leave this spot until Lokesh is gone. No matter what you see and hear, you *must not interfere*! Give me your warrior's vow."

Mr. Kadam clasped their hands. Together, they repeated a mantra I'd never heard before.

"Yours in life, yours in death. We vow to respect the wisdom of our leaders, remain ever vigilant in our duty, exhibit bravery in the face of death, and demonstrate compassion in the same way we would have it given to those we love."

Then together, Kishan and then Ren touched their foreheads to Mr. Kadam's.

Soberly, he said, "Your charge is Kelsey. Lokesh must not find her. Protect her at all costs. Think only of her and block out everything else. This is the only way to defeat him. No matter what happens, if you wish to honor me, you must do this."

With that said, Mr. Kadam disappeared into thin air.

"What's happening?" I whispered, more than just a little afraid.

At that moment we heard voices carried on the wind from the other side of the brush. Ren edged closer to the greenery, and we peered at our campsite through the thick branches. The fire we'd been standing next to a few moments before was crackling again. And in front of the dancing flames were Mr. Kadam and Lokesh.

I stood up, but before I could take a step, Ren and Kishan tackled me to the ground.

"What are you doing? We need to help him! We have all the weapons!"

Ren whispered, "We gave him the warrior's vow."

"So?"

"We won't break it. It's a warrior's code, and Kadam has never asked it of us before. It's only used when a plan needs to be followed without deviation. If even one person does not fulfill their duty, the endeavor is lost," Kishan explained.

"Well, he didn't think this through! Mr. Kadam's not in his right mind!" I argued futilely.

Through the shrubs, we could see Lokesh clearly. I stifled a gasp. Half of his face was burned badly and his damaged eyelid drooped. The hair on that side had been burned away. There were shiny scars around his neck where we'd strangled him, and he walked with a slight limp.

"Where have you taken them, my friend? It seems you still have some tricks up your sleeve." Lokesh asked in an almost desperate, raspy voice.

"Somewhere they will be safe," Mr. Kadam answered.

Mr. Kadam lifted his Samurai sword, blew on its surface, and slid his finger along the blade.

"I know you want the amulet. Unlike my sons, I have no weapon with which to fight you other than my old sword. Be that as it may, I will endeavor to protect them with my life."

"It will come to that in due time." Lokesh fixed his good eye on

Mr. Kadam's amulet greedily and asked, "Would you like to tell me of your amulet's power so that a few minutes of your life might be spared?"

Mr. Kadam shrugged. "It provides a healing power. From what I hear, you should be dead already." He gestured to Lokesh's face. "It would seem that your power doesn't heal you as well as mine does."

Lokesh spat at the dirt angrily. "We will test that out soon enough. How did you move them?"

"Would you like the opportunity to win my piece of the amulet fairly?" Mr. Kadam countered. "No amulets, sorcery, or black magic. Just two warriors fighting hand to hand, steel on steel, as if we were still a part of the old world."

Lokesh scrutinized his opponent for a moment, and then smoothly, with just a hint of mockery, he said, "You wish to die as a warrior. I have been a warrior long enough to understand and empathize with your request. I ask you, though, what of your healing? Surely, this fight would not be fair."

"The healing is not instantaneous. Deal me a crippling blow, and you will be able to easily remove my piece of the amulet. That is, unless you're afraid to fight an old man."

"Fear does not motivate me." Lokesh peered into the darkness focusing on right where we were sitting as if he were considering his options.

I sucked in a breath, and Ren quietly let the foliage fall back to its natural shape.

"It shames me to say this, old friend, but I find that I am not as enthusiastic to continue this discussion as I should be. My mind has been bewitched, and there will be no rest for me—not until the young Ms. Hayes and I are reconciled. I believe I'd rather seek my reluctant bride first and teach her a lesson. She's close, my comrade, even now. I can sense her. But, rest assured, I'll return to deal with you later."

He took a step toward the jungle, then halted when Mr. Kadam took a few practice swings with his sword and warned, "You won't find her easily."

Lokesh spun. "On the contrary, I found *you* in this wilderness. I've had spies watching the temples of Durga for some time. She's near, and I won't be thwarted any longer."

I gasped, and the sound was enough to make Lokesh and Mr. Kadam stop talking and peer into the trees.

Mr. Kadam swung his sword menacingly. Distracted, Lokesh turned back to watch. "You have a master's touch, my friend."

Mr. Kadam stopped and held up his sword so Lokesh could admire it. "It's exquisite, is it not?"

"Indeed it is. Very well, since you are so eager to die for your *charges*, I will accommodate you. Besides, it will be lovely to see the expression on my bride's face when I tell her of your death."

Mr. Kadam pointed his sword at Lokesh. "She will not be your bride. She is meant for my son. You will never touch her again, you vile demon."

"Demon?" He smiled evilly. "I like the sound of that."

Mr. Kadam whipped the sword quickly forward and left a slash along Lokesh's cheek. Astonished, Lokesh reached up to touch the wet blood dripping down his face. His surprise transformed to fury in an instant, and his fingertips crackled, unleashing a blast at Mr. Kadam. Mr. Kadam's body blurred slightly as the power rolled ineffectually through him in waves.

Frustrated, Lokesh summoned an earthquake, but his opponent still remained standing. Lokesh raised his hands into the air and mumbled an odd chant. A rumbling shook the dirt in front of him, and after a moment, a black sword rose into the air.

"It would seem you get your gentleman's death after all," he sneered.

Mr. Kadam smiled, raised his sword, and attacked. Lokesh's sword was thick and solid, and despite having the lighter and longer weapon, Mr. Kadam seemed to have difficulty maneuvering away from Lokesh's blows. The clang of swords rang stridently through the crisp night air. I could see the foggy breath of both men as they clashed.

Mr. Kadam was the more elegant fighter and quickly dealt wounds to Lokesh's arms and torso, but Lokesh played dirty and used his powers to try to break down his opponent. Lokesh swung a mighty blow that bit deeply into Mr. Kadam's shoulder. As his arm sagged, he tossed his sword to his other hand.

I whimpered. Kishan wrapped his arms around me and pressed his cheek to mine.

"He can use both hands equally well in battle," he whispered.

I itched to use my fire power to help, but as if reading my thoughts, Kishan purposefully threaded his fingers through mine. Minute by slow minute passed with neither man making headway. The minor wounds didn't seem to affect Lokesh at all, and he blazed into battle like a bull that had been stuck several times. His murderous attention was focused on Mr. Kadam, who neither backed down nor seemed to be influenced by it. Instead, he lithely danced away from the beast and continued to poke and prod.

Ren and Kishan lifted their heads at the same time and sniffed the air.

"What is it?" I whispered.

"Cats," Ren answered.

A moment later a pair of large snow leopards passed within a few feet of us. They paused and pricked their ears forward. With a hiss they continued through the brush and emerged from the tree line to creep behind Lokesh. A pack of wolves entered the clearing from the other side and a black bear ambled near the fire, stood up on his hind legs, and bawled ferociously at Mr. Kadam. The wolves snapped at his heels, and the cats crouched, waiting for a good time to pounce.

Lokesh laughed and welcomed his new friends. Mr. Kadam panted and constantly faded in and out of focus. A leopard jumped and landed on his back. He threw it off, and the creature fell awkwardly into the pack of wolves. The bear charged but passed right through Mr. Kadam's body as if he were a ghost. Despite this newfound ability, when he turned, I saw bloody claw marks covering Mr. Kadam's back.

"We have to help him," I demanded quietly.

"No," Kishan said.

"He'll die."

Ren touched my face. "He wants us to stay hidden. We have to trust that he has a plan."

A wolf bit Mr. Kadam's ankle. He ran it through with his sword, but he limped after that. Lokesh circled him gleefully.

"Do you surrender now, old man?"

"I will not," Mr. Kadam responded.

"Very well."

Lokesh advanced quickly, swinging his black blade in a fast series of thrusts that backed Mr. Kadam into the bear. The bear raked the back of Mr. Kadam's thigh, and he staggered to the ground, crying out. I hissed through my teeth and gripped Kishan's arm, feeling a sympathetic ache as I recalled the painful wounds a bear had given me in the same place.

With a grunt, I sucked in a breath, stood, and made a break for it. I'd been able to elude Kishan but not Ren. He yanked me off my feet. I wriggled and wrestled, pushing against him with all my might, but I couldn't escape. Tears leaked from my eyes and I begged, but the brothers did not let me go.

Stinging with my failure and the betrayal of the men I loved, I wept.

I couldn't see what was happening anymore. I heard the growls of the wolves, a whimper of pain, the roar of the bear, and the clash of the swords. Distraught, Kishan wiped the tears from my eyes and stroked my hair out of my face but Ren was immovable. His hold on me was absolute.

I heard the spray of pebbles against a rock, the clatter of a sword, a howl of pain, and then Ren jolted as I heard the unmistakable sound of a body hitting the ground. Ren's eyes filled with tears. He ducked his head and silently let them spill.

Kishan's body was stiff, his expression frozen. I jerked when I heard Lokesh's lecherous laugh.

"It pains me to see you brought to this, my friend. But I always win, you see. It's too bad, really, that you won't be around to give away the bride. I'm sure she would have liked that."

I heard the low murmur of a response, then a wet cough.

Lokesh replied, "Obstinacy must run in the family. Even now, you believe you're going to win. Given your current circumstances, your confidence is perhaps a bit excessive. I must give you some credit, however. You managed to bloody me more than I had anticipated."

I balled Ren's shirt in my fist and pulled myself up to see what was happening. Mr. Kadam was lying next to the fire, the sword pinning him to the ground through his chest. He was gasping for air, one hand reaching for the sword.

My lungs seized, and I began to hyperventilate.

Bored with the proceedings, Lokesh violently kicked Mr. Kadam in his wounded leg.

"That is for distracting me from my purpose."

He bent over Mr. Kadam's body and twisted the sword cruelly. An evil smile spread over his face as Mr. Kadam cried out in pain. "And that . . . is for mussing my suit."

Mr. Kadam panted and said between wet coughs, "Then . . . take . . . what you . . . came for."

His words trailed off, and he lifted a bloody hand to his collar. With a savage jerk, he tore the amulet from his neck and held it out to Lokesh, whose eyes fixed on the piece with delight. "She will be your doom," he proclaimed.

The moment Lokesh's hand closed around the stone, he and the amulet disappeared in a flash, and the beasts slunk off into the brush. Mr. Kadam slumped back to the ground. Together, the three of us ran into the clearing and slid to our knees next to our beloved mentor and father.

"Kadam! Kadam!" Ren and Kishan shouted in desperation.

Blood trickled out of Mr. Kadam's mouth. I ripped off one of my many shirts and wrapped it around the sword to try and staunch the blood that was gushing from his wound.

I yelled, "Kishan, where's the *kamandal*?"

Kishan reached for the shell that usually hung at his throat—only to find it missing. "I don't understand. I never take it off!"

As he tore through the tent, ripping bedding apart in a frantic search for the mermaid's gift, I wished up a cup of water, gently lifted Mr. Kadam's head, and pressed it to his lips.

I had the Necklace fill the cup again but Ren wrapped his hand around my wrist and stopped me.

"The sword has pierced his lung, Kelsey, and he's lost too much blood. Without the *kamandal* . . . we can't save him."

Kishan returned and sunk to his knees at my side. "It's gone. I can't find it," he mumbled desperately.

I heard a cough and a whisper. "Miss Kelsey."

"Please don't leave me," I begged. "I can help you. Just tell me what to do."

Mr. Kadam lifted a trembling hand and caressed my cheek. "There is nothing . . . you can do. Don't cry. I was . . . prepared for this. I took the *kamandal*. I knew it would happen. Was . . . nec . . . necessary."

"What? How can it be necessary that you die? We could have helped you, fought with you! Why did you hold us back?"

"If you had been here, the fight would . . . have changed. This was . . . the only way to . . . to defeat him."

I closed my eyes, and fat drops squeezed through the tight lids. I exhaled shallowly, and then Mr. Kadam whispered painfully again.

"I need to tell you—I . . . love you. So much."

"I love you too," I wept.

"I'm so proud of you. All of you," he wheezed and looked at Ren. "You must press on. Fin . . . finish what we started." Feebly, he gripped Ren's arm. "Ren, you must . . . find him," Mr. Kadam said. "Find him in the . . . past."

Ren nodded and sobbed openly. Tears ran down Kishan's face.

Mr. Kadam closed his eyes. His hand dropped to the ground, and he smiled at me faintly. I listened to the wet rattling in his lungs as he breathed in and out, once, twice, and then no more. The man who was our friend, advisor, mentor, and father slipped away. His life forfeited for a cause we didn't understand.

a farewell

Piercing grief swelled inside me and burst, leaving me empty, hollow, a collapsed version of myself. All of my questions about our quest and Mr. Kadam's strange words melted away into the shadowy recesses of my consciousness.

I picked up Mr. Kadam's limp hand and stroked it over and over, willing his fingers to clasp mine. But they didn't move. Gently, Kishan put his arms around me and tried to offer me comfort, but I sat stiffly, staring blankly at Mr. Kadam's body.

Ren pulled the sword from Mr. Kadam's chest and violently hurled the loathsome weapon into the jungle. Then he fell to his knees and sunk his face into his hands. The three of us sat this way until we heard a thumping sound in the sky.

Confused, I wondered briefly if it was a Stymphalian bird, but then sudden gusts of wind shook the trees and a spotlight touched the ground. I looked up to see the dark outline of a helicopter landing. Footsteps rushed toward us, and Nilima fell onto the ground next to me, crying out in grief and sorrow. Cradling her grandfather's head on her lap, she rocked back and forth. After some time, the night became silent again.

Kishan and Nilima spoke quietly in Hindi. The two of them

moved around the camp, gathering our things and stowing them in the helicopter. Kishan retrieved the Scarf from our backpack. Tenderly, he placed Mr. Kadam's arms over his chest, touched his forehead, and murmured words to the shimmering material.

Slowly, the Scarf twisted and shot out dark threads to wrap around Mr. Kadam's body. I watched in a mental fog as it created a burial shroud. When this was done, Kishan shook Ren to get his attention. He spoke in Hindi, and together they picked up Mr. Kadam's body.

I heard the engine of the helicopter start up again. I knew I needed to move, but I didn't seem able to. When Ren knelt before me, his eyes bright with tears, I felt my own well up again. I put my arms around his neck, and he swept me into his embrace and cried with me for a moment before carrying me to the helicopter. An emotional Nilima adjusted a few instruments, wiped her eyes, and took off.

As we rose into the night sky, I stared despondently at the wrapped form placed at our feet. Ren held me and rubbed my back, but his touch couldn't stop my trembling. At some point on that long journey home, he changed into his tiger form and rested his head in my lap. Every once in a while he growled softly, sorrowfully. I buried my face in his fur and wrapped my arms around his neck. Rhythmically, I stroked his back over and over, and found solace for my sadness while comforting my tiger. Eventually, I slept.

When we landed on the practice field near the house, it was two o'clock in the morning. Ren and Kishan carried Mr. Kadam's shrouded body to the dojo while Nilima and I walked upstairs. I slumped into the nearest chair, like a broken doll and when she brought me an icy lemon water, I started crying again.

The boys returned just as the front doorbell rang. Mr. Kadam's old pilot, Murphy, who had flown us over the Baiga camp, was standing at the doorstep.

"I'm sorry to call at such an hour, but Kadam asked me to come here at this exact time," Murphy explained. "A few weeks ago, Kadam gave me detailed instructions to fly here and deliver a letter. He said I was to fly you somewhere else after you read the letter. Is everything alright?"

"Please, won't you come inside?" Nilima asked numbly. "I'm afraid Mr. Kadam has . . . has died."

Murphy's face crumpled, and with a shaking hand, he gave Ren an envelope bearing Mr. Kadam's familiar script.

We all sat down in the living room as Ren skimmed through and read, "I would like to be placed in a simple wooden casket and buried next to Ren and Kishan's parents. A pressed suit is hanging in the entry-way closet." Ren paused. "He speaks so matter-of-factly about his own death."

Nilima patted Murphy's hand.

He gripped her fingers and said, "I'm so sorry, Miss. If there is anything I can do, please let me know. He was a remarkable man."

"Yes, he was." Her voice broke, and then we sat silently.

Time slowed. My mind was foggy and thick, and I sat there dull, heavy, and filled with sorrow, hardly listening to the rest of Mr. Kadam's letter. I looked up when Kishan knelt by my chair and stroked my cheek.

He spoke softly, "Murphy's going to fly us to the jungle where we first met. In Kadam's letter, he wrote that his casket is already there. He wanted to be laid to rest near Deschen's garden, so he would be remembered at the place where our lives came full circle. I'm not sure what that means but we will honor his wishes. If you don't want to go, you can remain behind. Would you prefer to stay here?"

I shook my head. "No. I want to go, but I need to find something more appropriate to wear to his funeral."

Somehow I made my way upstairs and washed my face and hands. I walked into my closet and discarded several items of clothing. Angrily,

I tore through my closet, ripping clothes off hangers and throwing them violently across the room. I shredded the plastic wrapping on new clothes, then wadded the skirts into balls and pitched them at the wall.

When that wasn't satisfying, I started on the shoes. I picked out the heaviest and hurled them. They each hit the wall with a gratifying bang. When I ran out of ammunition, I used my fists. I punched the wall over and over again until I tore the skin across my knuckles. Tears streamed down my face, and I collapsed into a wounded heap on top of my pile of shoes.

A shadow fell over my body. "What can I do?" Ren asked. He sat on the floor of my closet and pulled me onto his lap.

I sniffed. "I don't have anything to wear."

"I can see that. Someone destroyed your closet while we were away."

I laughed wetly and then sobbed. "Did . . . did I ever tell you about my parents' funeral? I wanted to give the eulogy. I was going to talk about my mom and dad, but when the time came, I couldn't say a word."

His fingertips wiped tears from my eyes. "That's a lot to expect of a traumatized teenager."

"I *wanted* to do it. I wanted everyone at that funeral to know what great parents I had. I wanted them to know how much I'd needed them. How important they were to me. I wanted them to know that I'd loved them."

He pushed the hair away from my sticky cheek and tucked it behind my ear.

"When the time came, I dissolved. I stood there staring at those two caskets and couldn't say one word. They deserved more than that. They deserved to be remembered and loved and talked about, and I let them down."

"I'm sure they wouldn't have thought that."

"That was the last thing I could do to honor them, and I screwed it up. I don't want to do the same thing to Mr. Kadam."

"Kells," he sighed. "You honor your parents every day of your life. You don't have to give a speech to show how much you loved them. They wouldn't have wanted you to carry this burden all this time. They loved you. Kadam loved you too. You don't have to say the right thing or wear the perfect dress. You honor them by living, by being the wonderful woman that you are."

"You always know the right things to say, don't you? Thank you," I whispered as I clutched my shoes.

Ren brushed his fingers along my jaw and left.

I showered quickly and scrubbed my puffy, tear-streaked face. After I dressed, I wound my hair into a bun at the nape of my neck and headed downstairs. Ren and Kishan had showered and changed too. Both men were wearing dress shirts and ties, and even though we'd be in the jungle, their more formal clothes seemed appropriate.

Kishan drove us to the private airport that was a few miles from the house.

As we climbed into the old propeller plane, Murphy bent over his controls and said, "Kadam loved this old plane. It's a Lockheed Electra 10E used in World War Two. He once told me that Amelia Earhart made her famous last trip in one of these."

The factoid made me smile and remember how fond Mr. Kadam was of sharing every little detail of his mechanical toys. But my smile fell when I stole a glance at Nilima across from us. Mr. Kadam's death had clearly affected her terribly. Her hair hung in tangles around her tear-stained face and something she had rubbed up against had left grease stains on her lovely white blouse. She rested her head, leaning back, and closed her eyes.

Murphy smoothly lifted us into the air, and with the hum of the engines and the emotional roller coaster ride of the past twenty-four hours, it wasn't long before I fell into a dark, confusing dream.

In the dream, a young Lokesh was standing over a monk, torturing him for information.

"Tell me of the amulet, old man," a desperate Lokesh threatened.

The monk screamed. "Please! I beg you to have mercy!"

"Mercy will be given when you tell me what I desire to hear."

The weakened man nodded and said, "A few centuries before the birth of my teacher, there was a great war. All the powerful kingdoms of Asia gathered together to battle a demon. A goddess arose with two faces: one face was dark and beautiful and the other was bright and more glorious than the sun. She led the armies of Asia against the armies of the demon. The armies of Asia were victorious, and, as a result, the goddess blessed each kingdom with a gift."

"What does this have to do with the amulet?" an impatient Lokesh screamed and wrenched the man's wrist cruelly.

"Let me . . . let me explain," the man panted. "The goddess took the amulet from her neck and broke it into five pieces. She gave one piece to each king and admonished them to keep secret its origin and to use its power to help and protect his people. They were instructed to pass it within their family to the eldest son."

"And which kingdoms fought in this battle?"

"The five that gathered were the people of the—"

The dream suddenly ended when Ren shook me awake.

"We're landing," he murmured quietly.

I looked out the window and only saw dense jungle below. "Landing where?" I asked.

The plane turned and Ren pointed out of one of the windows. "There."

The morning sun glinted in my eyes, blinding me for a moment, but then the plane banked to the right and I saw the sparkle of the river and a dirt runway below us. I knew the river eventually led to our old camp near Ren's waterfall, but I couldn't remember seeing the runway before.

"Where did that come from?" I asked.

"I have no idea," Kishan answered. "I know this jungle like the back of my hand and there was never a clearing there, let alone a space long enough to land a plane."

"Hold on, everybody," Murphy warned. "It's going to get a little bumpy."

He circled the jungle one more time and began his descent. The belly of the plane brushed across some tree tops as we dipped lower. When the wheels touched down, the old aircraft rumbled and bounced as if it were going to come apart, but Murphy landed us safely, and we all disembarked.

Mr. Kadam had left instructions for Ren and Kishan to dig his burial plot in the garden. They somberly carried Mr. Kadam's shrouded body down the hill while Murphy, Nilima, and I found a shady spot to wait.

"This is the darndest thing I've ever heard of," Murphy commented. "Why in the world would he want to be buried in the middle of nowhere? I just don't understand it."

I patted Murphy's arm in sympathy but said nothing as I tried to coax Nilima to drink some juice. It was hot. Even in December, the jungle was hotter than most summer days in Oregon. We'd gone from a Himalayan winter to a tropical zone in less than twenty-four hours.

Murphy continued to talk. He seemed almost able to carry the entire conversation by himself, which was a good thing as Nilima was practically mute.

"Did you know I first met Kadam in China during World War Two? I was in the navy then, part of the Flying Tigers. We went over before America joined the war as a part of the AVG—American Volunteer Group. During the war, Kadam helped us through some tough spots.

He sometimes served as an interpreter for our commander, Old Man Chennault. Kadam owned the company that supplied our aircraft, the Curtiss P-40s, and he had visited several times to ask the pilots questions so he could improve the aircraft design. Our normal translator was absent one day, and Kadam stepped in. After that, he made it a point to stop by headquarters whenever he was visiting.

"He always teased me about being a hellion, mostly because I was in the Hell's Angels squadron, but also because I was a very green eighteen-year-old intoxicated with flying. We had that in common. I've never seen a man more taken with aviation."

"You *have* known him a long time," I whispered.

"Yes, I have. We formed a fast friendship. After the war, I returned to the States. Imagine my shock when he found me a few decades later. He looked exactly the same as I remembered him. Said he was recruiting pilots for a new airline company, Flying Tiger Airlines. I didn't even hesitate. In all that time, that man never aged a day. I always asked him what his secret was, but he never told me."

I looked up at Murphy, startled and unsure where the conversation was headed, but the kind pilot just laughed and rambled on.

"Oh, I learned long ago not to ask Kadam too many questions. He was a man with secrets, but a more honorable one I never met. I thought my old bones would be laid to rest long before his."

The more Murphy talked, the more I reminisced about my own experiences with Mr. Kadam. Murphy's endless chatter seemed to even perk up Nilima a tiny bit, and before we knew it, Ren and Kishan had returned to collect us.

Kishan took my hand and helped me up. He whispered, "The dirt was soft and practically shoveled itself. It was very strange."

Ren and Kishan carried Mr. Kadam's coffin, and we walked in a slow procession to the grave site. The first thing I noticed was the old hut. I could see that it must have been beautiful a long time ago. It was connected to another building by a worn walkway that was raised off the jungle floor atop thick tree trunks. Though there were holes in the roofs where birds nested, I could see they had once been carefully shingled.

The small garden was surrounded by mango trees. Monkeys above us chattered noisily. Though dormant for the winter, I saw shriveled melon plants and even found a cluster of overgrown, rotting pumpkins.

The path curved, and I swallowed thickly as we stopped at an open grave. Ren and Kishan had removed the shroud and placed Mr. Kadam's body in a simple wooden casket. He looked distinguished and peaceful in his suit and with one jolt I realized it was the same suit he'd been wearing the first time we met at the circus. No longer able to look at him, I took a step to the side and brushed my fingers across large headstones. Vines had crawled over the stone markers. The ground was thick with ferns, and the canopy of tall trees shaded the old grave site. It was a peaceful, quiet place. In the shade, the air was cool and a breeze caused the leaves to quiver overhead.

"This is my father's. Kadam must have put these here recently. The old grave markers rotted into dust centuries ago," Kishan said, crouching down to trace the Sanskrit writing.

"What does it say?" I whispered as I admired its carved lotus flower.

"It says 'Rajaram, beloved husband and father, forgotten king of the Mujulaain Empire. He ruled with wisdom, vigilance, bravery, and compassion.'"

"Just like your seal."

"Yes. The marker is actually a replica if you look closely."

Kneeling at his mother's grave, Ren read, "'Deschen, dearly loved wife and mother.'"

The boys quietly paid respects to their mother while I thought about my own parents. Looking back at the hut on the hill, I wondered if the spirits of Deschen and Rajaram had watched over their old home and their sons all these years. Knowing Mr. Kadam would be laid to rest here in this beautiful place was somehow comforting. He belonged here.

"This is a lovely spot," I commented under my breath.

"It is," Kishan answered. "But we did find something odd when we were digging."

"*Tiger* bones," Ren added softly.

Tiger bones? I'll need to remember to ask Mr. Ka . . . oh. For the tiniest moment, I had forgotten. My eyes welled up. I sucked in a deep breath, knowing it was time.

Ren touched my cheek. "Are you ready?"

"Yes," I said in a small voice.

Ren took the lead and asked Murphy if he'd like to say anything. Murphy shook his head and wiped his nose with a handkerchief, blowing noisily.

"He . . . he already knew how I felt about him," he said.

Nilima waved the offer off as well, lifting her haunted eyes to us and shaking her head mutely.

It was Kishan who took a step forward and said, "Yours was the death of a warrior. You laid down your life for your king, your country, and your family. Today we honor you as you take your place among our ancestors. We are endowed richly, having been taught by you in all things. You have been our advisor, our example, our most trusted soldier, and our father. I honor your deeds. I honor your loyalty. I honor your generosity of spirit. It has been our privilege to fight by your side and to live in your presence. May your weary soul attain rest from earthly toil and find peace. We are not left desolate without you for you will abide evermore in our minds and in our hearts."

Kishan stepped back, and Ren squeezed my hand. It was my turn. I wiped tears from my face and began with a poem:

HOME THEY BROUGHT HER WARRIOR DEAD
By Alfred, Lord Tennyson

Home they brought her warrior dead:
She nor swooned, nor uttered cry:
All her maidens, watching, said,
She must weep or she will die.

Then they praised him, soft and low,
Called him worthy to be loved,
Truest friend and noblest foe;
Yet she neither spoke nor moved.

Stole a maiden from her place,
Lightly to the warrior stepped,
Took the face-cloth from the face;
Yet she neither moved nor wept.

Rose a nurse of ninety years,
Set his child upon her knee
Like summer tempest came her tears
Sweet my child, I live for thee.

Nilima wept softly at Kishan's side while I continued, "It's hard for me to express my feelings, much like the girl in the poem. Mr. Kadam, you were my surrogate parent, and I felt as connected to you as I did to my own." I choked, and my voice cracked. I whispered, "I don't know how I'm going to make it without you. I miss you so much already. I'll do my best to help your princes, and I will always try to honor you. I love you."

Kishan put his arm across my shoulders, and I stepped into his embrace, wrapping my arm around his waist. Ren stepped forward and spoke last.

"Kishan has given a warrior's eulogy and to it I would add my own. I honor you also my friend and father. You were steadfast in affliction and unwavering in support. You deserve a hero's memorial. Humbly, we offer our admiration, our respect, and our love."

Ren read a poem he'd brought with him.

THE DESERTED HOUSE
By Alfred, Lord Tennyson

Life and Thought have gone away
Side by side,
Leaving door and windows wide.
Careless tenants they!

All within is dark as night:
In the windows is no light;
And no murmur at the door,
So frequent on its hinge before.

Close the door; the shutters close;
Or through the windows we shall see
The nakedness and vacancy
Of the dark deserted house.

Come away: no more of mirth
Is here or merry-making sound.
The house was builded of the earth,
And shall fall again to ground.

Come away: for Life and Thought
Here no longer dwell;
But in a city glorious—
A great and distant city—have bought
A mansion incorruptible.
Would he could have stayed with us!

"We are diminished in your death, my friend, and can only pray that we can live on in such a way that would make you proud. I hope that you have found your mansion incorruptible, for if anyone deserves such a place, it is you."

Trembling, I watched as Ren and Kishan approached the casket to lower the lid. On a sudden impulse, I asked the Scarf to make me a white silk rose. The threads wound together in my hand and when it was finished, I placed it carefully inside. Then the lid was closed, shutting away the beloved face of Mr. Kadam forever.

9

Voices of the departed

Walking away from the grave site, I felt melancholy and heavy. I shaded my eyes so I could look up at the roof of the old hut. Palms, ferns, and thick gnarled trees were clumped in such a way that I could imagine they had once been meticulously landscaped. Old wooden steps with rustic branch railings led up to the jungle house, and a deck made of bamboo poles encircled the structure.

While Nilima and Murphy headed back to the plane, I dusted the bottom step and sat down to wait for Ren and Kishan, soothing my heart by vowing to return to this place after we broke the curse. I got lost in my thoughts until I heard the crunch of footsteps as Ren and Kishan turned the corner.

Trying to get all our minds momentarily off our loss, I asked the Necklace for tall, cool glasses of water, which we sipped quietly. Then I told them about the strange dream I had on the plane.

"What do you think it means?" I asked.

"I don't know," Ren said. "Maybe your connection to Lokesh has become more powerful since he took the fourth piece of the amulet."

"Or maybe Mr. Kadam is sending these dreams to her," Kishan offered. "Like the time she dreamt of him after we rescued her."

"I'd prefer to think it's the latter," I said.

Ren crouched before me and touched my cheek. "So do I."

"We'll figure out what it means, Kells," Kishan said. Flicking his head toward the house overhead where he and his family had taken refuge after the curse, he asked, "Would you like a tour?" He took my hand and guided me up the old steps. "We built these to last. Still, they could use some fixing up."

I ran my hand along the knobby wood railing. "It's in really good condition for how old it is."

The house was made of smooth wooden boards. The structure was simple in design. A braided bamboo rug covered the floor and next to it were a carved table and chairs. A set of shelves with a large basin was set into the other corner. Hollowed out gourd bowls were stacked neatly on a shelf, and I could see the remnants of a towel left on the wooden counter.

Blowing spiderwebs and dust off of a misshapen tool, I discovered a hairbrush with a carved ivory handle. "I'd like to keep it, if you don't mind."

Kishan smiled gently and said softly, "I don't mind, *bilauta*."

"Did you and Ren sleep here?"

He shook his head. "Because we were tigers all the time back then, we slept in the jungle or near the steps, keeping watch at night. Sometimes we slept in Kadam's house across the way. If there was a bad storm, Mother insisted we stay inside with them, but most of the time we tried to give our parents some privacy." He took my hand and headed to the door.

I asked, "Were they happy here, do you think? I mean, leaving their palace and their riches and coming here to live like this in the jungle?"

Kishan stopped by the table and turned. "Yes. They were happy here." He reached up to run his fingers delicately along my jaw. "When you have a life filled with love, you don't really need anything else."

I wandered the room slowly, thinking about Kishan's parents, Mr. Kadam, and all the things Mr. Kadam had seen and experienced in his long life. I barely knew a fraction of them. There were so many things about him I wanted to know. A tear slid down my cheek. *Now I'll never know.*

Kishan stood patiently as I touched each dusty item.

"Do you love him, Kells?"

"Yes," I replied, knowing exactly who he meant.

"Do you love me?"

"Yes."

"You're sure you want to choose me?"

"Yes."

Kishan smiled. "Good. I promise I'll do my best to make you happy." He put his arm around me.

I sighed and leaned my head on his shoulder. "Kishan . . . in order for us to work, we'll have to leave Ren. I can't be with you the way I should be with him around. It's too painful for all of us."

He kissed my forehead. "Then we'll leave. After we find the fourth object, we'll go."

"You'd leave India for me?"

"In a heartbeat."

Slowly, I let out a weary sigh. As we were leaving, I placed my hand on Kishan's arm. "I'd like to come back here someday. I want to plant some flowers at Mr. Kadam's grave and trim back the jungle."

Kishan smiled and kissed my forehead. "We'll return as often as you wish."

As we made our way down the back steps, I asked, "If you had some supplies do you think you could fix up the house?"

"Why do you want to do that?" He leapt over the last few broken steps and landed smoothly.

"It would be nice to stay here sometimes," I explained, jumping safely down. "This place is important to you, to your family. It's your home." I played with the leather band he wore on his wrist, the one I'd given him in Mahabalipuram. "I want you to feel like your heritage is remembered and honored."

He wrapped his arms around me. "You are my home, Kelsey. Wherever you are is where I belong."

We found Ren at the bottom of the front stairs, whittling a stick with an old knife. He looked up at our entwined hands and frowned. "I found Father's old hunting knife buried in the dirt."

"Ren, if it's alright with you, we'd like to come back here sometime and get the place fixed up," I said hesitantly. "Technically, you own the property since you are the heir."

He grunted and stood abruptly. "Being the heir means nothing." His eyes pierced Kishan's. "So, the two of you want to build a cozy nest. The lovebirds need a place to call home, do they?"

I took a step toward him. "Ren, don't."

"Don't what, Kelsey? Don't react? Don't feel? Don't speak? Which thing *don't* do you want me to do?"

"Ren, I don't want to fight. Not today. *Please.*"

He lifted watery eyes to my face and studied me for a moment, then wearily turned his head away. "Do what you want with the place. It doesn't matter. Nothing does anymore."

He stalked off toward the plane.

Just as quickly as we had arrived, Murphy flew us all back to Ren and Kishan's home in the jungle. The brothers and I lagged behind in the driveway, saying our goodbyes to Mr. Kadam's old pilot. We eventually made our way to the kitchen, where we found a tearful Nilima.

"He knew all of this would happen! Kadam planned everything!" she announced.

I put my hand on her trembling shoulders.

"What are you talking about?" I asked.

She sniffled loudly and turned to the kitchen table. Grabbing up a handful of papers and a manila envelope, she shook the fistful of documents and shouted, "I found this. He left it for us. He planned everything!"

Ren put his hand on her arm. He quickly scanned the documents and frowned. "I think you should read this aloud, Kells. Would you mind?"

The manila envelope had been sent priority mail from a law office in Mumbai. The first page was a letter. I began:

My Dear Ones,

When you receive this letter, I will be dead. I know you have many questions that I could not answer before, and there are still many things I cannot share with you now. As you may have guessed, the amulet I wore healed me of minor wounds, prevented disease, and kept me alive for centuries. It also has more power than we had previously thought.

It has the ability to control time and space. I discovered this potentially most dangerous of powers purely by accident when I tried to protect Nilima on the ship. The amulet physically removed us and set us adrift in the cosmos.

It took me a while to understand what had happened to us and to learn how to control the amulet. I was also able to erase Nilima's memory of the event. Forgive me, my dear, but I wanted at least one of us to recover from the experience and be able to live a normal life.

During that interval, I was able to see time unfold before me. I learned more of the universe than a man should know. It's a terrible burden to know the future. I didn't want that for you, Nilima.

If there had been any way to guarantee a successful outcome without my demise, I would not have sacrificed myself. Please believe this. I would have preferred to help you finish Durga's quest and would have enjoyed bouncing your children on my knee, Miss Kelsey. I had no desire to leave you, but it was necessary.

If I survived, one or all of you would have been killed. I could not let that happen. When Lokesh took the amulet, I used its power to send him into the past, for that is where he was fated to go. But this does not mean he is gone for good, and this does not mean you are safe from him.

I also know definitively that it has always been your destiny to overcome Lokesh, and there is only one way you are able to accomplish this—through the power of the tiger.

This power was destined for two worthy sons of India to wield, and though I cannot tell you more at this time, I will say that I can think of no men finer or braver than the two of you. Destiny has chosen well. The lives of many have been entrusted to your care. Consider your actions carefully. There is still much work to be done.

Miss Kelsey, I bequeath to you my library. All the books that I own now belong to you. This library will be the beginning of your own collection. Whether you leave them here or take them with you when you marry, they are yours. You are a daughter to me, and this gift is nothing compared to what you have given me.

Study the books that talk about Durga's creation. This knowledge will help you in your journey. Take care of Ren and

Kishan—they both need you—and guard your piece of the amulet well. It is the only object protecting the world from Lokesh, and he will stop at nothing to take it from you.

When you knew him, Lokesh was still a mortal, but in the past he has embraced evil and allowed his soul to fester in darkness. Through black magic and his manipulation of the amulet, he has become a demon and though he will fall into your hands, it will not be in this time or in this place. To defeat him, you must journey into the past and confront him when he is at his most powerful.

I have included the translation of the fourth prophecy to guide your way. Nilima can take you to the Andaman Islands where you will seek the City of Light. Do not fear the flame, Miss Kelsey, for if you are prepared, it will not hurt you. The object you are seeking is called the Rope of Fire. It will transport you to the time and place I sent Lokesh. There you shall meet a guide who will aid you in your battle. To use the Rope, simply think of when and where in time you need to go and whip it in a circle. A vortex will open, and you will be able to leap through time.

Nilima must stay behind and take care of all the difficulties that will arise in the company due to my death. If she journeys with you into the past, she will perish. She must not go!

I wish that I could be with you. I wish that I could tell you everything. But I promise you that I have seen your future, and I know that you will be victorious. You will overcome the monster. Rely upon one another; trust each other. Ahead lies a lifetime full of love and happiness for all of you.

There is a story about a king and his son that may give you some comfort: An oracle foretold that the boy would die by snakebite on the fourth day of his marriage. The king, distressed at this news, vowed that his son would never marry and taught his son to find fault with every princess who came to seek his hand.

Years passed, and then one day when the king was away, a young woman stormed through the castle doors and accused the prince of wrongly imprisoning her father.

The prince was shocked. No woman had ever spoken to him in that manner before. His eyes fixated on the smudge on her cheek and her one eye that was a shade bluer than the other. But as she continued to beseech him, those thoughts fell away, and he soon noticed the curve of her figure, the gleam in her eyes, and the shine of her black hair.

The prince demanded that her father be freed. Instead of pledging her undying thanks, the woman gave a stiff curtsey, which only made the prince love her more. The prince declared his feelings for the woman, who merely scoffed at him with disdain. However, his persistence won out in the end, and she came to love him as fiercely as she once reviled him.

Despite the king's misgivings, the two were married, and the king told the new bride of the oracle's prediction. On the fourth night of their marriage, the new bride set out every piece of gold, silver, and jewelry the couple had. Both she and the prince kept vigil all night long and waited for the serpent. She lit lamps, told her husband stories, and sang to him to keep him awake.

Late that night, the god of death, Yama, arrived in the guise of a cobra, but his eyes were dazzled by the lights and the wealth heaped on the floor. He swayed to the lilting songs and at dawn, unable to fulfill the prophecy, he slithered away.

I tell you this story for two reasons. First, I want you to remember that even though your feet have been set on a path that is not of your choosing you still have the freedom to decide your own destiny. I want nothing more than for you to be happy. This story is an excellent example of twisting fate to your benefit.

I would also have you know that I chose my fate and I could not have wished for a better death or have more hope for a beneficial outcome. Do not mourn me, but consider instead the blessings of a life well lived.

There is a saying, "When a father gives to his son, both laugh. When a son gives to his father, both cry." You have given me much, my sons. I am proud of you. I have often wept at the thought of leaving you, but I know that you will be able to go on without me. Take good care of my Miss Kelsey.

I will leave you with a sonnet. Perhaps the reading of it will soothe us all.

SONNET 30
William Shakespeare

When to the sessions of sweet silent thought
I summon up remembrance of things past,
I sigh the lack of many a thing I sought,
And with old woes new wail my dear time's waste:
Then can I drown an eye, unused to flow,
For precious friends hid in death's dateless night,
And weep afresh love's long-since-cancell'd woe,
And moan the expense of many a vanisht sight:
Then can I grieve at grievances foregone,
And heavily from woe to woe tell o'er

The sad account of fore-bemoaned moan,
Which I new pay as if not paid before.
But if the while I think on thee, dear friend,
All losses are restored, and sorrows end.

I will think on thee often, my dear friends. Until we meet again.
—Anik Kadam

As if in silent tribute, Ren and Kishan switched back to tigers. My hand dropped heavily to my lap, and I stared silently out the kitchen window. Nilima wept softly.

"Why didn't he tell me? I could have shared this burden with him," she declared emotionally.

"He didn't want that for you," I replied and rubbed her back. "He didn't want that for any of us."

Scooping up the papers, I read through Mr. Kadam's translation of the fourth prophecy.

Flames of the skies,
Sunset and Sunrise,
Await you with blazing breath.
Caldera descend
And Qilin defend
While Rakshasas seek your death.
When Bodha is near,
That which you fear
Will threaten to tear you in two.

But with armor and sword,
You will find your reward
And spells of illusion undo.
The Lords of the Fire
Intend to conspire
To keep you from what you need.
A burning lash
From Chimera's cache
Is a prize they surely won't cede.
Then when you have won
And your task is done,
It is time to cross to the past.
When destiny draws close,
Overcome your foes
And bring India peace at last.

"There's a note attached to the prophecy," I read. "'I have compiled this list of what I believe you will be up against in this last journey. First, you must travel to the Andaman Islands, where you will take a boat to Barren Island, a tiny volcanic isle that has a diameter of only three kilometers. There are directions on how to find Barren Island in the GPS I installed into the watercraft.

'Once you arrive on the island, climb to the top of the cliff and then descend into the caldera. You must proceed with caution. This volcano is active, and the cliff is precipitous. It erupted this year. This island is uninhabited by humans, but there will be other creatures that are not of this world. You must brave the flame to enter Bodha, a fabled City of Light that is found at the core of Earth.

'Not much is known about the city or its inhabitants, but there is an account written by Willis George Emerson of a lost sailor from Norway who found the entrance to the underground city through a cavern at the North Pole. The story by Jules Verne, *Journey to the Center of the Earth*, is reminiscent of Bodha as well. In that case, the adventurer journeyed to the center of Earth through volcanic tubes in Iceland to find a lost world.

'Some of the other creatures you may come across on this journey according to the prophecy are Qilin and Rakshasas. A Qilin is a creature from Chinese mythology. It has the head of a dragon and the antlers of a deer and is covered with fish scales. It is said to be a gentle creature and symbolizes good luck. Rakshasas are shape-shifting man-eaters that use magic and illusion to catch their prey. They are warriors and difficult to kill. They have venomous claws as well.

'Be wary of the Chimera, which Miss Kelsey most likely has already heard of. It is a lioness with a snake tail and an extra head that is usually represented by a goat. The Chimera breathes fire and is very dangerous.

'You will also cross paths with the Lords of the Flame, trickster twin brothers who are powerful and greedy. They can be played against each other, but if they unite against you, the result may be tragic. One of them fights with a *Gáe Bolga*—a notched javelin-like spear. Its tip opens into thirty barbs upon impact. The only way to remove the weapon is to cut it out. The other twin wields a pair of barbed whips.

'I do not know what types of creatures Sunset and Sunrise are, so I would plan for the worst and hope for the best. This is all I can prepare you for. Good luck to you all.'"

Nilima sniffled as I set the papers down and felt a tiger nose touch my leg. Ren looked pointedly at the stairs. I knew exactly what he wanted to say. It was time to put this long day behind us.

After Nilima and I said good night, I climbed the stairs with my two tigers trailing along behind me. They settled on the floor in my room and watched me move about through sleepy eyes narrowed into slits. I climbed into bed and tried to burn every detail of Mr. Kadam's face into my memory forever.

10

the birth of durga

It was a Hindu custom to mourn for thirteen days, but we decided to mourn for three days and then follow the tradition of keeping a lamp lit for another ten.

Mr. Kadam had said to look up Durga's creation, and I dutifully immersed myself in study that led me to an interesting theory. The Durga stories told of many weapons, and with Ren and Kishan researching at my side, we jotted down a quick list to keep track of them all.

<u>Weapons</u>

Disc (Chakram)

Conch (Kamandal—healing power)

Missile (Spear Darts from Trident?)

Arrows (Golden Bow and Arrows)

Thunder Bolt (Lightning Power?)

Bell (Needed to Awaken Durga)

Rod (Trident/Trishula)

Axe (Blade of Chakram?)

Magic Armor (New Weapon)

Mace (Gada)

Water pot (Other Name for Kamandal, I think)

Cudgel (Other Name for Gada)

Sword (Actually Two Swords)

Snake (Fanindra)

Rope (Rope of Fire?)

Jewels (Pearl Necklace)

New Clothing (Divine Scarf)

Garlands of Immortal Lotus (Gave to the mermaid
    Kaeliora—Durga said it had no power)

Noose (Rope of Fire?)

"It appears there are lots of different versions of how Durga was born," I explained, reading on. "In this text it says Durga was a goddess who was born from the flame. But other books claim she rose from a river, appeared out of a whirlwind, came from a ball of light, and emerged from the cave of a great mountain. Then there's also a story about Durga being created to battle a demon called Mahishasur."

"Okay, so the stories vary," said Kishan.

"Yes, but what's the common denominator?"

I paused, but they said nothing, waiting for me to fill in the blank. "The *amulet*!" I exclaimed.

"I don't get it," Ren said rubbing his jaw.

"We know that the amulet piece I wear has the properties of fire, and Mr. Kadam said his piece shot him into space. What if each amulet represents one of the elements—fire, air, water, earth, and space—and each of her 'birth' stories reflect a different element?" I proposed and handed over my notes on the amulet.

<u>Possible Powers</u>

The roar of Durga's tiger shook the world.

   (Earthquake? Earth Amulet)

Oceans boiled and surf flooded the land.

   (Water Amulet or Pearl Necklace)

Mountains crumbled in a thousand landslides.

   (Earth Amulet)

Used her divine breath to replenish her armies.

   (Food/water/clothing? Using gifts)

Great flames issued forth in all directions.

   (Fire Amulet/Rope of Fire)

Dodged mountains. (Earth Amulet)

Encompassed Mahishasur's army in a sandstorm.

   (Air Amulet)

"Okay, then which birth story is the accurate one?" Kishan asked.

"Maybe they all are," I suggested.

"Um . . . here's something," Ren added. "This book talks about a volcanic island that sounds an awful lot like the one Kadam told us to go to. It's called the Pit of Hell."

"Really?" I coughed on a bite of muffin. "That's marvelous."

"That's not the worst of it."

"Good," I mumbled sarcastically. "I wouldn't want it to be *too* easy. So a volcanic island and a battle between Durga and Mahishasur? I think it's possible that Durga may have had the whole amulet when she beat him, taking into account, of course, that we accept the story literally."

"It's a good theory," Kishan said. "There's no mention of anything strange happening in space or time though."

"No, there isn't. There's also no mention of anyone appearing or disappearing."

"Tell me the story of the battle, so I can picture it in my mind," Kishan asked.

"Alright. I'll start when Durga meets Mahishasur." I thumbed through pages until I found what I was looking for. "'When the goddess entered the battlefield astride her tiger, all eyes turned to her. The tiger paced slowly forward, and the awestruck men knelt while the demons panted softly at seeing the beautiful goddess. She was calm, fearless. Though she passed squadrons of demon archers, thousands of charioteers, and hundreds of battle elephants, none moved to harm her—each creature was totally awestruck at her power.

'When at last she reached the demon king, she was surrounded by men with glistening iron axes and black halberds'—wait, what are halberds?"

"It's like a long spear with an axe on the end," Ren answered.

"Got it. 'The battlefield was a river of blood but even the red river could not distract from the red of her lips or the lushness of her hair, so immensely beautiful was she. The demon king fell in love upon seeing her and announced he would take her for his bride. He instructed his men to capture the goddess, but none of them were aware that behind her great beauty was a creature of great strength.

'Like a whirlwind, she and her tiger rose up and slew each of the demon king's cohorts. She threw her noose around Mahishasur's neck, and while her tiger clamped onto his body with his jaws, she raised her sword and cut the demon in half.'"

Kishan whistled. "She sure sounds like my kind of woman."

I elbowed him in the ribs and Ren rolled his eyes, but Kishan ignored us.

"I would have loved to see her in battle," he continued.

"I think you're missing the point, Casanova."

Kishan grinned, captured my hand, and kissed it. "I wondered what it would take to make you jealous. By the way, I'm nothing like Casanova. I'm strictly a one-woman man," he said.

I looked up and locked eyes with Ren briefly before he buried his nose in a book again.

"The point is," I continued without remarking upon his comment, "I think we need to prepare to fight Lokesh the same way Durga fought Mahishasur."

Kishan blinked, and understanding lit his eyes. Soberly, he leaned forward and took my list from Ren. "I think you're right, Kelsey. Lokesh wants you in the same way the demon king wanted Durga. You'd better let me see those books."

I handed him a stack while he scooted closer and put his arm around me. Ren left, and after an hour more of studying, my eyes felt heavy. I nestled my head against Kishan's strong shoulder and just as I fell asleep, I heard him whisper, "I won't let him have you, Kelsey. You belong with me."

My subconscious batted his words back and forth until I imagined a different voice saying the same thing. Only then could my mind drift, comfortable at last.

On the fourth day, we began our final quest to find the City of Light through the volcanic island also known as the Pit of Hell. I hoped the place wasn't as ominous as it sounded.

Nilima flew us to Visakhapatnam, then over the Bay of Bengal, and we finally touched down in Port Blair. A car was waiting for us when we landed.

As we drove through the town of Port Blair, Nilima shared a fascinating story about Mr. Kadam, who had been captured by the native—and once cannibalistic—Andamanese. Mr. Kadam had shrewdly bargained for his life, eventually becoming an honorary tribal member.

I shook my head, smiled, and wondered how many other amazing stories I never got the chance to hear.

We wound through dense trees on a private road. As we climbed a hill I caught glimpses of the ocean and marveled at the bright colors. Finally, breaking through the tree line, we came upon a beautiful luxury villa on the coast overlooking the Andaman Sea.

The interior design reminded me more of Mr. Kadam's private jet than of the house in India. The villa was austere and decorated in black and chrome with clean lines. The side of the house facing the ocean was made entirely of glass. Each bedroom had a private balcony, and there was a large terrace, a Jacuzzi, and a marvelous outdoor lounge shaded by palm trees. A magnificent panoramic view of the ocean, a white sand beach, and a four-leveled infinity pool was spread before me. It was beyond spectacular, and I knew that Mr. Kadam wouldn't have settled for anything less—even in the middle of the Indian Ocean.

Near sunset, after I lit a lamp in honor of Mr. Kadam, Kishan kissed me and said he needed to go into town. Nilima too had preparations to make before we could continue our journey. After eating dinner alone, I decided to hunt down Ren, who had disappeared soon after we had arrived.

I finally found him sitting on his balcony. He was leaning back against the wall with his eyes closed. Soft music played, and a cool ocean breeze blew back my hair as I stepped onto the balcony and inhaled the scent of the sea.

"May I join you?" I asked softly.

He didn't bother opening his eyes. "If you like."

The moon in the dark sky looked like a giant white plate dipping its edge into the ocean. We sat quietly for a while. I closed my eyes too and listened to him hum along in harmony with the music.

"You haven't played your guitar in a long time. I miss it," I said when the song was finished.

Ren turned away. "I fear there is no music left in me."

I teased, "'The man that hath no music in himself, nor is not mov'd with concord of sweet sounds, is fit for treasons, stratagems, and spoils.'"

Abruptly standing up, Ren strode across the balcony and settled at the far end of the railing. He leaned out over the side, bracing himself on his elbows.

"I'm sorry," I said and moved next to him. Putting my hand on his forearm, I touched him lightly. "I didn't realize you were serious."

He clasped my hand in his and played with my fingers. "Music reminds me too much of what I can't have, and yet I can't stop listening." He laughed sardonically. "I never understood the connection until you left me and returned to Oregon. I realized then that music was a link to you, a way to keep you close, much the same as my poetry."

Ren turned toward me and pressed my hand against his heart. "Kelsey, my blood pounds and my heart races when you're near. I have to make a conscious effort to restrain myself from touching you. From taking you into my arms. From kissing you. I would almost rather be tortured by Lokesh again than be tormented everyday like this by seeing you with Kishan."

I swallowed and tore my gaze from the handsome man. Instead, I looked at our entwined hands covering his heart. I felt the beat against my palm and fingertips.

Quaking, I whispered, "I'm sorry, Ren," and slid my hand away.

I could feel the heat and warmth and passion circulate, wrapping tangibly around me. The heat was overwhelming and intense, and my muscles felt about as substantial as warm candle wax.

"I'm sorry," I repeated stubbornly, "but I just can't leave Kishan."

I took a step back, and Ren leaned over the railing again. A new song began. Quietly Ren quoted Shakespeare's *Twelfth Night* and murmured, "Then, 'if music be the food of love, play on, give me excess of it; that surfeiting, the appetite may sicken, and so die.'"

Silently, I went back into the house but turned to look at him once more. Standing in the moonlight, Ren really looked the part of Shakespeare's melancholic Duke Orsino pining for his Lady Olivia. Something wrenched in my heart, and I stifled a sob as I slipped away.

pledged

As we waited for Nilima to declare we were ready for our next adventure, Kishan took me on picnics, sightseeing, dancing, and window shopping. He bought every flower in the city and had them delivered to my room in fancy arrangements. He took me night swimming—or night wading, as I was still paranoid of sharks. We talked often of Mr. Kadam. Eventually, it became easier to get past the lump in my throat when I heard his name.

Though I was happy enjoying my time with Kishan and feeling closer to him than I had before, I couldn't help but notice that Ren was pulling further and further away. Kishan dismissed it and said that Ren needed space. Still, I worried.

One afternoon, Kishan suggested lunch on the beach. There were a couple dozen other people already out on the beach, but Kishan found us a spot away from the sunbathers. He set up a huge beach umbrella, and after slathering me with sunscreen, he set out our picnic lunch.

Kishan bustled about excessively happy. He pressed a flute of sparkling apple juice into my hands, he fed me grapes and crackers smeared with caviar. As I hesitantly took my first bite of the delicacy, I found it tasted like butter with a little pop that burst in my mouth with the faint flavor of the sea. After we'd eaten, he kicked off his shoes and took off his shirt and went for a swim while I read a book.

When Kishan came back and toweled off, he shifted the umbrella so he could lie in the sun but put his head on my lap in the shade. He laughed when I complained about his wet head but I soon got over that and stroked his hair and his warm shoulders absently as I read. He was so still and quiet, I thought he had fallen asleep, so it startled me when Kishan reached for my hand. He pressed it to his bare chest and looked at me tenderly.

"Kells, I feel like my life is starting to make sense. That everything I've been through has been for a reason, for a purpose."

"I think that's true."

He sat up and stroked my face. "I believe I was destined for this, to live this long, to experience what I did, so that I could be here, now, in this moment, with you."

I laughed. "Well, maybe not this exact moment. I think destiny had more in mind than the two of us eating caviar."

"It's not about the caviar. It's about something more important."

"What do you mean?"

Taking both my hands in his, Kishan continued, "Look, I know that we have another prize to win, and I know that we still have to defeat Lokesh. The timing could, of course, be better . . ."

"The timing for what?"

At that moment, my gaze flitted to the water as two blue eyes broke the surface. Next came a bronze torso, and a handsome man emerged and reached up to smooth back his dripping hair. Water sluiced off his powerful form as he stepped toward the shore. My mouth went dry, and 99 percent of my brain power and attention were riveted on him.

". . . and you know how I feel about you," Kishan went on. "You're the only girl for me. The one I want to spend the rest of my life with. The one I want to wake up with every morning."

I nodded absently, only half-listening to what he was saying and watching the other girls on the beach take notice of the dark Poseidon walking among them.

". . . used the ruby we found in the House of Gourds, and also the diamond teardrop Durga gave me. It's all just a formality anyway. I mean, we already know how we feel about each other."

"Right . . ." I said woodenly.

The most perfect man on Earth turned his sea-blue eyes on me, and I caught a hidden message in them as he walked toward me. He wanted *me*. Out of all the beautiful bikini-clad girls, he was heading toward me. Me—with my white skin, golden brown braids, and a floppy hat. Me—the girl cowering from the sun and the heat under my wide beach umbrella, wearing a one-piece and a cover-up.

I swallowed thickly. Time slowed and each long stride he made was imprinted on my brain. I took in everything. The stubbornness of his chin. The set of his sensual mouth. The determination in his brow. I noticed the wideness of his shoulders. The planes of his chest. The thick muscle of his arms.

I remembered how he touched me, how he held me, and how he liked to slide those very nice hands into my hair. I saw every water droplet on his chest and shoulders and, heaven help me, I wanted to kiss away each one.

Kishan interrupted my thoughts. "So what I'm trying to say is—"

"Yes?" I mumbled distractedly. "What are you trying to say?"

Kishan brushed a soft kiss on my bare shoulder where my cover-up had slid off and said tenderly, "What I'm trying to say, *Kelsey*, is that I want you to be my wife." He slipped something cool and smooth onto my fourth finger.

I blinked and shifted my focus to Kishan, who was looking at me with love and gentleness. On my left hand, I saw the glint of a diamond ring. Slack-jawed, I glanced up. Ren had frozen and was staring at my hand in shock. Slowly, seconds crawled by and his blue eyes met my brown ones. Trapped in his gaze, I saw a sort of purgatory that blazed behind them.

The moment seemed to last a lifetime. Then his demeanor became cold. I felt the freezing touch of his eyes caress me one last time and then Ren disappeared. The only reminder of him was the icy jewel sitting heavily on my finger. What felt like an hour of silent communication had happened in just a few seconds.

I took a deep breath and offered Kishan an emotional smile. I leaned over to kiss his cheek while tears filled my eyes. The sun hitting the diamond shot rainbows onto my bare thigh. I touched my leg briefly and flinched at how cold my skin was. A part of me wondered if I'd ever feel truly warm again.

Kishan wrapped his arms around me and asked, "What is it, love? You don't like the ring?"

I held my hand up and blinked the tears from my eyes so I could clearly see it. It was lovely. A teardrop diamond rested in the center while curved lotus petals cut from the ruby he'd found in the House of Gourds radiated outward. Clusters of diamonds shaped as leaves ran down either side of the white gold ring.

"It's beautiful," I whispered.

"It dims in comparison to the woman I love," he replied.

"I . . . I didn't think this would happen so fast."

His face lit in a slow, lazy smile. "When I see something I want, I go after it, remember?"

I shut my eyes for a moment and felt a tear plop onto my lap. "I remember."

Kishan brushed tears away from my cheeks and said soberly, "For the longest time I didn't think I deserved to find love again. You were right when you said I blamed myself for everything. I thought I was responsible for it all—the curse, Yesubai's death, Lokesh—but when I met you, something changed.

"I remembered who I was, who I am—Prince Sohan Kishan Rajaram. I'd always been the younger brother, the second in line to inherit the throne but that time is past and that kingdom is gone. Now I realize that none of those things mattered, that my regrets were preventing me from seeing," he trailed a finger lightly down my cheek and jaw, "the beauty the world offered."

Trailing warm, slow kisses over my shoulder and up my neck, he continued, "You made me believe that I still had something to offer to the world, something to offer to a woman."

Kishan smiled when I swayed unsteadily. Pirate gold eyes looked into mine, and I sucked in a breath as I realized a smoldering passion lay hidden there behind them. It was glossed over by layers of patience and love, but I could still feel the intensity humming between the two of us.

At that moment, I knew that Phet was right, that this handsome prince was an equally good choice and that it would only take a gentle nudge for me to be completely enveloped by him. Stroking his arm, I slid my hand up slowly over his muscular shoulder until I cupped his neck. His pulse thumped wildly, and in a blink, his eyes changed. It was like throwing a match into a barrel of oil.

A rumble sounded in his throat as he pulled me toward him. I placed my hands against his bare chest, warmed by the sun, and his lips found mine. Kishan's hands gently gripped my arms and pressed me closer. The kiss was wild, aggressive, and demanding, challenging me—not only to meet his ardor, but also to feel as passionate about him as he felt about me.

Soon the kiss changed, and the smolder that had escaped his control was once again hidden just below the surface. I stroked his hair and held him close. The untamed black tiger closed his golden eyes and kissed me again, this time sweetly. Squeezing my waist, he said tenderly, "Kelsey Hayes, I promise that I will always love you, and I will try my best to be a good husband."

I put my hand on his cheek and touched my forehead to his. "And I'll try my best to be a good wife."

Although I was happy to be Kishan's fiancée, there was one unraveled thread in my otherwise beautiful tapestry. The bittersweet tangle irritated and tickled, and it was all I could do not to grab hold of it and tug, but I knew if I did, I'd destroy this precious new life I was trying to create.

I truly loved Kishan, and I knew that marriage was where we were eventually heading, but a part of me, deep down, grieved. I felt like a shell of a person. On the outside, everything looked fine. I was healthy, happy, and had a great future all planned out. Kishan would love me passionately and be a good husband and father. We'd have a dozen sons who would all want to grow up to be little warriors like their dad.

On the inside, though, I was empty. I had nothing to give him. My goal in life would be to make him believe I had absolutely no regrets about my choice. To pretend that I was whole. Complete.

Mom? Durga? Mr. Kadam? What do I do? How do I stop loving Ren? Please, please, please, help me give Kishan all the love he deserves.

Oblivious to my thoughts, Kishan pulled me into his strong arms and whispered plans for our future. He stroked my arm and my hair and told me how much he loved me. I remained quiet. I leaned back against his warm chest, and we sat like that, watching the tide come in until it turned dark.

12

guise

the next afternoon I took a long walk by myself, partly to clear my head and partly to find Ren, who had disappeared after my . . . engagement on the beach. I wasn't sure what I was going to say if I found him, but somehow I knew I needed to.

The breeze drove the clouds across the sky, pushing the gray puffy mounds into one another. The scent of rain was in the air so I hurried out the door.

Winding my way through the jungle, I headed north and walked along a path for fifteen minutes or so. The trees felt cool and once in a while a plop of cold water hit my bare arms. Then I cupped my hands to my mouth and shouted, "Ren?"

I waited, watching for the familiar form of my white tiger, hoping to see him bounding over a fallen log and to my side.

Stepping away from the path and into the trees, I dropped my bag at my feet. "Ren?" I shouted again in a different direction.

Nothing. I sat on a log, my chin on my fists, and thought about my predicament. I'd always dreamed of a big wedding. Of walking down the aisle to the man I loved, the man of my dreams. *And Kishan more than adequately fits that description. In fact, as far as Prince Charmings go, he exceeds any girl's expectations.*

Loving Kishan wasn't the problem. He was a great guy. Better than great. He was fantastic. I ticked off his traits in my head. *Kishan is kind, handsome, brave, a good kisser, strong, he gives great massages, and he loves me. What else could a girl need? What is my problem?*

As I sat there stewing, I heard a noise. An old, wrinkled woman hobbled down the path carrying a large bag. Deep-set brown eyes studied me from a face that had seen too many years in the sun. She smiled and nodded but kept shuffling along with slow heavy steps. White hair peeped out from beneath her bright yellow *dupatta* and her flowing skirt was marked with stains from the forest.

Just before she passed me by, one of her woven shoes slipped off her foot, and she toppled heavily to the ground. Her bag split open, and brown fruits about the size of small potatoes rolled in every direction. She groaned, and I immediately went to help her stand.

When I deposited the fruit and missing shoe at her feet, the old woman smiled and said, "Thank you. I Saachi. I rest here few minute. Okay with you?"

"Sure. It's not like I own the log. I'm Kelsey. It's nice to meet you."

The woman inspected her bag of fruit, feeling them for bruises and then pulled one out of the bag. "Take. You must try. Sapota. Many grow here. Good to eat."

Handing me the brown fruit, she grinned, revealing a mouthful of surprisingly white teeth and then ate a piece herself, wiping the dribbling stray juice on her scarf.

Tentatively, I bit into the fruit. The flesh was yellow-brown and the texture was similar to a pear, but the flavor was like malt with just a hint of caramel.

"It's good. Thank you," I mumbled while turning the fruit to study it.

"Chinese call this heart fruit. You see?" she said and lifted another fruit to show me its shape. "It look like heart. All fall to ground when see you. Mean you broken heart, bruised. Bad luck to walk past you. Why your heart broken? You pretty girl. Strong back. What wrong? You got no mans?"

I laughed dryly. "No, I have too many mans. It's a long story."

"What you mean too many mans? I fix problem. Tell Saachi about the mans. They strong? Pretty?"

"They're both strong and both very pretty."

"Ah!" She grinned. "Saachi like story about pretty mans."

I couldn't help but smile. "Yes. Well, they're brothers. The older brother is named Ren and the younger is called Kishan."

She nodded. "Good name."

"Right. Anyway, the younger brother, Kishan, asked me to marry him."

I flashed the ring on my finger, and she inspected it closely.

"He want you wife? He a good man? Hard work? Lazy mans no good," Saachi said.

"Oh, he's not lazy. He's very brave. He takes care of me. It's just that . . . I love his brother too. I was with his brother first. We loved each other and then we were . . . apart for a while. During that time Kishan and I became close."

"Ah," she said as if understanding. "Happen my friend. Her man go away trip. Not come back long time. Then she marry other. Later her first mans come home but already too late. He go away again. No come back. Not too late for you. You no marry. You go back first mans. You still love him?"

"Of course I still love him. I never stopped loving him, but I can't go back. He . . . it's not safe when I'm with him."

"What you mean? He hurt you? He beat you? Why you no choose him?"

"No." In a tiny voice, I whispered, "That's not why I'm afraid."

She smacked her lips and shifted to a more comfortable place on the log. "You one crazy girl. You afraid handsome man who love you."

I groaned, stood up, and started to pace. "The problem is he has a superhero complex. He likes to rush off and save the day."

"That's good. Brave mans," she clucked.

"No. That's bad. Heroes get killed. Every time he tries to save me, he risks his life. He endangers himself constantly."

"Bah. Is no problem. Only problem your mind."

"No!" I whipped around. "Don't you understand? Mr. Kadam is *dead*! My parents are *dead*! If Ren dies, that's it for me. There's nothing else. The people I love die. I'm afraid that if I let myself love him, really love him . . . it's like giving him a death sentence."

I sat down heavily on the log again. "When the bad guys came for me—he stayed behind and got captured. When he couldn't give me CPR—he broke up with me and handed me off to Kishan. When an evil man got too close to finding me—he sacrificed his memories of us. Every time something threatens me, he rushes ahead to face it without thinking about what will happen to me if *he* dies. He was supposed to be a king. Maybe that's where he gets his overdeveloped sense of duty from."

"Then easy pick. You choose other brother," the old woman concluded.

"I want to be a good wife for Kishan. I'll love him, and we'll raise a family together. And hopefully that will mean that Ren will stop hurtling himself into the arms of death."

She clucked her tongue. "Is good but which mans make you happy? Make you feel so much?"

"I feel for both of them."

"Huh," she grunted. "You most happy time who?" she insisted while peering at me shrewdly.

I squirmed then admitted softly, "Ren." Her thick eyebrows rose and she wore an "Ah-Ha" expression. I quickly explained, "But it doesn't matter. I'm *choosing* Kishan. I promised Kishan I'd never let him be alone again. And he *will*, I mean he *does*, make me very happy. I love Kishan."

"But your heart is divide."

"Yes. And the truth of it is . . . most of my heart belongs to Ren. I never stopped loving him. When we were apart, nothing mattered. I was lost. The only thing that kept me going was the hope that someday we'd be together again. That, and Kishan needed me. Ren thinks that as long as I *live* I'll be okay. But he's wrong. If he is killed, and I have to put him into a grave next to Mr. Kadam, I won't recover."

I smiled wanly and turned to face the quiet jungle. "You see? I *can't live* without him. So to keep him safe, to keep my heart safe, we can't be together. Do you understand?"

A familiar voice answered, "I think I do."

The breath froze in my body. Saachi's voice had changed to a silky, smooth tone, like caramel and honey. It was a voice I was very familiar with. Closing my eyes, I turned to face the man standing behind me.

I took a deep breath. Slowly I opened my eyes, and my anguished heart beat thickly when I saw his expression.

"The Scarf . . ." I said, realizing how he had tricked me into admitting the truth.

"Yes," he said, his voice heavy with emotion. He lifted his hand to sweep his hair from his face and let out a shaky breath.

I took a step toward him. "Please, try to understand that none of this matters. It doesn't change anything. I've already decided upon a course of action, and I intend to follow through with it."

"I wanted to know. I needed to know. You've kept your true feelings from both of us. Kelsey, why didn't you share these worries? These fears?"

"Would it have changed anything? Does it really make a difference?"

"I don't know. Maybe. Maybe not. But at least all the cards are on the table now."

I bit my lip. "Are you going to tell him?"

"Don't you think he needs to know?"

"I don't see how it will help."

He stood quietly as he considered me and then sighed. "I suppose for now we can keep this just between the two of us."

"Thank you."

Feeling awkward, I gathered up my bag and turned on my heel to head back into town. My skin prickled with the awareness of the man following along silently behind me.

13

barren island

finally Nilima announced it was time to go. I stood on the dock yawning at four a.m. while Ren and Kishan peeled back a tarp covering a futuristic looking Disneyland type of ride that bobbed in the water.

"What . . . is that?" I asked Nilima with a slight accusatory edge to my voice.

Kishan moved past me as he untied some ropes. "We call it the Skimmer."

"But what is it?" I replied.

Nilima explained. "It's a prototype that Rajaram Industries has been developing."

Ren climbed on top of the structure. "Kadam said he modeled it after the giant jellyfish."

"But—" I stammered.

"I know. There wasn't time," Ren interrupted. "We haven't figured out how or when he started developing it. But here it is nonetheless."

Nilima shooed him away. "It's part submersible, part luxury cruiser but with the full sustainability of a nuclear submarine. We call it a Skimmer because it doesn't dive as deep as a sub. It's meant for exploring reefs and shallow waters in comfort, though it can cross oceans as well."

"It seems a bit small to cross oceans," I said nervously.

"You're only seeing the top deck," Kishan protested. "Most of it's underwater. It can stay submerged just as long as most modern submarines. We have the latest technology that creates oxygen from the ocean itself. Just wait until you see the bubble."

"A bubble? What do you mean? Is it safe?"

"He's referring to the observation bubble in the nose. That is the part modeled after your giant jellyfish, though this glass version is considerably larger. It provides a 360-degree view of the surrounding ocean," Nilima added. "The engine runs quietly on a top-secret fuel-cell technology that takes its power from the ocean so as not to disturb underwater ecosystems. We also installed a very unusual and not-yet-out-on-the-market type of underwater lighting so passengers can feel more a part of the ocean world. It's been through numerous trials, Miss Kelsey. We even have a small motorboat on board."

I put my hands on my hips. "That's just . . . just amazing," I marveled.

Ren moved past me, brushing against my shoulder softly without looking. He headed into the Skimmer's dark interior and disappeared.

"And you're sure they know how to drive this thing? It's a pretty expensive underwater bumper car, Nilima."

"Kelsey, relax. Ren's been up most of the night practicing with me. We know what we're doing."

I wasn't sure how to respond to that idea so I said nothing but the memory of Nilima dancing in Ren's arms at the beach party suddenly flooded my mind and I had a hard time focusing. When all three of us were aboard the craft, Nilima waved and hollered out from the pier. "Be careful at Barren Island."

"Why?"

"The volcano is active," she shouted.

"What? What! Why doesn't anybody tell me these things?"

Kishan laughed as he descended the ladder behind me. "Because we know you'll react like this. Come on. Let me show you your room."

As I shuffled through the boat, I mumbled about volcanoes and walking on hot lava, and about why Durga's prophecies never ended at a day spa. I remembered a movie in which the lava ate away a guy's legs to his knees, and his body melted into the pool of it. *All things considered, fighting Lokesh might be easier.*

Soon I forgot all about the volcano and marveled at the incredible invention Mr. Kadam had somehow been able to commission before his death. My room was decked out with a mini-fridge, a small sink, and cabinets on one side and a narrow table with a seating nook on the other. I had a luxurious private bath and a king-sized bed.

"Wait until you see your view," Kishan said proudly.

He walked over to a long set of panels and pushed a button. With a quiet whir, the panels slid back, revealing floor to ceiling glass and it wasn't until then that I realized that my room was a curved sort of pod. The glass mimicked the lining of the giant jellyfish, but the glass was crystal clear. The lights automatically dimmed, and I stepped forward on the invisible floor, gazing into the Andaman Sea.

"It's beautiful isn't it?" Kishan whispered.

"It's amazing! Are we moving already?" I asked, not being able to tell if a fish swam by us, or we moved past it.

"Yes. Can you feel it?"

I shook my head, impressed by how silent and still the craft was. Mr. Kishan had outdone himself.

Kishan left me to explore the rest of the ship, and rounding a corner, I found the observation bubble. Couches and soft chairs in silver were bolted somehow to the glass floor, and I sat there in silence for a time, surrounded by the ocean. A bit later, I climbed a set of stairs to find the control center where Ren sat in his own mini bubble above the waterline. Ren showed me some of the dials, and I admired the expansive view of the ocean through the curved glass.

"Too bad we can't enjoy the breeze," I mentioned.

Ren smiled softly and pushed a button. A section of the glass dome above us shifted and slid away. Instant sunroof.

I headed down some steps to the surface deck of our futuristic sci-fi craft. The wind blew the hair away from Ren's handsome face just as we rounded a section of beach and the city of Port Blair came into sight. Soon the only lights I could see were our own running lights and the fading stars.

Ren stood stiffly at his post and seemed to be doing a good job of ignoring me. I decided to watch the sunrise and made my way carefully to the front of the ship where I sat and let the ocean spray tickle my feet. After an hour, I was rewarded with a breathtaking view. The water turned pink, then gold, and then, as if I willed it into appearing, the round sun burst from the sea.

For some reason it made me think of Mr. Kadam. I smiled sadly and wondered what interesting facts he'd share if he were here. I sat there for another half hour, letting the sun warm my skin while I breathed the fresh scent of the ocean.

Ren and Kishan took turns steering the boat. A few hours later, we skirted Neill Island, then cruised by Havelock Islands, and headed out to open ocean. The weather was nice, and we made good time traveling the sixty-five nautical miles to Barren Island. As it came into view late in the afternoon, I could see that the volcano was definitely still active. Small wisps of steam and spirals of smoke rose into the air from the caldera. I marveled at the wide black path of cooled lava that had oozed from the center and had either punched or melted a hole through the mountain wall before sliding into the sea at a fairly gentle slope. It reminded me of a fried egg after the yolk had been broken.

Though a huge part of the island was covered in black ashes, there were still enough green trees and small shrubs around the circumference to see it had been beautiful once. There were no beaches; the mountain cliffs seemed to rise straight up out of the sea.

The three of us stood on the top deck looking at the island, and with a few murmured words, Ren and Kishan decided to drop anchor on the western side, upwind, where there would be less smoke. They both agreed that the best way to access the island would be hiking over the blackened lava bed and that we would start early the next morning.

As soon as Kishan wrapped his arms around me, Ren descended to the lower deck. The air was cool, causing goose bumps to shoot across my arms. I wrapped my arms around Kishan's waist, snuggled against his warm chest, and said, "This is really nice."

He grinned and brought his lips to mine. One hand slid into my hair and cupped the back of my head while the other rested gently on my neck. After a moment his fingertips began to massage the nape of my neck. I closed my eyes and let myself get lost in his kiss.

It was warm and sweet, and on his lips, I tasted just a hint of the salty sea. He stroked my jaw and after tilting my head slightly, his kiss deepened. I held onto him, knowing moments like these might not happen for a while once we started into the volcano.

He smiled at me, obviously pleased with my response, and pulled a small box from his pocket.

"What's this?" I asked.

"Merry Christmas, Kells."

"What? It's Christmas?"

"Well, tomorrow is. It's Christmas Eve. Did you forget?"

"I did. It's hard to remember Christmas when you're in a tropical zone." I picked up the present hesitantly. "Um, Kishan, I'm so sorry. I didn't remember to get you anything."

He pulled me toward him, cupped my face in his hands and gave me a soft kiss. "You agreed to be my wife, Kelsey. There's nothing else on this Earth that I want."

I teased him gently, "You're kind of a smooth talker."

"Hopefully that works in my favor," he said with a grin and a twinkle in his golden eyes.

Inside the box, I found an ancient-looking golden key. Raising an eyebrow, my mouth quirking up at the corner, I asked, "And what, pray tell, does this key unlock?"

"Technically nothing anymore. It used to open the treasure room of our old palace. Now it's more of a symbol of a home. Or homes. Wherever you want to live. I found it when we were looking through my parents' things. We can rebuild the jungle home where my parents and Kadam are buried, or we can buy a new home in the United States or India or we can do both or all three. It's nothing we have to decide on right now, but I know having a home is important to you. Leaving our old home will be hard, but we'll make new memories together, and," he laid his palm against my neck, "I'll make you happy, Kelsey, I promise."

"I know you will." I leaned up to kiss his cheek. "Thank you for my present."

"You're welcome." Kishan strung the old key onto the chain around my neck where it rested next to the amulet. "Someday," he said as he touched the key where it lay against my skin. "Someday we'll build a home."

He kissed me again in a long, lingering way, then abruptly turned me around and gave me a gentle nudge. "But first, I'm going to beat you at a game of Parcheesi."

"Deal."

I laughed and headed to retrieve the game from my room—only to discover another present. On my bed, Ren had left a gift carefully wrapped in golden paper. Inside was a wooden music box with a painted white tiger identical to Ren on the top.

I lifted the lid and my song began to play—the one Ren had written for me when we were apart, the one he struggled with when he lost his memory. I listened to the familiar notes, which were sad at first, and gasped when it continued past the point I remembered. The sad music of separation changed. I could almost hear the hope, the determination, in the sound. It crescendoed in a burst of happiness until the notes faded like twinkling stars at dawn. I shut the lid and closed my eyes.

I was so wrapped up with the music box that I almost didn't notice that Ren had also left me a note with the sprig of a little plant on my bed.

Kelsey,

You might think I am presumptuous in assuming the end of our song will be a joyful one, but I still believe there's a happy ending for us, that the promise in the song will someday be realized. I'll just have to practice patience until then. My heart is in your hands, take care of it for I cannot live without it.

Mistletoe
by Walter de la Mare

Sitting under the mistletoe
(Pale-green, fairy mistletoe),

One last candle burning low,
All the sleepy dancers gone,
Just one candle burning on,
Shadows lurking everywhere:
Someone came, and kissed me there.

Tired I was; my head would go
Nodding under the mistletoe
(Pale-green, fairy mistletoe),
No footsteps came, no voice, but only,
Just as I sat there, sleepy, lonely,
Stooped in the still and shadowy air
Lips unseen—and kissed me there.

Merry Christmas, iadala.

—Ren

With trembling fingers, I pressed the page and the mistletoe into my journal. I stood there fingering the leaves of the plant, imagining Ren dressed in a tux and yanking me under the mistletoe for a kiss. After a few seconds of delicious fantasy, I mentally rebuffed myself.

What kind of a person am I? How can I go from kissing one man, my fiancé, no less, to daydreaming about being swept away by his brother? Something is seriously wrong with me.

I quoted my personalized serenity prayer, rededicated myself to the path I'd chosen, and met Kishan at the table. He smoothly set up the game board, not noticing a thing.

The next morning, I woke bright and early, left the snoring black tiger on the floor, and headed up to Mr. Kadam's fabulous kitchen to make the best-ever Christmas breakfast for all three of us. The window panels slid back with the push of a button. With the amazing view for inspiration, I set the table for breakfast, humming until a noise startled me.

Ren stood framed in the doorway. My eyes darted up to his blue ones as he handed me a bouquet of lilacs.

"Merry Christmas," he said as he handed me the flowers.

I took them and said quietly, "You've already given me more than enough."

"When a man gives a woman a lilac. . . ."

"He's asking her a question," I finished.

"You remember."

I turned away. "Did you think I would forget?"

He put his hands on my shoulders and turned me around. "I love you, Kelsey. What I feel for you is more than gratitude, more than attraction, more than affection. I never wrote a poem with exclamation points until I met you. You're the air in my lungs, the blood in my veins, and the courage in my heart. I'm an empty shell without you."

He cupped my face with his palms. "You illuminate my soul with the warm glow of your love and devotion. Even now, I can feel it and it sustains me. You can deny what you feel with your words, but your heart is still mine, *iadala*."

I wrapped my fingers around his hands and with a tremendous effort stepped back.

Taking my rejection in stride, he teased, "Maybe I should've brought more mistletoe instead."

I turned my back to him and bustled about efficiently as if my every nerve wasn't focused on the mesmerizing man watching me.

"Why didn't you then?" I asked nonchalantly.

He shrugged and rested his body against the bulkhead. "I didn't want to give Kishan any more motivation."

"Oh." I picked up the Fruit and began asking for dishes. The Fruit became warm and shimmered like a disco ball as it made platter after platter. Steam rose from each, and the smells of the familiar foods wafted through the air.

Coolly, I smiled and said, "Merry Christmas, Ren. Thank you for the poem and music box." I made no mention of the rest of his note and didn't respond to the heartfelt words given to me along with the bunch of lilacs. Instead I pretended as if I weren't guiltily holding onto them, clutching them fervently to my fast-beating heart. Breezily, I said, "I totally forgot to get you a present, so I'm making you my grandma's famous Christmas brunch instead. Are you hungry?"

He folded his arms across his chest, and stared back with an intensity that threatened to swallow me whole. "Yes," he answered quietly.

I cleared my throat awkwardly and fluttered my hands toward the breakfast nook. "Well, take a seat then, and you can get started. Kishan's still sleeping."

Ren grunted but sat down. I handed him a linen napkin and silverware and, when he reached out to take them, his hand cupped mine for just a fraction longer than was necessary. I spun around quickly and began dishing large helpings from each platter onto his plate: biscuits slathered in sausage gravy, cheesy eggs, fried potatoes with onions and peppers, thick-sliced bacon, buttery baked cinnamon apples, and Grandma's homemade hot chocolate with whipped cream, chocolate sauce, chocolate sprinkles, a peppermint stick, and a cherry.

I served myself and took the seat across from him. He tasted a little of each dish and then picked up the cocoa.

"Is this breakfast a tradition in your family?"

"Yes," I answered. "Every year Grandma would sleep over on Christmas Eve. The next morning she would be up before everyone else making biscuits from scratch. I'd usually wake up just after she did and stir the gravy for her while she sliced potatoes and onions. Her cocoa was a special treat that evolved over time. I added the chocolate sprinkles, Dad added the peppermint, and Mom added the cherry. We usually waited until after breakfast was all cleaned up before we opened presents."

"When was the last time you ate this breakfast?"

"Just before my parents died. I took over making the eggs and potatoes, and Mom took over the biscuits. We used to talk about Grandma while we worked. My foster family wouldn't have liked this breakfast. Too many carbs. Even when they have cocoa at Christmas, it's diet and without whipped cream."

Ren reached across the table and took my hand. "It's important to keep our family traditions alive. It helps us remember who we are and where we came from."

"What about your grandmother?"

"She died when I was young, but I had a great-aunt who spent a lot of time with us. She was like a grandmother in many ways."

"Kells, I hope you saved me some breakfast!" Kishan bound into the room, planted a loud kiss on the top of my head, and picked up a plate.

Ren let go of my hand, moved, and lifted his eyes to mine. "Her name was Saachi."

I sucked in a quick breath. "*Oh.*"

Kishan looked from me to Ren then cleared his throat noisily. "Kells, I'm going to die if I don't get something to eat. Please make it in vast quantities if you don't mind."

I stood up abruptly, stumbled to the counter, and began mindlessly filling Kishan's plate.

After the somewhat awkward meal, it was time to start our last quest. I slid Fanindra onto my arm and hopped into the tiny motorboat. Kishan steered us smoothly across the water and then leapt onto the crumbly black surface of the lava path. Ren dragged the boat onshore, and I set foot on Barren Island.

phoenix

With Kishan holding my hand, we began carefully picking our way across the scarred alien terrain, Durga's weapons at the ready. We had brought all of the goddess's gifts, and it felt good to have the bow and arrows slung across my back again, especially since unbidden dark thoughts teased the edges of my mind. I imagined bristling beasts and feral creatures with jagged teeth lurking in the shadows of the mangled mangrove trees stripped of green and stretching leprous limbs that snagged at our clothing; their rooty claws made our progress difficult.

Our feet sank into the ash as if it were carbon snow, and the air felt heavy, hot, and menacing. Nervously, I mumbled as we moved through the frightening landscape. "Did . . . did I ever tell you about Mt. Vesuvius?"

Kishan shook his head but kept his eyes forward.

"It was a stratovolcano just like this one. It wiped out two cities. Most of the people were killed instantly, but some slowly suffocated under layers of ash. They've found intact skeletons. One was a pregnant woman who was lying on her bed; the skeleton of the fetus was still inside her. She was surrounded by others who were most likely her family members watching over her."

Kishan grunted and kept moving. Ren wrapped his hand around my other arm, squeezed slightly, and said, "We're going to be fine, Kells."

"I just feel like the ash is choking me. It's hard to breathe."

"If it helps, have the Scarf make you a mask. Try not to think about it. Focus your eyes on Kishan's over-developed biceps instead of the ash stirred up by your feet and take deep breaths."

I snorted nervously. Kishan abruptly stopped. He frowned at Ren, then said to me, "We'll go slower if you're feeling tired."

"I'm not tired. I'm just . . . what is *that*?" I exclaimed and pointed at the rustling leaves.

Kishan spun around and with a deft movement threw the *chakram* into the stunted trees. The *chakram* sank into a gnarled trunk. We heard a terrified bleating as several animals clumsily leapt from the area, their hooves sinking into the sound-deadening ash. They moved away from the trees, leaping up the perilous sides of the caldera and disappearing over the top.

"Goats? How did goats get here?" I asked.

Ren answered, "I read that livestock animals were often left on the smaller islands in case a ship ran aground and the sailors needed something to eat. We may also see bats and small rodents."

"Bats, goats, and rats, oh my." If that was all we were going to encounter, I'd consider myself lucky.

We continued to climb the side of the volcano. I often slipped in the soft, pebbly, and ashy dirt and had to use my hands to scramble ahead when the incline became a bit steeper. The ash was warm, hot even at times. Grabbing onto tree roots didn't help much as the roots either gave way or they broke apart into chunks. Kishan bulldozed ahead and often stretched out a hand to help me. Ren took up the rear and caught me twice when I slipped on the soft ground.

At the top, the view was amazing. It looked like we were standing on the broken lip of a large bowl. The caldera wall on either side was a thousand feet from the ocean surface. A slight breeze blew past, tickling my nose with the scent of the ocean mixed with the smell of wood smoke. Remnants of trees covered the rocky slopes, and I could even see bits of green peeking through here and there, but when my gaze slipped to the center of the caldera, I couldn't help but shiver.

I estimated the basin of the volcano to be about two miles in diameter. While Ren and Kishan discussed the best place to descend, I took in the desolation. The terrain looked like the surface of an evil moon circling a hellish planet. Pockmarked, ripped, and raw, the blackened interior was a festering boil on what was otherwise a beautiful tropic ocean. I sipped some water, hoping to clear the dry dust from my throat.

"We're going to make rope with the Divine Scarf and rappel down," Ren explained the plan.

"Are you sure the entrance to the City of Light is down there?"

Kishan replied, "It's not a big island, Kells. If it's not down there, then we'll search the island until we find it."

All three of us put on gloves, and then Kishan secured various ropes around my body and the trunk of a thick tree. We were going to walk down the rock face, using a pulley system of ropes to keep us from going too fast.

"Don't bounce. Don't push off. Just walk down slowly. Ren will be below you on the same rope, and I'll be right next to you. We won't let you fall. Ready?" Kishan asked calmly.

I was about as ready to rappel down a cliff as I was to stick my hand in lava.

Ren gripped his rope, let his body fall back, and disappeared. I cautiously peeked over the edge and found him a few feet below us, his feet braced on the rock wall. He looked up at me and said gently, "Come on, Kells. I'm right here."

Shaking and nervous, I moved into position and took hold of my ropes. At first I was alright and Kishan kept pace with me as I crept down the hill like a grandma on roller skates. Then when the rock face dipped in, leaving my feet dangling in the air, I panicked and lurched frantically, crying out. Twisting the rope, I spun in a circle, but Kishan caught me and straightened out my rope while I wrapped a leg around his desperately.

He smiled and said, "You're alright, *bilauta*. Loosen your grip and slide down to where Ren is."

I twisted my leg, letting him go, and he swung slightly away. I looked up and felt sick. I looked down and felt sicker. Swallowing, I let the rope slide through my fingers and went down quickly, only stopping when I finally felt solid rock against my feet again. Though we still descended in slow motion, we made it to the bottom without further incident. My hands shook, and my legs felt like Jell-O as I numbly let Ren remove the ropes from my body.

We left the ropes dangling and headed for the center of the caldera. The ash had been replaced with shiny black lobes that stretched toward us like knobby fingers. Ren tested the cooled crust by walking out a few paces. Declaring it safe, he followed a crooked tentacle, and Kishan and I joined him.

The hike across the barren surface was sluggish and complicated due to the boulders of massive rock that often barred our path. Giant cannonball stones had collided with the ropes of dried lava and shattered it, creating bizarre shapes with jagged, barbed surfaces in the crust. In other places, the lava had covered rocks as large as ten feet in diameter, like gritty fondant over a cake.

Occasionally, we stepped onto some of the charred bubbles, which burst into powdery granules. Sulfurous vapors rose from thin cracks. When Kishan's boot broke through the black crust in one spot, scalding steam blasted out of the hole and burned the skin on his arm.

Seeing my concerned expression, Kishan flashed me a reassuring smile. He tapped the *kamandal* hidden beneath his shirt.

"We'll heal, Kells, and if something happens to you, we'll use the mermaid's elixir."

I nodded and plodded ahead, wondering if the elixir was powerful enough to heal me after lava melted off my face. I used the Pearl Necklace to fill canteens of water, and we drank as much as we could. We continued on, and it wasn't long before we came to a large hole that glowed with a faint light.

Ren crouched down to peer in. "It's a lava tube. Probably an active one."

"So lava will come spurting out of there?" I asked.

"I don't know."

"Well, what should we do? Go on or go in?"

Kishan leaned over the opening, "It's too hot. She won't survive."

"What about you two?" I interjected. "I assume you don't want your fur burned off either."

"Then we move on," Ren said as he stood and shifted his pack.

Following in his footsteps, we started to walk away but then I stopped and turned.

"Did you hear that?"

"Hear what?" Kishan asked from behind me.

"It's a . . . a song."

"I didn't hear anything," Ren answered.

"Me neither," Kishan added.

I closed my eyes and listened. "There it is again. You can't pick it up with your tiger hearing?"

They shook their heads.

"I hate to say this but I feel like . . . this is the place."

"But it's too hot, Kells."

"Then we need to cool it off. Cooling myself off in the process wouldn't be a bad idea either." While brushing away the sweat that tickled the back of my neck, my fingers touched the Black Pearl Necklace.

"I have an idea," I said to Kishan. "Follow me."

We climbed onto the lip above the tunnel. I touched the pearl lotus flower on the Necklace at my throat and murmured a few words. A rumble shook the island, and I heard the rushing of water. Ren wrapped an arm around me when I stumbled as the ground moved.

"I hope I can control it," I mumbled nervously with arms raised.

I focused on the wall of the caldera. The trees shook wildly, and then a spray of ocean water rushed over the wall and plunged into the basin. Visualizing the flow of water, I willed it to come closer, and it quickly rolled over the black surface of the volcano.

Steam shot up in several places and hissed with the sound of a thousand snakes. I raised my hands, cupping them, and slowly brought them together. I tamed the water, shaped it, until it became exactly what I wanted it to be, guiding the flow toward the lava tube.

Cold sea water rushed forward and surged down the open mouth of the tube. I could feel the water moving through the island traveling through tunnels miles long and I willed more and more water to come until I'd displaced something the size of a small lake from the surrounding ocean. Spreading my fingertips, I sent the cold sea water underground to flow over lava that hissed and steamed and blackened as the two disparate elements met. I stood silently with closed eyes and felt the stream's progress until every last bit of it had evaporated.

When I opened my eyes, Ren and Kishan were watching me quizzically.

"How did you know to do that?" Kishan asked.

"I don't know. I think it was the song. Are you sure you didn't hear it?"

When they both shook their heads, I wondered if I was now hearing things in addition to having strange powers and control over magical objects. Whatever had been my inspiration seemed to work. The tunnel was warm but it had cooled significantly.

We stepped into the damp opening. As we descended, the tunnel twisted and became very dark, and only the glow of Fanindra's eyes lit our way. The air felt muggy and humid. Metallic veins of fibers clung to the sides of the tunnel, and I coughed as little wisps floated in the air.

We came to a fork in the tunnel, and I turned left, only hesitating when Kishan whispered, "How do you know where to go?"

"I don't know," I replied. "I just do."

My answer echoed sinisterly through the dark passages. I swiped the back of my neck and pulled my sticky T-shirt away from my lower back. To keep my mind off the heat and the danger, I hummed Christmas carols and thought about snow. To my surprise, Ren and Kishan joined me on "Jingle Bells," but the song was quiet, hesitant, and when the echo came back, we sounded more like the ghosts of holidays long since forgotten.

The lava tube was rounded and smooth as if a giant earthworm had tunneled it out for us. It was easily twelve feet in diameter, and two of us could walk comfortably side by side. We journeyed downward about a mile or so. *Surely we are well below sea level by now.* I heard a rushing sound ahead and wondered if some of my ocean water was still running through the tubes.

We came upon a broken section that glowed with an orange light. We stepped closer, and a rush of heat instantly dried the sweat all over my body.

Ren held me back, but the three of us craned forward to see into the opening. A hundred feet below, a river of lava flowed. Its rocky edges were dark and sluggish, but the middle was bright orange and moved quickly. A cooled dark skin cracked and floated on the surface in different places, making the lava look like a reddish-orange pudding left uncovered in the refrigerator.

Kishan pulled me away from the spectacle, and we continued downward through the maze of tubes until we finally came to a dead end. I placed my hand onto the coarse surface of a rock wall.

"I don't understand. This is the place," I murmured.

Ren placed his hands on the wall and brushed them over the surface, dusting off the grit. Kishan and I helped. My fingers sank into a slight depression, and I swept my hand over it, digging out the powdery dust. Loose gravel fell at my feet, and a moment later I called out.

"It's here. The handprint!"

I placed my hand into the depression and let the crackling sparks pour into the rock. My henna drawing surfaced and glowed, illuminating my hand from the inside out. The cavern shook, and the rock wall shifted. As dust rained down on us, Kishan grabbed me and pressed my head into his chest, covering me with his body. The stone groaned and rocked back and forth, then slowly rolled to the side and stopped. I wiped some feathery dust away that tickled my cheek and stepped through the opening.

We were standing on a ledge that overlooked a giant underground forest.

"Trees? How can there be trees here?" I asked in disbelief.

"I don't think those are normal trees. This must be like Kishkindha," Ren murmured, "an underground world."

"Yeah, except this world is hotter than Hades."

When Ren found a series of stone steps, we began to make our way down. As we moved along, I marveled at the beauty of the woodland. Thick, sooty trunks supported a vast canopy of limbs covered with leaves that softly flickered like the embers of a dying fire. Curly golden tendrils grew out of the branches and moved in our direction as we walked.

Ren watched them warily and removed the *gada* from his backpack, but I strode forward fearlessly and held out a finger. A small tendril stretched toward my hand almost hesitantly, and then slowly, gently, it wrapped around my finger and clung to me. Warmth reverberated through my body, and the amulet around my neck began to glow.

"Kelsey?" Ren stepped toward me.

I held out my hand to stop him. "It's okay. It's not hurting me." I smiled. "It's drawn to the power of the amulet."

Another thin vine with two quivering leaves brushed against my cheek. Kishan approached the tree, but the leaves flickered colors of alarm. I stroked the trunk to reassure it.

"They won't hurt you. You have nothing to fear from us."

The tree seemed to recover and let Kishan touch a limb.

Shivering delicately, the fire tree stretched out another vine with tiny buds that sprang open into bright orange petals with gold leaves.

"It's beautiful," I exclaimed.

Kishan grunted, saying, "They seem to like you."

The leaves trembled and turned toward us as we made our way down the slope.

We saw flickering ferns and fiery flowers that burst into radiant bloom as we walked by. Ren and Kishan found tracks and spied a red-orange animal that looked like a rabbit. The forest seemed to enclose us in warmth but spared us from the devastating heat of the volcano. The air was dry, and the ground was rich and dark like the most fertile potting soil. Thick glowing mosses in a variety of orange and red shades grew on black rocks and tree trunks.

We sat on a fallen trunk and ate a lunch made by the Golden Fruit, quietly talking of the strangeness of the place. Trees often stretched out curly vines to touch my hair or my arm. The amulet glowed upon contact, and warmth spread through my limbs. I felt as if they were recharging my batteries, and the heat no longer bothered me.

Though the forest was ablaze with light, the sky was dark and without stars. We started up a rise and, upon reaching the peak, Ren pointed at the distant horizon.

"Can you see them?"

"See what?" I asked.

"Over there. It's a mountain range. It's hard to see because the mountains are black on black."

Kishan said he could make out the outline, but all I saw was blackness.

"Your tiger vision must help. I can't see anything."

Ren nodded and suggested we make camp in the valley below. We had just started down when a bright light shot across the sky and burst into a quiet cascade that reminded me of Fourth of July fireworks. Then, as if someone had flipped a switch, all the trees went dark. I couldn't even see my hand in front of me.

"What happened?" I exclaimed nervously.

Ren took my hand and drew me to his side. "I'm not sure."

Fanindra's emerald eyes glowed, casting a welcome glimpse of green onto this strange, dark world. Ren made his way down the hill, holding tightly onto my hand.

At the bottom, we set up camp and made a large tent with the Scarf. When I reached out to touch a tree limb, I felt nothing. It didn't move or fill me with warmth. It seemed to be dead. I put my hand against the trunk and allowed some of my fire energy to seep into it. A faint thrumming confirmed the tree was alive, but I guessed that this was its version of sleeping.

When I crawled into the tent to join Ren and Kishan, they abruptly stopped talking.

"Keeping secrets, huh?" I teased. "I don't want to know anyway. I only wanted to tell you that the trees are all asleep. I think it's just a light's out kind of thing."

Ren nodded, "Fine. We're going to keep watch tonight. We think . . . it's possible you're being manipulated, Kells."

"What?" I laughed. "Are you serious?"

Neither of them made eye contact.

"You think the trees are leading me astray?"

Ren spoke softly. "We have to keep our minds open to the possibility."

Kishan added, "And for that reason we're keeping watch, and you are not allowed to participate in that."

I folded my arms across my chest. "I think I know when I'm being manipulated. And why do you two tigers always think you know what's best for me? You're such, such . . . men!"

"*Kells*," they both protested.

"Fine. Knock yourselves out. Go sit on a spark while you're at it."

I heard Kishan's sigh and a soft, "Goodnight, Kelsey," as I rolled over and stuffed my fist beneath my cheek. I twisted, kicking off my blanket in the heat, and fell asleep.

A bright flash penetrated the fabric tent and woke me. I heard a popping sound and a metallic hum, and suddenly everything was bathed in flickering firelight.

Ren was asleep. He had one arm raised over his head and the other resting on his stomach. I moved closer, and he sighed and angled his head better on his pillow.

I wanted to reach out to him, to touch him. I knew his golden skin would be smooth and warm, but instead I sat there listening to him quietly breathe and wondered how I could be engaged to one man and still long for another.

What a terrible person I am, I thought and stumbled out of the tent.

"Good morning, *bilauta*," Kishan said, still keeping watch. "Are you still angry?"

"No."

149

"Good."

He wrapped me in a bear hug and kissed my head. A tiny vine as soft as a kitten's paw touched the back of my hand. I let it curl around my pinky and felt its warmth.

Feeling sticky and grimy from the volcano, I walked off a ways and tried to set up a shower using the Necklace. But as soon as the drops of water touched them, the trees shook violently and their leaves turned brown and fell off.

Hmm . . . that's strange, I thought and stopped the flow of water. Remembering the trees' attraction to the fire amulet, I wondered if fire might be their energy source.

I tried to repair the damaged trees by warming them with my fire power. The first tree started to heal, but I could still feel the energy draining out of it. Heartbroken, I removed my hands from the trunk as silent tears ran down my face.

Ren found me a few minutes later, brushed away a tear, and asked, "Why are you crying?"

"I killed a tree," I said through a sniffle. "I think these trees feed off of fire and die when they come into contact with water. I tried to save them but I don't have enough power."

He studied the tree, and then picked up my hand and placed it onto the trunk. "Try again."

I closed my eyes and let the fire build up until it began to flow into the tree. I sensed the feeble glow deep within it respond to me and reach out with weak fingers. We stretched toward each other, but I knew we'd never bridge the gap. In despair, I sobbed anew, but then I felt a burst of golden energy radiate out of my hands and travel from the tree's roots to the once-fiery leaves. The liquid gold rushed through deadened limbs, invigorating dried, brown tendrils as it went.

Pulsing with new life, the tree reached toward me and softly stroked my hair and face. My tears dried in the warmth. A branch wrapped me into a leafy embrace, and I joyfully stood in its glow. Turning around, I realized that all the other trees had also been healed.

"How did one tree heal them all?" I asked out loud.

Ren answered, "Maybe their roots are connected."

Ren brushed the hair away from my neck and ran his thumb lightly across the sensitive place just behind my ear. I shivered, and my eyes met his.

"Maybe they responded to your touch," he said quietly, his lips just inches from mine.

"Why do you have to look at me like that?" I asked while stepping away and lowering my eyes.

His hand dropped from my neck. "How am I looking at you?"

"Like I'm an antelope. Same as before."

Ren smiled slightly, but then his expression became serious as he pulled me into his arms. "Maybe it's because I'm starving."

"Didn't you eat this morning?" My attempt to diffuse the tension with humor failed.

"I don't want food, Kelsey. I'm starving for you."

I was about to protest when he pressed his finger against my lips. "Shh . . . Just let me enjoy this moment. I get precious few of them. I promise I won't kiss you. I just want to hold you and not think of anything or anyone else."

Sighing, I let my head drop against his chest.

A minute or two later, an annoyed Kishan asked, "Are you done hugging my fiancée?"

Ren stiffened and backed away, saying nothing.

"We were healing the . . ."

Kishan spun on his heels and stormed off.

". . . trees," I said to his back as he retreated.

Clearly it was time to get moving again, and after an hour's hike made mostly in silence, we came upon a meadow full of glowing flowers bobbing on thin black stalks. The undergrowth was layered with golden hedges, vermillion bushes, crimson shrubs, and dead copper bracken, while the surrounding thicket burned with trees in lightning yellow, sunset orange, and scarlet.

We stopped to take in the beauty of the forest around us, and that's when I heard the thump of wings on the air. Kishan unhooked his *chakram* and Ren drew the golden sword, separated it into two, and tossed one to Kishan. He also twisted the Sai knife hanging at his side until it lengthened into the familiar form of the trident. He raised his arm, ready to throw it like a javelin.

We heard the unmistakable sound of a bird screeching. I swallowed and searched the dark sky, hoping it wasn't another set of iron birds. The creature shot toward us like a flaming comet, blackened around the edges but burning from within.

It circled in the sky, tilting its head to look at us with one white eye scanning the ground like a searchlight. The bird opened its curved eagle's beak and screeched again, then it flapped its wings quickly as it descended straight for us.

The flight feathers lining the bird's wings were soft—part angel hair and part flame. Broad wings ended in defined wingtips that were candlelight yellow nearer the body but ended in a red so dark, it was almost black.

Its beak was golden, and its feet were covered with dark orange feathers, ending with powerful, sharp talons. A fiery crest lifted from its head, and long crimson plumage protected its nape and reflected the flaming light. It had a long tail that fanned out behind it as it flew. The flickering colors matched the flora of the land, and as the wings, tail, and crest rippled in the wind, the bird truly looked as if it were on fire.

It landed on a fallen log and gripped the wood tightly with its talons. Dancing back and forth until it was balanced, the bird folded its wings and peered at the three of us. A masculine voice penetrated the meadow. Warm and musical, it seemed to shimmer like the world around us.

"Why have you come to my realm?" the bird asked.

Ren stepped forward. "We're looking for the Rope of Fire."

"What is your reason for seeking this?"

"We want to end our quest, bring Durga her prize, and regain our humanity," Kishan answered.

"To enter my realm, you must make a sacrifice to prove you are worthy."

"Tell us what to do, and we will see to it," Ren pledged.

A peal of soft laughter echoed around us. "This sacrifice is not yours to offer, white tiger. No, the sacrifice I require is that of a Sati wife. There is only one person here who is able to fulfill my request."

Ren and Kishan both leapt forward in front of me, lifted their weapons, and shouted, "No! You will not take her!"

Confused, I peered between their broad shoulders and was soon captivated by the bright eyes of the Phoenix.

15

sati wife

Ren and Kishan barred my way, keeping a safe distance between the Phoenix and me.

"Why are you two acting this way?" I asked, trying to get past. "We're here to negotiate, aren't we? We have plenty of things we can sacrifice. I can summon fruit or golden cloth or whatever it wants."

Kishan lowered his *chakram*, but kept his eyes on the bird. "The Phoenix doesn't want just any sacrifice, Kells. It wants a Sati wife."

"And what does that mean?"

Ren tightened his jaw and glanced at me in a way I'd never seen before. His bright eyes filled with the deepest of sorrows. He shook his head, refusing to answer me, tightened his grip on his weapons, and took a step forward, angling his body so he stood between me and the bird.

I turned to Kishan and spoke softly, "Tell me."

In a deadened tone, Kishan replied, "In ancient times, women were taught to devote themselves, body and soul, to their husbands. A Sati wife is a widow. She is stricken with such overwhelming grief at the death of her husband that she will not be separated from him. When his body is cremated, she throws herself onto his funeral pyre to show her dedication and love in this final, fatal act."

Ren added with disgust, "It's been outlawed in India for some time, and my parents had forbidden the ceremony in our kingdom."

I whispered quietly, "I see."

I turned to face the Phoenix and felt Ren's lips brush my ear.

"*Iadala*, we will *not* give you up."

I placed my hand on his rock-hard forearm and squeezed it lightly. Then I gripped Kishan's wrist with my other hand and asked the Phoenix with as much bravery as I could muster, "What is it you want from me?"

The bird tilted its head to study me and replied, "You said you seek the Rope of Fire. Only those who are worthy may pass through my mountains to find it. To deem your worthiness, I ask a sacrifice."

"If I offered myself up for this, would I die?"

"Perhaps. Perhaps not. The true test of a Sati wife lies in her heart, not in her flesh. If your heart is pure and your love is true then your flesh will not burn. If your heart deceives, then your body cannot pass through the flame."

My gut clenched as my heart beat double time. I registered Kishan protesting softly beside me, saying we'd find another way, but a part of me already knew that there was no other way. My mind flashed back to conversations I'd had with Mr. Kadam. I could almost hear his voice whispering in my mind.

"Do not fear the flame, Miss Kelsey, for if you are prepared, it will not hurt you."

But what if I die?

His voice came to me again. *"Reincarnation is an old spirit giving rise to a new one, like a dying flame igniting a new candle. The two candles are different but the flame comes from those who have gone before."*

But I don't believe in reincarnation. My eyes filled with tears that spilled over onto my cheeks despite the dryness of my surroundings, and memories of another conversation with Mr. Kadam flickered to mind. *"What if your child was trapped in a house of burning flame?"*

"I would run in and save him."

I knew then what my answer to the Phoenix must be. I lifted my head and said softly, "I will be the sacrifice."

The Phoenix raised its wings and called out a mournful cry. Kishan pleaded with me not to do this and threw the *chakram* at the bird, but the weapon simply circled around the Phoenix and returned to him.

Ren trembled next to me and tried to barter with the immortal guardian. The anguish he felt was obvious in his voice. "Please, I beg you to reconsider. Take me instead. There is precedent."

The Phoenix replied, "You are correct that the sacrifice was not always the Sati wife. Loved ones of all ages, both male and female, have given their lives in grief and suffering, but your heart has already been given."

"What do you mean?" I asked.

The wise Phoenix explained, "The white tiger was given a choice to forget his love in order to save her. His heart is pure. His love, certain."

"Then take me," Kishan offered.

The fiery bird considered Kishan for a moment. "I cannot. Your time for sacrifice has not yet come, but rest assured, you will be tested as well, though not by me. Come forth, young woman."

I took a hesitant step forward, which was pretty courageous, all things considered, but stopped to face Kishan.

He wrapped his arms around me and whispered, "The second it hurts you, its head comes off."

"I'll remember to duck," I teased and kissed him quickly.

I heard a sob of protest behind me. Ren had fallen to his knees. He locked his arms around my waist and pressed his cheek against my belly.

"Please don't go through with this, Kelsey. I'm begging you," Ren pleaded.

"I have to do it." I stroked his hair and kissed the top of his head.

"I love you," he whispered.

"I know," I answered simply.

Reluctantly, he let me go. He stood, angrily wiped away the tears that had turned his blue eyes even brighter and picked up his weapons with renewed determination. I stepped away from him and faced the Phoenix.

"I'm ready."

The great bird unfurled and flapped its wings, which sent billows of warm air swirling around my body. My hands shook so I pressed them to my sides and waited for the pain.

Dancing on taloned feet, the Phoenix opened its beak and sang. The notes were beautiful and sweet. When the song was finished, it said, "Now they cannot stop you."

"What?" I asked, spinning around.

Ren and Kishan were encased in a box of sparkling glass. They pounded and threw themselves at the clear walls in a futile effort to shatter the glass. I could see but not hear them.

"Can they breathe in there?" I asked.

"The diamond cage allows them to breathe. They will not be hurt but, more importantly, they will not disturb the sacrifice. Now, I must ask you to remove your amulet."

My hand darted to my throat. "Why?"

"The fire amulet protects you in this realm. If you keep it on, all the creatures of the forest, including the trees, will share your pain."

Immediately I reached behind my neck to unhook the clasp. "Will you promise to leave it here for Ren and Kishan? They'll need it."

"I have no interest in your amulet. It will not be disturbed if you set it aside."

I removed the amulet and Fanindra to protect both of them. The heat of the fire world immediately enveloped me. Sweat trickled down my face, and I licked my suddenly dry lips.

I attempted to ignore Ren and Kishan, who clearly thought that this was a bad idea, but as I turned to face the Phoenix, I knew I'd made the right choice.

Then the Phoenix sang again, and the ground peeled back, separating me from the fiery bird. Between us lay a burning bridge of rock and gravel.

"If you can walk the path of flame, you may cross my mountain."

"And if I can't?"

"Then your blackened bones will find a resting place here in this grove."

I swallowed dryly and placed my booted foot onto the white-hot coals. The heat overwhelmed me. My boot started smoking. Sweat dripped from my temples, ran down my neck, and beaded on my upper lip. I took another searing step and another. Although the path was rocky, I slid along as if it were an icy pond. Horrified, I realized that the rubber soles of my boots had melted into slick puddles.

When my socked heel touched the hot rocks, I screamed. I lifted my foot and was about to leap away when the Phoenix warned, "If you leave the path, your life is forfeit."

I set my foot down, careful to stand only on my tiptoes, and took another few steps. A tear rolled down my cheek as I hobbled forward.

The bird watched my progress and asked, "Why is your heart closed?"

I gasped in pain. "What do you mean?"

He didn't answer. I set my left foot down, which was now bare, and hopped to my right foot. The tiny piece of shoe that was left melted away. I screamed in agony but refused to step away. What was left of the top of my sock was burning. With inhuman strength, I ripped it away and stared at my blackened feet. The skin above the ankles was bright red and terribly blistered.

Soon the only pain I felt was up and down my calves, and I knew the fire had burned away the nerve endings in my feet. Determinedly, I took a few more steps.

The Phoenix posed another question, "Why aren't you with the man you love?"

I gritted my teeth. "I am. I love Kishan."

Flames burst around my feet, and my shorts caught fire. I patted it out and saw the skin on my shin bone was now blackened and cracking.

Calmly, the bird asked again, "Why aren't you with the man you love?"

Breathing quickly, I panted, "You're talking about Ren, aren't you?"

The Phoenix remained silent.

I took another step and cried out in pain. "Ren and I don't . . . don't match," I gasped. "He is a chocolate ganache layer cake, and I am a radish. He'll break my heart and leave me for another."

"You are lying. You know in your heart that he will not leave you."

Flames leapt around me. I screamed with a sound louder than I thought was physically possible.

The unruffled bird said, "Your heart is hidden. Speak the truth, and the pain will lessen."

"The truth is . . . he's a superhero, and I'm—"

A burst of flame encircled me, and I screamed again, trembling with weakness and emotion.

"I made a promise to Kishan. I can't leave him!"

When the crackling flames surrounded me, I screamed. The bird said nothing and after the inferno finally receded, I shouted, "Here's the truth: I'm afraid to be alone! I'm afraid he'll die! Like Mr. Kadam! Like my parents!"

"Death is the cause of your fear, but it is not the reason you keep him at a distance."

My hair was aflame. Every part of my body was burning. The red ribbon I'd tied to my hair floated away on a breeze. It was burning on one end, and I watched with fascination as it fell onto the path ahead of me and disintegrated in a puff of ash. My face felt wet. I touched it, and blackened skin flaked off.

No longer strong enough to stand, I collapsed to my hands and knees. "Please!" I begged. "Stop the pain!"

"Speak the truth, and the pain will stop. Why aren't you with the man you love?"

I gasped for breath and knew I was going to die. I stared at my ashen hands, sobbed dryly, and with my last breath, whispered, "I don't deserve to be happy when they're all dead."

"Your heart speaks true."

The pain washed away as if it had never been, but my torso was burned almost past the point of recognition. I didn't care. As long as the pain was gone, I'd contentedly lie on my bed of fire and fall into "that sleep of death."

The Phoenix continued, "What would you give to have your parents and Mr. Kadam back again?"

"Anything," I whispered roughly through burned, cracked lips.

"Would you sacrifice your young men?"

My drifting mind focused. *Would I sacrifice Ren and Kishan to get my parents back?* I thought of my family's little library, of baking cookies with my mom, of picnics by waterfalls. I remembered when I had graduated middle school, and my dad leapt to his feet, clapping, brushing tears away from beneath his glasses, even though none of the other parents stood up. I thought of Mr. Kadam and of how we enjoyed cooking dinner together in the evenings, how he loved to ramble on and on about fast cars and spices and of how much I missed him.

But then my thoughts drifted to Ren and Kishan. *I loved them both. Could I give up Kishan's teasing or Ren's smile? Could I give up Kishan's bear hugs or Ren's touch?*

I answered the Phoenix, "No, I will not trade their lives for my parents' or Mr. Kadam's. You can have my life though." I coughed, my voice sounding like crackling leaves. ". . . for what it's worth."

Tentatively, I reached up and felt my bald scalp. I lowered my trembling hand and managed to squeeze out a tear.

"Poor broken fledgling," the bird whispered. "You're right that your life isn't worth much. Certainly not worth the full lives of three souls who have passed beyond. Perhaps if you'd been willing to experience love and had had a few years of happiness, you might have amounted to something. As it is, your life is rather pathetic. What a waste."

I tried to nod in agreement, but I had lost control of my body. The Phoenix was right. I *was* pathetic. I had wasted my life. I'd been so afraid of losing that I'd never tried to win.

"Still, I suppose you might amount to something someday. You certainly seem important enough to those young men." After a moment he continued. "I think I'll take you up on your offer. Until I deem you ready to appreciate it, your life is mine. Come."

I heard the heavy thump of wings as the Phoenix rose in the air and stirred up a wind that blew around my blackened body. As it descended toward me, I heard its beautiful song once again. Then I felt the sensation of being picked up and flown through the sky. As we soared over the flaming forest through the dark sky, I fell into a deep slumber, gently rocked to sleep on the softest of clouds.

I dreamt of a great kingdom of the past. In an ancient library, Lokesh was torturing a lowly record keeper for information on Queen Panhtwar Beikthano, the Burmese Queen of Pyu, whose brother had given her a magic drum. When she beat upon the drum, the nearby river rose up and fell upon her enemies. It also brought rain during a drought and cast off floodwaters. The evil magician smiled and murmured, "The drum was a diversion." Lokesh's eyes blazed with fire before the vision shifted to a dark evening.

Next, I saw Lokesh try to barter with the queen's grandson for his piece of the amulet, but he refused to sell. Lokesh killed him and then bent over the dead man and slipped a gold ring from the grandson's finger onto his own hand. Lokesh smirked and stretched his hand over a fountain. Water lifted from the basin and swirled in a circle. Then the dream ended.

Water, I thought. *One of the pieces of Lokesh's amulet controlled water.*

When I woke, the first thing I noticed was the pink skin of my hand. My nails were perfectly round and shiny. The Phoenix was nowhere to be seen. I reached up to touch my hair and found it thick and full and silky. When I rubbed the skin on my arm it was as soft as down. My body was clothed in a golden dress, and instead of boots, I now wore soft slippers.

I sat up and realized I was in a large nest next to dozens of gem-like eggs. The nest was resting on a precarious ledge at the top of a black rock mountain thousands of feet high. There was no way for me to climb down, not without the Scarf's ropes. A forest of fire trees stretched out over the hills as far as I could see.

My stomach growled, and I guessed breakfast was several hours, if not days, behind me.

On a nearby mountain, a molten flow of lava plummeted over a jagged cliff. It tumbled through the air, slightly cooling in the process. The radiant falls dropped into a fiery pool below, and the molten liquid sprayed up in a lava fountain that splashed against the surrounding rocks, coating them with darkening layers. Woodland fire trees thickly ringed the pool and seemed to lap up the hot magma as if it was the freshest of spring water.

A musical voice broke the silence. "It's like a newborn's."

I raised my eyes to the Phoenix, who was perched on a ledge overhead, preening its feathers.

"What is like a newborn's?" I asked.

"Your skin. Your hair and nails."

"You healed me?"

"You healed yourself. When you admitted the truth, your heart healed you. A part of you fought to live." The Phoenix tilted its feathered head to peer at me. "I wonder if you will squander this gift."

"Did you need a companion? Is that why you wanted a Sati wife?"

"The Sati wife is a symbol of fidelity and devotion. It gave me no pleasure to see you burn, but I wanted to teach you that the body is immaterial. It is the fire, the passion of the heart, I wished to examine. This heart-fire never ebbs and will never still. It burns brightly, faithfully, for millennia. I could sense your troubled heart when you entered the forest and knew what you needed.

"I have offered you the rare opportunity to purge the sadness that weighs down your soul, but you now have a choice to make: the choice to either take up that burden once again or to remain free of it. Once, we Phoenixes offered our cleansing fire to humans all over Earth, but humankind has forgotten our power, and their hearts suffer all the more for it."

"Sometimes I think that the sadness helps me to remember them," I told the Phoenix.

"That is a false belief."

I drew my knees to my chest and inquired, "What would you do, if you were in my place?"

"And what place are you in exactly, young woman?"

"You know better than anyone. How do I get past my fears? Make a life for myself? Risk loving someone? When death is all that waits for you, what's the point in trying to have a life?"

The bird flapped its wings and then folded them and hopped into the nest beside me. "Do you know much about the life of a Phoenix?"

"Not really. Most of the myths I study end up being wrong."

"Most stories are fictionalized, but a careful reader can always find a smattering of truth. Would you like to learn about my kind while we wait for your young men?"

"They're coming here?"

"Undoubtedly. I released them from the diamond cage. They saw me fly off with you, and it's only a matter of time before they seek out my nest. They think you're dead, you see."

"But why would they seek you out if they thought I was dead?"

"Because," he laughed musically, "they want to kill me. I read the truth of their intentions in their hearts. The blue-eyed one regrets the act but is determined to kill or be killed and the brawnier one thinks only of wringing the life from me with his bare hands."

I picked up a turquoise egg and polished it gently on my shirt.

"Do I see regret in your heart?" the Phoenix asked gently.

"Did . . . did they hear everything I said?"

"No. They could only see what happened to you."

I sighed with momentary relief.

"It would have been easier for you if they knew."

I changed the subject. "Tell me what it's like being a Phoenix."

The majestic bird shifted in the nest, tapped on a ruby egg with its beak, and listened intently. After a moment it began to speak.

"A Phoenix can purify poisoned lakes or streams by dipping in its beak. With a blast of fiery breath, we can cleanse the earth, making wastelands fertile and thriving."

"Have you done that?"

"Regretfully, no. But I've seen it done through the eyes of my ancestors."

"How does that work, exactly? Do you have all their memories?"

"When a new Phoenix is born, the life-spark of those who came before enter its body. A Phoenix is born with the knowledge and the abilities possessed by its forebears. For example, I can cure illness, bring luck to those who glimpse me as I fly past, and I know every language of Earth, even those that have faded away over time. With a flap of my wings, I can level a mountain. I can sing men and beasts to sleep with my song. I can turn living creatures into stone or ash, though I've never had reason to do that. The less altruistic Phoenixes of the past have dried up lakes to dine on fresh fish and carried off elephants to eat, but this is the extent of our mischief making."

"How do you eat an elephant?"

"We eat the same way other raptors do. If the animal is alive, we carry it up to a great height and then drop it."

"Holy cow!"

"Exactly. In my mind, I've watched the destruction of the world and its subsequent rebirth three times. A Phoenix possesses the knowledge of the ages that has been passed to each of us with the expectation that we will guard it and grant wisdom to humankind only when they have proved their merit."

"Mr. Kadam sure would've liked to have had a conversation with you."

The Phoenix shook its head and ruffled its crest before relaxing.

I ventured, "So are you really born of the flame? I've heard that a Phoenix can live for a thousand years before dying and being reborn."

"A thousand years!" it scoffed. "If only that were true, I could accomplish so many, many things in that time."

"Then . . . how long do you live?"

"My time is not measured by even one of your days."

"What?"

It pierced me with a glowing eye. "I will live until this day is over. At dawn, a new Phoenix will rise. It was not always so."

"But then how did you accomplish so many things? How did you learn all those languages? Amass all that wisdom?"

"I didn't. My ancestors did. In ancient times, a Phoenix lived for eons. That was when humankind believed in us, needed us. We were their inspiration, their hope for a better future, a symbol of renewal, rebirth, truth, loyalty, and fidelity. We were asked to bless new marriages for we brought luck, and we helped young couples find harmony and contentment as they began their lives together.

"Then the world began to change. Humans forgot not only the Phoenix but also the ideas we'd come to symbolize. We were no longer needed, so we disappeared. Now we're caretakers of the fire forest. We nurture the flames at the center of this world, for in the center is the heart. You asked me before how to get past your fears and make a life for yourself. How you could risk loving someone when death was all that awaited you.

"The end of the day nears, and as I look into the eyes of my own death, I will tell you that love is the only thing in this universe worth risking all for. The purpose of life is to grow in wisdom and to follow the truths found in your own heart. If you do this, you will be happy, but if you waste your life being miserable due to your choices, or lack thereof, the deaths of your parents and of Mr. Kadam will have had no purpose, no meaning. Live each day as if it was the last. Do not forget."

"I won't."

The Phoenix stood up and stretched its wings to their full span. Flapping them lightly, it raised its head and sang softly. A comet streaked slowly through the dark sky, and the voice of the Phoenix vibrated through my body as it called out, "I am called Sunset, the twilight Phoenix. Accept my sacrifice so that the keeper of the Knowledge of the Ages, the Watcher of Mankind, the Fire Found in All Hearts, will live again!"

With that said it folded his wings around its body, tucked its head into its chest, and exploded in a fiery inferno that consumed its body completely in a matter of moments. As I shielded my eyes, I heard the Phoenix's triumphant song echo through the blaze. The comet streaked toward our mountain, and a white light rose from the still burning creature and shot into the ruby egg at its feet. The egg glowed briefly and then was covered in hot, black ash that rained down from the smoldering Phoenix.

The comet passed over the peak of the mountain and disappeared. With a snap, the fire trees extinguished, and I was plunged into darkness.

16

firefruit

As blackness surrounded me, I felt myself sinking into it, diminishing, as if I was drowning in a hot ocean. The air was thick and palpable. I blinked often hoping my eyes would adjust, so I'd be able to see something. Even the lava falls had gone dark. After a few minutes, I laid my head against the nest and tried to sleep.

A small knocking noise like that of a tiny woodpecker against a tree woke me. I could feel the vibrations on my palm where it rested on the nest. A warm breeze blew my hair over my shoulder. I sat up and pushed it out of the way. As I did so, I noticed the breeze had also cleared away some of the ashes covering the ruby Phoenix egg.

It glowed from the inside with a red, pulsing light. Careful not to damage any of the other Phoenix eggs, I crawled closer on my hands and knees and heard a soft scraping sound. The ruby egg shook slightly and a burst of white light appeared as the shell began to crack. With fascination, I watched the slow hatching of a new baby Phoenix.

After several minutes, a golden beak knocked a small hole into the shell, then retreated. With another burst of energy, a golden-taloned foot emerged and gripped the shell just as a light penetrated the darkness. When I looked over my shoulder, I saw the dawn comet streaking slowly across the black sky.

Another crack, and the shell broke further apart. I could see the bird's fiery reddish colors as it struggled, wrenching its body awkwardly back and forth to free itself from the egg. Its feathers were sticky and wet and clung to its crimson body. I could see the rapid beating of the Phoenix's heart thumping against its thin chest.

The baby Phoenix rested its head on the broken eggshell, lying half in and half out. It cheeped loudly and when it blinked and opened its eyes, they shone like tiny, white penlights. In a flash, I knew it had the intelligence of its sire.

The comet passed over the mountain, lighting up the valley to signal a new day. The Phoenix seemed to gain strength from the fire and began to preen its feathers. Within a matter of minutes, its beautiful feathers and tail were dry, and the bird moved around with strength. It hopped over to me. I reached out a finger to touch its head. The Phoenix raised its crest and closed its eyes, tilting its neck toward me. For the next hour, I watched the bird mature rapidly.

Though similar in form, its coloring was different from Sunset's. Its entire body was covered in reddish hues except for its golden feet and beak.

"Greetings," the new Phoenix chirped squeakily for the first time. "I am Sunrise."

"It's nice to meet you, Sunrise. You must be hungry. Maybe I can find you something."

"I . . . will not eat."

"Why not?"

"I only live for a short time. I will not hunt and kill another creature to sate my appetite."

"What about fruit?" I asked.

"Phoenixes love firefruit," it answered. "But, alas! None have grown here for many centuries."

"When the brothers come, I'll try to create some firefruit for you."

"Yes, if they survive the climb. The white and black tigers are on their way to you now."

I looked down the mountain anxiously but didn't see them.

"It is time for me to choose a new egg," the Phoenix announced.

"Already? But you just hatched," I answered, confused.

"The young Phoenix inside must be given time to develop before my time is done. If you'd like to help, you may bring the eggs to me so I can choose the right one."

I gathered dozens of Phoenix eggs. Each sparkled, lit with its own inner fire. When I had built up a rather large pile of gemstone eggs, I held them up one at a time for the young Phoenix to inspect. It peered into the heart of each egg and declared each of them not ready. When I'd exhausted the pile in the nest, it asked for more.

"There are eggs in the hidden cracks and crags of the mountain."

Quickly, I set aside the amethyst egg I'd been polishing and hunted for more of the precious eggs. "Will you be laying more eggs today?"

"No. All Phoenixes are males. We don't lay eggs."

"Then how did they get here?"

"We have no mother that we know of. Even the wisdom of the ages does not explain where we come from, but we have always known that when the eggs run out, it will be the end of our lineage."

"There aren't a lot of eggs considering you only live for one day," I commented, doing the math as I looked over the nest.

"We do not fear for the future. Each of us is allotted our time. When the eggs are gone, we will cease to exist. I do not dwell on things I cannot control."

"I can't imagine what it would be like to live only for one day."

"One day, if you make the most of it, can be more satisfactory than a lifetime squandered," the wise young bird replied.

I slipped on some loose rock and almost dropped a delicate opal egg, but managed to right myself just in time. As I set it down before the Phoenix, I asked, "Does each bird have different coloring?"

"Yes, each bird is unique. The coloring of the egg is similar to the feathers of the bird." It peered at the opal egg and dismissed it. "No, not that one either."

Directed by the Phoenix, I climbed farther and farther away from the nest to find more eggs. The cliff was perilous so I edged carefully along. As I shimmied my way onto a thin ledge, I saw a gleaming, topaz-yellow egg on a shelf just beyond my reach.

I wedged my foot into a crack and hoisted my body upward several feet until I could just touch the egg with my fingertips. I needed to climb higher. Lifting my other foot, I stepped onto a protruding rock and tested my weight on it. Confident it would hold, I continued the climb.

The egg was beautiful. It sparkled like a yellow diamond and was about the size of a football. I gently tucked it inside my dress above the belt. My skin turned warm where it rested. I started to move down, feeling blindly for a foothold.

My foot dangled in the air and suddenly the rock that held my weight started to give way. It dislodged and tumbled down to the valley below, slamming my body into the cliff on my right. Clinging to the ledge with only my fingertips, I desperately shouted to the Phoenix for help. Then my fingers slipped off the edge and I screamed and tumbled through the sky.

Luckily, after only a moment of freefall, something stopped my descent. At first, I thought I was caught on a tree limb, but then I looked up and saw the face of my rescuer.

"Are you alright?" Ren asked.

I wrapped my arms around his neck, hugged him tightly, and exclaimed, "Thank you! Thank you! Thank you!" as I kissed him on both cheeks repeatedly.

He touched my cheek gently. "You're welcome." Ren hugged my body to his and then pulled back with an expression of confusion on his face as his eyes scanned my protruding belly. He raised an eyebrow and stared.

I glanced down at the bulge hidden under my clothes, wrapped my arms around my precious cargo, and cried out, "My egg! Ren, quick! Let me down!"

As soon as he set me on my feet, I retrieved the yellow egg and examined it for fractures.

"It's fine." I smiled in relief and set it carefully onto the floor of the nest.

I heard the sounds of a struggle and spun around to find Kishan wrestling with Sunrise. The Phoenix had grown again and was nearing the size of its predecessor. Kishan hollered at the bird as he slowly strangled it. Fat tears streamed down Kishan's handsome face.

I grabbed his arm and tugged with all my strength, but Kishan just shoved me roughly aside and shouted, "Leave me alone, Ren. It's my right!"

Ren helped me to my feet. "He still thinks you're dead."

I rushed around the nest to face Kishan—who only had eyes for the Phoenix. Kishan tried unsuccessfully to wring its neck and tear its wings from its body but the Phoenix was unbreakable.

"Kishan, please stop," I said softly.

Kishan froze and then dashed tears from his eyes and looked up. "Kelsey?"

I nodded and held out a hand. He let go of the Phoenix, who moved away a few paces and shook itself vigorously. Sunrise flapped its wings several times and then flew to an overhead ledge beyond our reach.

"You're alive?" Kishan took my hand and yanked me into a tight embrace, stroking my hair as his body shook with relief. "I thought . . . I thought I'd never see you again. That I wouldn't even be able to find your body and take it home."

"I tried to tell you she wasn't dead," Ren said quietly but matter of factly.

"How did you know I was alive?" I asked, still crushed to Kishan's chest. "I was pretty badly burned."

Ren's blue eyes pierced mine as he admitted softly. "I didn't at first, but then I realized I'd know. I'd feel it if you were gone." He broke eye contact and picked up an egg. "I didn't know you'd be healed, however."

I gave Kishan a final squeeze, cleared my throat, and announced, "Ren, Kishan, I'd like you to meet Sunrise."

"And what a memorable greeting it was," the Phoenix hissed sulkily.

"Are you injured?" I asked.

"Would it matter to you if I was?"

"Of course it would."

I heard a musical sigh. "No, I am not injured. No thanks to the brute standing at your side."

Kishan, still angry, threatened, "I held you responsible for her death."

"She is very much alive. And even better than she was before, in fact."

"What do you mean better?" I asked.

"The scars on your legs are gone."

"What?"

Ren crouched down and examined my calves for the scars from the shark and the Kraken. I turned my leg back and forth and only found healthy pink skin as soft as a fawn's.

The Phoenix eyed our group shrewdly. "I congratulate the two of you on successfully scaling my mountain. As is your right for such a feat, I will grant you passage to the other side as promised and will even give each of you a boon. You may each take something from my mountain with you to the other world. Make your choice when you're ready. And to show what a magnanimous creature I am, the black tiger may begin."

Kishan grunted and went for a Phoenix egg. I bit my lip, knowing he'd have to give it back because the eggs were so rare. He chose an egg that was creamy ivory with golden-orange striations running through it. I was about to say something when the Phoenix spoke.

"Have you made your choice then, black tiger?"

Kishan nodded.

"You know not what you have taken, but I will give you this egg on the condition that you guard it all of your days and that it will remain in your family. When you take it from this place, it will change from an egg into a truth stone, and it will never grow to become a Phoenix. When held, you will recognize if those around you speak the truth and you will be able to see into their hearts. It will grant you wisdom if you seek it to be of aid to others, but if you use it to manipulate or exploit, the heart of the Phoenix will destroy you. This is a very precious gift."

Kishan inclined his head. "Thank you and I . . . apologize for trying to kill you."

"Protect the egg, and I will accept your apology . . . eventually." The Phoenix shifted on its talons and settled on the ledge. "And now you, white tiger."

Ren replied, "I would ask to take Kelsey with me."

The bird laughed musically while Kishan frowned. "You are wise to ask for the girl, for I was sorely tempted to keep her with me. I would have enjoyed having a companion as would the other Phoenixes, but a promise is a promise. You may take her with you. It is now your turn, my dear. What would you like for your prize?"

"But I didn't scale the mountain."

"In a way, you did. Phoenixes don't make offers twice. I suggest you take me up on my hospitality."

"Okay. Then . . . I would like some of your wisdom."

"The wisdom of the ages is more than a mortal mind can comprehend. The corporeal form you now possess would be overwhelmed and damaged to the point of death, but perhaps I can answer a question for you instead."

"Alright." I paused briefly as I thought of what I wanted to ask. "My question is this . . . will I ever see my parents or Mr. Kadam again?"

"Are you sure you want me to answer that question? Scholars, priests, kings, and laymen throughout the centuries have pondered on and debated the afterlife. Humankind has always needed to look outward, to aspire to something greater than themselves. It is because they do not know the future that they find the hope that gives them the motivation to change. Do you still wish to know the answer?"

"Yes," I whispered.

The Phoenix opened its wings and leapt to the edge of the nest, considered me, and said, "Then your answer is yes, though you may not recognize them when they are near. Do you remember when Sunset said that love was the only thing in the universe worth risking everything for? The reason is because love is enduring. It flows through not just this mortal world but also beyond."

"Thank you." I wiped a tear from my cheek, took a few steps closer to the bird, and wrapped my arms gently around its neck.

"You're welcome," Sunrise sang softly in my ear. "Now perhaps you will show me that egg you risked your life for."

Ren picked up the topaz egg and handed it to me. I held it up so the Phoenix could peer into it with a blinding gaze. Twin beams shot into the egg, and the center lit up with a small red light the size of a quarter. The little light pulsed, and the Phoenix sang a happy burst of melody.

"What is it?" I asked.

"That is the heart of the next Phoenix."

Reverently, I made a special place in the center of the nest and placed the egg on top of a soft bed of crackling fire leaves. The bird watched me with approval and then stretched its wings and dove off the edge of the nest. Arcing in a circle, it gathered speed and sang loudly. The echo rang through the valley. The mountain shook and a short distance to the side of the nest, rock blasted out in a great explosion. When the dust settled, I saw a dark tunnel in the rocky face.

The Phoenix alit on the nest again and said, "This opening will lead you to a cavern called the Cave of Sleep and Death. Pass through the cavern quickly. If you are fast, you can cross it in two days. Do not delay, for if you tire and fall asleep you will not wake up.

"Beware the Rakshasas in the forest on the other side. You will find the Rope of Fire hidden near the City of Light, but you will have to defeat the Lords of the Flame to take it. Also, should you have the opportunity, try to save the herd of Qilin that used to roam freely in the fire forest. If they are freed, they will make their way back here on their own."

The Phoenix addressed Kishan. "She will need her amulet to travel. Once past the safety of my nest, the heat will soon kill her without it. The two of you regenerate well enough on your own to survive."

Kishan nodded, placed his precious Phoenix egg into his backpack, and then took off the fire amulet and fixed the clasp behind my neck.

Ren took Fanindra from his bag and slid her onto my arm. "Are you ready?" he asked.

"Yes," I answered.

Kishan tested the climb to the cave and back while Ren guided him verbally. I stepped onto the edge of the nest, took Kishan's outstretched hand, and then abruptly turned back.

"I almost forgot," I explained and then mumbled a few words.

The nest filled with mounds of large, reddish-orange fruit that looked like a cross between a dragon fruit and a prickly pear cactus fruit. The pineapple-sized fruit had a leathery-looking skin with soft leaves that narrowed into a sharp point, much like the Phoenix's talons.

Sunrise flapped its wings with excitement. "Ah! Firefruit!"

"Maybe when you're done eating them you can plant the seeds and grow more trees."

"I will plant a grove! Please, take one with you to taste. The juice will revitalize you."

I thanked the Phoenix, stuck my firefruit into the backpack, and stepped from the nest onto the ledge with Kishan. He clung to the side with feet firmly planted, one hand wrapped protectively around my waist. Only when Ren came behind to hold me did Kishan move forward.

We didn't have far to go. Kishan swung his body into the tunnel and reached out for my hand. I squealed when he yanked me into his arms but recovered quickly. Soon, Ren joined us, and we began making our way down the dark passage. Fanindra's eyes gleamed as we descended into the heart of the black cliffs heading toward the mysterious place not even mentioned in Mr. Kadam's prophecy called the Cave of Sleep and Death.

17

the cave of sleep and death

I trailed my fingers across the surface of the tunnel and found it was smooth in sections, almost like the facet of a cut stone. Chunks of loose black gemstone lay on the floor of the tunnel and jagged stalactites hung overhead. I shivered as I passed under them, remembering the Kraken's underwater tunnel.

I told Ren and Kishan about my new vision of Lokesh and that the queen's piece of the amulet controlled water. In great detail, I explained what happened and caught Ren and Kishan glancing at each other, obviously worried that my connection to Lokesh was getting stronger. I didn't blame them. I was worried, too.

Changing the subject, I asked the Scarf to make me new clothes underneath what I was wearing, because a golden dress didn't fit my idea of hiking-through-a-scary-tunnel wear.

After ten minutes of walking, I started to feel claustrophobic and jittery. I knew we had to get through the tunnel without sleeping and that it would take two days at best. Ren and Kishan talked of their childhoods to pass the time and to distract me from hyperventilating.

We stopped to rest often because my new skin bruised easily, and I no longer had calluses protecting my feet or heels. At the end of the first day, I had so many blisters that Ren bandaged my feet, made me a pair of soft slippers, and he and Kishan took turns carrying me. While the royal treatment felt nice, my eyes soon started to droop.

I fought off sleep and tried to keep up an animated conversation with Kishan, but during the long evening, cradled in Kishan's arms, I actually nodded off and quickly came to understand the Phoenix's warning. As my eyes fluttered closed, something dark sucked at my consciousness. My head became heavy, and I could actually feel the flow of blood in my veins slow to a stop.

Alarmed, I tried to rouse myself but couldn't. It was as if I was back with Sunrise and the topaz-colored egg, teetering on the edge of a cliff and had just lost my footing.

I drifted into another vision of Lokesh. My mind seemed to lock with his, and I knew he sought information about another piece of the amulet from a poor servant.

The man, who had been beaten severely, held out a fistful of crumpled papers and mumbled, "According to the records, two great warriors, Chandragupta and Seleucus, frequently met in battle prior to 305 BCE but then mysteriously, all war ceased, and they signed a peace treaty. Seleucus, who served under Alexander the Great, presented his daughter to the emperor to take as his wife, and the emperor sent him five hundred battle elephants in return. Seleucus took over his East Asian territories after the emperor died."

"Continue," Lokesh said to the frightened man after kicking him viciously. I felt Lokesh's delight in the abuse, and I recoiled in horror.

The servant read Lokesh a letter. "Seleucus had offered Chandragupta lands that bordered the Indus River in exchange for goods and soldiers. Chandragupta replied, 'I will consider your offer if you will agree to level the mountain that blocks the view from my palace. You have the power, after all.'"

"Stop!" Lokesh ordered and demanded to see the letters. When the servant handed them over, Lokesh used his magic, and wind swirled around him. Blue lightning crackled at his fingertips and shot into the unsuspecting man, who fell to the floor. Black lightning marks streaked his chest.

The vision shifted, and I was once again with Lokesh in a strange land. "You were hard to find, old man," Lokesh smiled at the aged grandfather he had cornered in a hut. "Fortunately for me your ancestor Seleucus had a birthmark that was passed down to his sons and grandsons."

Lokesh laughed derisively, "Do you know that Seleucus's mother told him his real father was the god Apollo and that his anchor-shaped birthmark was the sign of his favor?"

The frightened man shook his head.

"Seleucus thought he was destined for great things. Perhaps he was in his own small way." Bending over the elderly man, Lokesh continued, "Between you and me, a great man makes himself great. Sadly, your chance to become great has long since passed. Perhaps you'd like to know how long I have been searching for you."

Pulling a knife from his belt, a knife I recognized, Lokesh tested it with his thumb. "Five hundred years," he said, "And that's a long time. Even for me."

The false smile Lokesh wore faded. "But, rest assured, I *will* punish you for every year I've had to wait. Incidentally, the last two years were the most interesting of my search. I traced Apama, the wife of Seleucus, to her Persian hometown of Susa. Then, several months and many deaths led me to you. They all wanted to protect you—their ancient grandfather who claimed to be one hundred and twelve years old."

Lokesh leaned forward and narrowed his eyes. "But between you and me, my friend, I believe that you are much, much older."

The old man's eyes gave him away. In a flash, he used the power of his amulet to shake the ground, but he was as feeble as he appeared. Lokesh froze the old man's entire body in an instant and with his earthquake still rumbling; the man's body slid from the chair and broke apart into scattered pieces.

Lokesh shoved aside the old man's remains and pulled the amulet from his neck. Then he picked up a ring that had rolled away from the shattered hand. It had a smooth oval gem encased in a thick gold, molded edging. The stone's flat blue surface had a marbled appearance that made it look slightly like a weathered map. Lokesh rubbed the Persian turquoise stone and slid it over the knuckle of his thumb.

Frowning, Lokesh kicked aside what was left of the old man's body and mumbled, "I need to learn how to better control the water piece. They die entirely too quickly."

He joined the new piece of the amulet to the others, and I felt the rush of power. The amulet invigorated Lokesh, and somehow I knew he'd found the earth piece. I watched as he tested its range and the scope of its power. With the old man's piece of the amulet, Lokesh was able to bring precious gems to the surface, shift rock, and cause tremors. Together with his other two pieces of the Damon Amulet, Lokesh could call forth predators of the earth and sea to do his bidding.

The sharks! That was how he called them. It was also how he was able to use the bear, wolves, and snow leopards to distract Mr. Kadam during the swordfight.

Satisfied only momentarily with his new power, Lokesh set his sights on India and the remaining two pieces of the amulet.

My body jerked, and I snapped awake to find I was lying in the tunnel with my head pillowed on Kishan's backpack. My connection to Lokesh was indeed getting stronger. It was becoming harder to remain at a distance, and I shook with revulsion at the thought.

Kishan leaned over me and asked, "Another dream?"

I nodded. My cheek stung, and I rubbed the tingling skin. The tips of my fingers were gray and had no feeling. "What happened?" I asked.

With a strange expression, Ren answered, "You fell asleep. We couldn't wake you. I'm sorry, Kells."

"Sorry for what?"

"I had to slap you to get you to wake up."

"Oh. Don't worry about it," I said as I caressed my slightly numb cheek. "It barely hurts."

"That's what worries me. Can you move your legs?"

"Of course I can."

I tried but nothing happened. Grabbing Ren's arm, I painfully pulled my body into a sitting position and looked at my legs. The skin was gray. I poked my calf and found the muscle hard, almost like stone.

"What's happening to me?" I whispered desperately.

Ren took my hand and massaged my fingers gently. "Your face was gray too but it's starting to return to normal color. We just need to get your blood moving."

My fingers began to turn pink, but the tips stung as if they'd been stuck with thousands of hot needles. I whimpered despite my attempt to tough out the pain, and my eyes stung with tears. Kishan pulled off my socks and began rubbing my feet. It wasn't long until I felt burning prickles shoot through my feet and legs.

"It hurts!" I exclaimed.

Ren pressed a kiss on my forehead and wiped away a tear. "We need to do it, Kells. Can you stand it for a little while longer?"

I nodded and he worked on the other leg while Kishan focused on my toes. The fingertips on both of my hands ached, but the sharp pain was gone. After a half hour, Kishan announced that my legs were no longer gray and offered his arm to support me standing up. I did and hobbled around, feeling shooting pains travel up my legs.

Leaning heavily on Kishan, I continued down the path, grateful for my painful blisters that ensured I would stay awake. Ren asked me to tell him all about my dream and kept me talking until my muscles screamed in protest from the constant walking.

I was dead tired. A new body, combined with sleeping in a nest and almost burning to death, had exhausted me. I felt like a walking zombie, and all I could think of was my soft bed back home at Ren's house. Every footstep I took seemed to repeatedly whisper, "Bed, bed, bed." It was late into the night, or perhaps early morning, when Ren suggested we take a short break and taste the firefruit.

Kishan produced a knife and cut into the layers of leathery skin. The fruit separated into two halves. A thick red rind surrounded the soft, reddish-orange flesh. Like a kiwi, the fragile interior was filled with black seeds. Kishan handed me a wedge, and I bit into the juicy fruit.

It had a slightly sour but refreshing tang. The seeds were crunchy but edible and had a nutty flavor. The fruit had the texture of a soft grainy fig but the flavor was like a burst of watermelon and grapefruit combined. As I reached for another piece, I felt heat on the back of my tongue as if I had eaten something mildly spicy.

When we finished eating the fruit and began walking on through the cavern, I felt invigorated, suddenly realizing the pain was gone. I inspected my heels and murmured with awe, "I'm better! The firefruit healed my feet!"

Ren and Kishan felt recharged as well and decided I needed to constantly munch on firefruit as we walked. Instead of eating the messy and sticky fruit, I created a gourd filled with firefruit juice and sipped it whenever my feet started to hurt. We came to a fork in the tunnel and while Ren took Fanindra and explored ahead a short ways, I stopped to rest with Kishan. He leaned against the tunnel wall, and closed his eyes.

I was talking to Kishan while rummaging through the bag when

Ren returned. Immediately, he ran to his brother and shook him. I spun around and gasped. In the few short moments I'd had my back turned, Kishan had fallen asleep. His face had turned gray and his body slumped against the ground as if he were dead.

We shouted and Ren even slapped him twice, but Kishan wouldn't awaken. The gray color visibly crept from his fingertips up his forearms and inched from his face down to his neck. I worried that if it reached his heart he wouldn't be able to recover. As Ren tried to shake him awake, I doused him with water, but the life-giving liquid, though safe to us, was poisonous in the fire realm. It hissed on the rocks and ate through several large stones like acid.

I lifted my gourd of firefruit juice to his lips and though most of it trickled down his neck, he stirred slightly. I gave him more and soon he was able to swallow. The gray began to retreat, and finally Kishan blinked open his golden eyes.

I kissed his still stony lips and admonished softly, "Don't scare me like that."

He tried to speak, but I pressed my finger against his lips. "Don't talk yet. Just drink."

Two bottles of firefruit juice later, he seemed to be fully recovered and stood up, but Ren still draped Kishan's arm around his shoulder and helped him walk off the numbness. I winced when Kishan grunted in pain, completely empathizing with the terrible sting he felt. Soon we were on our way again, headed down the tunnel Ren and Fanindra had chosen.

Kishan regained his strength, and, as the tunnel narrowed, he took the lead, followed by Ren and then me.

After helping me over a large rock blocking our path, Ren said, "I want to ask you something, but if it makes you uncomfortable, you don't have to talk about it."

"What's your question?"

"When you sacrificed yourself to the Phoenix, we saw you burn."

"Yes," I answered softly.

"What happened?"

"The Phoenix asked me some questions that I had a hard time answering, and the burning was the result. There were some things I needed to learn, to admit to myself. Sunset said that my heart called out to it when we entered the forest. It . . . it wanted to heal me."

"Its methods of healing leave something to be desired."

"Perhaps." We walked in silence for a moment and then I added, "The Phoenix didn't ask more of me than it expected from itself though."

"What do you mean?"

"When the night comet streaked across the sky, I watched it burn. Sunset gave its life so the new Phoenix, Sunrise, could be born."

Ren's eyes fixed on me briefly, and then he looked away. Gently, he inquired, "What did he ask you, Kelsey?"

I let out a soft sigh and walked beside him quietly for a few seconds. He didn't press me while I considered how much to share with him.

Finally, I responded, "My heart has been hurting for a long time, and I've clung to the pain. The Phoenix made me face that. And now that I've recognized it, I'm trying to figure out my next steps. As for the questions he asked me . . ." I stopped walking and reached for his hand. "I want to keep that to myself for a while. I promise that I will tell you about it someday. Just not right now."

Ren lifted my hand to his lips and pressed a soft kiss on my fingers. "Then I'll just have to wait for someday."

Six hours later the tunnel widened, and my golden snake suddenly came alive. Fanindra brushed her head against my cheek and squeezed my upper arm with her coils, an unnerving sensation I still hadn't gotten used to. She peered into the darkness ahead of us and flicked her tongue in and out several times. When she angled her head toward the ground, I crouched down and set her onto the gritty black path.

Lifting her head, Fanindra opened her hood and swayed back and forth as she studied the terrain ahead. Then she hissed slightly and moved off in a different direction. We followed her across a rugged trail that was covered with sharp black stones. Her golden body wove between the rocks, and though we lost speed, we all agreed it was safer to follow the snake.

Soon we felt a change in our surroundings. The tunnel opened into a large cavern. Echoes of our voices bounced around us. As we progressed farther forward, I felt a cold wind brush against me and then disappear abruptly. Goose bumps fanned out on my arms, and I rubbed them anxiously.

The movement of cold air was strange enough in the fire world, but it was also accompanied by several unnerving noises. The current of air twisted through holes in the rocks, creating a soft rattling, or fluttering, noise, and the rocks slowly strangulated with dull gasping sounds. The wind continued to brush against my new skin with long intervals in between, and I conjured up the image of a dying colossus exhaling his last cold breath.

Fanindra stopped abruptly and lifted her head, sensing something we couldn't. Not even Ren or Kishan could hear or see far beyond the light cast by the golden cobra. All of us sensed danger. Ren responded by unhooking the sword from his belt. As he grasped the hilt, it lengthened into its full span. With a twist of his wrist, the sword separated into two blades. He handed one to Kishan and by unspoken agreement, both brothers moved slightly ahead of me.

After an hour of this slow movement, I felt the energy drain from my body again. I'd just uncorked the stopper to take a sip of the firefruit juice when Fanindra suddenly coiled and elevated almost the entire upper half of her body. She spread the ribs below her head wider than she ever had before, which showed off the elaborate coloring of her hood and made her look three times larger than she was.

She spat a loud series of hisses in warning, either for us or to try and scare off whatever was frightening her. Her mouth opened and closed several times as if tasting the wind. Her forked tongue tickled the air over and over, waving vertically like a loose ribbon in the breeze as she tried to get a sense of her surroundings.

A pop on our left, like that of a rock falling, echoed through the cavern, startling us. Not a moment later, we heard the quick skittering sound of something being dragged across rocks. It continued to move, circling closer, and the noise reminded me of a child carelessly dragging a heavy toy down stairs. The rhythmic thumps fell in sequence on the landscape, and I felt like something evil was tapping a jittery rhythm down my spine. My vertebrae pinged in sequence with the noise.

Kishan tensed. "Do you smell that?"

"Smell what?" I whispered.

Grimly, Ren nodded. "The stench of death."

Ren reached behind him and took my hand. He nestled me between his strong back and Kishan's. That's when the smell hit me. I gagged immediately, and my eyes began watering. A vapor of decay encircled us, and I had to cover my mouth and nose with my hand. Ren's nostrils flared, but that was the only sign that either brother was uncomfortable.

The smell was worse than a ripe garbage dump. A dead animal would be a pleasant perfume compared to it. It was almost tangible. I could even taste the stench on my tongue and feel it permeate my clothing and my hair. It was a smoldering, caustic, corruption—a sticky, biting tang that was somehow both toxic and sickly sweet at the same time.

The thumping noise came closer and suddenly stopped. The thick air made my eyes sting from the gassy vinegar smell. Fanindra's body waved briefly and then she struck at something in the darkness. She hissed and struck again. I peered into the blackness ahead of her and felt Kishan tense.

A ghostly gray shape shuffled slowly toward us. The hairs on my body stood on end as I realized it was a corpse. The body moved stiffly. The belly was grotesquely distended, and the mouth gaped open slackly. Where there should have been gums was the white jaw of a skeleton. I shuddered when I saw that the skin around the rotting flesh was bloated around the face and was blackened, as if bruised.

Hair hung limply from what remained of the scalp, and I quivered and moved closer to Kishan's back as the creature scratched its forehead, and the scalp slipped, exposing part of its white skull.

Ren spoke first. "What are you? What do you want from us?"

The creature hesitated briefly but began moving toward us again. It seemed fascinated with Fanindra. The snake struck at the creature several times, but it was either unaffected by the poison of her bites or couldn't feel them. When it reached down to take hold of her, she quickly slithered out of its grasp and wound back toward me, wrapping around my leg.

I picked Fanindra up, and she immediately coiled into her jeweled armband shape. Placing her on my arm, I noticed the walking corpse straighten its body and move toward us. Its rheumy white eyes were fixed on Fanindra and me.

Ren raised his sword. "Stop! If you continue to approach, we'll injure you."

The walking corpse didn't even look at him. Ren raised his sword and hacked violently at the creature, slicing cleanly through its right arm. The moldering limb fell to the ground but the lifeless being was only slightly hindered by the lost appendage as the arm slid away from its body. It obviously felt no pain.

Kishan leapt forward then and drew his blade across the corpse's distended belly, splitting open its midsection with a liquid pop. Biting fumes and a thick liquid gushed out. The smell of putrefaction and raw sewage eddied through the air, and as I raised my hand to blast it with lightning power, the corpse clamped its hand on my wrist.

With a strong tug, I escaped its grasp. But to my horror, its skin peeled off and stuck to my wrist. I screamed and flung my arm about, trying to dislodge the fluttering gray epidermis. Calmly, Ren took my arm and peeled off the glove of skin that had slipped cleanly from the gleaming white bones of the corpse's hand.

I, for one, had had enough. With Fanindra's eyes aglow, I turned and ran. I heard Kishan and Ren following behind me, and we quickly distanced ourselves from our pursuer.

As we moved through the cavern, we found other bodies in various states of decomposition. A woman lay over the rocks as if she had fallen in a swoon. Moist flesh still clung to her bones, and her liquefied brains were oozing from her ears and nose. The syrupy smell of musty blood and rotting flesh stayed with us long after we left her behind. We found bleached skeletons with some sort of vegetation growing in the bones and a skull that had had some kind of rodent gnawing on it.

Most of the bodies weren't moving enough to bother me too much, though every once in a while we came across one with rupturing cells, sloughing skin, and the smell of ammonia. When we saw them, we skirted them widely. Still, their heads, when able, turned to watch us.

After passing one particularly ghastly looking fellow, I asked, "What do you think they want?"

Ren answered, "They seem interested in Fanindra. Perhaps they crave the light she casts."

I shivered and clung to his arm as we made our way through the cavern.

Kishan mused thoughtfully, "The Phoenix said this was the Cave of Sleep and Death."

"I'll have to thank him for his literal translation," I remarked.

We skirted another woman who was reaching toward us with an almost motherly expression on what was left of her face. As we moved past, she lowered her arms and her long hair covered her ghostly countenance.

"I'm not afraid of them anymore," Ren said.

"What? Why not?" I asked.

"I think . . . I think they could be us."

Kishan replied, "What do you mean?"

"When the two of you fell asleep, your skin turned gray. If you had never awakened, perhaps either one of you might've shared their fate. They can't help what is happening to them. I feel sad that they are somehow aware enough to experience the decay of their own bodies."

I added softly, "If I was trapped in the dark for years, I'd want some light too."

"Perhaps it is better for them to be spared from seeing their fate," Kishan said.

We moved through the cave quietly. The once frightening feeling of being surrounded by decaying zombies had been replaced with a somber melancholy, and as I passed around the gray bodies, I whispered the quiet words of respect I would have said in the cemetery where my parents were buried, knowing every moment that the difference between one of them and me was simply the slight gesture of closing my eyes.

18

rakshasa

small light appeared far ahead of us and, for a time, I thought it was an illusion. The brothers headed in that direction though, so I assumed they could see it too. Fanindra had decided to remain safely wrapped upon my arm and only gave us the eerie viridian-green light from her eyes, muting her golden luminosity after it had attracted too much cave-of-death-zombie attention. Without her bright glow, we stumbled on our way through the blackness a bit more, but we also remained blissfully ignorant of our surroundings.

Despite the creepy knowledge that I was surrounded by death, and that the smell of rotting corpses had permeated my clothes, hair, and skin, I became numb enough from my exhaustion to not only ignore it, but also to start thinking that laying down next to a rotting skeleton for a brief snooze was a pretty good idea. Ren caught me closing my eyes as I walked, took my hand, and began pulling me along. Kishan moved into a position behind me and gave me a pushy nudge on my back every time I started to slow.

We finally neared the cave opening and peered through to the other side. Thick fire trees stretched ahead of us as far as I could see. Ren and Kishan scanned the fire forest for movement while keeping us hidden in the darkness.

"What is it?" I whispered. "Why aren't we headed for a long nap in the forest?"

Kishan answered, "We have to look out for the Rakshasa. The Phoenix warned us. Remember?"

I glanced out at the trees, looking for scary demons. "I don't see anything."

"That's what worries me," Ren answered.

"Well, what's the big deal? We've faced demons before and survived. They can't be worse than the Kappa, can they?"

"Rakshasas are hunters," Ren explained. "They're night-walkers, blood drinkers. Their hunger is insatiable."

Kishan added, "They're demons from Indian mythology. It's said that they were vile, evil humans cursed to live for eternity as monsters. They can only be destroyed by using special weapons or with a wooden arrow through the heart. They're tricky and use mental powers to confuse their victims and draw them out of their homes."

I blinked and said quietly, "You're talking about vampires."

Ren nodded. "They are much like the European version of vampires."

Kishan snorted. "Kelsey convinced me to watch a vampire movie with her fairly recently, and I have to say that Rakshasas are about as much like the brooding American vampires as the Kraken is like an octopus. These vampires not only drink blood, but also consume flesh, especially rotting flesh."

"Oh," I stammered lamely. "And right now we smell particularly . . . fragrant."

Ren dipped his head slightly in agreement, his concentration still focused on the forest. "It seems safe enough for now, but I suggest we take turns sleeping and travel through the forest as quickly as possible."

We stepped through the cave opening into the fire forest, and it was like stepping from an igloo onto a balmy tropical island. I felt the warmth of the fire trees almost immediately. They stretched out long vines to brush against my arms and clothes as we passed.

I stopped underneath a large tree, and a leafy tendril wrapped around my finger.

As I examined a particularly beautiful fire flower, Ren cautioned, "We have to address our problem. We stink like the dead."

Kishan sighed, "We're leaving a trail."

"I think I can help with that," I said.

"What do you mean?" Ren asked.

"The trees can burn the smell off of us. It's something the Phoenix mentioned when I asked how I healed from being so badly burned. They can't do anything about our clothes but we can make more."

"What do we do?"

"Put your hands on a tree and concentrate on its energy. The heat will be drawn from its roots. Allow it to cycle around you and cleanse your body. It will burn your clothes away and might sting a little, but the warmth will also heal you. You two go into the clearing over there and I'll stay here."

Kishan and Ren reluctantly left their weapons with me and headed to the clearing. The fact that they were willing to leave their weapons behind showed just how tired they were. *We all are*, I amended. I set Fanindra down next to their weapons and backpacks and placed my palms on the tree.

The limbs of the surrounding trees began to quiver and shake, and I heard a hum reverberate in the air. The glowing leaves grew brighter and brighter and the air sizzled. Then with a burst of light, the leaves turned so white hot I had to close my eyes. The blue ribbon I'd tied my hair with disintegrated, along with my clothing. A searing tickling vibration moved from my toes all the way up my body. Then a sudden wind blew my loose hair straight up into the air and caressed my bare skin as it whisked away the smell of death.

I heard a distant yelp and knew the boys were being cleansed in a similar manner and wondered briefly if it burned their skin. To me it felt like a tingle. Finally the strong wind disappeared, and I felt more than warm. I felt . . . flushed. I was relaxed and sleepy, as if I'd been languishing in a hot tub and then placed under a blow dryer while someone massaged my shoulders and brushed out my hair.

I picked up the Divine Scarf and lifted it to my nose. It was mimicking the glowing pattern on the leaves of the fire trees, which had faded again to orange and yellow. The Scarf smelled clean and fresh, retaining no odor from the caves. I wished for new clothes for myself and quickly dressed.

Ren and Kishan made an appearance soon after in the white and black clothing that always appeared after they became tigers. They debated the merits of hiking farther. Ren felt our previous smell was strong enough to be easily tracked, but Kishan argued that it would be just as easy to track our new smell when the old one disappeared. I figured we were safe since we no longer smelled like prey and sided with Kishan mostly because I wanted to sleep. We compromised by hiking just a bit farther before striking camp.

Kishan used the Scarf to create a tent and bedding while Ren replaced the backpacks that had been melted away with our clothing. With my white and black tigers positioned on either side of me, I was unconscious as soon as my head hit the pillow.

This time I dreamed about Lokesh as a young boy. An older man who I soon realized was his father, the emperor, was tutoring him.

Shifting his hands in the air, Lokesh's father instructed, "To control the movement of air, use your mind. Imagine the wind swirling between your fingers or around your body, and it will happen. Once you have practiced and have more control, you can summon something as powerful as a cyclone or simply lift a leaf on the wind."

The emperor showed his young son how to manipulate the air to lift a kite into the sky. He flicked his fingers, and the kite bucked and wove in the air. When it was the boy's turn, the emperor placed the amulet around his son's neck, and the kite plummeted. With a determined expression, the boy lifted his hands, and at the last moment, the kite circled around the two of them and rose again.

"Good," the father said. "Now try calling your falcon."

The boy closed his eyes and soon a bird screeched high overhead.

His father explained, "All creatures of the air are subject to you but you must learn control."

Soberly the boy nodded.

Someone touched my arm, and I jerked awake. "There's movement in the trees," Kishan hissed desperately.

Immediately alert, Ren and Kishan moved silently through the tent, collecting weapons. They gestured for me to remain quiet before the two of them crawled out of the tent and disappeared into the forest. It was completely dark outside, which meant the night comet had passed.

After waiting for what seemed like too long, I decided to risk looking for Ren and Kishan. Fanindra led me to them. They had backtracked and were crouched behind a rock, watching the opening to the cave.

As I approached, I accidentally stepped on a twig and both Ren and Kishan whipped around, saw me, and yanked me down next to them in a matter of seconds. At the same time, what looked like torches flared to life ahead of us in the forest. The flickering lights bobbed and converged in one spot. I heard hissing, clicking noises that moved closer to us.

I sucked in a breath as the lights grew brighter and saw a mob of dark-skinned demons with glowing tattoos covering their bodies. Their long locks of hair flickered in the darkness like small campfires. The radiant strands were brushed back from their foreheads and fire leaves were braided through them.

The male demons were large with powerful arms and bare chests. Two sets of horns grew out from their foreheads—the longer set on the outside. A female approached the largest male and lifted her hand to his shoulder. With a fast swipe, she raked wicked claws down his chest and hissed at him. He stood mutely by as she licked wet droplets from her claws, and I noticed that her tattoos glowed brighter red while his faded to a dull orange.

As she spoke to him in harsh tones, the inside of her mouth glowed yellow as if her throat burned with an inner flame. I sucked in a breath, and she turned quickly toward our hiding place. Her shrewd eyes gleamed, and with an abrupt whisper, all the lights, including their hair, eyes, and tattoos, quickly extinguished.

We sat quietly for a long time, taking shallow breaths and not daring to move. I could sense their presence around us. It was as if they were waiting for us to bolt, wanting to flush us out from our hiding place.

Soon, we heard a familiar shuffling noise, and we peeked out through the darkened leaves toward the cave opening. A stumbling zombie, bald and thin, with wrinkled mummified skin, staggered into the jungle. He stopped as if confused, and I heard a slight hissing. Glowing hair and tattoos flared to life as the Rakshasas surrounded the zombie. Moving as one, they attacked, wrapped it in vines, and carried it off.

It was a long time before Ren and Kishan allowed me to stand. My knees felt locked into place as we made our way quietly back to camp. Without a word, we packed up and hiked in the exact opposite direction in which the Rakshasas had carried off their dinner.

On the way, the three of us reviewed all the visions I'd had. I told them that I now knew for sure that Lokesh had the power to manipulate water, air, earth, and space, thanks to Mr. Kadam's piece, and could also call forth creatures from each of the realms. Lokesh had four segments of the Damon Amulet now, and all he needed was the one hanging around my neck. We finally had all the pieces of the puzzle. It was time to begin putting the picture together.

When the morning comet flew overhead, the trees lit up and touched my cheeks in feather-light strokes. Kishan was worried but said that according to stories the Rakshasa typically hunted at night though they'd been known to venture out during the day if they were very hungry.

Ren wanted to get as far away from the demons as possible, so we hiked all day and only stopped when the evening comet flew overhead. Ren found a secluded place to camp and was keeping watch with Kishan so I decided to head to a nearby clearing with the Scarf for a fire bath.

"Just make sure you're back soon, or I'll come looking for you," Kishan warned as I kissed him on the cheek. "And if I happen to catch you undressed, then that's just too bad."

He grinned while Ren frowned. "Be careful, Kells," he added.

"I will. You won't even miss me."

I gave a good jolt of my fire power to a young tree to compensate for the energy it would soon expend, and it returned the favor by giving me a gentle fire bath. After I dressed, I sat on a nearby rock and brushed out my newly cleansed hair as the little tree went back to its normal mode. The fire baths included the added benefit of straightening my hair, and I liked the soft feel of it hanging down my back.

Refreshed, I took the Scarf and Fanindra and returned to our little tent only to find the fabric ripped apart and our belongings strewn about. Ren and Kishan were missing along with all of our weapons. I turned in a slow circle and listened carefully to the dark forest. I heard nothing. Despairing, I headed back to the rock near the young tree and paced the ground.

"Well, we've got to save them. There's no question about that," I mumbled to Fanindra. "But how?"

Fanindra's golden scales shimmered to life, and she led me through the forest. Her eyes only glowed enough so that I didn't trip over rocks or tree roots. After a good hour's hike, I made out the glowing light of the demon camp.

Untying the Scarf from my waist, I shook it out, wrapped it around my body, and said, "Disguise. Rakshasi queen."

My body tingled as the Scarf did its magic and when I lifted it away, I pulled my long fiery hair over my shoulder and ran my hand through it. It was thick and coarse, and when I reached up to touch my head, I found a circlet of fire leaves. My dark arms glowed with red tattoos, and I ran my tongue over my teeth. The canines were pointed and sharp. I wore a dress of burnished orange that seemed to smolder when I walked.

With my head held high and Fanindra showcased in all her gleaming glory on my arm, we walked toward the camp. Sentries spotted me almost instantly and called out in low hoots. I was soon surrounded by the clan, but before long, the throng parted and a female sauntered toward me. I'd correctly guessed this was a matriarchal society and that she was the queen.

She was beautiful for a demon. Her dress, though not as fine as mine, was long and of better quality than the clothing of those around her. An orange spark lit her eyes when she saw me, and when she blinked, I saw her pupils were elongated like a cat's. Boldly, I withstood her inspection and took my own time appraising her. She wore a necklace of little silver interlocking wishbones. Thin bone earrings pierced her ears and hanging below dangled the tiny claws of some small raptor.

A silver circlet with a veil of fire leaves adorned her flaming tresses. Hanging from it was a crescent-shaped bone that rested in the middle of her forehead. Red tattoos that looked like clawed hands covered her eyes and cheeks. Her ears were long and pointed like an elf, and her horns were much thinner and more delicate than the males surrounding her. There were no other females in sight.

Her painted orange lips parted, and her cheeks glowed as if lit under the skin by a flashlight. She ran her tongue across her pointed teeth before speaking.

"Worthy wanderer. Carcass of contamination. How shall I address you?" she asked.

"You may call me . . . Malevolence," I answered.

The group surrounding me shifted in surprise, and the queen smiled at me dangerously and responded. "Are you a vanquisher or are you our prey?" She tilted her head. "I wonder why you are here alone. Could this be some kind of a clever trick?"

She gave a sign, and some of the warriors took up arms and surrounded me while others disappeared into forest. Slowly, she circled me and plucked at the fabric of my dress, peering at it with obvious covetousness. When she dared to touch Fanindra, the cobra came alive and hissed at her. The queen stepped away but showed no surprise or fear of the snake.

Warriors returned and whispered reports in her ear. She smiled.

"I am called Desecration," she announced, "the Rakshasi queen of this clan. For now, I will open my hand to you. At least until you present more of a . . . challenge. Come."

She snarled at the burly demons surrounding us until they dispersed, leaving only the two of us and a few guards. She ran a hand over one of the demon's biceps appreciatively and indicated that I should follow her.

Leading me to a tent, she ducked inside. Two guards stayed close by while I entered and sat across from the queen. After sprinkling some kind of powder into a cup of steaming drink, she handed it to me. It smelled sweet and coppery, and I immediately suspected it was blood.

I set it aside and proceeded as if I had no time for small talk. "I have come on a matter of great importance."

The tattoos on her face flared momentarily then returned to their normal color. She sipped from her cup, indicating to me that I should go on.

"My two best hunters are missing from my clan and I believe they have been taken by your people."

She shrugged. "My hunters have the right to take anything from the forest that they can overpower."

"So you *do* have them."

"And if I did?"

"I was hoping you'd be willing to barter for their lives."

"Barter? What does this word mean?"

"It means trade. I'll give you something of value in exchange for their freedom."

"Trade? Rakshasas do not trade." She licked her lips greedily and shifted in such a way that made me think she was ready to spring. Tilting her head, she studied me suspiciously. "What are you? You are no Rakshasi queen," she spat. "Your teeth are as dull as those we eat and you do not even extend your claws when threatened. Your venom must be as weak as your hunters. I do have your men, pale and sickly though they are."

She swirled her drink thoughtfully. "If you wish to take them with you, you must first prove yourself in battle." Desecration smiled evilly. "If you win, they go free. If you lose," her eyes sparkled, "we eat you. The flesh of a queen, even a weak one, is luscious."

Fear and disgust merged, and I felt a burst of emotion inside me that grew into a hot flame. My new body responded and my fingers elongated, producing another knuckle. My nails extended into sharp daggers and stretched out from my hands several inches. The tips of my claws tingled, and a shiny black drop that fell to the ground where I knelt hissed when it hit the soil.

I moved into a crouch. My legs were strong and I felt powerful. With all the cruelty I could muster, I leapt toward her, and slashed the air near her face. I sneered and replied, "I accept your challenge."

Desecration smiled as if pleased with my display. "Very well. We will fight at twilight tomorrow, for tonight is a feast."

I was taken out to the revelry and had to watch in revulsion as they feasted on the remains of the zombie they'd captured earlier. I shivered at the sound of bones cracking, bones being almost all that remained from the previous night's feast. There was no sign of Ren or Kishan anywhere, and I hoped that with their healing ability they were at least alive.

I caught one of the largest demons smiling wickedly at me. Bony protrusions pierced the skin of his shoulders and his forearms were so thick, they looked like tree trunks. When he turned in the firelight a certain way, the handsome illusion slipped, and I saw that beneath it, his face was a frightening skull with glowing eyes.

The queen watched my reaction to the feast with a mocking expression and noticed the demon that was paying particular attention to me. She called him over and whispered words in his ear as the two of them looked at me.

Grinning widely, he approached me and bowed low. "My queen has given me over to you for the evening."

"Oh. How very . . . generous of her. And what exactly does she expect me to do with you?" I asked nervously.

"You may use me in whatever way you wish," he answered hungrily.

I smiled at the watchful queen and inclined my head, then threaded my arm through the burly Rakshasa's. Weighing the risks against the possible benefits, I said, "Then perhaps you could take me on a tour of your camp. If you are finished feasting, that is."

He smiled rakishly. "I was instructed to indulge you in your every whim. A tour of the camp is only the *beginning* of the things I could do for you," he bragged and boldly ran a hand down my hair. Hoping I could keep his claws off of me long enough to figure out where they were holding Ren and Kishan, I let him lead me off alone.

He took me to the largest tent and showed me a trophy wall of sorts that sported bones and skulls arranged in a gruesome display. "This place is dedicated to our best hunters." He picked up a necklace made from tiny bones and handed it to me. "It belonged to the greatest hunter of our generation, Thunder Cloud. I am his descendant and was named for him."

"You're called Thunder Cloud as well?"

"No. I am Lightning, Thunder Cloud's son."

"Oh? Is he here? Did I meet him?"

"He has gone the way of all the infirm."

"What happened to him?"

"He was injured in a hunt. Every year the greatest hunter enters the cave and tries to capture the Phoenix. He returned to us alive but unsuccessful. His arm had been broken."

"So his arm didn't heal?"

He hissed. "True Rakshasa hunters have no desire to heal. They sacrifice themselves for the clan. Their energy is absorbed and rechanneled."

I swallowed thickly. "You mean . . . you ate him."

He set down a painted skull and looked at me. "Do you not do this honor for your injured hunters?"

"Oh, we do, we do. It's just that . . . my hunters have the power to regenerate. They're never permanently injured, and they don't age."

He caught my arm and whispered conspiratorially, "I knew from your appearance that you were a special queen. You must grant me this power. Discard your weak hunters, and you and I could slip away and start a new clan, our own clan."

He looked me up and down, smiled, and stepped closer. His sharp, pointed teeth glistened in the flickering light created by our hair. "Of all the hunters here, I am the most . . . gifted." He stroked my arm with his long claws, not piercing my skin, but leaving wicked scratches along the length of it. "I assure you, I would be a most loyal companion."

I gripped his forearm and allowed my claws to dig into his skin. He groaned as if I'd kissed him.

"I'll consider it," I promised suggestively. "Now . . . I'd like to see the rest of your clan's relics."

He showed me a crude painting of the first Rakshasa leader, which was a male, not a female. *Interesting.*

"He was a great magician and illusionist," Lightning explained. "He could shape-shift into an owl, a monkey, a human, or even a great black cat."

"Really?" I remarked, studying the painting with interest. "Can your queen still do this?"

"Our queen claims she has the ability, but I have not seen it. She can create illusion though. She is very powerful."

"I see. Do all of you have this ability?"

"The people of our clan are all experts at cloaking our life force. Does your clan not have this power?"

"My clan has . . . a different kind of magic." I placed my hand on his arm. "Perhaps I'll be able to demonstrate some of my abilities later."

His grin was frightening. "I look forward to it."

He showed me other truly vile keepsakes—a dried wreath of entrails, a collection of scalps and furs, and several frightening masks, as if their own faces weren't already vile enough. Their handsome façade no longer fooled me. Now that I knew how to look, if I squinted just right, I could see his skull peeping through his skin, but it was easier to pretend he was just a handsome demon.

When I'd had my fill of the place, he took me outside and showed me a sort of corral. He hooted softly and I heard the thunder of hooves as a large herd of animals approached. Dark shapes moved toward us and then, as if someone had clicked a switch, the animals blazed into color. They were the most beautiful creatures I'd ever seen.

"What are they?" I whispered as one of the animals approached me and stretched out its neck.

"They are Qilin. We captured them from the forest of the Phoenix."

"Ah."

The Qilin were the size and shape of a horse but had the face and teeth of a dragon. Smooth fish scales covered their bodies, but they still had flowing manes and tails. They came in a variety of colors—red, green, orange, gold, blue, and silver. And, like the Rakshasa, the hair of the animals glowed as if on fire.

My guide shouted a command, and the animals jumped in fear and galloped in a circle. Flickering flames spread out from their hooves, manes, and tails as they ran.

I climbed the fence and held out my hand. A bold, blue Qilin walked toward me. It flared its nostrils and blew out a hot breath into my hand when I touched its muzzle. When I patted its smooth cheek and ran my hand through its blue flaming mane, I could hear its thoughts: *Fiery one, you are not of them. I can smell your humanity. We are of the other side of the mountain. They feed us on the flesh of our brothers. You must save us, princess!*

I allowed my fire power to blaze into the Qilin's side and it shuddered at the warmth. I sent a silent message. *I will save you. Watch for me and prepare your herd.*

I will watch for you, fire princess.

"The morning comet approaches, my queen. You must rest so that you may be victorious in your battle."

"Very well. Let's return to the camp."

The demon escorted me to my tent and tried to follow me in. I put my hands on his broad chest and stopped him. "The time for such things is not yet. First, I must defeat your queen."

He growled in frustration. "I will leave you alone for now, so that you may prepare, but I will not be set aside so easily in the future."

I nodded and turned to leave when he took my arm and whispered a few of the brutal things he wanted to do either to me or with me. I wasn't sure which, and I really didn't want to know. I just smiled at him and hissed slightly, which he took as a good sign, and then he finally left me alone.

Inside my tent, I pulled back the blanket on the bed—and found a box full of dead insects. I figured they were used either as a mattress or as a late night snack.

I curled up in a corner and spent the next hour wondering what I'd gotten myself into. So far, I'd seen no sign of Ren or Kishan and for all I knew, Queen Desecration was bluffing and didn't even have them in the first place. Knowing I needed rest, I pillowed my head in my hands, figured out how to dim my hair and tattoos, and tried to sleep.

I quickly learned that the Rakshasi queen didn't really leave me to my own devices. Two huge guards stood just outside my tent and squashed any ideas I had of sneaking out to find Ren and Kishan. I napped on and off during the day, worrying about my tigers.

When the night comet passed overhead and the fire trees extinguished, I was summoned for battle. The queen had dressed for the occasion in some kind of bone armor, and her hair was teased out to look like a bonfire. The tattoos on her face glowed vivid red as if someone had slapped her across her face with red paint.

We marched to a large clearing, and the Rakshasa demons melted into the surrounding trees so that only their torch-like hair was visible.

The queen faced off from me and raised her arms into the air. "Rakshasas! Witness the power of your queen!"

She circled her arms dramatically and produced sparks and black smoke that swirled around her. The smoke moved as if alive and twisted toward me. It circled around my body and then back to the queen. She shouted, and two bolts of lightning hit the ground.

The smoke cleared and two stone altars appeared—with Ren and Kishan tied to them. They looked around in confusion and struggled vainly against the ropes. Their shirts hung in ribbons, but other than that, I could see no injury.

The queen walked up to Ren and ran a dagger-like nail down his bare chest. She clucked, "Now, now, my pretty. Don't jostle around so." She touched his lip with her grotesque claw. "I like my meat . . . tender."

She moved as if to kiss him, and Ren turned his head in disgust. In retaliation, she ran her claws across his cheek. Bloody gashes dripped rivulets down his neck. Desecration turned to Kishan. "Perhaps this one will be more cooperative."

She smoothed her hand across Kishan's broad shoulders and down his arm. He snarled angrily at her.

The demon laughed throatily. "Perhaps I'll let you live just a bit longer. Your aggressiveness is charming. Well, don't despair, my fragile hunters. Your queen has come to redeem you, for as much good as it will do her."

Both Ren and Kishan desperately sought the surrounding forest for me but their eyes passed over my new form.

I stepped forward and shouted, "You've wasted enough of my time and have insulted me by abusing my warriors before my eyes. I don't think you have the venom necessary to defeat me."

Smoke swirled around Desecration, and her eyes glinted dangerously. "I will suck the marrow from your bones as you choke slowly on your own blood."

I put my hands on my hips and smiled, baring my fangs. "If only your bite were as strong as your rank perfume."

Ren and Kishan were gaping openly at me, and the Rakshasa hunter from the night before stepped out of the tree line and grinned triumphantly.

Just when I was starting to feel like I had the upper hand, a streak of smoke slammed into my stomach and threw me to the ground. It wrapped around my throat, cutting off my oxygen. Quickly, I untied the Scarf from my waist and whispered painfully, "Gather the winds."

Smoke billowed and pulsed into the bag the Scarf had created. The air swirled around the clearing and blew my hair in every direction. Finally, the winds were gone and the bag danced in my hands. I smiled at the woman glaring at me from across the clearing, lifted my eyebrow, and opened the bag. Smoke shot toward the queen, circled her, and began choking her. She coughed, raised her arms into the air, and brought them suddenly down. The smoke disappeared.

Desecration snapped her fingers, and the light of her hair and body went out. I took a battle stance, turned off my own inner light, and watched the darkness carefully. I heard her laughter as she appeared briefly and was gone again. I tried to sense her, but she moved stealthily. A hiss came from my right, and as I spun around, her claws raked across my arm and shoulder.

She jumped onto me and pushed me to the ground, but I thrust her back and attacked with my own claws, managing to get her thigh and calf. My shoulder began to burn horribly like acid was gnawing its way into my muscle. I'd thought the bear scratches on my leg were excruciatingly painful. This was far worse.

She disappeared again, only to materialize a few feet away. She whispered some words, and with a flourish, the trident appeared in her hands. She aimed it at me.

"Perhaps you are missing this?" She brandished the weapon and circled. "I have to admit I was surprised to see your collection of war prizes. For such a weak queen, you have accomplished much."

"Come a little closer," I threatened with an evil smile, "and I'll show you how much more I can accomplish."

She attacked with the trident, but I stepped aside and blasted her in the back with my fire power. I heard the collective hisses and shifting of the demons in the trees and smiled until I heard the queen laugh excitedly.

"Now *that* felt good." She turned and stretched languidly. "You must tell me the secret for that power before you die, my little queen."

"Not likely," I hissed and crouched for the next assault. *Stupid! Fire is good for them. Time to change tactics.*

I sprung at the queen and pushed her to the ground. She blew a palmful of some kind of dust that ignited and sent sparks flying everywhere. I couldn't see anything but white flashes. Still, I slammed into her blindly, and we tore at each other with claws until I had stinging hurts everywhere.

The queen overpowered me, pinned me with her muscular legs, and wrapped her claws around my throat. The tips pierced my neck, and I could feel her poison entering my body.

"What have you to say now, tiny queen?"

I bared my fangs and smiled. "How about some rain?"

Her eyes narrowed in confusion. I whispered to the Pearl Necklace to rain only on the Rakshasi queen. I could smell the water before it touched me. It gathered in the air above us as a white mist. The cloud darkened and rumbled, then a light rain shower began to fall. The queen screamed as the drops hit her back and arms. It hissed when it touched her skin and her tattoos faded.

I punched the demon queen in the face and pushed her aside. Rolling away, I stopped the rain shower and whispered to the Scarf to tie her up and gag her. Threads shot out from the Scarf and wrapped Desecration's legs and arms. She used her claws to break the threads several times, but the Scarf just thickened the ropes.

I blinked, trying to clear my vision and bring all the shapes around me into focus. I felt for one of the stone altars and bumped into human flesh.

Ren spoke proudly, "You make a beautiful demon."

"Thanks." I smiled weakly and raked my claws across the stone. Sparks flew, and the tight ropes binding Ren fell away from his body. He freed himself the rest of the way while I stumbled to the other altar to cut Kishan loose. My blood was boiling from the venom, and I knew it would soon overpower me.

The fallen queen struggled on the ground. I slashed the ropes holding Kishan and stood as tall as I could. "Lightning. Come forward."

The powerful demon strode into the clearing boldly and prostrated himself before me. "My queen," he said and lifted his head. "Let me dispose of those weakling warriors who couldn't protect you and then take my place at your side."

I placed my hand on his shoulder and smiled almost lovingly at him. "I have other plans for you, great hunter." I could feel Ren and Kishan standing at my back. "I would not have you kill these two warriors, for they are special and far from weak. I promised you a demonstration, didn't I?"

The Rakshasa demon lifted his head. I staggered slightly, and Ren reached for my elbow.

I pushed him away, not wanting the Rakshasas to see me weakened, and shouted, "My hunters, come to me."

Ren and Kishan positioned themselves at my side. With a dramatic flourish of my arms, I declared, "Your queen commands you to show this clan your claws."

Ren tilted his head and Kishan studied me quietly for a second. Then both men morphed into their tiger forms. The Rakshasas who had since stepped into the clearing collectively gasped. Ren growled menacingly and Kishan roared and slashed the air before they began pacing protectively in front of me. A few demons immediately prostrated themselves on the ground. Even the queen stopped struggling and watched us though she lay tied and gagged.

"Lightning," I continued, "My wish as your new queen is that you hunt the creatures from the cave no more. You will dine only on the flesh of animals found in the forest and you will leave the Phoenix alone."

"Yes, my queen."

"The Qilin shall be freed and instead of eating your infirm, you will allow them to heal." *So much for the Prime Directive. Sorry, Captain Picard!*

He inclined his head. "As you wish."

"We shall celebrate with a victory feast."

The demon stood and smiled. "Yes! We shall eat the former queen!"

"No!" I called out. "You will treat her with respect, but you will no longer bow to her wishes."

He responded with confusion. "If that is your desire."

"It is, and I have decided to appoint you, Lightning, the new leader of this clan."

He hesitated, and then said, "But our clan has had a female leader since the time of my grandfather."

"You told me that once it was led by a male, correct?"

"That is true." He paused, then stood taller and shouted. "I *will* lead. Are there any here that challenge me?"

No one stepped forward. He hissed smugly and then approached me and boldly ran his claws down my arm. "Venomous one, stay here as my queen and rule by my side," he offered. "Share with me your power, and you shall want for nothing."

Both tigers growled and crouched to pounce, but he completely ignored them.

I raised my chin haughtily and brushed his arm away. He smiled at my hostility. Brashly, I answered, "I must return to care for my own clan, but I will produce a feast for you before I go."

I swayed on my feet and sucked in a deep breath. Closing my eyes, I wished for a meat-lover's feast and was rewarded with suckling pigs, rare beef roasts, and fat turkeys. Dishes appeared all around us, and any of the demons who were still standing knelt on the ground and bowed before me. Only Lightning stood, and he directed the hunters to take the queen and the food back to the camp.

When he looked to me for approval, I smiled at him and promptly collapsed into his arms. I heard a terrible roar from one of the tigers, a variety of hisses and calls of distress from the Rakshasa, the throaty laughter of the bound queen, and then heard nothing more.

19

qilin

When I finally came to, I blinked and tried to lift my head—only to lower it again carefully when I felt an excruciating pain explode behind my eyeballs.

Kishan knelt next to me and touched his palm lightly to my cheek and neck. "How are you feeling?"

"Like the Kraken chewed me up and spat me out," I mumbled and tried to rub my aching forehead.

Kishan caught my wrist before I made contact. "Hold on there. You've got to be careful with those things. You might put your eye out."

Confused, I glanced at my hand and groaned softly when I saw that I was still disguised as a Rakshasi queen. My fingers sported deadly black claws dripping with venom. I placed my arm at my side. "Lovely. How long have I been out?"

"A few hours."

"Where's Ren?"

"He's supervising the feast and distracting the warriors while I use my considerable magic to heal you." Kishan tapped the *kamandal* at his throat and then readjusted my pillow. "You have no idea how many demons are absolutely enamored with you. He has to keep them at bay, in fact."

I snorted. "They aren't interested in me. It's my power they desire."

Kishan raised an eyebrow, looked me up and down in my Rakshasa disguise, and then grinned. "I think you may be underestimating your appeal."

I felt my face go hot at the compliment, and my tattoos flared red. Kishan's smile widened. He softly traced the outline of the tattoo on my cheek.

"The light flickers under your skin, especially when I touch you."

Uncomfortable with the attention, I shifted slightly and hissed in pain.

Kishan pulled back to examine my healing shoulder. "Just lie still and let the elixir work until you fully heal. The scratches weren't mortal wounds. I wonder why they affected you so badly."

I took the cup of water he offered and sipped while he helped me lift my head. "It was the poison in her claws," I answered between swallows.

I twitched my dangerous digits and concentrated to retract the claws. Kishan then took my hand and brought it to his lips for a kiss and said, "The most beautiful creatures are often the most deadly. At least the mermaid's elixir is healing you."

I closed my eyes and leaned into his broad chest. Kishan massaged the back of my neck to help with my throbbing headache.

A short time later, Ren ducked his head into the tent and frowned. "You are supposed to be healing her, not taking advantage of her weakened state."

"Her shoulder is healed," Kishan explained, "but her head still hurts."

Ren crouched down across from me, and his expression changed to one of concern. The pain was so sharp I had to squint at him though the tent was lit by only firelight.

"What is it?" I asked.

Ren studied me quietly for a moment, and then said, "I won't be able to hold them back much longer. They want to see the new queen. Apparently, your victory is not complete unless you prove to them that you are alive and well and that Desecration's venom didn't kill you."

I nodded slightly and was grateful that the motion didn't hurt. "Can you buy me five more minutes?" I asked.

He leaned over and pecked my forehead. "I will. She's hot, Kishan," he said as he ducked out of the tent.

"It's okay," I explained to Kishan. "Hot is my natural state as a demon."

He laughed softly and continued massaging my head with his fingertips. "Hot is your natural state all the time, *bilauta*. Just relax and breathe. Focus on your heartbeat."

The quiet crackling fire in the tent soothed me. I concentrated on inhaling and exhaling, and little by little the pain diminished. I peacefully drifted in Kishan's arms until we were disturbed by a clamor outside the tent.

Ren's voice was raised. "I promise you that she is alive. She has been resting these last few hours."

"We want to see her!" a demon insisted.

"Let her walk among us," another shouted.

"You monopolize her. Shut her away from the clan."

Ren threatened, "She has provided you with a sumptuous feast. She has expended much energy on your behalf. Allow her time to recuperate."

"*Recuperate*? What does this word mean?"

The uproar outside drowned out Ren's reply.

I whispered to Kishan, "They don't understand him. Their way is to speak spitefully, derisively to one another. They don't show kindness. They only know weakness and strength. You'd better help me up."

"Are you sure?"

"I think I can manage."

I stood on wobbly legs while Kishan took my arm and escorted me outside. A hush fell over the crowd as I made my appearance. Narrowing my eyes at the demons, I hissed, "I trust your feast was satisfactory?"

Several demons murmured, "It was, my queen."

"Then why have I been disturbed?" I shouted.

Lightning approached and inclined his head. "We are . . . confused."

"Perhaps these others with more simple minds are confused, but surely you, Lighting, are not. Please explain this confusion."

He quirked the side of his mouth in a small smile then explained, "A clan lives for its queen. If the queen is injured, then so are her hunters. They simply wish to reassure themselves that you are well." As he lustily studied my body, he added, "I can see that you have recovered sufficiently from your wounds."

Ren and Kishan growled.

"Yes, I have," I replied.

Lightning smiled suggestively. "Then it is time for you to choose your consort for the night."

"My consort? Very well. I choose to remain with my warriors."

"You may not choose them. Another night, yes, but on the night of your victory celebration, you must select a man from our clan."

"Why?"

"This man will journey to your new clan with you. He will become yours. It is the way of all Rakshasa. Surely you know this."

The demons murmured quietly at my strange reactions.

Thinking quickly, I laughed mockingly, approached Lightning, and extended my claws again to run them down his arm. "And were you hoping that you would be my choice, newly made king of the Rakshasa clan?"

He grabbed my arm and squeezed, causing me to utter a cry of pain that I somehow managed to turn into a snicker. Lightning smiled and replied, "Of course you would choose me. Who else here is as worthy?"

I looked up into his eyes and licked my lips. His attention moved to my mouth and he growled appreciatively. He ducked his head to kiss me but, before he made contact, I shoved him roughly away and announced, "Any of you who wish to be my consort will have a fair chance to . . . capture my attention. Tonight you will hunt."

Murmurs of excitement spread through the camp.

"You will not hunt for flesh, however. Tonight you will bring me a," I paused while I racked my brain trying to think of something, "a white fire flower. The first man to do so may be my companion this evening."

One by one, the men doused the light of their bodies and slunk off into the woods. Lightning remained behind, studying me.

"Well?" I asked. "I thought you were interested in becoming my consort."

"I am." He cocked his head. "I was just wondering why your two warriors didn't leave with the others to seek your trophy. Have they no interest in pleasing their queen?"

Kishan strode forward boldly, shoved Lightning, and spat, "Do not presume you understand the wishes of our queen."

I intercepted. "Of course they will hunt. I expect nothing less from them. But first they will escort me to the tree where I will watch for the first hunter to return."

Ren and Kishan each took an arm and walked me over to a stand of fire trees that were darkened in sleep. I handed Ren a handkerchief that I'd had the Scarf make. He read the embroidered message and handed it to Kishan. Both men changed to tigers and trotted out of camp. Lightning gave me a suspicious look and then dimmed his light and left the camp as well.

Dawn would come soon, and I had a lot to do while everyone was gone. Using the Fruit, I filled a goblet with firefruit juice and drank it down. After two more cups I felt much better.

Renewed, I returned to my tent and gathered the weapons, the Phoenix egg, and our other belongings that had been confiscated from our packs. With Fanindra on my arm and a newly made backpack, I dimmed my light and moved through the darkness until I'd found the corral Lightning had shown me the night before.

Closing my eyes, I sent out a message to the animals I sensed resting not far away. A soft whicker and a clop of hooves was my answer as several of the beasts drew near the fence. The lead Qilin approached me. It nudged my hand and blew a hot burst of air from its nostrils.

You have returned, princess. We have waited for you.

Are you ready to be free once again? I asked the animals.

They stomped their hooves excitedly, which created a shower of different-colored sparks over the ground in the otherwise dark night.

Do you know the way through the cave? I asked.

We do, but many of us will be lost on the journey.

Not if you eat these firefruit, I thought and asked the Golden Fruit to create a mound of firefruits in the Qilin's corral. *They will heal you and help you to stay awake.*

Firefruit! These have been lost for generations! It is a precious gift you've given us, princess.

The Qilin devoured the fruit noisily, biting through the tough outer skin with their dragon teeth. I made more until they'd all eaten their fill.

We are ready now for our journey.

Please be careful. The hunters are out tonight. Move swiftly to the cave. They are unlikely to follow you inside.

I made my way over to the gate, which was secured by a complicated system of braided ropes. Simply untying them was impossible because they were so tightly knotted.

Taking the Scarf, I tried to use it to loosen the ropes. Threads shot out and touched the cords but after a few attempts, the threads recoiled. Alarming patterns and colors flickered over its surface momentarily before stopping.

Once again I tried to wiggle a section loose. My long fingers were awkward to use and, frustrated, I yanked my index finger free of the section I'd dug into and angrily ripped my Rakshasa claw across the surface of the rope. The knot fell to the ground.

Quickly, I used my claws to cut the other ropes. Curious, I picked up a severed piece of the silky rope.

One of the Qilin explained, *The cords are made from the manes and tails of our dead brothers. It is very strong, and the demons know we cannot break it.*

I'm sorry that I had to cut them then.

Do not be sorry. They would have been happy that we are freed.

The Qilin directly in front of me snorted and whispered a warning in my mind: *Someone comes, princess!*

I tensed and crouched in the dark shadows. The dragon-horses were so still, I couldn't even hear their breathing, though I could feel the presence of the herd behind me. My Rakshasa eyes could just make out the shape of a man carefully walking toward me.

As he neared, I heard his quiet whisper, "Kells?"

"Kishan? Over here," I whispered back.

He skirted some trees and edged behind some undergrowth until he could grasp my hand. "Are you alright?" he asked.

"Took you long enough to find me," I said with a smile. "Where's Ren?"

"We were followed. We had to split up and circle back around."

Kishan lifted the locking mechanism and pulled the gate open far enough to accommodate the animals shifting excitedly in the dark. As he moved back to me, he said, "I've never smelled anything like them in my life. What are they?"

One of the beasts blew out a breath. *We've never smelled anything like you before either.*

I laughed softly. "They are Qilin, and they can communicate with me. I think you've slightly offended them."

"I apologize," Kishan told the animals. "I only meant that I'd never met a creature such as you."

"They accept," I translated, "and we need to move the broken ropes on the ground. They are all that remains of the Qilin that the Rakshasas killed, and the Qilin herd does not want to accidentally trample them."

Together, Kishan and I crouched down and collected the silky cords. Startled by a touch on my shoulder, I dropped the bunch of ropes I had picked up. Standing abruptly, I jumped back and raised my deadly claws.

"It's okay. It's just me, Ren."

I lowered my arms to retrieve the ropes and let out a shaky breath. "Ren! We've been waiting for you. There's just one more thing to do."

Wrapping the Scarf around my body, I whispered the words that would return my form to its natural state. When I pulled the Scarf away and tied it around my waist, I ran my hands through my hair and quickly secured it with a ribbon. "Now that feels much better," I mumbled.

Out of the corner of my eye, fire erupted in the darkness.

"Betrayer! You are no Rakshasa queen!"

Lightning strode toward us, his tattoos and hair ablaze with anger.

I put my arm on Kishan's, knowing he was ready to turn this into a brawl. Directing my comments to Lightning, I said firmly, "I am the same woman you have admired, with the same heart and courage. I just choose to take a different form right now."

"And do you also choose to free the animals we have rightly captured? You break the Rakshasa law! What have you done?"

I stretched out my arms and rubbed my hands slowly. "Rakshasa law says that whatever you are strong enough to capture is yours. I have taken these creatures from you. It's true that in this form, it appears as if I am powerless, as if I am prey," I narrowed my eyes, "but make no mistake, Lightning, I still have the ability to bring harm to you and your clan. I have no desire to do so . . . presently, but if a challenge is presented, then—" I shrugged.

He studied me in my new form as Ren and Kishan tensed next to me. Seeming to come to a decision, Lightning smiled evilly, and said, "This is a test. A test that will cement my claim as leader of the Rakshasa clan forever, and I will not fail."

He sprung at me, claws extended, and Ren and Kishan switched to tigers and met him in mid-air. While they rolled around on the ground, claws ripping, I encouraged the Qilin to make their escape while they could. I stood out of the way as one by one the large beasts moved silently through the dark trees toward the distant cave, and then I turned to help Ren and Kishan.

Murmuring a few words and touching the Pearl Necklace at my throat, I cause a wet fog to surround the men. Lightning gasped and panted as if he was breathing poison. With a mighty cry, Lightning threw both tigers off of him, doused his light, and escaped into the trees. Ren and Kishan were about to chase after him when I called softly, "Ren, Kishan, let him go. We need to get out of here before he brings the whole clan down on our heads."

The two tigers trotted back to me, and I felt a nudge on my back, which was accompanied by a soft whicker. Three Qilin remained.

We will take you far from here, princess.

But how can you? I asked the leader. *You must stay with your herd.*

You have done us a great service, and we will return the favor. Come. Climb onto our backs, and we will speed you away from this place.

I crouched down near the tigers and stroked their heads. The black tiger licked my arm. "They want us to ride them to safety," I explained. "They said they are fast and they want to repay their debt."

Kishan changed into a man and smiled. "Then what are we waiting for?"

The Qilin turned on their lights and stomped the ground eagerly. Kishan lifted me onto the back of the herd leader, and as I grabbed a hold of his flickering blue mane, Kishan leapt onto the back of a beast with green coloring. Ren changed into a man and bent to pick something up, then approached a glimmering purple beast dancing nearby. He leapt onto the back of the animal and deftly maneuvered it closer to me.

Leaning down to pat my blue Qilin, he spoke quietly, "Be careful with her. She hasn't ridden before."

After a pause, I smiled. "The Qilin will take care of me."

"Good," Ren answered before tucking something between my fingers.

Kishan called out, "Follow me," and kneed his mount forward.

With a burst of speed, Ren's Qilin followed and mine raced along behind. Green and purple fire trailed behind Ren's and Kishan's Qilin, and I marveled at the beauty of the creatures once again. The Qilin I rode moved so smoothly and so gracefully, through the darkened forest that I could relax and turn my attention to the gift Ren twined through my fingers: a white fire flower. I lifted the soft petals to my nose and allowed my thoughts to fly away as fast as the Qilin's hooves would take me.

20

bodha—city of light

Atop a rise, we caught our first glimpse of a beautiful, sprawling city. The City of Light stretched from one end of the valley to the other, bisected by a lava river that flowed from a black mountaintop, ran underneath the city's center, and disappeared between the hills at the other end. All of the buildings twinkled brightly despite being surrounded by fire trees, and at the heart of the community was a glowing, dazzling temple that sparkled like a diamond. The view was breathtaking.

Ren, Kishan, and I let out a sigh, partly at the splendor before us and partly from relief at having finally made it to our destination. It certainly wasn't home, but it was one step closer.

Somewhere down there is the Rope of Fire, I thought.

With renewed determination, I dismounted from the Qilin leader, brushed the hair from its eyes, and thanked it for taking us to safety. With a whinny, the three animals trotted through the trees and soon disappeared.

We slept all afternoon and into the early evening. At nightfall, the fire trees slept, dark as usual, but the city was alive with light and activity. Carefully we made our way into the valley toward the outskirts of town. Everyone seemed to be headed to the temple for some kind of holiday celebration or ceremonial gathering.

Spying through darkened trees, we learned that the citizens were called Bodha. They glowed like the Rakshasa, but the skin of the Bodha twinkled with a golden light, and the tattoos they wore seemed to be just decoration. The Bodha didn't appear aggressive, though they had the muscled physiques of warriors.

As we studied the golden city, Ren whispered the words of a poem.

ELDORADO
By Edgar Allan Poe

Gaily bedight,
A gallant knight,
In sunshine and in shadow,
Had journeyed long,
Singing a song,
In search of Eldorado.

But he grew old—
This knight so bold—
And o'er his heart a shadow
Fell as he found
No spot of ground
That looked like Eldorado.

And, as his strength
Failed him at length,
He met a pilgrim shadow—
"Shadow," said he,
"Where can it be—
This land of Eldorado?"

> *"Over the Mountains*
> *Of the Moon,*
> *Down the Valley of the Shadow,*
> *Ride, boldly ride,"*
> *The shade replied—*
> *"If you seek for Eldorado!"*

"Do you think this is where the legend of Eldorado came from?" I asked Ren.

He replied, "I don't know, but it certainly looks like a city of gold."

Kishan turned to me and asked for the Divine Scarf. Wrapping it around his body, he whispered a few words and emerged from the Scarf dressed as a citizen of Bodha. I stretched out my fingers to touch his arm. His skin was textured and iridescent, almost like the scales of the Qilin. A sarong hung from his waist, and though he wore glimmering arm and wristbands with red jewels, the rest of his upper body was bare. His golden skin was heavily tattooed with crimson and black patterns and his thick black hair had become a pearly white. Even his eyebrows and lashes gleamed with a pearly luster, and the scales around his eyes were pronounced, making it look as if his golden eyes were lined with clusters of gemstone.

Ren took the Scarf and changed as well, only his color scheme was blue, green, and purple. He handed me the Scarf, but I just stood and stared at the two golden gods standing before me until Ren gave me a nudge and Kishan snickered.

After I'd changed into a Bodha woman and removed the Scarf, Ren and Kishan circled me, admiring my costume.

"Not bad," Kishan said after giving me the once over.

"Good," I mumbled. I studied my arm, which was covered with emerald butterflies and twisting black vines, and tried unsuccessfully to dim the light emanating from my skin. Reaching up to touch my hair, I pulled some over my shoulder. It was long, ivory, and coarse, very different from my natural hair, which was thick, brown, and had a natural wave. I wore golden jewelry crusted with what looked like emeralds but were actually Scarf-made fabrications and a dress seemingly spun from strands of starlight.

"What does my face look like?" I asked.

"It's pretty," Kishan replied.

Ren had crouched down to pack our bags and responded without even looking at me.

"Your eyelids are covered with tiny emeralds that radiate out and down your cheekbones. Topaz stones dot your forehead from your eyebrows to your hairline. The skin of your cheeks and forehead are tinged a greenish hue that spills down your neck and shoulders and then fades to gold."

He rose and walked toward me. "Your lips," his eyes lingered on them for the briefest of moments, "are gold too. The only thing missing . . . is this." He took the still glowing white fire flower from my fingers and placed it in my hair, twisting the stem into the tresses just over my ear. My pulse jumped at his touch. "She's not merely pretty, Kishan. She's perfect."

Before I could react, Ren scooped up the bag and headed into the city. Kishan growled unhappily at Ren's retreating back, mumbling something I didn't catch, and then offered me his hand. Without a word, we joined the parade of people walking toward the pyramid-shaped temple in the City of Light.

"They seem to be very excited about something. Whatever's going on hasn't happened in a long time. This must be a special occasion," Ren whispered after using his tiger hearing to eavesdrop on a pair of old men nearby.

A group of people had formed a circle and were clapping and singing along with musicians who played drums and instruments similar to flutes or pipes. As the music rose in tempo, some of the Bodha began dancing. The energy in the crowd was palpable. Flowers were thrown onto the lava pool where they floated without burning. The scent they gave off was heady and thick.

We wandered closer to the massive temple, and I couldn't tear my eyes away from it. It not only reflected the light of everyone surrounding it, but also it glowed with its own internal fire. The surface was multi-faceted like a brilliant cut jewel, and its light danced around us as if we were standing beneath a twirling disco ball. I couldn't see the top from where I stood but I'd estimate the building was around twenty stories tall. It looked similar to pictures I'd seen of Mayan temples.

The temple was a giant crystal carved in a tetrahedron shape and had a steep, terraced staircase leading to the top. Guards armed with spears stood on each step from the base of the temple up. Though they were impressive in appearance, they smiled breezily along with the crowd and didn't seem to expect any trouble.

Suddenly, two young, handsome men appeared through an entryway halfway up the staircase. Together the pair descended several steps until they were just above the crowd. Their bodies were dusted in gold, and they wore sarongs similar to Ren's and Kishan's but much more detailed. Bands of gold circled their upper arms, forearms, and lower legs, and plumes of firebirds were woven through the white hair that hung down their backs.

"The Lords!" the crowd cheered. One of the men lifted his hand, and the shouts and hoots stilled.

"My people, it has been many, many years since we've added to our clan. Some have even wondered if the time for gathering new ones had passed forever. Now we know it has not. This liquid energy that runs beneath our city and sustains us has not lost its fire after all. It still speaks to the world above and brings us new life."

"And new hope for our Lords!" the Bodha crowd hollered in response.

The man who spoke smiled and clapped his companion on the shoulder. "Yes. New hope, brother."

"To hope!" he replied and raised a golden goblet.

With the toast still hanging in the festive air, drinks were passed out to the crowd.

The Lords once again raised golden goblets. "To hope. May this new addition be the lost lady we seek!"

"To hope!" the crowd shouted, and then everyone sipped the golden drink.

Kishan took a glass and tasted it. "It's good," he assured us quietly. "Kind of like a cross between firefruit and apples."

"Do you feel it, brother? She is coming," one of the Lords said as the pair descended into the crowd.

Guards flanked the men as they walked among the Bodha along the black sand beach. Approaching the fiery lava lake, they stepped to the edge and watched the surface intently.

I winced seeing how close their toes came to burning off and had a flashback of my own body burning and the agony I felt. I grasped Ren's arm. He looked at me with concern but I took a deep breath and whispered, "Come on. Let's move closer."

We found an unobstructed view. It wasn't long before I noticed some bubbles rising to the surface and then a ripple. The ripple grew larger, and the crowd pointed excitedly as a young girl emerged from the lava. I gasped. She was shivering and clearly afraid. As she strode toward the shore, she wiped the lava from her arms, and I saw that her skin was bright red.

The Lords strode into the lava river to greet her, totally unaffected by the heat and flame. One wrapped a beautiful robe around the girl and the other placed a circlet of fire flowers onto her hair. Gently, they guided her to the black sand.

One of the brothers spoke: "Welcome to the City of Light, little one. Here we will take care of you. Your every need will be attended to. Come with us."

As the two men led her to the temple, the Bodha cheered and threw flowers at her feet. When she reached the edifice, she flashed a tiny smile before disappearing inside with the brothers. The guards moved back to their original positions on the staircase.

As soon as the ceremony was over, the celebration began in earnest. Music started up again, food was brought out, and the crowd reveled near the temple. We mingled as best we could and discovered the food to be delicious but spicy. I happily learned that the drink they passed around diminished the fire on my tongue.

Ren, Kishan, and I eavesdropped some more and learned that the party would continue for most of night. The Bodha hoped the Lords would reappear with the happy news that this girl was the one they'd been waiting for. I couldn't help but empathize with her and found the entire situation a little familiar.

To our left, a group of people began to chant, "Tell us the tale!"

I wanted to listen and figure out what was going on, so I edged in closer. My silent protectors Kishan and Ren vigilantly took up spots next to me and watched the crowd.

After fending off the repeated shouts, an elderly man eventually held up his hands and spoke. "Above us are the smoking mountains—doorways from the world above to our world here below."

The people murmured and nodded their heads.

"The Ancients knew our people suffered, that we could no longer care for the sacred flame on our own. This is when the Lords of the Flame, Shala and Wyea, came to govern us."

A young girl added, "But they left someone behind."

"That's correct, Dormida. The beautiful girl, Lawala, did not come with them. Lawala was loved by both brothers, and she was to choose between them. Before each Lord departed through a different smoking mountain, she was asked to choose and follow the brother she wanted. They waited for her to come but she never came. Distraught, Shala and Wyea left their posts and sought her in the world above, but the lovely Lawala was not to be found.

"Soon it became apparent that the brothers were neglecting their duties so the Ancients promised that if the Lords would return to our world to tend the eternal flames at the center of creation, they would seek Lawala themselves and send her to the two brothers through the smoking mountains."

Fascinated, I asked a question. "Why don't the brothers recognize her when they see her?"

The man smiled at me. "The Ancients only know to look for a young and virtuous girl. She may have been reborn into another form, but the brothers insist they will know her regardless of what form she takes."

"What happens to the girl if she is not the one they seek?" I asked.

"She becomes one of us and adds to our numbers." The old man looked up at the dark night. "Tonight the smoking mountains will be still, for the brothers are content, but if this girl is not their lady, their anger will shake the sky and the lake of fire will explode into the world above."

I grabbed Ren's hand and motioned to Kishan that we should go. We made our way to the fire forest and set up camp.

After a brief discussion about what we'd seen, I proposed, "I think he was talking about volcanoes. When the brothers are upset, a volcano erupts aboveground . . . and I also think the girls get here by being sacrificed to a volcano god."

"Why do you think that?" Ren asked.

"Because the man said they sought young, virtuous women and in myths, books, and movies, virgins are sacrificed to volcanoes. Also each Lord traveled here through a smoking mountain. It makes sense. Somehow, instead of burning up, the girls emerge safely in the lava pool near the temple."

Kishan replied, "It's a plausible explanation. Tell me what Durga's prophecy says about the Lords of the Flame."

I leafed through a notebook until I found what I was looking for. "Mr. Kadam's translation says, 'The Lords of the Fire intend to conspire to keep you from what you need.' And don't forget the Phoenix said we'd need to defeat them to get the Rope of Fire."

"So it doesn't sound like they're going to be very cooperative," Ren murmured.

"The good news is the guards don't appear to be very well trained," Kishan commented.

"How can you tell?" I asked. "They're all muscle."

Kishan rubbed his jaw. "Having muscle doesn't mean they have the fighting skills of a warrior. The guards had spears, but they didn't carry them at the ready. Their manner spoke of comfort."

Ren nodded silently as Kishan went on with his assessment.

"Besides, there doesn't seem to be any warfare here. The Rakshasa are far enough away not to cause too much trouble, and I don't see any divisive factions among the citizens."

"He's right," Ren stated. "They seem to be a peaceful people. Still, it's best not to take chances or underestimate them. You are staying here tomorrow, Kells."

"What? Why? Haven't I proved myself in battle enough for you?

Let's not forget who saved the two of you when the Rakshasa took you prisoner."

"She has a point, Ren."

Ren seemed to wage an inner battle before acquiescing. "Alright, but stay close to us."

I saluted him. "Yes, sir, general, sir. Cadet Kelsey Hayes, reporting for duty as assigned," I teased.

Ren grinned and threw a newly made pillow at my head. "Get some shut-eye, *Private* Hayes."

I punched the pillow a few times and lay down. "Where on Earth did you learn the word *shut-eye*?"

Ren laughed. "Good night, Kells."

Giggling, I rolled over to find a quiet Kishan watching me. He was brooding. He had his could-tempt-any-girl-to-run-away-with-him lost expression on his handsome face. I smiled, but he just looked away and folded the Divine Scarf. I watched him as he moved silently in the tent, preparing to keep first watch. He positioned himself at the tent door.

Bunching my fist under my cheek, I studied his strong back and wide shoulders and could almost sense Kishan's disappointment with me. I'd been aloof with him since my experience with the Phoenix, and I knew he could sense it. We'd have to talk, and soon, but for the moment, I didn't want anything to distract us from our goal.

lords of the flame

Disguised once again as citizens of Bodha, we made our way to the temple. The townspeople had long since dispersed to their homes, and the city streets were quiet. We'd slept only a few hours, wanting to be up with the sun so as not to miss the goings on in the city.

I did not think it was possible, but the temple was even more dazzlingly in the predawn hour. We walked in without any fanfare, and the guards completely ignored us until Ren leapt onto the temple staircase. Kishan lifted me up to Ren, and by the time the three of us were standing on the first terrace of the temple, we were surrounded.

"Why have you come here?" a guard interrogated. "Why do you disturb our leaders at this most sacrosanct time?"

Ren lifted an eyebrow, but I jumped in before he could say anything.

"Brave warriors, we did not mean to cause alarm. We have been traveling and have news of the Rakshasa queen. We believe that the information is important enough to justify this intrusion.

"The Rakshasa queen has worked a terrible magic upon us. She tried to prevent us from warning your people."

Ren added a personal story of the Rakshasa queen torturing him. I assumed that it had really happened, and it wasn't a stretch for me to murmur sympathetically and take his hand. I dropped my head sadly and managed to squeeze out a tear.

This seemed to convince the guards that we were sincere.

"Come with us," a warrior ordered.

We followed two of the guards up the temple staircase while the others resumed their positions. At a terrace halfway up, we turned into a marble hallway and descended a crystal staircase that led to the center of the structure. The sides of the pyramid stretched upward until they met at a peak high above us. From this vantage point, the facets of the crystal looked like sparkling windows set at multiple angles.

Like the hallway, the floor of the temple's inner chamber was ivory marble streaked with gold. Fire trees stretched their leafy fingers to the top of the pyramid and framed a pair of statues depicting the Lords of the Flame seated on golden thrones. Life-sized Qilin, a likeness of the Phoenix, and other beasts were carved out of gleaming stone and served as the centerpieces for assorted fountains that flowed with bright reddish-orange lava. Warm steam rose from the fountains.

As we walked past, Ren and Kishan gingerly touched the hot liquid and said it felt refreshing.

The guard led us to a new section of the temple that was more beautiful than what I'd already seen. There were more statues, including a towering ivory marble carving of a lovely woman kneeling. Long hair swept past her waist and fire flowers were braided through her tresses. Her chiseled lips were full and lush, and the folds of her draped gown pooled onto the smooth floor. Fresh flowers were strewn around her. This lovely girl could be none other than the beloved Lawala.

The guard pulled back a sheer curtain, and I saw the Lords of the Flame reclining comfortably near the young woman from the lava lake. The two men fed her tidbits and filled her goblet as they murmured to her softly. A woman was brushing the girl's long brown tresses while another rubbed cream onto her skin.

The girl didn't look like a Bodha. Her skin was white and unblemished by tattoos. The Lords kept finding reasons to touch her. They held her hand and kissed her fingers. The women were constantly ordered to do one thing or another to make her comfortable. They fluffed her pillows and smoothed her dress. Nobody noticed us. It was almost as if we were invisible.

I took a step forward, but the guard held me back and whispered, "We must wait for the ritual to be finished."

"What ritual?" I asked quietly.

He shook his head and pressed his finger to his lips. Puzzled, I turned to watch.

One of the Lords leaned toward the girl and said, "It is time, young one."

The other brother sat up and clapped his hands. Servants entered carrying a rectangular object draped with a silky material. The Lords of the Flame stood, gently pulled the young girl to her feet, and led her toward it.

One of the Lords pulled off the silk covering to reveal a shining mirror and explained, "This mirror belonged to our beloved Lawala. We were promised that one day she would return to us."

The other man took over. "We ask you to gaze upon your reflection. If you are indeed our Lawala, you will assume your true form and we will rejoice together. If you are merely a girl sacrificed to the smoking mountains above, your body will change. You will become Bodha, a citizen of light." He kissed her hand and added, "If you are my Lawala, you must choose me."

"If she is Lawala, she will recognize me as the one she loves," the other brother replied darkly.

The girl seemed frightened at his abrupt tone, but when he noticed, his expression lightened.

"Are you ready?" he asked softly.

She nodded and turned to the mirror. At first, nothing happened, but then a light seemed to grow from inside the curtained area. The girl pressed her hands to her face and shivered lightly. Her hair moved as if in a breeze and slowly the brown strands were replaced by thick white ones. Her skin lightened and began to glow, and when she took her hands from her face, I saw, reflected in the mirror, the flash of pink jewels over her eyes.

I heard her soft voice, "I . . . I am Bodha," she whispered as she looked at herself, admiring her gleaming skin and the jewels adorning her body.

Then the Lords of the Flame's hands tightened in fists. Their chests heaved, their bright skin dimmed, and their handsome faces twisted with bitter disappointment. They shook with an emotion so powerful, they could no longer contain it, and the floor under us rumbled.

The temple plunged into shadow. Ren and Kishan took my arms when the floor rumbled again. The mirror cracked; broken pieces splintered and shattered onto the ground. I looked up through the panes of the temple and saw dark, angry clouds covering the entire sky.

The girl screamed in alarm, and the servants quickly ushered her away.

One of the brothers cried out, "Lawala!" and sunk to his knees while the other, in a feverish gesture, flung his hands out to the statue of Lawala. The lovely marble statue cracked. The fracture splintered across her face and down her torso and arms.

"No, Shala!" Wyea shouted at his brother, but it was too late.

The ivory marble had split. A broken arm crashed to the floor, and then the entire thing bent toward me, lips puckered, as if Lawala wanted to lay a smooth kiss upon my brow. Kishan scooped me in his arms, and he and Ren darted out of the way just before the heavy stone broke in pieces and fell right where we'd been standing.

"I'm all right," I reassured them, as Kishan set me on my feet. "Not even a scrape."

I felt Kishan tense, and I peeked around Ren to see what was going on. The two Lords of the Flame were quiet. The darkness in them diminished as they finally took notice of us. My heart fluttered in alarm as I realized both men had actually taken notice of *me*. They stared at me as if I was the center of the universe and strode purposely forward.

Ren stepped instinctively in front of me and partially blocked their view, but the men didn't waver.

"I am Shala," the Lord of the Flame announced and extended his hand to me.

Gracefully, Wyea put a hand on Ren's and Kishan's shoulders and pushed gently. It was the softest of touches, but somehow it sent Ren and Kishan flying to the opposite sides of the room. They slid across the golden floor and thumped hard, unconscious, against the temple wall.

I swallowed nervously and said the first dumb thing that came to my mind, "You . . . you're twins!"

Without missing a beat, Wyea asked, "Is there enough time?"

"We have until the setting of the sun. At that time the cycle will be complete," Shala replied.

Then, as if on cue, the brothers smiled and said, "Welcome to Bodha, young one."

"You already met Shala. I am Wyea. Would you care for some refreshment?" Wyea offered. He tucked my hand under his arm and walked me to a chaise lounge.

"I know what you're thinking," I said nervously, sending a mental flare to my tigers. "But I'm not Lawala."

Wyea chided, "Only the mirror can tell."

"Yeah? Well, I'm already Bodha, see?" I pointed to my jeweled forehead. "I already passed your mirror test thing, and it didn't pick me."

Shala touched my nose softly and smiled. "We would know if you were truly Bodha."

He snapped his fingers, and a tiny flame burned at his fingertips.

It shot toward my body, and my Bodha disguise melted into my normal appearance. My brown hair was braided. I even wore my regular clothes down to my favorite pair of sneakers.

I sputtered, "Fine. You caught me. I'm not Bodha, but I didn't come here through a volcano like your other girls either."

Thankfully, Ren and Kishan stirred and sprang to their feet. But the Lords of the Flame completely ignored them.

"It matters not in the least how you came to be here," Wyea declared.

"And you are still a maiden, otherwise you wouldn't have been able to enter the inner chamber of the temple," Shala said. "This means you are eligible for the test."

I blushed furiously and glanced briefly from Ren to Kishan to see if they'd overheard. *Of course they did.* Ren and Kishan both grinned until they saw each other's smiles. As they crept closer, their bodies tensed. I could tell they were ready to pounce at any moment.

Before I knew it, I had taken the place of the other girl from only a moment ago. Servants were bringing me delicious things to eat. The broken mirror was gone, and the statue of Lawala had mysteriously been rebuilt. The Lords of the Flame sat by my side, falling over themselves as they fawned over me.

I craned my neck to see what Ren and Kishan were up to. Shala saw me looking for them and with a wave of his hand put up clear glass walls around us. I could no longer hear them, though I could see them call out to me. It was the exact opposite of Sunset's crystal cage. Instead of being on the outside, now I was on the inside with a pair of twins I could hardly tell apart, and the two of them couldn't seem to keep their hands to themselves.

I pushed aside their hands and said, "Look, I already have more male attention than I know what to do with and though I'm flattered that you might think I'm your chosen one, I'm not interested."

Shala peered at Ren and Kishan. "Are they distracting you, my love?

We can dispense with your young men easily enough." He lifted his hand, and I quickly covered it with my own.

"No, they aren't a distraction. Please don't hurt them."

He kissed my fingers. "As you wish."

"We desire only to please you," added Wyea.

"Yeah, I got that from watching your other date. You want to please me until you discover I'm not Lawala. Then you'll have temper tantrums and the skies will darken and all the light will leech out of the city while you two feel sorry for yourselves."

"These dark feelings do not last," Wyea explained. "And you will remain ours whether you are Lawala or not."

"What do you mean, 'remain yours'?"

"You will become one of our concubines until you are too old to please us. Then you will join the citizens of light."

I snorted. "Like I said, I'm not interested."

"Do not worry," Shala quickly added, "you will not age rapidly. You will be ours for centuries."

"Okay. See, I'm planning on living happily ever after with one of *them*," I said, gesturing to Ren and Kishan. "You could learn a thing or two about women from them. You see, neither of them would simply set me aside when I became old. Also, neither would have a harem on the side. What you're offering simply doesn't compare."

"But we can provide whatever you desire. Tell us what you wish for, and we will give it to you," said Wyea.

"Fine. What I wish for is a man who loves *me*—not a man who enslaves me so he can fill his lonely days with a warm body while he pines for another. What I desire is true love, and I don't think that you can offer me that. You don't even know what it means. If you truly loved this woman, Lawala, you would keep the memory of her in your hearts and not use other women in a sad attempt to find her. I don't think she would have wanted that."

Wyea gripped my wrist and twisted it painfully. "You dare to assume what Lawala thought and felt?"

"I've been loved by two brothers as well. That puts me in a unique position to understand your girlfriend, doesn't it?" I rebuked abrasively.

Shala took my elbow and turned me sharply toward him. His face was dark and angry.

I laughed roughly. "Guess the honeymoon is over, huh?"

He threatened, "You will take the test whether you wish to or not, my sweet, and you will learn to respect us and our power."

"Your power doesn't concern me. Ren and Kishan have *earned* my respect. They're better men than the two of you could ever be. I will never belong to either of you."

The twin Lords thrust me away, and I fell back onto some pillows. Shala shouted, "Bring the mirror! Now!"

Servants bustled in with the newly restored mirror. Each man took one of my arms and dragged me to face the looking glass.

Wyea ordered, "Look inside and tell me what you see."

Having had just about enough, I smiled at my reflection, lifted my palm, and blasted the mirror. Sharp pieces of glass shot into every direction. I ducked but was still cut in several places. Nothing serious, but I sucked in a breath at the sting. The Lords dropped my hands and took a step back.

On the other side of the glass, Ren attacked the departing servant and pushed him through the wall face-first. The glass melted in front of him, allowing Ren and Kishan to tumble in after. They threw themselves between me and the Lords of the Flame.

Pulling the golden sword from his belt, Kishan whipped it to the side and when he brought it back in front of him, it was full length. With a twist, the sword separated, and he tossed one to Ren.

Kishan brandished his sword and asked, "Why don't you two try bullying someone a little more your own size?"

The twin brothers eyed Kishan . . . and laughed.

"How entertaining," Wyea remarked. "They wish to battle for their woman."

"Perhaps we should indulge them," the other said. "They remind me of what we were like many, many lifetimes ago."

They sized up Ren and Kishan and seemed to come to a decision. Shala clapped his hands. A servant appeared, and Shala issued instructions. "Have the battlefield prepared and bring our weapons."

The servant hurried away, and a trumpet was sounded outside.

"We'll allow you some time to prepare yourselves," Wyea offered. He snapped his fingers and fire leapt around us.

"Wait! Listen!" I called out. "What we really came for is the—"

It was too late. The fire encompassed us, and I felt a rush of nausea and dizziness.

When the flames diminished, we were standing on a flat, rocky terrain high above the valley. It would be difficult if not impossible to get down. The temple twinkled beckoningly below. Across the valley expanse lay the black mountain.

Briefly exploring our new locale, I discovered the stones underfoot were black and crumbled to dust when stepped on.

"We're on some kind of plateau on the edge of a mountaintop. The only way off is to leap across that chasm to the mountain or go down the cliff's sheer face. It looks pretty far," Kishan reported.

We were discussing using the Divine Scarf to make a rope bridge when the ground shook. Two pillars of fire rose from the temple far below and twisted in the air. They wove back and forth like burning tornados, then touched down on the black soil where we stood. Circling flames diminished until they disappeared altogether.

Standing before us were the Lords of the Flame. Shala's long white hair was now a glossy black with deep red highlights, and it hung loose.

He wore crimson armor and a coat of mail similar to the scales of the red dragon, Lóngjūn. The devilish color seemed to suit his mood. Shala pursed his lips and twirled his weapon, a wicked double-bladed staff, menacingly. A pair of barbed whips hung from his belt as well. His eyes burned as he watched us.

Wyea's long hair was dark as well, but it was tied back at the nape of his neck. His copper-colored cape billowed in the breeze as he strode toward us. He carried a long spear, and I couldn't help but notice the glint of weapons attached to his belt. Wyea's armor was black and copper and a fierce lion was carved onto his breastplate.

The Lords of the Flame bowed to me, Ren, and Kishan and held out their weapons.

"What is this?" Kishan asked cautiously.

"It is our custom to present our weapons to our opponents before we engage in battle," Wyea explained.

I didn't even have time to protest before Ren and Kishan took the offered weapons and bowed back, offering their golden swords, the *chakram*, and the trident for inspection.

I hissed, "Don't trust them!" but my disapproval fell onto deaf ears.

Ren and Kishan bent their heads together, examining the weapons while the Lords of the Flame barely glanced at Durga's gleaming arsenal. Instead, they spent their time inspecting me in a very disconcerting way. To get away from Wyea's stripping-me-with-his-eyes and Shala's wonder-what-you'd-be-like-as-my-concubine gazes, I moved behind Ren.

Ren and Kishan briefly studied Shala's staff, which I knew a little about, having heard Li go on about weapons after each martial arts film we watched. The shaft along the middle ended in polished gold guards and was crisscrossed with leather thongs, which would make it easier to grip. Long razor-sharp blades sprung from both ends. Each blade faced in an opposite direction and had a pointed tip.

Wyea's weapon appeared to be a morning star, a heavy studded mace attached with a chain on one side and a polished black spear with a large, pointed head on the other. But when Ren ran his thumb across the top, the head snapped as quickly as a mousetrap. Sharp barbs sprung out at every angle, and try as he might, Ren couldn't get the weapon to reset. Wyea took it from him, and the barbs slid back into their hiding place. The handsome Lord handed Ren his trident and sword and admired his own weapon.

"It's beautiful, is it not?" Wyea asked, looking directly at me. With a cocky grin and a wink, he turned and said, "Whenever the two of you are ready."

Ren nodded mutely while the twin Lords moved toward the center of the battlefield.

I put my hand onto Ren's arm. "I know what that weapon is," I whispered. "Mr. Kadam mentioned it. It's a *Gáe Bolga*."

Kishan frowned. "What's that?"

"It's from Norse mythology. I won't go into all the details but when the weapon enters flesh, the barbs pop out. The only way to remove it is to," I swallowed thickly, "cut it out."

Ren grunted. "Good to know."

"Are you prepared?" Shala called across the battlefield.

I pressed Durga's brooch into Kishan's hand and heard him mumble, "Armor and shield."

The brooch grew, encompassing his upper arm in gold and swiftly moved across his entire body, covering him in gleaming black and gold armor. The brooch became a handle, and circular segments flipped out, snapping into place until Kishan had a large shield with a roaring black tiger on the front.

Ren held out his hand for the other brooch. His fingers clasped mine briefly before he whispered some words in Hindi and his own brooch began to grow. Segments flipped over and around his limbs, connecting with a weighty snap. Soon his body was protected as well, encased in armor of silver and black. His heavy shield sported a snarling white tiger.

I helped thread the trident through Ren's belt and then knelt to pull my bow and arrows from my pack.

Ren's gloved hand soon covered mine. "What are you doing, Kelsey?"

"Fighting with you," I replied and pushed some stray hair from my eyes.

He shook his head and sighed. "I don't want you hurt."

"I'll shoot from a distance."

Ren was about to say something else when a fire erupted in my hands. The bow and arrows burst into flame and disappeared.

Wyea suddenly appeared behind me in a circle of flame. "You are the prize, my dear, not a warrior."

"I think I've heard this before. I'm done sitting on the sidelines. I wish to fight for my own freedom. Surly you can't begrudge me that."

The burning form of Shala materialized next to his brother. "Why are we waiting?"

"She wishes to fight," Wyea explained.

"She may not."

Wyea wiped some black dust from his armor. "I admire her spirit. Perhaps we should let her."

"No," Ren and Kishan admonished at the same time.

"See how protective they are? This battle will be memorable."

Biting my lip, I came to a decision. "Alright. I'll watch this time—under one condition. You two," I pointed to the twins, "have to make it a fair fight. No . . . dematerializing or throwing them over the cliff."

The Lords of the Flame shrugged.

"It will be fair," Wyea said, "but you will accept the winners without argument, whomever they may be. Agreed?"

"Wait a second, Kells," Ren started.

"Agreed," I announced and shook their hands before Ren or Kishan could intervene. "But understand one thing . . . you cheat and it's no holds barred. I get to use all the power at my disposal on you."

"We accept." Wyea grinned and boldly stroked my cheek.

With a grunt I shoved his hand away. "You haven't won anything yet so keep your hands to yourself."

The twin brothers laughed then disappeared, and a trumpet was sounded.

"I guess that means it's time," I mumbled. I kissed Kishan on the cheek and whispered, "That's for good luck."

He smiled, and I turned to Ren. "*Bhagyashalin*, Ren."

"See you on the other side, Kells."

I pressed my lips to his cheek. "Be careful," I admonished as I brushed the hair from his eyes, and the two men I loved headed into battle with the Lords of the Flame.

As they walked away, I wondered if my promise to remain on the sidelines would end up costing one or both of them their lives.

22

the heat of battle

en and Kishan moved into position. Wyea made the first move and charged at Ren with his deadly spear. He spun at the last moment, and the morning star struck Ren's shield with a loud clash. Ren attacked with his sword, but the heavy weapon only glanced off Wyea's armguard.

Kishan and Shala circled each other until, with a battle cry, Kishan attacked. He went straight for Shala's head. The fire Lord parried with the edge of his staff, but Kishan's blow was so powerful that Shala staggered back a few steps and had to readjust his helmet. Then he smiled, twirled his staff a few times, and hit Kishan so hard that Kishan spun off balance.

Quick as a bullet, Shala rolled his weapon across his shoulders and jabbed the sharp end into the unprotected spot where the armor met at Kishan's shoulder. Kishan grunted and moved away. The blade came out slick with Kishan's blood.

Shala laughed and called out, "I drew first blood, brother."

"But I will have the first defeat," Wyea boasted.

He'd been effectively clubbing Ren's shield until it was bent with the force of his attacks, and when Ren made a risky move to plunge his sword into Wyea's chest, the Lord simply disappeared and reappeared next to Ren. With a mighty blow from the fire Lord, Ren's shield flew from his grasp and he fell to one knee.

I shouted, "That's cheating!" but they ignored me.

Deftly, Ren rolled away from his opponent and stood ready with his sword in one hand and the trident in the other. He struck away the spear with his sword and shot darts with the trident. The missiles dented Wyea's armor and one grazed his neck. Wyea touched the wound and rubbed the wet blood between his fingers.

"So you have some claws after all!"

"You have no idea," Ren responded and charged.

Wyea renewed his attack.

Meanwhile, Kishan leapt over Shala's blade as he swept Kishan's feet. The other end of the staff was racing in a perfect arc to decapitate Kishan, but Kishan raised his shield and fortunately the weapon glanced off. With Shala's back turned, Kishan stabbed him under the arm, twisting his sword as he withdrew. Shala cried out and spun angrily, raising his weapon over his head.

Shala brought his weapon down with a heavy clash—just as Kishan's sword rose to meet it. The two men shoved off each other, and Shala threw a fire ball at Kishan's head. Kishan ducked and launched the *chakram* into the air. It struck Shala's back on its return and imbedded itself into his armor.

Enraged, Shala yanked the *chakram* out and dropped it onto the black soil. His blood coated the sharp edge.

"Now we're even," Kishan said.

Shala sneered. "You won't be saying that when I take your woman."

"Not in this lifetime."

"You forget. I'm immortal. Your lifetimes are as the blink of an eye to me."

Shala snapped the flat side of the blade across Kishan's neck in a mocking blow. Kishan fell to the ground, grabbed the *chakram*, and did a kick-stand, ending with the *chakram* positioned across the fire Lord's throat.

"Here's some news," Kishan said, "I'm immortal too, and I'll remove your head in the blink of an eye before I let you anywhere near Kelsey." He pressed the *chakram* into Shala's throat. "Now . . . do you concede?" he asked.

The Lord of the Flame smiled. "Fire never concedes."

Shala's body grew red hot, but still Kishan held on though he grunted in pain. The skin on the fire Lord's face sizzled and his entire body turned black. A stiff wind blew around him and the ashes of his form were swept to a new location a short distance from Kishan. There the ashes swirled into the shape of the man and, with the snap of his fingers, he was whole once more. Shala had cheated again.

"Nice trick," Kishan admitted.

Shala smiled. "It comes in handy. Now where were we? Ah, I was about to kill you and take your woman."

"That's not how I remember it."

Kishan ran, flipping over the fire Lord entirely, twisting in the air and attempting to carve Shala's back as he came down, but Shala sidestepped before Kishan made contact. As Kishan landed nimbly on his feet, Shala whipped his staff in a windmill, attacking with a flurry of strikes until Kishan staggered under the assault and dropped his shield. With a triumphant shout, Shala thrust the sharp edge of his blade into the middle of Kishan's breastplate. Kishan's armor seemed to stop the weapon, or at least most of its progress. Shala was unable to dislodge the staff so Kishan wrapped his hands around it and held on. The two engaged in a tug-of-war for the staff until finally Kishan raised the *chakram* and brought it down, severing it.

Shala reeled away with the broken piece of his weapon while Kishan yanked the other piece from his armor. It made an awful shearing sound. His hands shook, and I gasped when I saw the tip was covered with blood. Panting, he bent over and threw the broken end of the staff at the fire Lord's feet.

Furious, Shala picked up his ruined weapon and circled Kishan. "Did you think this would stop me? I *told* you! Fire . . . doesn't . . . yield!"

Flames shot down his arms and ignited the pieces of the staff. He twirled them, one in each hand and attacked again.

Another burst of flame from the other side of the field caught my attention. Ren had wrestled Wyea to the ground, and the two were rolling dangerously close to the edge of the cliff. Ren's sword and trident were missing, and the *Gáe Bolga* was nowhere to be seen. The fire Lord stopped them at the cliff edge and pressed Ren's head back as if trying to push him over.

Chunks of broken turf cascaded over the side and dropped to the valley floor far below. Ren brought up his hands and wrapped them around Wyea's throat. With a mighty shove, Ren rolled the two of them away from the cliff and proceeded to strangle Wyea. But the twin Lord brought his palms up to Ren's chest and a stream of fire shot out from each hand like a flamethrower. Crying out, Ren rolled away and got to his feet. His armor was smoking and charred.

Wyea stood, cracked his neck, and said, "I think it's time we made this more interesting."

The ground began to shake. Wyea mumbled something and raised his hands slowly into the air. As black soil cracked, sooty puffs exhaled all over the ground, leaving the arena riddled with holes. Still the fire Lord chanted.

Shala shoved Kishan to the ground near his brother. They looked down on my tigers with a maniacal gleam in their eyes. The arena shifted. All four fighters rose into the air, positioned on top of black poles that emerged from the ground. The battlefield looked like the bulletin board in the language lab at Western Oregon University where Artie worked— no notes, just hundreds of pins placed in perfect symmetry, Artie style. For a minute, I almost wished we were back in the safety of my hometown, where my biggest foe was Artie and his datebook planner.

Each pillar was no bigger than six inches in diameter and positioned two feet apart on every side. I walked up to the wall of posts high above my head and rubbed my fingers against one. It was blackish brown in color and as smooth and shiny as glass. Looking at my tigers perched precariously above reminded me of the crane move from *The Karate Kid*. But I knew this was no movie, and it was going to take a lot more than just the power of the underdog to win a happy ending.

Wasting no time, I asked the Scarf to weave a ladder between two pillars and scrambled up quickly. When I reached the top, I carefully placed each foot on a post and balanced my weight between them. A burst of flame hit Ren, and he fell between the black posts. Worried, I scanned the dangerous path ahead and saw the twin Lords gleefully balancing on their respective poles while Kishan jumped from pillar to pillar to get to Ren.

Kishan lay across the top of several posts, steadied himself, and held out a hand.

"Jump!" he shouted.

With a tremendous effort, he pulled Ren up between the obsidian trunks and rolled to the side to make room for his brother.

As Ren got to his feet, he touched a place on his chest and his armor folded up and shrunk back into a brooch form. Kishan hooked his *chakram* onto his belt and did the same thing. The Lords of the Flame bowed in a mocking way and with the snap of their fingers, their armor disappeared as well.

Kishan waved his golden sword, but the only weapon Ren had left was the trident. The fire Lords moved closer. Ren jumped from pole to pole and executed an aerial corkscrew. His feet impacted solidly with Shala's chest, causing the fire twin to fall heavily atop the columns. Ren landed with perfect balance and resumed a fighting stance. Shala almost fell between the pillars but clutched the top of one and rolled to his feet.

As Ren moved in to attack again, Shala recovered, twisted his hand,

and threw a ball of fire. The blast hit Ren squarely in the chest. He flew back several feet and started to fall between the pillars. At the last moment, Ren extended the trident to its full length across two poles. When he whipped his body back into the air like a gymnast on a high bar, Shala was prepared for him. He brought out his barbed whips and snapped them one after the other, pummeling Ren mercilessly. Ren spun in the air, rolled across the top of the pillars, and dropped the trident. I sucked in a breath as the weapon fell between the columns, landing too far below to retrieve.

In an impressive display, Ren charged Shala, twisting his body in the air, and grabbed the end of first one whip, then the other. He snapped his arms violently apart and wrenched the weapons from Shala's grasp. The ends slithered down the pillars as Shala tackled Ren—the two of them rolling dangerously atop the pillars.

Kishan fought Wyea with his sword and managed to dislodge the spear from Wyea's hands. It soared through the air until the heavy morning star propelled the weapon down between the pillars. Wyea backflipped impressively and reached down between the columns to grab his spear, but Kishan was on him too fast. Wyea rolled away a split second before Kishan's foot crashed down.

Using his momentum to rotate in a backward crescent kick, Kishan regained his balance and tornado-kicked Wyea in the face. He brought his sword up under Wyea's chin, but the fire Lord murmured a few words and Kishan's sword grew so hot he could no longer hold it. Kishan's scorched flesh healed as his weapon fell to the ground.

With no weapons left, Ren and Kishan turned the battle into a martial arts brawl unlike anything I'd seen before. Ren targeted Shala's vulnerable spots with the eagle claw technique. Kishan employed the monkey approach. He stayed very close to Wyea, tearing at his torso and arms and even darted up Wyea's leg only to leap over him to land on Shala's turned back.

Ren had to constantly block the spinning blades of Shala, and he and Kishan ended up switching places often throughout the battle. Ren heel-kicked Shala and reverse-punched Wyea while Kishan grabbed Wyea's arm and flipped him. Then Kishan hook-punched Shala before he could attack Ren.

Just as quickly, the tables turned and the fire Lords claimed the upper hand. Wyea shot a stream of flame at Kishan's chest. In pain and seriously injured, Kishan ripped off his shirt before it engulfed him and collapsed on top of the pillars. Seconds later, Shala flung a broken piece of his staff at Ren. The razor-sharp edge glinted in the light as it rotated in the air and imbedded itself in Ren's back. Kishan caught Ren as he fell and somehow managed to keep them on top of the pillars.

Pulling the weapon out, Kishan threw it violently down between the poles and held onto his brother while the twin Lords mocked.

"Was that the best you could do?" Wyea taunted.

"They barely put up a fight at all. It's disappointing, really." Shala sighed and ran his thumb along the edge of his remaining blade.

Wyea smiled smugly in my direction. "At least we won the girl. Come, brother, we don't have much time."

"It's for the best," Shala said, picking up Ren by the shirt. "Neither of you were man enough to keep your woman anyway."

He thrust Ren back into Kishan's arms, and the twins started toward me.

I narrowed my eyes as they approached and brought my hand to the Pearl Necklace, remembering that my fire power was useless in this realm. There was no way I was going to go without a fight.

The brothers were halfway to me when I saw Ren and Kishan rise up as tigers behind them. They leapt, claws extended, and pushed the fire Lords down. They ripped at their backs and arms with claws and teeth until the twins fell between the pillars. The cats nimbly circled, heads angled down, watching the Lords of the Flame as if they were mice chased into a hole. Ren and Kishan snarled and growled as they paced.

Suddenly a stream of fire shot up between the pillars, and the tigers darted away from the flames. Implacable, the fire Lords emerged in a swirl of flame and stood on top of the columns.

Shala spat, "Got a second wind, did you?"

Ren and Kishan morphed back into men. I let out a pent-up breath, seeing that they were completely healed.

Kishan smiled menacingly. "It will take a much stronger *man* than either of you to bring us down."

"Kelsey will never belong to you. That I promise," Ren threatened.

Shala and Wyea lifted their arms. Fire flowed down Wyea's extended limbs and shot toward Ren. What looked like throwing stars made of flame just missed Kishan as he leapt to the side.

Kishan turned on Wyea and landed a series of punches and elbow strikes, then pivoted and did an inside sweep on Shala. Meanwhile, Ren leapt over the fallen Shala and cross-blocked a downward hammer-fist strike Wyea had aimed at Kishan's head. Unsuccessfully, Ren tried to target pressure points: joints, the throat, the eyes, and the ears. But the twin fire Lords recovered too quickly for the open-handed jabs to be effective.

The Lords of the Flame repeatedly shot streams of fire and burning throwing stars at Ren and Kishan. I shouted that they were cheating again, but they ignored me.

Finally, Ren and Kishan seemed to have the advantage. They pressed the twins until the Lords of the Flame stood back to back. All four of the men were now extremely weary.

Kishan kicked Wyea across the face, and the fire Lord collapsed. Leaning over him, Kishan yelled through gritted teeth, "Do you submit?"

Wyea spat blood, and the crimson liquid trickled from his mouth. "Never."

The twin closed his eyes and mumbled some words. A clicking noise surrounded us on all sides.

"What is it?" I called out. "What did you do?"

The clicking sound got closer, and I gaped in horror as a giant red creature emerged to crawl across the top of the pillar near me. It was a scorpion! It popped up on the top of the column, followed by dozens more. One of them struck at me with its tail. Panicking, I blasted it with a lightning bolt, but it absorbed the power and actually grew bigger.

"Alright! That's it!" I spat.

I'd had enough. The Lords of the Flame were cheating, which meant I had every right to intervene. I stroked the Pearl Necklace at my throat and felt a cooling rush of water hiss through my limbs. My anger calmed and my head cleared. I felt waves pulsing, almost lapping gently at my fingertips. Raising my hand, I struck the giant scorpion next to me with a burst of water. It emitted a high pitched screech as it fell over the side of the pillar.

Spreading my fingers, I let the waves of water rush down my arms, and I blasted two creatures that slid away to the dark ground below. One by one, I pounded the scorpions, making my way closer and closer to the fighting men. Ren and Kishan had been able to kick the monster arthropods off the posts, but the scorpions just turned around and climbed back up again. I manipulated the water, taking out almost all of the scorpions.

"Call off your creatures," I shouted to the Lords. "This fight is over."

The men stopped and looked at me.

Shala smiled. "The fight isn't over until someone wins."

"It's over . . . because *I* win." I narrowed my eyes at the fire Lord.

"Prove it," Wyea taunted.

He launched a fireball at me. I lifted my hand and caught it, bounced it up and down a few times and then threw it back, aiming for his head. I missed, but the action caused the Lords of the Flame to stare in shock.

"You have the power of the flame?" Shala murmured in wonder.

"It's her!" Wyea declared. "It must be! Lawala has returned." He waved his hand and all the remaining scorpions disappeared.

The Lords of the Flame leapt across pillars to reach me but were intercepted by Ren and Kishan, who knocked them over. The twin Lords' skin began to glow, and fire and light swirled around Ren and Kishan in a cyclone. Ren and Kishan were lifted into the air and set on fire. They writhed in pain and screamed.

"Stop it! Put them down! Now!" I yelled.

"They are of no consequence. We must complete the ritual. You will come with us." Shala threatened.

"I will not." I summoned the water within and threatened, "I'm warning you. Let them go, or you will suffer greatly."

Shala and Wyea smiled haughtily and moved closer. With a mighty push, I sent a huge wave of water toward them. A great hissing cloud of vapor rose around them when it hit their chests. They seemed unharmed but confused, as if they'd never seen water before.

I dropped my hands. "Let them go."

Wyea straightened, tilted his head, and twirled his finger. Fire exploded around Ren and Kishan until they were completely enveloped. Desperate, I turned my power toward Ren and Kishan, trying to douse the flames.

The Lords of the Flame laughed. "Your power is not as strong as ours."

"Oh yeah?"

I turned my inner valve on full blast. Water circled around the men I loved, but Ren and Kishan were still suffering. Every second that ticked by was agony. I needed to stop the Lords of the Flame before it was too late. The strength of my emotions turned the water ice cold. I couldn't overcome the flames surrounding my tigers, so I turned my icy focus on the twins. They screamed when the freezing water hit them. The fire cyclone twirling around Ren and Kishan subsided, dropping them slowly to the tops of the pillars. Immediately, they switched into tigers to accelerate their healing process.

I could see that the fur was burned off their bodies. Pushing every drop of energy I could muster, I encased the fire Lords in ice and hurried as fast as I could to Ren and Kishan's side. My tigers were panting in short bursts as they tried to breathe. I touched Kishan gently, and burned skin peeled away and clung to my fingertips. Crying, I gingerly took the *kamandal* from his neck and poured a few drops onto his tongue. Kishan licked his chops weakly, and I turned to Ren.

His fur was sloughing off in clumps too, but his black stripes were still prominent against the white of his skin. His whiskers and eyelashes were gone, and the sensitive hairs in his ears were missing as well.

"My poor tigers," I gasped with a sob.

I gave Ren a few drops of the mermaid's elixir as well and prayed it would lessen their pain. I sat with them, stroking their heads as their labored breathing eased. It wasn't long before I touched soft fur again.

Mussing Ren's head, I whispered, "Next time I fight with you." I kissed Kishan's head and said, "You got that?"

I heard a quiet huff from both brothers and then a mocking voice interrupted us. "Hiding behind a woman's skirt, are we?"

I turned. *Shala*! He was standing a short distance away. He looked a bit blue, but he'd still had enough power to melt the ice I'd encased him in.

"Are you back for more?" I challenged.

Shala rubbed his jaw, and I saw little flames burst in his eyes. "Of you? No. We want no more of you. Lawala would never damage us like you did."

"No kidding."

"Unfortunately, we are the jealous type, and if we can't be happy with our woman, nobody can."

He raised his hands and pointed them at Ren and Kishan. Fire flew down his arms. I flung my hands at Shala, and a wall of water met his fire in a terrible hiss. Vapor billowed around us in waves.

A nagging thought invaded by mind. *Where was Wyea?*

Just then, I heard running footsteps and heard Ren shout, *"Kelsey! No!"*

Before I knew what was happening, Ren threw himself between me and Shala, who laughed gleefully. Ren fell heavily against me. I clutched him desperately as we collapsed in Kishan's outstretched arms.

Kishan pulled Ren off me, and I cried out as Ren's blood trickled over my hands. Quivering rigidly, deeply imbedded in the middle of Ren's chest, was the *Gáe Bolga*.

23

chimera

I could hear the sound of the horrible weapon as the spear discharged in Ren's chest. Sharp barbs sunk deep, ripping him apart from the inside. He screamed as blood gushed from his wound and trickled from his mouth. The soft mocking laugh of the twins behind me became mere background noise as I stared at the protruding weapon in shock. For a brief moment, I flashed back to the loss of Mr. Kadam. The grief and suffering flowed into me anew, and I was crippled, unable to move.

I thought of my parents and the burning of the Phoenix. Only the gentle touch of Kishan's hand brought me back to the present. Though it was one of the hardest things I ever had to do, I left the care of Ren to Kishan.

Steeling my resolve, I turned to the twins. Wyea was worse off than his brother; he could barely stand. Acting purely on impulse and with the heaviness of loss and guilt still flowing through my veins, I attacked. But this time I concentrated all of my efforts on Wyea.

Icy water hit the fire Lord and knocked him off the column. Determined to finish what I'd started, I made my way over the pillars until I found him on the ground, his limbs twisted around the obsidian pillars. I lifted my hands and allowed the cold emptiness I felt inside to become a weapon. It was only a few moments later that I realized the water coming from my hands had turned to sleet. Frosty air swirled around me and with a twitch of my fingers, the sleet turned to icy daggers.

Shala had come after me, of course, but this time his attacks were no match for me. When his plumes of fire came close, my wintry wind blew them out. When Wyea was no longer moving, I lifted my arms up to the sky, turned to Shala, and shouted, "You will not take Ren from me. If I have to use my power against everyone and everything in your realm, even to the point of destroying your world, I will."

My mind twitched briefly with sadness at the thought of destroying the fire trees but the pain of losing Ren overwhelmed me enough that I was able to push the guilt aside. In all honesty I didn't even know if I had the power to carry through with my threat, but at that moment I felt as if I could. If I were a Jedi, I had definitely turned to the dark side of the Force, for in truth my thoughts and feelings dwelled on pain, wrath, and vengeance. But I didn't care.

Seeing his brother so severely injured, Shala stared at me bitterly, and then nodded his head. "Your life is your own. You are free to go. I concede the battle."

He crouched down to peer at his brother. Stretching out his hands, he gave his twin some of his own waning heat.

"There's something else," I added, high on my victory. "I demand a boon for winning."

Shala sighed heavily and pivoted on the balls of his feet to look at me. "What is it you wish?"

"I want the Rope of Fire."

"How do you know of such things?" Shala sputtered, shocked by my request.

"It doesn't matter. I just do. We need the Rope of Fire to complete a task."

The Lord of the Flame stood, raised his hands into the air, and lowered them slowly. The poles shifted slightly, then began to descend back into the ground. I balanced myself carefully.

"The Rope was given to us by an Ancient. We were told that only when we were defeated in battle could the Rope leave our realm. Take it."

He dismissed me with a wave of his hand and leapt down to assist his injured twin.

"How do we get it?" I asked, grateful to step firmly back on the black soil.

As he leaned over Wyea, Shala replied, "It's wound around a fire tree at the base of this mountain. I can send you there, but you will have to get past the guardian who protects it."

"Fine."

"And . . . Kelsey, you are a formidable opponent, but I'd suggest you leave for the above world before we are fully recovered."

Shala smiled slightly and nodded before both twins disappeared in a swirl of flame.

I ran over to Ren and knelt next to Kishan. "How is he?"

"His body is trying to heal, but I've been unable to remove the weapon."

My hands shook as I gingerly touched Ren's quivering stomach. "It has to be cut out. Remember? Can he heal from that?" I asked.

"It will have to be done quickly, carefully, and we should have the elixir ready."

My eyes filled with tears at the thought of the pain Ren would continue to suffer. Kishan went to gather all our weapons so he could choose which one would be best for removing the *Gáe Bolga*. I put Ren's head in my lap and stroked his hair. A tear dropped from my cheek to his forehead.

"Please don't die," I whispered.

He moaned and shifted.

"Shh. Try not to move."

I used the Necklace to make a cup of water and pressed the rim to his lips. He drank but his chest bled again.

"It's okay. This will all be okay," I crooned, as much for myself as for him. I touched my lips to his forehead. "There's so much I need to tell you. Please don't leave me."

He mumbled something but I didn't understand. He whispered the word again.

Asambhava.

The translation came to my mind quickly—*impossible*.

I laughed wetly and said, "Good. Because I plan to keep you around for a while."

Kishan returned with the trident and the swords. Pressing the golden blades together until they clicked, he twisted the handle and shrank the weapons down to the size of a knife. He knelt beside Ren and warned, "This is going to be difficult. The darts are in his lungs and heart."

"Lokesh stabbed him in the heart before and drained all his blood, and he still came back," I said hopefully.

"I've never been injured this badly before," Kishan said frankly. "I don't know how long this will take to heal. Give him a few drops of the elixir right after I remove the spear."

I nodded mutely as I watched Kishan bring the knife to Ren's chest. He plunged the blade in swiftly and began sawing. I couldn't watch. I closed my eyes and kept stroking his hair, but I felt Ren's twitching and then the jerk of his body as Kishan finally lifted the spear from his chest.

Immediately, I attempted to give him the elixir but he was gasping for breath and thrashing due to the damage in his lungs. Kishan grabbed his head and held him steady while I got some drops in his mouth. I couldn't help but see the gaping hole in his chest. Crying, I used the Scarf to cover his exposed wound.

How can anyone recover from something like that?

Ren stopped thrashing and lay still as if dead. Fresh tears slid down my cheeks.

"Kishan . . . ?"

I couldn't finish the question. I couldn't ask if he was still alive or not.

Kishan cocked his head and listened. "He's not breathing and his heart isn't beating."

"No. *No.*"

I cried and rocked back and forth, cradling his head in my arms.

"Please come back to me, Ren. Come back."

I said this over and over until Kishan whispered, "Kelsey, shh. Wait." Kishan touched Ren's arm briefly. "I feel a faint pulse."

It was several long, agonizing moments later when Ren first took a breath. Wetness rattled in his chest, and his body barely moved.

"He's been a long time without oxygen," I whispered, more to myself than to Kishan.

Kishan rubbed my back and inspected Ren's chest. "All we can do is wait, Kells. He's still a mess, but he's starting to heal."

I held onto Ren, clutching him desperately as if to physically keep death at bay and didn't realize that I was pouring fire power into him until I saw a twinkle through my tears. I blinked to clear my vision and gasped when I saw that the two of us were bathed in a golden light. The special magic that happened when we touched was helping him to heal.

After I realized what was happening, I concentrated my efforts and kept pushing the energy back into his weakened frame as it circled between us. Before long, his breathing settled and deepened as if he were asleep. Kishan announced that Ren's heart had a stronger beat and that the hole in his chest had closed.

My eyes grew heavy. I was so tired. I shifted to a more comfortable position and lay my head on Ren's shoulder. I almost blacked out, but then a hand caught my wrist.

A warm voice said softly, "*Priya*, you must stop."

"Can't stop," I mumbled. "Ren needs me."

"I will always need you."

The body I'd been lying against moved, and I moaned in protest. Suddenly I was weightless. Someone had picked me up. I felt a soft kiss against my cheek and heard quiet voices.

"She wore herself out trying to save you," Kishan said.

I felt the rumbling of a chest against my arm.

"She needs time to recover, to rest."

Ren. Ren was holding me. But how? He was injured.

"I can take her. You're still weak."

"I'm strong enough."

Ren had said it in a way that brooked no argument, but Kishan tried to protest anyway. Finally, Ren said quietly, "She'll be yours for the rest of your life, brother. Let me hold her for now."

There was no response from Kishan, and the quiet lulled me into a deeper sleep. I felt a brief burning sensation in my stomach, and then I was aware of nothing.

When I woke, I was ravenous. Ren and Kishan were sleeping on either side of me, and we were no longer atop the mountain. Instead, fire trees surrounded us.

Ren stirred first and touched my arm. "Kelsey? How do you feel?"

"Hungry," I whispered. "And thirsty too. Where are we?"

"We called to the Lords of the Flame, and they set us down here, along with our weapons. Your bow and arrows were returned, and we have the Scarf and the Fruit as well."

"Are you . . . healed?"

"I am well. And you?"

"I'm just really hungry."

"Will you two be quiet?" a sleepy Kishan grumbled.

I patted his back and kissed his cheek. "I'm sorry. Go back to sleep."

Kishan was soon dreaming again, but Ren watched me through cobalt blue eyes. We spent a long time just looking at each other. Neither of us spoke. I felt safe. We weren't touching at all, but it felt as if he was cradling me in his arms. My hunger diminished, twisting into something else, a different need entirely and all I could do was return the gaze of my blue-eyed tiger.

Too soon, Kishan opened his eyes and decided it was time to break camp.

I was sore and stiff all over my body. Even my pinkies hurt. I tried to stretch out. "Ugh. I'm not at my best this morning," I announced.

Ren started walking over to me but he hesitated when Kishan approached me instead.

Kishan hugged me close. "Are you strong enough to continue on today? There's still a guardian to fight."

Ren intervened. "There's no rush. She expended a lot of energy yesterday. She may need more time."

I grimaced. "There *is* sort of a reason to rush. The Lords of the Flame made it pretty clear that we should vacate the premises before they get back to full strength."

Kishan reassured, "We'll take it slow. We'll keep Kelsey on the sidelines while we battle the creature."

Ren gave me a long look; then he turned and gathered our belongings.

I nodded to Kishan and wandered over to a fire tree. I felt guilty as I greedily lapped up whatever energy the trees were willing to share. If I'd had to choose between destroying them and saving Ren, there was no contest, but I would have grieved for the friendly trees later. The warm vines slithered around my arms and stroked me gently. It wasn't long before I felt renewed and refreshed, but my mind was still tired.

I was exhausted from the constant battle, the stress of being in danger, and the monsters and villains who waited for us around every corner. I thought of my little home in Oregon. How content and happy I was. A deep longing for a lost dream swept through me. All I wanted was to be surrounded by those I loved. To know they were safe and nearby. One by one, the people who were the most important to me had been taken away.

I thought of the Phoenix again and the lessons it taught me. Sunrise had promised that I'd see my parents and Mr. Kadam again. It also said that I needed to follow the truths and the love in my heart. I stood up, brushed the dust from my jeans, and made my way back to camp.

Throwing my arms around the one I loved, I said, "I'm ready."

Half an hour later, the three of us were crouched behind some bushes.

"So the Chimera is a cat?" Kishan asked. His nose twitched, and he ran his fingers lightly along some claw marks on a fire tree.

"Sort of," I replied. "It's built a bit like a lioness but also has the head of a goat and a snake for a tail."

"We're in its territory," Ren added.

"Yes," Kishan rubbed his jaw. "Do you smell it?"

Ren nodded.

Just then a series of rumbling roars echoed through the trees.

"That cinches it," Kishan said.

"What?" I asked. "What is it?"

The brothers looked at each other knowingly. Ren shrugged, then Kishan said, "*She's* looking for a mate."

"*Oh.*" I stammered lamely. "What . . . um . . . what does that mean for us? Is that a good thing or a bad thing?"

"It could be a good thing. We could work it to our advantage," Kishan said.

At my look of confusion, Ren explained, "What he means is that she will be easily distracted."

Kishan cleared his throat with a deep chuckle. "And I vote that you should be the one to *distract* her while I get the Rope."

"How about you distract her, and I'll get the Rope," Ren countered.

"Why don't you both go, and I'll get the Rope," I suggested.

"No," they both answered in unison.

"I'll go," Ren volunteered with a sigh. A low moan shook the ground. He grimaced. "Just make it fast."

"Of course." Kishan grinned and winked at me as Ren disappeared through the trees.

When we next heard the plaintive roar, it was answered with a deep growl.

"That's the signal." Kishan kissed me quickly and slunk off through the trees.

I sat there listening to a loud series of snarls, growls, and hissing. Time passed, and the noises grew louder. It still didn't seem angry or violent. I was trying to figure out which sounds were coming from which parts of the Chimera when a new roar split the air. It was answered with a matching roar. I knew both of those voices well, even as tigers. Kishan had joined the pair for some reason. I was needed.

Carefully and quietly, I made my way through the trees, skirting the area where the racket was coming from. Finding a good place to hide, I peered through the undergrowth and saw Ren and Kishan fighting as tigers. The female cat lay nearby, licking her paws while surreptitiously watching the two tigers battle.

She didn't look exactly like I expected. From all my reading, I thought the Chimera would be a double-headed monster with a snake head on its tail, but she was more like the Qilin. Though she appeared to have the traits of many different creatures, the Chimera had only one head and six legs. Her body was the basic shape of a cat, a lioness maybe, but much larger. I'd say she was around twice the size of a lion.

Instead of having the coat of a cat though, the Chimera's skin appeared a tawny reptilian gold. It was scaled like the Qilin except for a flickering mane of fur that was aflame. Two long horns sprung from the top of her head. Chimera's feet were clawed and her tail moved back and forth sinuously like a snake, but I could see no head or fangs on the tip.

The Chimera sat at the base of a large tree. I scanned the branches for the Rope of Fire but couldn't make anything out from where I was hidden. I bit my lip trying to figure out what my next move should be. Ren and Kishan appeared to be making a lot of noise, but they were mostly posturing. They pushed each other around and snarled loudly but didn't really use their claws or teeth.

As soon as I started to move, the creature immediately turned her head into my direction. The beast sniffed the air and got to her feet. When the Chimera leapt toward my hiding place, Ren ran to her side and batted her feet with his paw. Distracted, the creature turned to him and rubbed her head over his back while peering at Kishan. Her snake-like tail wound around Ren's.

Kishan roared as if challenging Ren once again for the Chimera's affection. The Chimera moved off as the two of them recommenced their feigned battle. The beast arched her back while lowering her fore body, then settled next to a boulder to watch. She growled softly and snapped the air with several sharp teeth. Restlessly, she kneaded her claws in the soil and thumped her horns against the rock. The sound was like a woodpecker drilling into a tree. *If the woodpecker was the size of a rhinoceros.*

I took advantage of the noise and began making my way over to the tree the Chimera was guarding. Ren shoved Kishan, who rolled next to the Chimera. The female hissed, showing more of her teeth. Kishan stared her down, quietly growled back, and fanned his whiskers. He snapped at the creature's hindquarters. She snarled, rolled onto her back, and nipped at his forelegs. A small burst of fire emitted from her mouth as the Chimera waved a few paws into the air.

Kishan darted away from the flames. The Chimera licked her chops and sneezed, then rolled to six feet and took off after the black tiger. While the three cats chased one another, I made my way to the tree.

The Rope of Fire was on an uppermost limb and just as I placed my hands on the trunk to climb it, the vines began whipping back and forth. A thin vine dipped under the Rope and began unwinding it from the tree.

I would have preferred for the tree to remain still, but the vines were already in motion. The Chimera was nuzzling Ren when it suddenly froze and swung its head toward the tree. I'd hidden behind the trunk, but the creature sniffed the air, lowered its head, and growled softly. It stalked toward the tree and despite the "love" bites Ren gave her and the snorting and stomping of Kishan's feet, they could no longer distract the creature from the call of duty.

I looked up and saw the tree was lowering a plaited length of black rope. The Chimera was almost upon me. She crouched on one side of the tree and sniffed the air.

Ren changed into a man and shouted, "Kelsey! Run to me as fast as you can!"

I heard the snarl of the Chimera, but she didn't waver from her stance. I gathered my courage, then darted around the other side of the tree and ran toward Ren just as Kishan leapt on the Chimera's back. The two cats rolled, but the Chimera shoved the black tiger aside and galloped quickly toward me. Kishan morphed back into human form, unsure what the Chimera would do next.

Instead of attacking, the beast leapt over me and positioned herself in front of Ren, as if defending him—even though Ren was no longer a tiger.

The Chimera snarled, and I felt the heat of her breath wash over me.

"What do I do?" I whispered quietly.

The Chimera circled Ren's human body, licked his arm, and rubbed her head against his leg.

"She's defending her mate," Kishan answered as he carefully approached me.

"But he's a man now," I hissed.

"She still sees him as a cat. She has his scent."

"What am I supposed to do?" I repeated.

"Come here," Kishan answered. "Hold my hand."

I took Kishan's hand.

"Now circle me and growl.".

"What?"

"Do it."

"Fine."

I walked around Kishan and made feeble attempts to growl.

"Louder," he instructed. "Stroke my arms."

I ran my hands up and down his arms and stroked his chest while making as much noise as possible.

"Good. Now follow me."

Slowly the two of us moved toward the tree. Ren watched us and when we were well hidden, he changed to the white tiger form and calmly trotted to the other side of the clearing. The Chimera followed him like an exuberant puppy. She nipped at his hind legs as he ran.

I stretched up my arms, and the waiting tree lowered the Rope of Fire. It looked more like a whip than a rope. The end of one side had a stiff section that could be used like a handle, and instead of leather, the length was scaled similar to the Chimera and the Qilin. The dark and iridescent scales twinkled like the tail of a small, dusky dragon. The Rope tapered to a sharp point, and I couldn't help but think that this "gift" might also be used as a weapon.

"I guess I really am Indiana Jones," I mumbled.

Kishan stopped me as I reached out to unwind it from the branch.

"What is it?" I asked as he gently pulled my hands away.

"The minute you touch it, you could be swept away in a vision like before."

In my fascination with Durga's beautiful gift, I had forgotten the consequences of taking it. I had no interest in spending time trapped with Lokesh in a vision, especially knowing that Mr. Kadam would no longer be there to support me. Still, we needed the Rope.

"We're going to have to get it sometime," I said.

"Maybe it won't affect you if I take it instead."

"I guess you could try."

He put an arm around my waist to support me just in case and then stretched out his fingers to take the rope. After touching it, he peered at me but I was still in control of my faculties.

Braver, he took the Rope from the tree and smiled. "So that's how we avoid the visions. You just won't be allowed to touch it."

I let out a pent-up breath and moved to the side as Kishan shook out the length of the Rope and snapped it in the clearing. The sharp crack it made proved it could be used like a whip.

"Wait," I said. "Mr. Kadam's letter said we were to use the Rope to time travel. We're supposed to use it to open a vortex."

Kishan swung the Rope of Fire over his head in a fast circle. Nothing happened. I heard Ren roar loudly and saw the Chimera chasing him again. Kishan tried making little circles and big circles, but nothing happened.

The Chimera was getting desperate. She didn't understand why her mate was running from her. She growled plaintively and bit Ren hard enough on the shoulder to draw blood.

"We need to hurry," I said.

Kishan whipped faster.

Frustrated, the Chimera shot a plume of fire from her mouth as Ren twisted away from her. That gave me an idea.

"Maybe the Rope of Fire needs to be on fire," I suggested.

Kishan nodded but watched me warily. I used my hands to try to light the Rope without touching it. It sparked, but the flame didn't stay lit no matter how long I blasted it and no matter how much power I used. It was like trying to light a burned out wick.

"It won't stay lit." Rubbing my hands together, I tapped them against my bottom lip as I thought about the problem. Somberly, I lowered my arms to my side as I realized I'd picked up the habit from watching Mr. Kadam, and then I sighed in resignation, knowing what I had to do.

"I'm going to have to hold it, Kishan."

"No."

"It's only going to work if I'm touching it."

"Kelsey, I don't want—"

Squeezing his arm, I said, "I'll be okay. He can't hurt me. Not really. My body will be here with you."

Kishan opened his hand, dropped the Rope, and was next to me in an instant. "I don't care if it works or not, Kells."

Taking my left hand, he fingered our engagement ring. As he touched the delicate lotus flower, he said quietly, "I don't want you to have to go through any more of this, *bilauta*." His golden eyes pierced mine with a fierce determination. "My only wish is to shield you. To protect your body and soul from fiends such as he."

I grasped his hand and leaned forward to kiss him softly. My lips clung to his briefly, and I smiled.

"I know you do, and believe me, there's nothing I'd like better but to stay in your arms and never face any of these things again but—"

"But nothing. We have the Rope now. Durga may grant us our freedom. We may be able to live as men all the time now."

"But clearly Ren is still a tiger. Taking the Rope didn't fix everything."

"We've existed as tigers for centuries, Kells. I can live with six hours a day if that's what this means and so can Ren. We can stop. Here. Now. We can just go home." He wrapped his arms around me and pulled me close. "It's not worth the risk. Ren would agree. I have no desire to seek Lokesh in the past. Not if it means losing you."

I cupped his face with my hands. "But it's our destiny, Kishan. Your destiny. You and Ren were chosen, given the power of the tiger to be able to defeat Lokesh. We are meant to do this. It's not just about us. Mr. Kadam said we are to protect the lives of those Lokesh would harm."

Kishan's eyes glittered fiercely. "I don't care about my destiny. I only care about you."

"You don't really mean that. Your destiny calls to you the same way mine calls to me. The Phoenix taught me that. It knew that its death would bring new life. Mr. Kadam sacrificed himself for this cause. How can I stand back and hide like a coward when he died for us?"

Pressing his forehead against mine, Kishan sighed. "I know that you are right and that we must press on, if for no other reason, than to honor Kadam's death. But in my heart, Kelsey, all I want is to sweep you away from here and keep you in my heart and in my home forever."

He kissed me sweetly, then, resigned, he kept his arm wrapped around my waist, picked up the Rope, and shook it out.

I placed one hand over Kishan's and the other on the Rope. Summoning my inner fire power, I let the heat bubble up from my core and flow down my arm. I poured energy from my palm into the Rope until the scales along the surface began to glow. They sparkled and shimmered until they burst into blinding flame. The Rope hummed, and I felt energy building. The last thought I had was that the white light reminded me of the fire flower Ren had given me.

Then I was swept away into a vision.

Thick darkness surrounded me. I heard a deep voice and a laugh as a wind whipped around my body and squeezed. I couldn't tell where it came from, though the noise rumbled across my skin like a rough caress.

"I've been waiting for you, my dear."

"Lokesh?" I spun, but I still couldn't see him. His voice sounded different—deeper and gravelly, as if he was laboring to push the words through his lips.

My eyes adjusted, the mist thinned, and I caught a warm twinkle of a fire tree. I could see Kishan and Ren, but they couldn't see or hear me. Then a cold wind blew.

I rubbed my arms, confused. *Why am I feeling the cold? I never felt temperature before. . . .*

Peering into the dark, I realized I was in a forest full of ominous, thick-trunked trees. Something shifted among the branches. I heard the scrape of heavy feet, and a dark form drew close.

I sucked in a shaky breath and heard the rumble of a rolling chuckle that echoed first on my right side, then behind me. It drifted far away and then snuck up close on my left. I felt hot breath on my neck that prickled goose bumps on my skin. I turned, but whatever had been behind me had vanished.

Then I felt him—a huge, dangerous presence—beside me. Slowly, I turned to face Lokesh and gasped. His body had been dramatically transformed and now towered over mine. He was easily three feet taller than me and three times as wide. His skin was black. Lokesh's expensive business suits had been replaced by a sarong that hung from his waist to mid-thigh.

"Don't you recognize me, my sweet?"

Lokesh took a step closer, and my mouth gaped open at the sight of him. His horned head was bony with protective ridges over the eyes, and his once tamed hair sprouted in wooly curls. One brown eye still looked human, but the other had a bright red iris and was surrounded by scars. His torso, arms, and silvery scarred neck were thick and bulging with muscle. Instead of feet, his legs tapered into two massive, cloven hooves.

Alarmed, I shuffled several steps back. Mr. Kadam said that Lokesh had used his power to become a demon. Having seen his contorted face, it was clear Mr. Kadam had been right. Lokesh looked like a dark devil, like whatever evil coursed through his veins had finally surfaced.

Lokesh flexed his hand, and his arm muscles bulged at the slight movement. He watched my reaction to him with a burning, hungry intensity. The almost completely formed amulet glowed where it hung against his wide chest.

"Lokesh? What . . . what have you done?"

He lifted his arms to examine his dark limbs. "Do you like it?"

"It's . . . it's monstrous!"

He snorted and steam shot from his nostrils. "It's power."

Lokesh twisted his lips into an evil grimace. Lifting one huge hand, he ran a finger down my bare arm. The pads of his fingers were rough like an animal's and left my skin raw.

I took a step back as he took another step forward. I felt nauseous and wondered again, *How can I feel this?*

A gleam lit his eyes when Lokesh realized we had a physical connection, and he stretched his fingers toward my throat. I tried to run, but he grabbed my arm, wrenched me around, and wrapped his hand around my neck. He merely tightened his grip when I tried to twist free. Gasping for air, I felt tears leak from my eyes. I knew what he wanted. When I stopped thrashing, he let me breathe again. With an almost delicate touch, he reached for the fire amulet hanging around my neck. I flinched, waiting for him to rip the necklace away.

Lokesh's bony brow furrowed in concentration as his thick fingers passed through the amulet as if it was made of air. Enraged, he threw me to the ground. Blood trickled down my elbow where I skinned it. I touched my bruised throat and hoped that the pain was only temporary and would disappear with this vision. *How long will it last?*

He dragged me to my feet. His covetous gaze turned lustful as he brusquely perused the amulet on my body.

"If I cannot have the amulet, then fate has at least given me the woman. I think we have some unfinished business, my pet."

Hoping to distract him, I said hoarsely, "I think I preferred you more as a man."

"I am now a man *and* a beast. Much like your pathetic princes." Lokesh grabbed my shoulders and squeezed them mercilessly as his head descended toward mine. His horns scraped the side of my head and ripped out some of my hair by the root. I cried out, and my eyes teared. Moist air from his nostrils fanned over my face.

He breathed hotly, almost panting, as he said, "You won't escape me again, my sweet."

Lokesh yanked me against him and mashed his lips to mine. I tried to kick and bite, but he only laughed and hurt me more. He was too powerful. I screamed as he raked his fingers down my back. His nails dug into my flesh, and I felt the wet trickle of blood. The press of his body against mine was unbearable. He was smothering me. Wrenching away from him, I struggled to escape.

"Please, someone help me," I sobbed.

Soon, I felt lighter than air. Though I was still in Lokesh's clutches, I could no longer feel his touch.

He bellowed in frustration as his hand suddenly passed through my now intangible body.

Relieved, I wiped tears from my hot, abused face and stepped away. He could no longer hold me in his grip, and he violently swung his arms at my ghost-like form. I moved farther away from him, putting as much distance between us as I could. Soon, Lokesh's body began to fade as well. When he was almost gone, he narrowed his eyes and lowered his head. With a mighty roar, he charged toward me at full speed, like a bull at a matador. Froth foamed at his mouth, and there was a crazed look in his eyes.

The ground shook as he thunderously charged. I raised my arms to protect myself when the points of his horns made contact. A horrible roar echoed in my mind as his dark wind passed through my body. I screamed and fainted.

When the vision was over, I opened my eyes to see Ren and Kishan leaning over me. Kishan was using the Scarf to bandage my elbow, and Ren was examining my throat. Both had stony expressions but asked no questions. My back stung until Kishan applied a salve from the Golden Fruit.

I gulped the life-saving elixir from the *kamandal*, and within a few minutes, I began to feel better.

"She's starting to heal," Kishan remarked.

Ren nodded.

"Where's—" I tried to clear my raspy throat, but it hurt too much. "Chimera," I whispered.

"I used the Rope to whip her," Ren said, stroking my bruised throat. "She ran off and hasn't returned yet."

I saw regret in his eyes, but then he touched my arm and the steely determination returned. I knew how much it pained him to abuse an animal, even one that would have killed us. But I couldn't help but feel grateful that the Chimera wasn't around.

"She'll come back soon," Kishan said. "We need to leave."

I nodded my agreement. Ren gently lifted my arms to help me put on a new T-shirt. After he slipped it over my old torn one, he asked the Scarf to reabsorb the ripped and bloody shirt underneath. Threads flew out from under the hem and sleeves, and soon the Scarf was quiet.

Kishan and Ren helped me stand, and then Kishan picked up the Rope of Fire. I took hold of the Rope in one hand and placed the other on top of Kishan's.

"Try it now, Kishan," I encouraged, my voice just a bit stronger.

He whipped the Rope in a wide circle in front of him. I channeled my fire power into the Rope, and the entire length caught on fire. I sent in more energy, and he whipped faster and faster until the inner circle became a black vortex. Flames danced along the edges.

"Tell it where you want to go," Kishan said.

I whispered, "Take us to the past. To the place where we are to meet our destiny."

The blackness flickered and a green forest materialized.

Ren put on the backpack, picked me up, and ran toward the vortex just as the Chimera shot out from the trees. As he and Kishan leapt through the circle of flame, Ren twisted in the air to shield me from her. The Chimera's jaws snapped, but her teeth missed us, and we fell backward into the void. I was wrenched away from Ren, and then the three of us tumbled around one another in the vortex.

At first, I felt nothing. Then gravity took over, and my stomach heaved as I plummeted downward into an abyss. I screamed, terrified, as my body tumbled into blackness. The echoes of voices calling my name swirled around me.

I closed my eyes as a wave of dizziness overtook me. I heard a snarl, a roar. Then I felt heat and flame rush over my skin. Just as quickly, all motion ceased, and I felt my consciousness start to slip away until it disappeared altogether.

a new world

"Get up!" shouted a woman's no-nonsense voice.

I opened my eyes to see a lovely leg in a mile-long, thigh-high boot connect with my stomach. I curled into a protective ball, blinking and groaning at the aches and pains in my body. *Who is kicking me? And why won't she stop?*

The woman kicked me again and hissed, "Get up!"

Twisting into a sitting position, I looked up and saw a tall, striking woman in front of me. A helmet covered most of her face, but her eyes were a brilliant green, and her skin was an exotic buttery-brown of sugar caramel. Her long black hair fell well past her waist. I also noticed the sharp tip of her spear hovering dangerously close to my nose.

I shuffled slowly to my feet, trying to get a grip on my current situation. Once again, I was in a forest. I was surrounded by armored warriors who had confiscated our backpack and weapons and were pointing various spears directly at me. Ren and Kishan were bound with coarse ropes and still unconscious. The Rope of Fire lay idly on the ground.

"Who are you?" I asked the beautiful Amazon who could have doubled as a swimsuit cover–model. "What do you want with us?"

The men spoke to her in a foreign language until she silenced them with a signal.

"I am called Anamika."

I shifted carefully around her spear. "Nice to meet you," I said, surprised at her fluency in English.

Anamika kept her eyes trained on me. As I moved, I noticed her tiny waist was cinched in by the armored dress's heavy belt where several other weapons dangled.

"Do you mind pointing that thing somewhere else?" I asked.

She narrowed her eyes and then planted the blunt end of her spear on the ground, whipping her long hair back as if annoyed with it.

"What is your name?" she asked.

"Kelsey," I answered. "And you can call your warriors off. We won't hurt you."

Anamika translated my statement to her men, and I heard several snickers and a rumble of comments from the soldiers. Then she clipped off a command, and the warriors picked up Ren and Kishan.

Alarmed, I demanded, "Where are you taking them?"

"Come, Kelsey. There is much to do."

Because Ren and Kishan were still unconscious, and we didn't seem to be in any immediate danger, I followed her through the forest.

"Where are we headed?" I asked again.

"Back to my camp. It is not far," she smirked. "Though it may seem far to one as soft as you."

Did the Amazon just insult me?

"I may not be wearing armor on the outside, but I've seen my share of battle."

Anamika rubbed her fingers together and then moodily shifted her spear to the other hand. Her green eyes glittered.

"Really?" she said in a mocking tone. "It's hard to imagine you engaged in warfare with anything more substantial than a cooking pot." She boldly gave me the once-over, looking down at me from her freakishly tall Amazonian height.

I stuck my chin in the air and clenched my fists, deliberately tamping down the fire that raged through my blood. This woman was ticking me off.

"Please," she laughed insultingly, "tell me of your battles."

Tight lipped, I hissed, "Maybe later."

Determined to keep up with her though she covered twice as much distance per stride, I followed along and tried my best to take note of my whereabouts and study my captors. The forest was cold, especially after spending the last few weeks in the heat of lava falls and fire trees. Rubbing my arms, I wished that I could figure out a way to make warmer clothes using the Scarf without being noticed.

The leggy warrior-woman saw my twitching and smirked, so I ramped up my speed, determined to tough out the nippy temperature. Thinking quickly, I used the power of the amulet to warm me. A pocket of heat swirled around my body, and I smiled secretly as I moved along.

The going became rough as we descended a stony face. When the afternoon sun broke through the trees and my forehead broke out into a sweat, I turned off the heat and let the still, cooler air envelop me. Toward the bottom, the trees parted, and I looked up to find a very familiar sight. Towering snowcapped mountains loomed on all sides.

"We're in the Himalayas?" I gasped.

"We are near the great mountains," Anamika corrected.

"That's just fantastic," I mumbled. "It was bad enough the first time."

"You have been to this place before?" Warrior Barbie asked.

"Not this place exactly, but close enough."

She made no further comment, and I concentrated on getting to the bottom of the incline without breaking my neck while still keeping an eye on the men jostling Ren and Kishan. They'd been unconscious for a long time. I mused on their condition, thinking that maybe I'd recovered faster because of the mermaid's elixir.

Anamika must have read my thoughts. She pointed to Ren and Kishan. "Your men are weak. I found no injuries on their bodies, but still they sleep."

"You don't know what they've been through," I responded.

"Perhaps they are soft like you."

"I'd really appreciate it if you'd stop using that word."

"Very well. Then I will use the word *slow* or perhaps *wilting*."

I gaped at her. "You're pretty quick to judge, aren't you?"

"I must make quick assessments of my warriors, yes."

"Have you heard the phrase, 'Don't judge a book by its cover'?"

"I do not spend my time judging books."

I snorted and tripped on a rock. Anamika helped me to right myself, but I shoved her away, pointed my finger, and threatened, "Don't you dare call me soft."

She bowed her head slightly and continued on with a small grin on her face.

Looking around, I noticed that several of her warriors had fresh injuries. One man had a bandage-wrapped leg, another sported a nasty cut across his brow, and a third limped painfully.

"Have you been in recent battle?" I asked.

Anamika frowned. "Yes, we have been engaged in war. There have been many casualties."

I bit my lip. "Have you heard of a man called Lokesh? Is that the man you fought?"

She shook her head. "We are fighting the demon Mahishasur."

"Mahishasur?"

The name sounded familiar, but I couldn't remember what it meant. I'd have to consult Mr. Kadam's research—that is, after I ditched the bossy Barbie in calf-hugging boots.

At sundown, we wound our way through a narrow passage to a

valley surrounded by towering mountains. Ahead was the camp. Tents dotted the valley as far as I could see.

Surprised at the numbers, I remarked, "You have a lot of men."

"Not as many as I came with," she said softly.

Anamika led us to the largest tent somewhere in the middle of the camp. After having her men untie Ren and Kishan and depositing them onto a soft rug, she dismissed all but one and conferred briefly with him before sending him out too. With a weariness she didn't show in front of her men, she sank onto a chair, removed her boots, and massaged her feet. They were cracked and crusted with blood.

I knelt on the straw rug between Ren and Kishan and casually commented, "You are indeed tough if you can maneuver long distances with feet as injured as yours."

She set her feet on the floor as if embarrassed. "Do you expect the commander of the last of the Vedic Aryans to coddle herself, bathe her skin in milk, and anoint her hair with fragrant soaps like you?"

"I'll have you know that I've never bathed in milk. Who are the Vedic Aryans?"

Anamika sighed heavily. "We are the last of our people. Once we were one of sixteen *Mahājanapadas*. Our republic flourished under the rule of my grandfather, but one by one each of the sixteen kingdoms was conquered. Now we serve the Maurya Empire and answer to its head, Chandragupta Maurya. I was the captain's advisor, but he has been . . . lost. Now his duties have fallen onto me."

I berated myself for not studying Indian history more. If I had, I could at least figure out what time we were in. Ren and Kishan might know. Still the name Chandragupta sounded familiar. I'd read about him or heard of him somewhere before. *But where?*

Anamika turned her back to remove her armor. I heard the thump of her helmet as it hit the floor and ignored her while I tried to awaken

Ren and Kishan. They were breathing and their hearts were beating, but Ren's pulse was very slow. When I found I couldn't rouse them on my own, I took the *kamandal* from Kishan's neck and wet their lips with a few drops.

After splashing water on her face and arms, the long-legged warrior returned and stood behind me, watching my efforts as she brushed out her long hair. I bristled under her scrutiny but wouldn't give her the satisfaction of making eye contact. When she caught her brush on a snarl, I leaned over Ren and Kishan, hoping she wasn't paying attention, and took the opportunity to pour a little fire power into both brothers. Color returned to their faces, and they stirred.

Cobalt blue eyes blinked, and Ren sat up.

"Are you okay, Kells?"

"I'm fine."

Kishan rolled his upper body and leaned onto one arm while he rubbed his eyes. "Is the Rope still here?" he mumbled sleepily.

"Yes, I've got it."

"Good."

He opened his eyes and froze. Ren wasn't moving either. Both men were staring at Anamika, who'd gone suddenly quiet as well. I rolled my eyes and got to my feet.

"Ren and Kishan, I'd like to introduce you to, Ana . . ." The breath flew from my lips. ". . . mika."

The woman standing behind me clutching her brush was the same fiery green-eyed Barbie that I'd been talking with for the last few hours, but without her helmet I realized something that should have been obvious before. I knew her. I stared at her dumbly while she narrowed her eyes and pursed her lips.

"Why do you all stare at me like large-eyed puppies waiting for a bone?" she hissed.

Kishan was the first to react. He twisted around and prostrated himself before her. He bowed his head, and said, "How may I serve you?"

"Durga?" I whispered.

She looked exactly like the goddess we'd visited four times. Only this version had two arms instead of eight.

"What is a Durga?" she spat sharply, "and why is that one putting his face onto the floor? Has he lost control of his faculties? Perhaps his mind is as feeble as his body." She leaned over and addressed Kishan in a loud voice as if he were hard of hearing. "You may stand up now. You have mistaken me for someone else."

Kishan raised his bowed head and narrowed his gaze at the woman. Growling, he rolled quickly to his feet.

"What's going on?" Ren whispered.

Anamika answered. "What's going on is that we are at war, and I don't have time to coddle weaklings."

"Weaklings?" Kishan spat. He took a step toward the woman, but she only raised an eyebrow and looked him up and down with a disdainful expression.

I squeezed Kishan's arm, and he stopped moving but continued his stare-down with our hostess. "Anamika, this is Dhiren Rajaram, and this is his brother, Kishan."

"Anamika?" Kishan said. "Is that what she's calling herself?" he mumbled hotly.

The goddess-like woman put her hand onto a dagger strapped to her waist. "Are you suggesting I am not who I say I am? I am Anamika Kalinga, advisor to Chandragupta, the most esteemed female champion in the history of my people, and the daughter of great kings." She fixed a stormy gaze on Kishan. "I have bested men larger and smarter than you. You would be wise to treat me with respect, *durbala*."

"*Durbala?*"

Whatever that word meant caused Kishan to lose it. He strode toward Anamika and seized her wrist before she could pull her knife. Even though he was a few inches taller, she still managed to look down at him. If steam could have billowed out from his nose and his ears, it would have. I'd never seen him so angry before.

"Kishan," I said softly and held out my hand.

Settling down, he let go of Anamika's wrist and returned to my side.

Ren deftly inserted himself between Kishan and Anamika. He bowed slightly and said, "Forgive us. We have traveled far from our homeland, and despite appearances," he turned and gave Kishan a warning look, "we are grateful for the hospitality you've shown to us."

He then launched into Hindi and introduced himself and Kishan more formally. I caught the names but that was about it. Anamika switched languages easily, and words flowed silkily between Ren and the leggy woman. The ease with which she talked with Ren and the change in her demeanor irked me. She lowered her guard with Ren, and soon she was all smiles and laughs.

Kishan and I watched and listened, and I honestly didn't know whether to trust her. Frowning, I shifted, uneasily wishing I could understand what was being said.

At one point, Kishan interrupted, changing back to English. "My fiancée is weary. Might I ask for some food and a place where she may rest?"

Ren turned to look at me. I flushed under his scrutiny. I couldn't help but feel like he was comparing me with Anamika—and I fell short. Through tight lips I protested, "I'm fine. I don't need to rest."

"Perhaps that would be for the best," Ren argued quietly.

With a smirk, Anamika replied, "I'll have my men prepare the *softest* bedding they can find."

I bristled again while Kishan added, "I'm sure Kelsey would find that most welcome."

As soon as Anamika stepped outside the tent, I folded my arms across my chest and turned to Ren and Kishan. "Let's get one thing straight right now. I don't care what century we're in or even what planet we're on. You two don't speak for me. If either of you has got it into your heads to make me play the role of the little fiancée who needs a big strong man to think for me, you'd be wise to reassess your position! You are not going to send me off to my room so that I miss out on all the important discussions."

Kishan said, "Kells, I didn't mean . . . I wasn't trying to get rid of you. I just wanted you to be comfortable."

"I'm perfectly capable of making myself comfortable."

"I know, it's just . . ."

"Just what?"

"It's just that we don't exactly fit in. Our clothes are different, our speech, our mannerisms. Kelsey, I announced our betrothal and made efforts to see to your comfort to protect you. A single woman doesn't fend for herself. Not in this kind of environment."

"What about the Queen Bee over there? I don't see a ring on her finger, and she seems to be fending for herself just fine."

"It's different for royalty," Kishan explained. "She is likely protected by her man-at-arms or even a group of bodyguards."

"But you're forgetting that I can protect myself."

"It doesn't hurt to keep up appearances."

As I stewed over his words, Ren added, "I apologize for leaving you out of our conversation. I was simply trying to assess who she is and what languages she speaks. It will help us to determine where we are and what point in history we are in without asking outright." He took my hand. "I didn't intend to brush you aside. I'm sorry."

"Oh," I sighed. "Well, I don't like her, and I don't trust her. We should leave."

"Where else do you expect us to go, Kelsey?" Ren asked.

"We should be looking for Lokesh."

"We don't know where to find him," Kishan stated. "I don't like the harridan either, but our best option is find out what she knows."

The harridan? I raised my eyebrows. Kishan had never treated a woman with anything but respect.

"What exactly does *durbala* mean?" I asked Ren as Kishan busied himself inspecting the tent.

"It depends on how it's used, but the word can mean 'small,' 'sickly,' or . . . 'impotent.'"

I clapped my hand over my mouth to stifle my giggle. "No wonder he's mad."

Ren gave me a lopsided smile, retrieved our backpack, and sorted through everything to count all of our weapons.

Picking up Anamika's fallen hairbrush, I twirled it thoughtfully and remembered her blistered feet. "Well, she's obviously not the goddess, so why does she look like Durga?" I wondered aloud.

Ren took the trident from his belt and ran his fingertips down the length of it before placing it into the backpack. "I don't know, Kells. But we were brought here for a reason. We just need time to figure out what that reason is."

"Are you hiding our weapons?"

He nodded. "For now. They are of exceptional quality. I wouldn't want someone to see the gold and make plans to take them. Speaking of which . . ." Ren rose and gently lifted the sleeve of my T-shirt. His fingers brushed against my skin, and I shivered as he slid Fanindra down my arm. Bright blue eyes sought mine, and a familiar lopsided smile appeared as he watched my reaction to his touch. Saying nothing, he let out a soft sigh and placed Fanindra into the backpack; then he moved on to retrieve Kishan's weapons.

Anamika returned, followed by several men carrying rugs, pillows, and platters of food. They positioned the bedding behind a curtain, set the food on a low table, and waited at the entrance.

"Kelsey will stay in my tent," Anamika announced.

Kishan was about to protest when Anamika raised her hand.

"I allow no impropriety among my men, and I won't make any exceptions for you and your betrothed. I will, however, give you my vow that she will remain safe with me. The two of you will be assigned a tent to share and will be given proper clothing and . . . boots."

I had forgotten that Ren and Kishan had no shoes. They'd switched from tigers to leap through the vortex and wore only their loose shirts and pants.

Anamika examined my jeans and T-shirt with a puzzled expression. "Perhaps some of my clothing can be cut down to accommodate your smallish stature," she offered.

No one had ever called me small before. I stood up as tall as I could. "Just because you're freakishly large does not mean I am small. My height is considered slightly above average in my homeland, I'll have you know."

"Indeed." Her mouth twitched.

I took the backpack from Ren and slammed it over my shoulders. "I have my own clothes anyway. There is no need to cut any of your precious warrior-Barbie outfits."

Anamika made a noise suspiciously like a growl and signaled a guard. "Take the men to their tent."

As the brothers were being escorted away, she said to Kishan, "You may return to visit your little woman at the morning meal."

Kishan and Ren both paused at the tent opening to look at me. I jiggled the backpack to reassure them I could take care of myself. They nodded and disappeared.

A servant entered and poured water into our goblets. Anamika sank onto the floor to make herself comfortable on the pillows. Placing my backpack as close as possible, I joined her and picked up my cup. The liquid was icy and fresh—the most delicious water I'd ever tasted.

"It's wonderful!" I remarked after draining my cup.

Anamika grunted. "The water comes directly from the mountains. I also find it refreshing. Now, please, eat. I wouldn't want your fiancé to accuse me of starving you."

There were several different dishes, including bowls of toasted almonds, spicy chickpeas, pickled potatoes, lentils, and a few small pieces of fire-roasted meat. Anamika nibbled on a fragrant white fruit called lychee.

I picked up some flatbread and used it to scoop up chickpeas and the meat. "How did you hurt your feet?" I asked.

"My feet are none of your affair."

"They looked pretty bad," I remarked as I tried the potatoes.

She grunted but didn't say anything more. I watched her as I ate. *Who is she and why does she look like Durga?*

After she pulled off a small piece of flatbread and ate it, she turned her body away from the table as if she couldn't look at the food any longer.

"What's wrong?" I asked. "You don't like the food? A woman like you probably doesn't like to eat anything she didn't hunt down and kill herself, right?"

"I am no longer hungry."

I paused with a piece of plump lychee fruit pinched between my fingers. "You're full?" I was confused, but only for a moment. I'd met women like her before, women like Ren's annoying girlfriend, Randi. "Oh, you've got an Amazon figure to maintain."

"I do not understand 'Amazon figure.'"

"A figure is the shape of your body, and Amazons are these tall, beautiful women who live in South America. They are warriors who don't need men to take care of them."

"I have no concern for the shape of my body as long as it is strong. An Amazon, as you call me, may be what I am now but I was not always so. I like men."

She'd said it with such sincerity that I couldn't help laughing. "I understand. I like men too," I said. "So why are you an Amazon now?"

Anamika brought her knees up to her chest and wrapped her arms around them. "I was not always alone. I had a brother . . . Sunil. He was my twin." The ghost of a smile appeared on her lips. "He was the *senani*, in command of our forces."

"What happened to him?"

"He was taken. Captured by our enemy." She paused. "He is likely dead or so my men would have me believe. You asked about my feet. I dreamed my brother called to me, and I left my tent to find him. His voice compelled me forward, and I pressed on, not caring that my feet were cut by sharp rocks and torn by thorns and brambles. When I woke, I found I had experienced a walking dream and was far from my camp."

"I'm sorry about your brother, Anamika."

"We came here with thirty thousand foot soldiers, twenty thousand chariots, and five thousand battle elephants, along with dozens of spies and messengers. In the last battle, my brother was lost and our *sena*, our army, was struck down, hobbled. Hundreds of our elephants were overcome, and all that is now left of our proud warriors are a few thousand, most of whom are injured."

"Your enemy sounds formidable."

"He is a demon," she said tiredly.

"Why don't you eat a bit more?" I pressed. "You need to keep up your strength."

She turned to me with piercing eyes. "I will not. This food is more than most of my men get in a month. How can I eat more when they are starving?"

I paused in reaching for another piece of flatbread. "Your men are hungry?"

"Hunger is the most trivial of their sufferings. I have asked them to return home, but they refuse to desert me, and I cannot leave until I determine what has happened to my brother."

With a pointed glare, she got up and thrust aside the sheer curtain dividing the sleeping area. Anamika lay down on the floor of the tent and wrapped a thin blanket around her body. Whispering hushed words, I used the Golden Fruit to refill the bowls of food and even add a few more. Then I asked the guard outside the tent if he would distribute the food to the men.

The bowls were quietly removed and a hush fell over the camp as the men sought their tents for warm blankets. I peered up at the bright stars and wondered which tent belonged to Ren and Kishan. Shivering, I closed the flap and rubbed my arms.

Finding my pile of blankets, I wiggled between them and attempted to sleep. I lay there thinking about how warm I'd be if I was nestled between my tigers and clutched my blankets tightly as the night cooled to freezing temperatures. Finally, I could no longer stand it. Glancing at Anamika's inert form, I asked the Divine Scarf to make thick blankets and to soften the thin pallet I'd been given. I also made cozy mittens, cushioned socks, and a knit hat to cover my ears.

I was finally comfortable, but I still couldn't rest knowing that Anamika had only a thin blanket and threadbare clothing. Commanding the Scarf once again, I hoped that she wouldn't hear the whisper of threads as they covered her body. When the Scarf's work was done, Anamika moaned and rolled in her newly made thick blankets. Her sore feet were now encased in cashmere socks, and a soft pillow cushioned her head. I risked a peek through the sheer curtain. She'd drawn the blankets up to her nose, and her long black hair spilled across the pillow.

Annoying as she was, Anamika was definitely gorgeous. The memory of her talking to Ren in Hindi disturbed me more than I liked to admit. I was jealous, but at the same time, I felt a connection, a kinship to the woman. She'd lost her brother, and she was in pain. I also couldn't help but admire her strength and her dedication to her men.

Sighing softly, I snuggled under my blankets to finally sleep. I don't know how long I'd been asleep—hours or mere minutes—when I awoke to the sound of Anamika's scream.

25

sibling rivalry

A dark intruder wrestled with Anamika. I threw off my blankets and turned my backpack over, spilling out our golden weapons. Nocking an arrow and thrusting the curtain aside, I aimed at the shadows. The torch had gone out as we slept, and I couldn't tell who was who. I heard Anamika let out her breath in a rush as the trespasser punched her.

Desperate for a better weapon, I ran my hands over my blanket and felt for the *chakram*, but then my hand brushed against Fanindra.

"Fanindra, I need your eyes," I coaxed.

Immediately the snake's jeweled emerald eyes glowed and a viridian light filled the room, casting an eerie shade of green. Now I could tell that the intruder was a man, and he had his arms around Anamika from behind. Her eyes were hard and alert, and they widened upon seeing me.

Thanks to Fanindra, I had a clear shot. I raised my bow and yelled, "Anamika, duck!" but I realized quickly by the small shake of her head that she didn't understand. The man spun her around so she could look him in the eye.

She gasped. "Sunil?"

I was just about to release my arrow but hesitated at the name of Anamika's brother.

"You *are* alive!" she cried out.

He ignored her and turned his attention to me. Even in the low light I could see that he was tall, strong, muscled, and ready for war. Like his sister, his eyes were green and his hair was dark, but his had a curl to it. There was a little cleft in his unshaven chin. Even though he was attacking us, I could see that Sunil was very handsome.

After a brief assessment of me, a wide smile lit his face. In a cold voice, he said, "You! We've been waiting for you," he said. "My master will be pleased."

Sunil violently thrust Anamika aside and headed toward me. Brother or no brother, I let loose my arrow at close range. It sunk deeply into his thigh. Sunil didn't even flinch, even with an arrow in his leg. Grabbing me roughly, he began wrestling me out the tent door.

Anamika shouted for the guards and commanded them to subdue her brother. I could tell from the tears in her voice that she begged them not to hurt him.

Wrenched from his clutches, I stumbled on the cold ground. Sunil seemed to acknowledge that he'd failed. With a shout, he threw aside the men holding him as if they were mere rag dolls and ran off into the forest. Anamika's warriors followed but returned after a few moments. They told Anamika that her brother, once their leader, was faster than their quickest runners, even with his leg injury. They had lost him in the mist.

Ren and Kishan caught up to us and quickly positioned themselves alongside me.

"We heard shouts. What has happened?" Ren demanded.

"We were attacked by an unexpected adversary," Anamika answered.

After she explained that an intruder had almost abducted me, Kishan stepped forward, volunteering to track the man.

Anamika waved him off. "I know where he is now," she explained. "Sunil has fallen under the power of the demon. I have seen this power used on others. They forget themselves and those they care about."

"The demon you fight has powers?" Ren asked.

Anamika glanced at her men and then pressed her finger to her lips and entered the tent. I followed, trailed by Ren and Kishan. The four of us sat around her table.

"I do not wish my men to fear the enemy more than they already do," she cautioned.

She picked up a blanket and wrapped it around her body. Then she wiped away her tears with the corner. Stopping suddenly, Anamika pulled the soft blanket away from her face and stared at it. She tilted her head, considering me, before finally answering Ren.

"He has many extraordinary powers. He's used them to raise a demon army."

"A demon army?" Something was creeping around the edges of my brain. An old memory was leeching into my consciousness. My mouth suddenly went dry. I licked my chapped lips. "Anamika, what does your enemy look like?"

"His skin is black, and he has long horns like a bull. He uses his power to shake the earth and rain destruction on all who oppose him."

Wheels turned in my mind and pieces of an ancient puzzle began to click into place.

"A goddess arose," I whispered, "to slay the demon Mahishasur." I swallowed and looked at Ren and Kishan. "We need to talk."

Anamika stood. "You may converse at your leisure here. You should be safe enough. I must see to my men and send out the morning hunters."

"Hunters?" Kishan asked with piqued enthusiasm.

"Yes." She headed to the chair where she'd dropped her armor and boots. "The game has long since fled this land, but perhaps we will still find some food to fill the bellies of those under my care."

She removed the cozy socks I'd given her and set them aside while giving me a look that said we'll-get-to-the-bottom-of-this-later. Then she pulled on her boots and gear and was gone.

"I know why she looks like Durga," I exclaimed the minute she was out of hearing range. "She *is* Durga or . . . she's going to be once she slays Mahishasur. I read about how she killed him when I was studying the birth of Durga."

"But Durga was created by the gods," Kishan said.

"Yes, but remember, she was created to defeat Mahishasur. I think we were sent here to create Durga."

"We were sent here to defeat Lokesh," Ren countered.

I put my hand on his arm. "Ren, Lokesh *is* Mahishasur."

"I don't follow," Kishan said.

"I never got the chance to tell you, but in my vision Lokesh had become a demon. He was as Anamika described. His body is huge and black. He shoots steam from his nostrils, and he has two sets of horns." Something else clicked. "Wasn't Mahishasur supposed to be half man and half bull?"

Kishan nodded. "Buffalo, actually."

"Mr. Kadam said in his letter that Lokesh had become a demon in the past. This is it. This is why we're here."

"Kelsey—" Kishan began.

Absorbed in my theorizing, I interrupted, "Also, I think he used his tiger-making zombie charm on Anamika's brother."

"She has a brother?" Ren asked.

"Yes, a twin brother. His name is Sunil. He's the one who attacked us this morning."

"She didn't say he was her brother," Ren said.

"She thought he was dead."

"He hurt you." Ren gently ran his fingers over the red marks on my arms.

"I'll be fine," I mumbled distractedly. Clearing my throat to divert my attention from Ren's touch, I went on, "When Sunil saw me, he said,

'My master will be pleased.' I think Lokesh has been keeping a lookout for me. But he originally wanted to take Anamika. That must mean that Lokesh is after her too."

Kishan grunted. "Then it's simple. You and Anamika will stay here while we kill Lokesh." He stood and went to the backpack to retrieve his weapons.

"No," I said as I scrambled to my feet. "The demon Mahishasur could not be killed by a man. Remember? Durga was created to defeat him."

"So what do we do now?" Ren asked.

I gave him a tight smile. "We convince Anamika that she is a goddess."

The first step in convincing the Amazon that she needed to be a goddess was easier said than done. First, we had to locate her. It took several hours to find the woman. As soon as we'd arrive at one tent where she'd been tending to a wounded man, we'd discover she'd moved on to carry firewood to add to the stockpile. After questioning her men there, we learned she had set out hunting.

Tired of chasing the woman around the campsite, Kishan caught her scent heading into the forest. An hour later we came upon her returning to camp with a freshly caught rabbit slung over her shoulder.

Anamika briefly stopped in her tracks when she saw us, but stuck her nose into the air and kept walking. "What's wrong now?" she asked as she passed us. "Are your accommodations still lacking? Here to complain about my brother bruising your precious fiancé?" Her voice dripped with sarcasm.

This time her words didn't bother me. She brushed her hair back from her face, and I noticed the dark circles under her eyes and a purple welt on her jaw. Kishan growled and stepped forward to confront her, but I put my hand on his arm.

"We're here to help you," I said.

She paused and looked down at me. "And how can one as weak as you be of assistance?" she asked.

I scrambled and said the first thing that came to my mind. "Ren and Kishan are good hunters. Perhaps they can find some meat."

She sneered and thrust the dead rabbit in my face. "This skinny creature is more meat than we've caught in weeks."

"Trust me. They are exceptional hunters."

Anamika peered at Ren and Kishan, not bothering to hide her expression of doubt and then waved her hand. "I do not care how you amuse yourselves. The forest is yours."

With nimble leaps, she made her way down the stony path and headed back to camp.

"I thought we were going to talk to her," Kishan said while I removed the backpack from his shoulders and dug through it.

"We need to get her to trust us first, or she won't believe anything we say."

I handed Ren the Golden Fruit and said, "You two go off and hunt down some food via the Golden Fruit and bring back as much as you can carry. I'm going to help Anamika take care of her men. May I please borrow this?" I asked Kishan as I fingered the *kamandal*.

He kissed my hand, took the charm from his neck, and pressed it into my palm.

We agreed to regroup at sundown.

The first thing I did was head to the outskirts of camp. Once there, I used the Divine Scarf to create a tent filled with stacks of clothing in a variety of sizes, blankets, soft slippers, thick socks, mittens, hats, and a giant stockpile of bandages.

Once the tent was full to capacity, I sought out the perfect location for a hot spring. Using the magic of the Pearl Necklace, I used steam to blast loose dirt away from a rocky steppe and called forth bubbling mineral water from deep beneath Earth's surface. Then the power of the amulet flowed through my fingers, heating the ground below. I made the bed of rocks beneath it hot enough to last for several days. Finally, I dribbled several drops from the *kamandal* in the water. I wasn't sure if it would work topically, but I figured it couldn't hurt to try. The spring could be used for bathing as well as for soaking muscles sore from battle.

My next task was healing those who were too weak to bathe in the spring. I found the camp's main water supply: fifty barrels full of cold water. Picking up a dipper, I uncovered the top of one barrel and poured several drops from the *kamandal* into the water. After a quick stir, I moved on to the next barrel and the next. It took about an hour to finish with all the barrels, and then I sought out Anamika.

She was kneeling at the side of a soldier who had just died. Tears flowed freely down her face as she spoke with his friends. I felt immense guilt overwhelm me for a moment and berated myself for not seeing to the worst cases of the wounded first. Seeing the concern Anamika felt for her mourning men and the way they responded to her with obvious devotion and loyalty made my calling clear.

She will be the one thousands look to, and I am here to help her.

I was saddened that I could not save the man, but I knew that if I constantly second-guessed my actions, I would miss opportunities to save others.

Finishing with her soldiers, the warrior woman saw me standing at the tent opening and stepped outside.

"What do you want?" she asked testily.

"I'm sorry for your friend's death, Anamika."

"Your sorrow does not give me back his life."

"No, it does not." I stood by her mutely for a moment before saying, "You aren't to blame, Anamika."

"Every death here is my responsibility."

"Death comes," I said. "There's no stopping it. You can only do your best to help as many as you can."

She wiped angry tears from her cheeks and turned away, "What do you know about death?"

"More than you might think." I played with the *kamandal* hanging at my throat and confessed, "I used to be afraid of death. Not for myself, but I feared the death of those I loved. It crippled me. I wouldn't allow myself to be happy. I have since come to realize that I was wrong."

Anamika whispered, "There is no escape from death."

"No, there isn't," I admitted, "but there is still life."

I found a bag of water hanging from the side of the tent and held it out to her. She took a long drink and wiped her mouth with the back of her hand.

I said quietly, "It dishonors the deaths of our loved ones to shut out happiness. We throw away what we could have been and waste our opportunities. We each have a purpose, a destiny, and to realize it, we must reach beyond what we think we are capable of." My eyes locked with hers intently as I said, "A wise woman once told me that I needed to learn the lesson of the lotus flower: All of our human experience, both the good and the bad, grounds us like the sludge in a river. We may be rooted in pain or suffering but our job is to rise above it, find the sun, and bloom. Only then can you brighten the world for others."

She took another drink of water and snorted. "You sound like my aged grandmother."

"Aged? Speak for yourself. You are much older than me. Trust me."

"Then why should I listen to the wisdom of the young?"

I shrugged. "You'll have to decide for yourself if you're going to take my advice or not."

Anamika replaced the waterskin bag and asked, "Why are you here?"

I put my hand on her shoulder. "We've come to help you."

She gave me a small smile and asked, "And how can one as tiny as you be of any help to me?"

I grinned and said, "Follow me and see."

We wound our way through the ocean of tents, and once again, I marveled at how many people were gathered here. It wasn't just men either. There were several women and even some children in the camp.

Anamika explained, "Before my brother was taken, I sometimes stayed back to run the camp with these women. I was at his side constantly until my brother was captured and fell prey to the demon.

"When we were young, our father taught us together. We were inseparable. Our nursemaids said we were two halves of a bitter melon, especially when our tempers were roused." She smiled at the memory.

"It quickly became obvious that while Sunil was a powerful warrior and natural leader, I was gifted at organizing armies. Though he overpowered me in strength, I often beat him with cunning. Together we were unstoppable. Sunil always respected my opinions, and between us, we won every squabble, were successful in every maneuver, and overcame every obstacle. We were an unbreakable team, until now." She lightly stroked her bruised jaw.

I felt pity and a newfound respect for her as she talked more of her upbringing and her family. She loved her brother, and she was truly devastated that he had been turned against her.

Spotting the copse of trees near a rocky outcropping, I guided her to my secret stockpiled tent. When we got there, I pulled back the tent flap.

"It was set up on the outskirts of camp so I think your men forgot it was here," I explained, hoping she'd accept the flimsy excuse.

Anamika entered the tent and paused. As if stepping inside a temple, she fingered the fabrics in an almost loving way. "It is a gift from the gods," she exclaimed.

I smiled. "Something like that." I let her examine the textiles for a few minutes, and then said, "There's more. Come outside."

I led her to my new soaking tub, and her eyes lit. She dipped her hand into the warm, bubbling water. A look of intense longing swept over her face. "I have not been able to bathe fully for weeks," she said and let out a soft sigh. "The men will be able to relax here."

"I was thinking the same thing," I said. "So what should we do first?"

Anamika's all-business expression took over again. "I will have the goods immediately distributed and inform our medics of the hot spring." She turned to me and said, "Thank you, Kelsey."

"You're welcome."

She smiled at me and, for the first time, I glimpsed the goddess who had been my protector for the last few years.

For the rest of the day, I helped Anamika go from tent to tent to tend to her soldiers. Well after lunchtime, she touched my shoulder, smiled, and offered me half of her small flatbread. My stomach growled in protest, but I felt good staying by her side. There were so many who were wounded and starving. She left me late in the afternoon to see to the returning hunters.

I moved on to the next tent, encouraged the men to drink from the water barrels, and offered sips from a waterskin with a higher concentration of the mermaid's elixir. I also made sure they had enough clothes and bedding to keep them warm. None of the soldiers spoke English, but the wounded tried to communicate in Hindi.

"*Svargaduuta*," one man said as I lowered his head gently to the new pillow that had just been brought in.

I pulled the warm blanket up to his chin and wiped his face with a wet towel. "I'm sorry, I don't know what *svargaduuta* means," I said, "but you should be feeling better soon."

"It means 'angel,'" a warm voice behind me explained.

I flushed and looked up to see Ren standing at the tent opening, watching me. His eyes were filled with emotion, but he looked away when a man on the other side of the tent moaned in pain. Quickly, Ren bent over the man and questioned him before I could get there.

We worked together quietly for a time, and then I asked, "Were you able to bring back meat?"

"There is more than enough to feed everyone tonight. You've been busy, I see," he said.

I nodded and touched a wounded man's hand. "Drink this. You'll feel better soon."

The man managed to swallow a few mouthfuls of water, but most of it dribbled out of his mouth. Satisfied that he'd gotten enough, I spun on my feet and stood wearily.

"Where's Kishan?"

"Anamika has recruited him to distribute clothing and blankets. There will be something of a celebration tonight—a hearty stew for the wounded and roasted venison for the rest of us."

He guided me from the tent and took my elbow as he whispered, "Anamika was right about there being no game. We had to use the Fruit to create the roasts we brought in."

"They'll need more than meat to sustain them. They'll need fruits and vegetables as well."

"I don't know how we'll be able to provide that without suspicion."

I bit my lip. "We'll just have to figure out something."

Ren nodded. "I have discovered that we are roughly between 330 and 320 BC, more likely closer to 320."

"How do you know?"

"Her leader is Chandragupta Maurya. He led the Mauryan Empire that encompassed the lands my father and grandfather ruled, so I have studied him. He is a young man now, which means he has just begun his reign."

303

"Is that a good thing?"

Ren shrugged. "He is far away from here. Anamika is, for all intents and purposes, the leader of this army on his behalf. Her word is thereby considered his law."

"I suppose that's good then."

Ren nodded and lightened the mood. "Shall we attend the celebration?"

"I'd be happy to."

Ren escorted me to his horse waiting outside the tent. His white smile penetrated the looming darkness.

"I don't know how to ride," I protested.

"You rode the Qilin just fine," he answered as he lifted me, and I threw a leg over the horse's back.

"That's because the Qilin was driving," I said, managing to pull myself awkwardly atop the animal.

Ren mounted the horse right behind me, settling an arm around my waist and starting the horse at a walk. Whispering in my ear, he said, "To properly ride a horse, you have to form a bond, feel his strength, the power in his muscles. Pay attention to his gait, his stride. Close your eyes. Can you feel how his body rises and falls? He'll take you wherever you want to go. All you need to do is to learn to work with him and not against him."

I swallowed thickly and tried desperately to remember we were talking about a horse. During Ren's little speech, I had melted back against his chest, and all I could think of doing was taking over the reins and riding into the mountains with Ren.

Clearing my throat noisily after an indulgent moment of fantasy, I sat as far away as I could get from Ren and told him about the sick and injured men I'd helped during the day. Soon it was no longer just a distraction. I was proud of the work I had done and felt a newfound peace in my soul.

Though I was tired, I knew that the gifts of Durga had been created for this very purpose—to end suffering. The thought occurred to me that Mr. Kadam would have been pleased with our efforts and that he would have loved to discuss battle strategy with Anamika.

My warm inner glow and high spirits continued when we arrived at a huge fire in the center of the camp. Due to my Florence Nightingale efforts, the same men who had looked at me with suspicion and outright dislike the day before warmly received me now. They shifted positions and gave me the best seat in the house, on a worn log near the fire.

Ren brought trenchers of food for the both of us then sat at my feet. He translated some of the comments the men made. The general consensus around the camp was that we were good luck charms and that having us there meant there may be hope for winning this war after all.

Our peaceful meal was interrupted by raised voices that grew increasingly louder as they came closer.

"I am not a pack mule!"

"Your mulish behavior labels you as such!"

"I'm only mulish because you are a harpy."

"I do not understand this word, *harpy*."

"A harpy is a hag, a nag, a witch."

"How dare you call me thus?"

"I call it as I see it, Anamika."

"I do not wish to speak to you further. Leave my side, now!"

"That is music to my ears!"

Kishan stormed into the circle where we were eating, shooed Ren aside, and planted himself next to me. His face and neck were flushed, and he watched Anamika with a heated glare as she took a plate of food and perched on a log. She whipped her long hair over her shoulder and across her lap so it wouldn't drag in the dirt. As she dug into her food, she glanced my way, nodded to me and Ren, and then frowned at Kishan.

When dinner was finished, Anamika approached us and said, "Come, Kelsey. It is time to retire." I stood, but Kishan took my arm.

"Goodnight, *bilauta*." He dipped his head and kissed me, but as I was about to end it, he grunted and pulled me tightly against him. His kiss deepened and though I let it happen without struggling, I felt embarrassed by the very public display of an intimate embrace. Kishan finally let me go and smiled happily as I wobbled a few steps away toward Anamika.

She narrowed her eyes at Kishan and then turned to Ren and asked, "Would you mind helping me tomorrow? It is clear that your brother would be happier trailing after his *kitten* and nipping her heels."

Ren nodded his head in agreement. His eyes glittered as he watched us, but before I could say anything, Anamika linked her arm with mine and led me into the direction of her tent.

The next day there was a dappled gray mare left outside my tent with a note from Ren. He and Anamika were spending the day working together, but he arranged for me to have the mare to practice riding.

I found Kishan patiently waiting for me at breakfast. He smiled when I climbed down from my horse on my own and tied her to a post.

"I'll teach you how to tend to her properly," he offered.

I nodded and smiled proudly. "She's beautiful, isn't she?"

"One of Anamika's personal stock."

"Oh." I bit my lip, wondering what Ren had offered to Anamika in exchange for such a wonderful gift.

"What's our task today?" I asked, suddenly moody.

"We're in charge of food. I thought we could pretend we'd been fishing and bring back some edible plants and roots as well."

"Fine."

After a stop at the supply tent to refill the depleted stock, we set off toward the river.

We worked all day, traveling back and forth between the camp and the river, carrying bags of salad greens, roots, and lines of fish. My mind was only able to focus on two things: the ache of my muscles and the jealous green-headed monster that reared whenever I wondered what Ren and Anamika were doing. By the time I'd hauled in the last giant sack of greens and helped Kishan position the poles of freshly caught fish near the cooking fire, I desperately wished we could just drop the pretenses and use the Golden Fruit in front of everyone. I knew we still needed to guard the gift, but using it out in the open would be so much easier.

I waited a while for Ren and Anamika to return, but I was so exhausted from all the heavy lifting that shortly after the evening meal, I returned to my pallet and collapsed upon it.

It was Anamika who woke me.

"See," she whispered by torchlight, "too soft." She giggled quietly and said, "Kelsey, come with me."

"What time is it?" I yawned sleepily.

"It is very early in the morning. Only the guards are awake. Are you hungry?"

She'd brought me a breakfast bowl of cold fish stew. I wasn't quite hungry enough yet to eat fish for breakfast so I set it down. "Maybe later."

Anamika took my hand and pulled me out of the tent. "Come."

We wound our way through the quiet camp. The moonlight peeked through clouds and settled upon the tents, mushrooming up by the thousands at the base of the Himalayan Mountains. The air was crisply cold and as we walked, I wondered what would stand on this spot in my own time.

Will there be a bustling city here? A farm? Herds of animals? Or will there be only the moonlight, the bite of a cold breeze, and the forgotten ghosts of these people?

Steam billowed ahead. When we arrived at the supply tent and the hot spring, I peered into the moonlight.

"Where's the spring?"

"It is here."

Almost gleeful, Anamika brushed her hand across a sheet of draped fabric, parted it, and disappeared behind it.

"What is this?" I asked as I followed her.

"Dhiren did this for me tonight."

"Ren?"

"Yes. He is very kind." Her eyes twinkled in a way that disturbed me. "He noticed how I wished to bathe and set up these curtains for our privacy."

"Our privacy?"

"Yes. We can bathe and relax. Look. He even gave me soaps for my hair."

Anamika stripped and stepped into the bath, letting out a soft sigh. "Why do you hesitate, Kelsey? We won't be left alone long. The men will be up soon."

The desire for cleanliness overwhelmed my feelings of modesty, and I soon joined her in the warm spring. It was divine. Soft cloths had been left on a clean rock, and Anamika handed me the bowl of soaps.

As I scrubbed my scalp until it tingled, Anamika said, "After the morning meal, Dhiren will accompany me to the other camps."

"Other camps? What other camps?"

"Surely you did not believe we are the only ones fighting the demon?"

"Well, I guess I didn't really think about it."

"We are one of five. The peoples of China, Burma, and Persia, and the tribes from east of the great mountains join us in this struggle."

"I see."

She lifted a foot and sucked in a breath as she touched the raw flesh.

"Your feet still hurt?" I questioned.

"Yes."

"Have you ever heard of firefruit? I may have just one left in my bag. It should heal you right up." I rinsed my hair and began scrubbing my arms.

"Your bag of magic, you mean."

I paused to find her watching me. "I don't know what you mean," I said as I dipped the washcloth into the water and then pressed it to my face.

"Don't you think it's time to tell me the truth?"

Sighing, I scooped up some soap and washed my neck. "Look, the truth is . . . very complicated."

"Then tell me what you can. Can you get more food?" she asked.

I nodded.

"Enough to load many pack animals?"

I bit my lip. "Yes. We have an unlimited supply of whatever food you need. But pack animals are not necessary."

She tilted her head as she considered the information. "And what of clothes and blankets?"

"It is the same."

"And medicines?"

When I hedged uncomfortably, she pressed, "Most of my men are healed even from the gravest of wounds. You did this."

After a moment, I nodded again.

She blew out an awestruck breath that drifted away into the air. "Do Dhiren and Kishan also know how to use this power?"

"Yes."

"Then we will stockpile enough supplies here to last for a week and Dhiren will use this power to help the other armies. When we have provided for their needs, we will ask their leaders to meet with us and we will join together to defeat our enemy."

After a quiet moment, I whispered, "All right."

Anamika studied me thoughtfully. "This power must be protected at all costs. We must supply these things secretly. It would be wise to provide the men with a diversion, so they are not aware that the three of you have this power."

I hesitated and asked, "Would the men believe that a benevolent goddess was watching over them?"

She peered at me and though it was dark, I could still make out the flash of green in her eyes. "A goddess? With the power you wield, yes, they would believe in that."

"Then perhaps you would be willing to spread this rumor to the other camps when you meet with them?"

She considered for a moment then answered, "Yes. It is a good plan." She swiped a towel over her shoulders and said uncertainly, "Kelsey, do you care that I take Dhiren from your side? I will leave you with your betrothed, of course."

My jaw tightened, but I shook my head, indicating that it was okay, though inside my heart wrenched.

"Good. I like Dhiren." As she spread the wet towel on the rock, she said quietly, "He fills the empty place at my side."

I found that I suddenly couldn't swallow, and my eyes felt hot.

Anamika left the spring. Briskly, she dried off and began dressing in the dark. "These new clothes Dhiren made for me are of the softest material. I haven't worn anything so fine since I left India."

The empty place. Why do I suddenly feel like my heart has an empty place?

"He made clothes for you too. Here." She placed them on a rock nearby and crouched down before speaking again. "I have a favor to ask."

"What is it?" I replied with a solid lump in my throat.

"I want to ask you to take care of my camp until I return in a week's time. Kishan will help you. I do not find him an easy man like his brother, but you love him so I will tolerate his presence. My men will be instructed to obey your orders."

I nodded weakly and with a whisper of fabric, Anamika disappeared.

Our secrets were unraveling, spiraling out of control, and I felt them spin in my mind and heart. I rose from the spring, dried, and dressed, then made my way back to the main part of camp.

Back in our tent, I found Kishan helping Anamika and Ren prepare for their journey. Ren had a sword strapped to his side. He wore a heavy tunic over a thick pair of leggings. A cloak hung over his arm, which he set down along with a helmet to show me that the Scarf and the Golden Fruit were hidden within his bag. I took the *kamandal* from my neck and tied it around his.

He looked unbelievably handsome—an ancient Indian warrior come to life from the pages of a history book. A twist of fate had given him to me although he should have died centuries before I was born. I had set aside that precious gift, and now I didn't know how to get it back. Regret pierced my heart.

As Kishan made sure they had all they needed, I wished for a waterskin filled with firefruit juice. It materialized on Anamika's table with a shimmer. I handed it to her, saying it was medicine and that she should drink it all.

She clutched my upper arm and said, "Be safe, Kelsey," then Ren placed a cloak identical to his around her shoulders and gallantly tied it into place. She smiled shyly up at him, and the pair slipped through the tent flap and disappeared with Kishan trailing along behind to see them off.

A moment later, I heard the galloping of horse hooves receding. I returned to my bed to hide the backpack and noticed a sheet of parchment placed on top. In Ren's beautiful script, I read Shakespeare's "Sonnet 50" and a note:

SONNET 50
by William Shakespeare

How heavy do I journey on the way,
When what I seek, my weary travel's end,
Doth teach that ease and that repose to say
'Thus far the miles are measured from
    thy friend!'
The beast that bears me, tired with my woe,
Plods dully on, to bear that weight in me,
As if by some instinct the wretch did know
His rider loved not speed, being made
    from thee:
The bloody spur cannot provoke him on
That sometimes anger thrusts into his hide;
Which heavily he answers with a groan,
More sharp to me than spurring to his side;
For that same groan doth put this in
    my mind;
My grief lies onward and my joy behind.

Kelsey,

This parting is difficult for me though I believe it is necessary. Kishan will keep you safe. Our task is nearly complete. Lokesh will be destroyed, and we will be set free to live as men. I should feel exultation at that idea, but instead, my heart grows heavy. I know the distance from you is only temporary, and yet, my mind is burdened with the awareness of a final, impending separation to come. It is nearly impossible for me to leave you now. I don't know how I will bear it when you are gone forever. But still, I will meet my destiny.

—Ren

Stifling a flood of tears, I stepped out of the tent into the crisp air. The sky, beautiful and full of stars an hour before, was now bleak and empty. The light on the horizon was a nauseating shade of pink. Panic rose in me like a fluttering bird, beating its wings against my swollen heart. My stomach twisted. As the men stirred in their tents and the sky brightened, I felt an impending doom.

allies

Ren and Anamika were gone for almost three weeks. We'd been busy while they were gone but not busy enough for me to forget about Ren those eighteen long days. I couldn't help but feel that every day that we were apart, I was losing more of him.

Kishan trained the men to fight as one unified army and helped the wounded regain their strength. Ren and Kishan had built a new tent near the cooking fires and filled it with all kinds of food—fruits, meats, vegetables (both dried and fresh)—and there were barrels and bags of whole grains, beans, and rice.

Now that the men were eating heartily and were stronger, they yearned for something to do other than to perform battle exercises. Kishan's training as a military advisor quickly became apparent, and it was fascinating to watch him change from the modern man I knew back into the Indian prince he once was. As he eased into the role, I could see a different side of him, and I felt a sense of pride and amazement for the man who was my fiancé.

He worked alongside the men every day, taking very little time to tend to his own needs. I often brought him meals and found him doing everything from chopping wood and filling water barrels to patiently teaching young soldiers the correct way to throw a spear. Every time I approached, he gave me a soft smile and kissed my cheek.

In the evenings, he came to my tent and rested his head wearily in my lap. He'd tell me about his day as I stroked his hair and then as the camp settled for the night, he'd kiss me tenderly before heading to his own tent.

The men were more than willing to follow his direction, and he sent several groups out to hunt to supplement our food supply or out on scouting parties to assess the whereabouts of Lokesh and his army. Kishan had me and some of the women practicing drills also. He said if Lokesh was to be defeated by a woman, then it made sense to teach some of the women at least the rudimentary basics of battle.

I stood alongside old grandmothers and young wives as Kishan ran us through drills to strengthen our muscles and to train us in the use of knives and small swords. All the women remarked that I was such a lucky girl to have someone like Kishan as my fiancé, and the few unmarried women watched him covetously and flirted shamelessly as he patiently guided them in the use of light hand weapons.

I was happy being with Kishan and working with him. Exhaustion at the end of each day made me seek my tent at nightfall. Although I could barely keep my eyes open, I still scanned the horizon continually, watching for Ren and Anamika's return.

When Anamika's group of warriors finally rode into camp one evening, we all cheered and gave them heroes' welcomes. The clattering sound of their armor and their sheer size alone was intimidating. There was a call for water and for someone to take the horses. I heard Kishan bark out instructions. The sounds of many languages floated upon the air. I scanned the group seeking just one man, the one with the piercing blue eyes.

Without thinking, I cast aside my bow and wove through the stamping horses. Kishan shouted my name, but I continued on and ducked between armored bodies until I came upon Ren at last.

Ren turned and saw me. He still held the reins of his horse in one hand.

Emotions running wild, all I managed to say with a tight voice was, "I missed you."

He took a step toward me and scooped me into his arms. Though he wore plates of armor on his chest and shoulders, he held me tightly against him and pressed his cheek to mine. "I missed you too, *iadala.*"

The Chinese warrior standing behind him clapped Ren on the shoulder and made a few rather loud comments in either Mandarin or Cantonese. Ren set me down, and I turned to find several people staring at us. Kishan had pursued me through the crowd, his sword at the ready, until he saw me with Ren. Though his grip on his sword relaxed, his muscles remained tensed and his eyes were like hard flint. Stonily, he stared at Ren.

Anamika came up behind Kishan; her piercing gaze studied each of us in turn, her face had an unreadable expression. The crowd stilled and became uncomfortably silent as they watched the four of us. Anamika called out a command and then turned away, heading for her tent.

The returning soldiers started moving again but looked at me over their shoulders quizzically.

After handing off his horse to a waiting soldier, Ren gave me a brief smile and squeezed my arm before turning away. He quickly instructed men to set up accommodations and provide meals for the guests. Many of Anamika's soldiers, though they treated Ren deferentially, paused at his commands and explained that Kishan had already begun organizing the new arrivals. Ren accompanied the Chinese warrior to the cooking fire in the center of camp.

I looked for Kishan, but he had vanished. Figuring he was as busy as Ren, I ducked into the tent I shared with Anamika and came upon her shedding her armor. She kept her back to me.

"I'm glad to see you've returned safely," I said.

She didn't respond.

"Are you hungry?"

The goddess-like warrior shook her head and removed her boots, replacing them with softer, more comfortable slippers.

"I see your feet have healed. So the juice worked?"

She finally turned to me, and her tight expression softened a bit. "Yes, my feet are healed. Thank you."

"I'm just glad you're back." I smiled.

"Yes, I can see that." She let out a sigh and stood. "How are my men?"

"They are good. Almost all of them are ready for battle. Kishan has been training them—and the women as well."

Anamika raised an eyebrow. "He has trained the women?"

I shrugged. "He believes a woman should know how to defend herself."

She puzzled over this for a moment before nodding and stepping to the tent flap. As she parted it to go, she turned her head. "Our guests are beginning to believe that we are being helped by a goddess, and a few of them have the notion that the goddess is personified in me."

I nodded cautiously.

"They also believe that Dhiren is my consort," she stated frankly. "It might be wise to allow them to continue in this belief, at least until the war is over."

"I . . . I understand," I whispered thickly as she exited.

I stood there wondering if being a consort meant what I thought it meant or if there was some back-in-time different meaning of the word.

Consort.

The term crossed my tongue roughly. It was an ugly word. In fact, I didn't think I'd ever heard a word I detested more.

"Ren is her *consort*," I whispered.

I wandered toward the center of camp. There was a great deal of noise coming from the cooking area. Kishan stood on the outskirts with arms folded across his chest and a frown on his face. The warriors had refreshed themselves and were emerging from the food tent as Ren spoke with them enthusiastically. The new warriors hung on his every word and the men of the camp, though they nodded in respect to Kishan as they passed, flocked around the "goddess" and her new "companion."

I noticed Anamika stood next to Ren and often deferred to him when they were asked questions.

"What's going on?" I asked Kishan.

His eyes glittered as he watched Ren and Anamika. "My brother is stealing the show, as usual. Warriors I trained for two weeks now turn to him, Anamika fawns over him, and even my own fiancée can't keep her hands off of him."

"You're jealous."

Kishan finally turned to me. "Of course I'm jealous."

I looked into his golden eyes and apologized. "I'm sorry, Kishan. It's me you should be mad at. I missed Ren, but it wasn't appropriate for me to seek him out like that."

Kishan let out a deep sigh, took my hands, and kissed them one by one. "I'm overreacting. Forgive me."

"If you'll forgive me."

"Always."

He put his arm around my shoulders, and we stood there watching the spectacle for a moment before I asked, "Kishan, what exactly does it mean to be a consort? Is it like a bosom companion? That sort of thing?"

"Do you mean in our time or now?"

"Now."

"It means life companion. Usually a consort is the spouse of a ruling monarch. Why do you ask?"

A lump formed in my throat, and my eyes burned.

"It means marriage?" I stammered.

"It could mean betrothed as well." Kishan placed a hand on my shoulders and turned me to face him. "What's wrong, Kelsey?"

"Anamika told me that Ren is to act as her consort until the war is over."

"I see."

Kishan lifted his head and quietly studied Anamika and Ren as they mingled with the crowd.

Ineffectually trying to push away the horrible emotions I was feeling, I said, "I don't want to put any of us in a dangerous position because I can't seem to follow the proper rules of etiquette for this time. You are my fiancé and Ren is . . . hers. I should have stayed by your side."

Kishan nodded distractedly.

As I linked my arm with Kishan's, I wondered if this consort thing was truly temporary or if Ren had feelings for Anamika. *In his letter, he mentioned a parting. Did he intend to stay here and really become Anamika's consort? It sure didn't look like Anamika would object to the idea. I still love Ren. The Phoenix made me acknowledge that. Should I tell him or leave it alone? What if he rejects me and chooses Anamika? Acknowledging I loved him didn't necessarily mean I'd get him back. She is beautiful. Why would Ren choose me when he could have a goddess? He could be a king, a god standing by her side.*

I bit back a quiet sob and acknowledged for the first time that Ren's destiny might not match with mine. I might not get to keep him in my life at all, even as a friend.

I am going to lose him . . . forever. And what about Kishan? He had promised to always forgive me and he would learn to live with it if I should choose another. If I told him that I'm still in love with Ren, what would he do? Is that much forgiveness even possible? Would he hate me forever? Return to the jungle to live a life of loneliness and isolation?

In that moment, I knew it didn't matter. It made no difference if Ren decided to be with Anamika or if Kishan ever forgave me. They both needed to know everything. They both needed to be aware of how I felt. I would have to get each of them alone and share what was in my heart. If one or both of them chose to leave me, then I'd just have to deal with it. I couldn't continue to run away from heartache. I owed them that much. Phet was right when he said both men were good choices. Both of them were noble and brave, handsome and kind, and they deserved more than I had given them.

Kishan stayed by me as I watched the proceedings and told me what everyone was saying. I squeezed his arm, grateful for the good man that he was.

After some political posturing, Anamika asked everyone to gather for a banquet. Tables were brought and with the flourish of her hand, Anamika used the power of the Scarf (which was tied around her wrist) to create the finest of cloths to lay upon them. The threads of the Scarf wove its magic, and the warriors and Anamika's men gasped in wonder.

I made a small sound of protest and took a step forward, but Kishan held me back.

"What's done is done, Kelsey. Ren has obviously instructed her in the use of Durga's gifts."

Anamika filled the table with plates of food, and the men sitting at the banquet cheered as she moved from place to place, filling cups and trenchers with special treats from each man's homeland. She then took her place at the head of the table with Ren sitting at her side. He squeezed her hand, and at the same moment, I felt as if something black had squeezed my heart.

A place was made for me and Kishan, and after he pulled out my chair, I sat stiffly. I smiled when someone offered me food and accepted it gratefully, but everything I tasted turned to ash in my mouth, and no amount of drink could wet my dry throat.

I watched Ren and Anamika together and imagined him as her king. The prick of bitter jealousy tore through my heart—and not only because of Ren. I knew that the Divine Scarf and the Golden Fruit were for Durga and that Anamika was or would become Durga, but it was hard letting those gifts go. To give over that kind of power and be left with nothing was difficult.

Kishan had been envious of Ren getting the glory, and here I was feeling the same way about Anamika. I sat at dinner telling myself over and over that the Scarf and the Golden Fruit belonged to her, not to me. I fingered the Pearl Necklace at my throat and wondered if there was a way I could at least keep that gift to myself.

I'd fought hard for them, I rationalized. I had almost been killed many times. And all Anamika had to do was become a beautiful goddess and take the man I love as her consort. I thought about the Kappa bite, the monkeys, the giant shark, the Kraken, and the Stymphalian birds. Then there was Lokesh himself. *It isn't fair.*

I knew it was wrong, but I couldn't help feeling cheated sitting at the other end of the table. It was like I'd been summarily dismissed. Used. My perspective of the goddess shifted. As I mulled it over in my mind, I thought back to all of our meetings in the temples. When she'd promised to protect Ren, it wasn't for me at all, my resentful heart shouted. It was for her! She made him forget me. *Me!* If I'd only known that her plan was to take him for herself, I would have stayed in Oregon and let her go after her own gifts.

"Learn the lesson of the lotus flower," she'd said. Well, if I was a lotus flower, then she had essentially plucked me from the water and ground me into the dirt under her feet.

My eyes were captured by a flash of gold from Kishan's tunic. Durga's brooch. I sighed and remembered that she didn't have everything. I still had my golden bow and arrows, the Fire Amulet, the Pearl Necklace, and Fanindra.

I repeated over and over as I pushed the food around my plate, "This is why we're here. This is why we're here."

The glorious goddess and her power washed over me from the other side of the table like heavy waves, leaving me feeling as pale and as dank as rotten seaweed.

That's what I am, I mused darkly. *I'm as rotten on the outside as I am on the inside. I'm a power-hungry girl from the future who craves the love of two brothers and wants to keep all the magic too.* There was nothing I wanted more at that moment than to cheat Anamika of her destiny and take it all for myself.

Then she touched Ren and whispered something into his ear.

Ren bowed his head as they conversed quietly, intimately, together, and I realized that there was something else I wanted more than the Pearl Necklace, more than the Golden Fruit and the Divine Scarf. More than Durga's destiny, Fanindra, and more than the Fire Amulet.

I wanted *Ren*.

The force of the emotion came on like a hurricane. I'd been jealous before when Ren had danced with Nilima and all of the girls at the beach party, but even then, a part of me knew that it wasn't my Ren doing those things. That Ren had lost his memory of me. Now I was faced with the sight of a man who was very much *my* Ren being close to another woman. I couldn't stand it. I felt like I was being torn into two. My world was unraveling even faster than the Scarf could.

I sank my head into my hands and stared at the uneaten food on my plate. The scent of cinnamon and saffron wafted to my nose. Kishan asked if I was feeling well, and when I shook my head, he rose and led me back to my tent.

Kishan stayed for a while, but I told him I needed to be alone to think. I rubbed a pearl on the Necklace between my fingers and realized I'd been doing that since dinner started. Just because I could, I filled a cup with water using the Pearl Necklace. Then, in a vengeful mood, I soaked all of Anamika's clothes and filled her boots with water. Next, I created fog and made it rain on her bed. After her side of the tent was dripping, I got rid of all the water. I was surprised and slightly disappointed that her cot and her boots were completely dry.

When Anamika finally entered the tent several hours later and sank into a chair across from me, I was playing with my cup of water, draining and refilling it over and over using the Pearl Necklace.

Anamika watched me for a time and asked what I was doing.

"Wouldn't you like to know?"

I'd tried to muster a snarky, sarcastic tone, but it came off as sad and pathetic.

"What is wrong with you?" she asked. "Are you ill?"

"Maybe. What if I was?"

"Bah, you are not sick, except perhaps in the head."

I rose and pointed my finger into her face angrily. "If anyone here has brain damage it's you. Why were you showing off your powers to those men? Did you need some more followers? Is that it? What's wrong? Ren isn't enough for you anymore?"

She folded her arms and stared at me. "I thought the point was for me to impersonate a goddess. That is difficult to do without showing them powers." She angled her head. "This is not really about the Fruit or the Scarf, is it?"

"Partially," I grumbled moodily.

"You are the one who told me to do this, Kelsey. I didn't ask to take on this role."

I pointed out glumly, "And yet you fill it so well, don't you?"

She sighed. "Is this about Dhiren?"

I froze and stammered, "Why do you think that?"

She considered my question. "It is natural to be concerned for your brother. You wish him to be happy. If my brother brought home a woman, it would be difficult to see her take my place at his side."

"Ren is *not* my brother."

"You are betrothed to Kishan, and Ren obviously holds you in great esteem. You are close. He is like a brother to you, and you want to see to his welfare."

"I—"

I couldn't even respond to what she was saying.

Anamika put her hands over mine. "I do not know if Dhiren wishes to remain my consort after we kill the demon, but I will disclose to you that I hope he does." Her expression brightened. "I find him to be thoughtful and kind, and he has the mind of a great warrior and politician."

Her eyes twinkled. "I also find him to be very attractive. I would be honored to call you a sister. A *little* sister perhaps, but a sister in spirit, nonetheless. I will try to make him happy, Kelsey. I give you my oath." She squeezed my hands and stood. "There are many things that need doing tomorrow. I suggest you get some sleep."

I sat mutely as she prepared for bed and was still sitting when she looked at me, shrugged, and then blew out her lamp and climbed onto her dry mattress. I don't know how long I sat there, but it felt like time had stopped, and I was in a numbed, blackened hell.

Finally climbing into bed, I tucked my hand under my cheek and didn't realize I was crying until I felt a tear drip between my fingers. I fell asleep repeating the same words over and over in my mind: "She'll make him happy."

Anamika was gone when I awoke the next day. I reached behind my pillow for my backpack with the hidden weapons and Ren's poem. I wanted to read it again with new eyes to see if he was really saying good-bye to me. But the backpack was missing. I scrambled to my feet and quickly searched the tent.

After dressing, I headed to the campfire to see if I could find Ren or Kishan or even Anamika, but the cook told me that Ren and Anamika had eaten before dawn and had headed to the forest. Kishan was seeing to the needs of the visiting soldiers.

I finally found Kishan in the middle of a conference with the warriors. When he spied me at the tent flap, he invited me in and introduced me in several languages. The men nodded respectfully.

Kishan explained, "We are discussing battle strategy, and I am their translator. Each leader was just getting ready to discuss what they've seen in the war so far and will talk about the assets they will bring to the alliance. We are to keep a record of everything."

I nodded. "Okay, but our bag is missing. Do you know where it is?"

"Yes, Ren and Anamika are practicing with the weapons."

"Fanindra too?"

"Fanindra too. We need to continue now, Kells. Will you stay and take notes?"

My gut twisted at the thought of all my weapons being handed over without Ren even consulting me, and my eyes burned hotly.

I replied darkly, "Why not? Apparently I'm not needed elsewhere."

Kishan grunted, oblivious to my inner turmoil, and acknowledged the first leader, General Xi-Wong.

The Chinese warrior began speaking. Even without his battle armor, he was impressive. Kishan translated his words into two other languages while two other men also listened and translated for their leaders. He handed me a tablet, a pot of some potent-smelling ink, and a sharpened stick so I could keep track of the statistics. Somehow, he managed to translate for them and then feed me the highlights while waiting for the other men to finish interpreting. I struggled at first with the old-fashioned pen but finally figured out how to make it work and jotted on the paper.

General Xi-Wong didn't seem as war-weary as the others. His clothing was well cared for, and he had a beautiful yellow silk scarf wrapped around his neck. It made me think of Lady Silkworm.

I noted that General Xi-Wong's army uses iron weapons, and his battle philosophy was called the Hundred Schools of Thought. Of all the army leaders, his group was contributing the most men and weapons—including chariots, infantry, spearmen, archers, and dagger-axes (long spears with a blade on one end)—but he had also lost the most men to the demon, more than a hundred thousand.

General Xi-Wong said that he first learned of the demon when he began recruiting in China. Whole gangs of criminals went missing and then entire towns would simply disappear. Multiple cities seemed to be swallowed up by the earth, and even the women and children were taken. A few survivors reported that a sorcerer had come and enslaved all the people. Later, men spoke of a monster, a half man and half bull, that had terrorized the countryside.

I spilled some ink on the corner of the page and blotted it away as Kishan and General Xi-Wong finished and introduced Jangbu, a Tibetan, or someone from the area I thought of as Tibet.

Jangbu preferred to be called Tashi, and his army was completely made of volunteers recruited from various tribes living in that region. They specialized in archery and guerilla warfare. Jangbu's boots, fur, vest, and hat were edged with shaggy brown fur. I briefly wondered if he was wearing an ancestor of the brown bear Kishan and I had faced on Mount Everest.

Zeyar and Rithisak were from what would be the modern countries of Thailand, Myanmar/Burma, and Cambodia if they were all combined. They'd journeyed here from the Mon capital of Thaton—a port on the

Andaman Sea. I noticed worn holes in their boots and that the warriors were thin. If the leaders of the armies were starving, then I imagined their men were far worse. I made a side note to have Kishan ask if they needed more food.

According to Zeyar and Rithisak, their greatest strength was their defense. They built strongholds and advanced only when they recognized an opportunity and could achieve it with minimal loss. Interestingly, they claimed to be skilled in the use of fire as a weapon, had great faith in Anamika, who they thought was a goddess, and they also believed the demon was raising the dead to fight again. They seemed very frightened.

Kishan listened to the last group who spoke and then announced, "This is General Amphimachus, who was a Parthian and now serves under his king called Alexander."

My hand froze. "As in Alexander the *Great*?" I whispered.

Kishan translated my question into Greek before I could stop him. The general leaned forward and stared at me in a very uncomfortable way before Kishan added, "He *is* a wise and *great* leader."

I squeaked at the man's direct gaze, slouched down, and began scratching furiously with my writing utensil. The general introduced his men as well: Leonnatus, Demetrius, Stasandor, and Eumenes.

"We have not heard of the lands you come from. That is, except India, of course," he said with a politician's smile. "My king will be . . . pleased to learn more of your cities."

Under my breath, I mumbled, "I bet he would be."

The general went on, "Perhaps when this battle is over we can speak of establishing trade?"

The men from Tibet and Myanmar seemed interested in this offer but not General Xi-Wong.

I kept my eyes down and scribbled furiously. I had to tell Kishan what I knew. Several facts that I'd memorized in college and high school sprung to mind, and I was alarmed that the Macedonian Empire might become interested in Asia. As far as I knew, Alexander the Great never conquered anything beyond the Himalayas. We could be changing the course of history by being here, and I'd seen way too many *Star Trek* time-travel episodes to be fooled into believing that was a good thing.

I took notes dutifully and was shocked at the numbers and resources the various battle leaders provided. What worried me the most about working with them was the interest they had in Anamika. General Amphimachus seemed to believe that a goddess with her power needed to be seated on the throne next to Alexander. I grunted and perused my notes.

Amphimachus spoke of his assets. He had deadly Persian chariots, catapults, and panoplies, and he said that his men could fight in heavily armored phalanxes with spears, pikes, and *sarrisas*. Continuing to brag, he recounted how he lost an eye in the Battle of the Persian Gate. As a reward for his bravery, he was granted property and a foal sired by Alexander's famous horse, Bucephalus. I couldn't help but be fascinated. He smiled and lifted his patch to show me the gaping hole where his eye used to be. I shuddered and shifted closer to Kishan while Amphimachus delighted in my discomfort.

Finally, it was Kishan's turn to talk. He shared his philosophy of battle, some I recognized from the training Mr. Kadam had given us, and some was new to me. Anamika's numbers surprised me. He spoke of forty thousand horsemen, one hundred thousand footmen, over one thousand chariots, and two thousand battle elephants. From what I'd seen, Anamika didn't have anywhere near that number of men. Her army had almost been annihilated. I wondered if it was standard wartime practice to exaggerate numbers.

I did some quick calculations. According to what the leaders had said, combined they had fifteen thousand archers, two hundred fifty thousand cavalry, almost one hundred fifty thousand infantry, a thousand chariots, fifty catapults, and two thousand elephants. We were just shy of a half-million soldiers.

Plans were then made to have each leader return to his camp in a week and march his army to the base of Mount Kailash, which is where Lokesh had reportedly taken up residence. In the meantime, everyone was to enjoy the hospitality of the goddess and witness firsthand the skills of Anamika's soldiers.

As the leaders of many nations stood, Kishan thanked everyone for his contributions and said, "Each of you has experienced great losses, but I feel that together we will achieve victory and rid our lands of this demon."

He clapped General Xi-Wong on the shoulder. "My friends, we will be as fast as the wind, as silent as a forest, as ferocious as a fire, and as immovable as the mountain itself."

General Amphimachus was the last to leave. He leered at me when Kishan was distracted. One of his men fastened a black cape made of raven feathers around the general's shoulders before he exited with a flourish.

As they made their way to their tents, I complimented Kishan. "You were amazing. I think they were all impressed."

Kishan grinned. "I borrowed that speech from one of my old martial arts instructors. Technically, the daimyo in Japan who came up with the concept of *Fūrinkazan*, or wind, forest, fire, and mountain, won't be alive for another century."

I wrung my hands nervously. "Well, maybe you were meant to be the ancient source that inspired him."

He gently pried my hands apart and held them in his own. "What's wrong, Kelsey?"

Sighing softly, I said, "I know that we were destined to do this, to defeat Mahishasur or whatever Lokesh is calling himself these days. I just want to be careful that we're not rewriting history. I mean, what if

Alexander the Great now decides to go off and conquer China? What if we mess up our future so badly that we can't even go home?"

Kishan pressed his lips to my fingers and studied me with his warm golden eyes. "Would it be so bad if we can't?" he asked.

"What do you mean?"

"I mean other than Nilima and missing some of your friends, could you," he paused, "learn to be happy living here, with me, in the past?"

"I . . . I suppose I could learn to live without modern day comforts as long as you and Ren were here."

He let go of my hands, took hold of my shoulders, and smiled. "There's a part of me that feels at home here, Kells. Don't get me wrong. If you were in the future, I'd move mountains to get there, but as long as you're at my side, I feel . . . well, I want for nothing. There's nothing else I need in the universe except you."

Kishan kissed me softly before he led me off in search of lunch. I sighed, knowing that there was something else in the universe I needed. It wasn't really appropriate given the circumstances, but the something else I needed was . . . Ren.

After lunch, I went in search of him. Kishan had said that he was showing Anamika how to use all of our weapons. I touched the Pearl Necklace and swallowed the guilt I felt at keeping it to myself.

It took a while because our cell phone tracking devices no longer worked, but I finally found a soldier who told me of a clearing where Ren and Anamika might be practicing. As I wound my way through the trees, I heard the sounds of quiet murmuring ahead.

"I don't know how I would have done all this without you. Surely the gods sent you into my life."

"Something like that."

"Then my hope," the female voice responded softly, "is to never give you cause to leave."

I skirted a prickly bush and stopped dead in my tracks. Ren and Anamika stood entwined. She was enrobed as the goddess Durga in a gown of royal blue and had all eight of her arms. Each set of them were wrapped around Ren. Golden weapons lay at their feet except for Fanindra, who was coiled on the ground. She was awake and watching Ren and Anamika as they embraced.

For a brief moment, I stood there numb but then the shock pierced me. Tears blurred my vision. The salty liquid trembled there, threatening to spill over my lashes. Ren, still holding Durga, opened his blue eyes and saw me. I gasped softly as I recognized for the first time a sort of resigned distance in his glance. I couldn't even look at Durga, for that's who she was when she turned.

As the tears spilled onto my cheeks, I dashed them away angrily and looked down at the ground. Fanindra turned her head toward me and tasted the air with her tongue.

"Fanindra?" I whispered and held out my hand toward her.

The golden snake considered me for a few seconds and then unwound her body and began moving. Mistakenly, I thought she was heading toward me, but instead she made her way to the goddess, who leaned down and lifted the snake into position on her arm. As Fanindra wound her body around the dainty limb, something inside me snapped.

I felt utterly betrayed. Not even Fanindra wanted anything to do with me anymore.

Messily, I dashed my hand over my eyes, yanked the precious Pearl Necklace from my throat, and threw it at the goddess's feet. I could feel Ren's gaze, but I refused to look at him.

As the new Durga picked up the Necklace, I spat, "You forgot something."

Then I turned on my heels and fled back to camp.

27

war

Anamika called out to me, but I ignored her and ran back to my tent. *Her* tent. Scanning my sleeping area, I realized that there was nothing there that belonged to me. Ren had the backpack. All I owned in the world now were the clothes on my back. My pulse pounded as my vision turned red. I clutched the amulet hanging around my neck and realized that I wanted to burn something. I swallowed thickly, tamping down my inner fire. Destruction might ease the pain, but causing damage would undermine what we were doing and I knew it would only be a temporary fix.

Closing my eyes and pressing my fists against them, I whispered, "Mr. Kadam, if only you were here."

Kishan found me an hour later after a passing soldier tipped him off that he had seen me near the supply tent. I had confiscated the tent and attempted to set it up myself. Failing that, I took the heavy canvas, climbed a tree, and made a makeshift shelter. Stubbornly, I sat inside with my back against the trunk, cross legged, my chin resting on my fists.

Kishan sat down and watched me for a full minute before saying anything.

"What are you trying to do, Kelsey?"

"Get some distance," was my abrupt reply.

"From me?" he asked softly.

"From . . . everything," I mumbled.

Kishan tugged gently on my tent wall. "The canvas is heavy. I'm surprised you got it up in the tree by yourself."

I grunted, "Hell hath no fury . . ."

Kishan sat with me for a while, but I refused to talk, and he finally gave up. Confused and hurt by my silence, he prepared to leave and said quietly, "If you would like your own tent away from all of us, I will arrange it, but I won't leave you unprotected. I will assign soldiers to set one up for you in the midst of those I trust. Will that be agreeable?"

Not being able to meet his eyes, I nodded and he disappeared. A short time later, a man escorted me to a tent of my own, complete with my own pitcher of water, blankets, and wash basin.

I was left to myself for the rest of the week even though it appeared that either Ren or Kishan or both were checking upon me through the bodyguards who had been assigned to watch over me. I still trained with the women every day, but Kishan had selected a replacement instructor as he was spending much of his time with the other military leaders.

Sometimes I passed the training grounds and heard the clash of swords or the cheering of soldiers, and I skirted the area without investigating. I just couldn't bring myself to see Ren and Anamika together or to see her with all of *my* golden weapons. I longed for my bow and arrow, though I acknowledged that I mostly wanted to sink a golden arrow into Ren's unfaithful heart.

After a week had gone by, the leaders of the other camps left and preparations were made to relocate Anamika's camp. When it was time to move, my personal bodyguards packed my tent with a small bag of supplies and helped me onto my beautiful dapple-gray horse with its beautiful black mane and nose.

My mare stamped in anticipation, and the breath from her nostrils rose into the air in icy puffs. Specks of snow swirled in the early morning sky but didn't stick to the ground. Someone wrapped a cloak lined with soft fur around my shoulders. The soldiers treated me like a queen, though I felt more like a cast-off woman. I lifted the fur-lined hood over my hair and nodded that I was ready.

We rode northeast for two days and struck camp at the edge of Lake Rakshastal. The weather was cold but not yet freezing. I figured that for the Himalayas this must be early fall. I used my fire power to warm the air around me and my group of bodyguards, and they figured out pretty quickly that the closer they stayed by my side the more comfortable they were.

It wasn't long after we camped that we saw more soldiers on the horizon. I recognized the flag of General Xi-Wong's army on our left and the colors of General Amphimachus's on the right. Runners ran back and forth between the generals all day, and though I felt I was just an afterthought to Ren and Kishan and that it was probably best to stay out of the way and let the goddess do her thing, I couldn't help but be worried for them.

A day later, when I awoke, the camp was unusually silent. I felt a tug at my heart, knowing they were gone. I'd developed a rudimentary sign language with the guard at my tent door, and he confirmed my suspicions and handed me two folded papers. I sank onto a thick rug and opened the first one. It was from Kishan.

We are heading into battle today, Kelsey. The three of us decided that it would be best if you stayed behind. Having you in the war would only be a distraction for us, and we want this fight to be over as soon as possible. Please

understand that we only wish to keep you safe. Last week,
I instructed your guards to bring you to me the instant
you asked for me, but you never came. I love you, Kelsey. I
wish I knew what we were fighting about.

—Kishan

I set the letter aside and opened the second. It was from Ren. Inside
the folded paper was a ring. Sunlight hit the bright blue sapphire, and
it twinkled with an even deeper blue than Ren's eyes. The princess-cut
sapphire was surrounded by round diamonds and sat atop what looked
like two silver bands woven together with another diamond set at each
loop. The ring was breathtaking.

Kelsey,
I've been holding onto this ring for many
months. I bartered with the golden dragon for
it when we were in his realm. It was once worn
by a princess and when I saw it, I wanted it
for you. I'd intended to give it to you when
our task was complete and the time was right
to ask for your hand. Now I know that the
right time has come and gone. I regret many
things that have happened but I'll never
regret loving you. Please keep it. Soldiers use

the stars in the heavens to guide them safely home. You have been and forever will be my guiding star. Each time I look to the heavens, I will think of you.

—Ren

I slid the ring onto my finger next to Kishan's and let the facets of Kishan's ruby and Ren's sapphire catch the light for a moment. Then I closed my fist. Stepping outside the tent, I motioned for the guard to bring my horse. He shook his head vehemently. I persisted, but he still refused until I opened my palm and allowed the energy of the amulet to fill me. I produced a fireball that crackled with sparks and gave off enough heat to singe his eyebrows if he got too close.

His mouth fell open, and he stumbled back, calling for my horse. With a small, triumphant smile, I closed my hand, and the fireball disappeared in a burst of flame. By the time I'd yanked on my boots and donned the wide-legged pants and tunic in the style of the Chinese warriors that I'd taken from the supply tent, the horse was ready, as were my bodyguards. I set my sights on Mount Kailash and allowed my heart to guide me.

When we neared the edge of the army, the men surrounded me and motioned to a rise that overlooked the valley. I kneed my mare, turning her head toward the slope, and gasped at what I saw when we had reached the edge.

The valley was filled with soldiers standing in perfect formations. My guards gripped the handles of their long, curved swords as they leaned forward and discussed the upcoming fight. Catapults were set between the columns of men. I could hear the creak of saddles, the scrape of metal on metal, and the trumpeting of battle elephants.

As the columns marched into position, drums kept time. Couriers rushed from group to group on horseback, passing information along the front lines, and birds flew through the air. Some were carrion anticipating their next meal, but some were messenger birds—falcons or hawks trained to fly to the man carrying the commander's standard. Flag bearers clutching different colored pennants moved into position, ready to relay the General's orders to distant officers.

The fast Persian chariots and cavalry filled the north side of the valley while the remaining battle elephants of Anamika's army flanked by General Xi-Wong's infantry were on the south side. Somewhere in the middle were the combined soldiers of the Tibetan tribes and the Myanmar warriors. I couldn't distinguish Ren, Kishan, or Anamika, but I assumed they were near the front lines.

When all was ready, the noises quieted, and there was a palpable tension in the air. At first, I saw nothing and wondered if anyone would come to fight a combined army of this size, but then I saw it. Fog rolled down the mountain in waves so thick, it obscured the entire peak.

It crept along the ground with ominous pulpy fingers, as if the fog itself was tearing up the very earth and gnashing its teeth in anticipation of the battle ahead. When the mists began to clear, dark forms became visible, and our combined armies shuffled noisily in response. What lay ahead of our forces was horrible to behold.

Hunched forms—not human, not animal, and some, not even living—stood ready to obey their master. They dug at the earth with deformed claws. They snarled, howling and wheezing heavily. Some held weapons and spears like infantry, some crouched on all fours and paced restlessly like wild cats, And others—half horse, half men-like centaurs—tore at the ground with thick hooves.

One man moved to the forefront and seemed to be in charge. He shouted a command, and the demons next to him wobbled forward awkwardly and lifted their limbs to reveal wings. The demon bird-men took to the sky and called out to ranks and ranks of enemy soldiers. They veered out over our armies and screeched horribly. A volley of arrows chased them back to their side.

Lokesh was nowhere to be seen, but the soldiers next to me pointed at the leader of his army. It was Sunil, Anamika's brother. The deep unearthly sound of a horn shook the valley, and at that signal, the demon army began bellowing a war chant. They pounded the ground, roared, screeched, and hollered in unison. The cacophony resonated like a hellish nightmare.

Our armies struck the first blow. Catapults launched heavy stones that crushed dozens of demon creatures. Stones hit the mountain and chunks of rock broke off and plummeted, knocking over many of the creatures. But even with broken limbs and wings, they soon stood again, waiting for their master's signal to attack.

While the siege engines worked, a signal was given, and the demon army abruptly ceased their clamoring. Lokesh's army surged forward. Thousands of our archers sent a hailstorm of arrows into the sky. Most of them met their marks, but the creatures didn't even register pain. They simply yanked out the arrows, dropped them to the ground, and ran toward our armies.

Anamika's army rushed to meet them, and the two opposing forces crashed together like two tidal waves. The enemies swarmed over one another like angry hornets over a disturbed nest. The clash of metal and the cries of men in pain filled my ears. More men poured into the fight, running in formation and scattering as they fought the beasts of Lokesh. Then the Chinese cavalry thundered in and cut a hole through the center of the demon army, but were set upon by eagle-like creatures that swooped from the sky and ripped at their backs with sharp talons.

Next to fight was a group of canine zombies, resembling dogs, wolves, hyenas, and jackals. Long, thin muzzles hid sharp, deadly teeth. Loping on all fours, they moved in packs and took down our chariots.

The battle elephants charged, and the sight and sound of thousands of elephants plunging into war was so extraordinary that I couldn't look away. With protective armor deflecting spears and arrows, the six-ton animals thundered from our reserve lines to the front and trampled over anything that couldn't get out of the way fast enough.

Sweeping their heavy heads back and forth, the battle elephants pressed the demon army back, cornering them against the mountain as the archers riding in the towering howdahs kept the demons at bay. In retaliation, Sunil sent Lokesh's bird messengers into the sky. They shrieked out commands to the cat-like demons who managed to avoid the spiked cuffs and swords attached to the elephants' tusks and leapt onto their backs. The big animals bellowed loudly in pain as the cats' claws tore through their leathery skin before the elephants trumpeted their death throughout the valley.

One elephant shook itself violently to dislodge the destructive hitchhikers but caused the carriage on top to jar loose. The heavy platform fell and was crushed under the feet of the frightened animal. Cat demons quickly dispatched the men still alive while others leapt onto the elephant's back. The animal trumpeted loudly and twisted, rearing up onto its hind legs. Then it fell heavily with a boom that echoed across the valley, and demons swarmed over the creature.

Another elephant under attack swerved into a catapult that broke into pieces. Some men fell upon the swords attached to its tusks and were killed instantly. Others fell into the waiting arms of demons. The battle elephant trumpeted in fear before it was also taken down.

I saw the Mon banner of Rithisak head through the middle of the fight toward Sunil. His soldiers were met by huge demons with wide horns and heavy spiked maces. The demons raced forward with their heads down and gored several men with a flick of their powerful necks before finding another target. In closer quarters they swung the mace, striking several men at once who blew back into their fellow soldiers and crumpled to the ground.

Another segment of Lokesh's army was filled with bug demons. A horde of them scurried over the dead, dispatching those that might still be alive with stingers, claws, pinchers, and scorpion-like tails.

The fighting continued, and a wall of bodies piled up between the two armies. We were losing.

Where is Anamika?

I scanned the field and finally saw her as the goddess Durga. Strangely, she was not wearing her blue dress, and she only had one set of arms. She was using the golden bow and arrows in a large chariot flanked by two men in armor on horseback. My heart told me that it was Ren and Kishan.

The brothers fought only with swords and wooden shields, and they wore armor similar to the other soldiers, not the armor from Durga's brooch. It didn't make sense.

Why practice with all eight arms and then not use all the weapons in battle? Why create a goddess and not show her off in the fight? Where are Durga's other weapons?

General Amphimachus's troops had lost very few men. They gained some significant ground and were pressing forward in rectangular phalanxes. From where I sat, the formation looked like a giant red porcupine lumbering to its mountain nest. But even they were not victorious. A demon bird screeched overhead, and the cat-like demons jumped on top of the shields and tore at spears with sharp teeth. Soon tens of thousands of soldiers lay on the ground like a spent deck of cards.

As the day passed, more and more of our men were lost. An army of more than a half a million was mercilessly cut down to just more than half that number. One of my bodyguards pointed out a waving banner that signaled retreat, and soon our warriors escaped the battlefield, making their way back to their camps as best they could. Riders ran through the fallen soldiers seeking to help the wounded before the vermin demons could finish them off.

A horn was sounded, and Lokesh's army retreated into the shadows of the mountains. My horse, which I tied to a nearby tree, began stamping and neighing loudly. She bucked at her restraints, and the other horses did the same thing. On the field, men lost control of the elephants. They trumpeted loudly and made a beeline for safe cover. Birds of all kinds rose into the air, including the falcons used for communication by the Chinese army. Animals of all types left the surrounding forest and headed toward the scene of battle, overcome by a powerful instinct.

I called upon the power in my amulet and wrapped a bubble of calming heat around me, my horse, and the remaining animals near us. But it was too late to save them all. A king cobra rose up next to me, hissed, and then quickly made its way down the hill. I shivered.

I saw Anamika's horse and many of the horses still connected to chariots running toward Mount Kailash. When they reached the hill of dead bodies, they stopped and reared up on their hind legs. A powerful wind rose and lifted the bodies of the dead and then the animals were also pulled up into the sky. They hung there limply, dormant, tossed about in the wind as if they were merely autumn leaves caught in a swirling eddy.

Dead men wearing the red cloaks, the short tunics, and the knee-high armored boots of Alexander the Great's army swirled amid the dark green-garbed Chinese warriors. As their heads lolled back, the heavy helmets fell to the ground below, rolling to a stop amid the shields and weapons that littered the ground.

The animals and humans formed pairs that spun together in a vortex of black magic. Tremors shook the ground as if Mother Nature herself was watching in horror and trembling at the darkness that had stolen over the entire valley.

Circling each other faster and faster until the images blurred in the dark mist of twilight, the animal and the human merged into one being, a thing of darkness, an unholy coupling of man and beast.

Demon birds flapped new wings, rising higher in the air. Beasts—half bear or half wolf—blinked yellow eyes and, when released from the vortex, lumbered off toward the mountain. Creatures rained from the sky, profane imitations of what they once were. Zombie men that were now part wolverine, part snake, or part snow leopard also turned and made their way to their new master. They rose by the hundreds; then by the thousands.

I closed my eyes, sickened by the lack of respect for the dead. The dead soldiers would not be honored for their sacrifice in the manner of their country, but instead they would be conscripted against their will and enslaved to fight for a monster intent on destroying us all.

Who would stop him? Who could stop him?

Then the earth shook, and I saw the camp of the Macedonian army disappear, swallowed up in a fissure that inhaled tents, supplies, and war-weary men. A tornado whipped across the clearing, devastating the camp of the Chinese. Tents, men, weapons, and supplies were sucked into the storm and then, after dancing in the turbulent sky, streamed down on top of the broken camp. Something small pelted my cheek and I cupped my hand to catch what I thought was hail. It was raining rice.

A huge wave lifted from Lake Rakshastal and demolished the Indian camp completely. Most of the tents were swept away in a great flood, and the camp was devastated by the impact. Then the mountain settled and became quiet. Our armies had been decimated after a single day of fighting. Our deceased were now swelling the ranks of the demon army, and our camps were destroyed.

I told the men with me that they needed to return to camp to help. They refused to leave me—probably because Ren and/or Kishan had severely threatened them—but I used the power of my amulet to nudge them back down the hill, slightly toasting their backsides when they resisted. I tried my best to convey to them that I would be fine and that I would return soon as troubled questions filled my mind.

Would Lokesh be satisfied if I give myself up? Would he make a trade? The fire amulet and me for the zombie-making token he had? Which is worse? Giving him ultimate power through uniting the Damon Amulet or letting him keep on making zombies?

It seemed like he would win either way. Lokesh was a dangerous puzzle.

"He's like Ugra Narasimha," I mumbled. "Nearly invincible. There's got to be a way to destroy him. I just need to figure out how."

"You could start by using the gifts of Durga the way they were intended, Kahl-see," a familiar singsong voice behind me admonished.

I spun around. "Phet?"

two sides of the same coin

The wiry man found an overturned log and sat. He smiled at me and said, "I told you I would see you again in a happier time."

"Does this look like a happier time to you? And why are you talking like that?"

"Talking like what?" He picked at a speck of dirt from his robes and flicked it away.

"Your English has improved." I put my hand on my hip. "Significantly."

Phet still looked the same. Voluminous robes wrapped around his thin frame, but they still couldn't hide his knobby brown knees and elbows. His funny gap-toothed smile lit up his wrinkled face, and small tufts of gray hair stuck out from the back of his bald head.

He wrapped his hands around a knee. "My English was always good, *Kahl-see*. It's not my fault you saw something different."

"I saw something different because you showed me something different."

He pointed a finger in the air and smiled. "Precisely. I told the princes that you were a smart girl." Phet patted the log next to him, offering me a place to sit down.

"I showed you the man you needed to see," he explained. "The man you would trust to guide you to ancient prophecies. Let me ask you, would you have believed me if I had spoken to you like I am now?"

"Maybe," I responded, still confused.

"I think you wouldn't have. In fact, I think you would have returned to Mr. Kadam and taken the first plane out of India."

"There's no way to know how I would have reacted."

"Oh, there are ways to know, young lady. There are ways."

"That still doesn't explain why you're here now."

"I am here to ensure your victory."

"Well, because you mysteriously came all this way and obviously are not the man I thought you were, why the heck not. So, Phet, if that's even your real name, tell me, how do I defeat Lokesh?"

"It's simple. Do to him what I did to you."

"What? Talk to him in broken English?"

"No. You must trick him into believing that you are something that you're not."

"And what would that be?" I queried hesitantly.

"A goddess," Phet said in all seriousness.

I sputtered, "Perhaps you are unaware, but we already have one of those in stock."

"Phet is aware of everything, young one, and things are not always as they seem."

"Obviously." I gave him a pointed look.

He bowed slightly as if acknowledging his own magical presence, took my hand between his, and patted it. "You have become a beautiful blossom, Kahl-see."

He tilted his head considering me. "A stubborn one, perhaps, but on your different journeys, you needed that resolute strength. Your iron will and determination has kept you alive. That and the sacrifices of your tigers. Still, your experiences did not harden your heart. Your vulnerability, your softness, remain for all to see. I am very proud of you, my dear."

"Phet, if you knew all along that we'd end up here, then why didn't you send us here in the first place?"

He sighed deeply. "No victory is ever achieved without first making the decision to leave home. Each step that you've taken, each foe that you've overcome, each hardship that you've endured, has led you here, now, to this moment. It is the eve of your destiny, Kahl-see. It is meant to be, because it has always been so. Even I don't have the power to protect you from providence—no matter how dear you are to me."

A tear fell on his wrinkled cheek, and I squeezed his thin hand. Somehow Phet was suddenly here, advising me, and speaking of my destiny, and it didn't stun me speechless. He'd set my feet on this journey years ago, or would, sometime in the distant future, and in a way it felt right to end this quest with him.

"You are dear to me too," I said softly.

"Do you remember when I told you that you must choose between Ren and Kishan?"

I nodded and looked down at the two rings on my finger. "My love life has become a little . . . complicated. I'm afraid the choice has already been made for me."

Phet studied me quietly. Rising, he said, "I see. Then shall we find the others and figure out how to help destiny along?"

Rising too, I put my hand on his shoulder and agreed, "Yes. And Phet, thank you for coming. You don't know how much I need your guidance."

He smiled toothily. "Guidance is my specialty. Guidance and herbs. I wanted to see you again too, Kahl-see."

Phet used the log as a stepping stone to mount my horse, and together we set off through the moonlit landscape in search of the others.

When we reached the valley floor, we wove among injured stragglers making their way to a newly constructed camp farther back from the mountain. The air was heavy and thick with the tang of spilt blood and shattered hope. There didn't seem to be many men left alive and those who were stumbled along in the dark by twos and threes, disfigured in spirit as much as they were in body.

When I tried to stop to offer aid, Phet put his hand over mine and said that the others needed me more than these poor souls did. The night was quiet, almost peaceful in the aftermath of battle. The stars shone crisply, vividly, as if the pale light could reach into our lost and despairing troops and heal their pain.

It wasn't long before I heard a *clump, clump, clump* that grew louder. I reined in my horse and whipped my head back and forth in the dark, wishing that I had Fanindra's eyes. *Is it one of the equine demons? Is Lokesh after me?* My heart leapt into my throat, and I lifted my hand to use the only weapon I had left—flame.

Phet held onto my waist and sat calmly, completely unafraid of whatever or whoever approached. His steady presence gave me some measure of courage. Out of the darkness a great beast materialized. Breath steamed from its nostrils as it pounded toward me. The thundering figure was a white stallion, and my heart told me who rode it before I could even make out his features. Ren.

He barreled toward me, and before I knew what was happening, Ren had pulled me off my horse and into his arms. Phet was soon left far behind.

Ren was holding the reins in one hand and was pinning my body so tightly against him, I could barely breathe. I could feel his racing pulse where my wrist touched his neck. Almost instinctively, I stroked his back, hoping to knead away some of his tension.

I said softly, "It's okay, Ren. I'm alright," repeating it over and over.

Ren slowed his horse to a canter and then to a walk. He pressed his cheek against mine and murmured, "I thought you were in the camp when the flood came. I was so relieved when your guards returned and told me they left you on the cliff."

"I made them go. I used the fire amulet and toasted them just a bit."

I saw a hint of his brilliant white smile appear briefly. Then it was gone so fast I thought it must have been my imagination.

He sighed, "Kelsey, my love, I can always trust you to do exactly the opposite of what I would prefer."

"If I would have stayed in camp like you preferred, you might not have had this wonderful opportunity to lecture me."

He looked into my eyes, and my breath caught. I felt like I was leaning toward him, slowly, by incremental degrees. The chasm I'd built between us was narrowing. My heart beat faster. My internal compass pointed toward him. He was my north. He was beautiful, and he was amazing, and he was perfect, and he was . . . bleeding.

"Ren! You're hurt! Why haven't you healed yet?"

I yanked the sleeve of my shirt over my hand and dabbed at a bloody gash on his scalp that was hidden in his hair.

He shifted me slightly and squeezed my waist. "It would seem that Kishan and I no longer have the ability to spontaneously heal."

"What? How is that possible? Can you still become tigers here?"

Ren nodded. "Perhaps the beasts have become mortal like the prophecy said."

"No. No! We didn't go through all of that so you could become *vulnerable*! You're supposed to become *human*! When we get to camp, Phet will have some explaining to do."

"Phet? What are you talking about?"

"Phet was riding with me."

"You mean the man who kidnapped you was Phet?"

I snorted. "Kidnapped? Did I look like I was being held against my will?"

"I rescue first and ask questions later. Speaking of which, you don't sound much like a grateful maiden who was just rescued."

I bunched the fabric at my wrist and pressed it against his wound, which brought my face that much closer to his. He winced but wouldn't look away from me.

"I didn't need any rescuing," I muttered.

He brought his hand up, eased the hood away from my face, and softly trailed his fingertips over my cheek and lips. "The truth is, I would rip you away from the arms of any man, villain or no."

"You would?" I inquired softly and drew even nearer.

He angled closer too until our lips were almost touching. "Yes, *hridaya patni*, I would."

Delicate tension wove between us but we were soon joined by other riders. Before I could blink, we were back at camp. The moment was gone.

Ren dismounted and swung me down from the horse. Broken and wounded men from all of the different armies were clustered into groups around small fires. Some were tending to their weapons and armor, some slept, and some sat quietly, staring straight ahead. We set off in search of Anamika, who was tending the wounded.

She glanced up when we approached and gave me a long look.

"So you are safe after all, little sister. General Xi-Wong is dead, and Amphimachus has lost a leg," she said flatly. "The Tibetan leaders are here, but there are only a handful of men from Myanmar left alive. They believe their leaders have been taken by the demon."

She stood, and I took note of how weary she seemed. Her clothes were caked with dried blood, and her hair hung messily around her face.

"Anamika, let me," Ren offered and held out his hand for the *kamandal*.

She stared at him for a brief moment, as if asking a silent question, and then shook her head. "These men belong to me. I will care for them. Perhaps you could have helped earlier but instead you ran off to placate our little sister after another one of her temper tantrums."

"Now wait just a minute," I started.

Ren held up his hand. "You aren't angry with her, Anamika. You're mad at me." He stepped closer to her and put his hand on her arm. "You believe that I abandoned you, but I was only gone for a short time. The men were out of danger, and there are many able bodies to help. Besides, Kelsey is just the first of many who need rescue tonight. You would do the same for your brother, would you not?"

I'm just the first of many? Does he think of me as his sister now? What happened to ripping me away from the arms of any man?

Anamika sighed softly and nodded. "I would."

At that moment I was scooped up into some very muscular arms and cuddled against a broad chest.

"Are you alright? Are you hurt anywhere?" Kishan asked.

"If she is hurt at all, it is likely due to the over attentiveness the both of you lavish upon her," Anamika responded testily. "There is much work here to do."

"I'm afraid that work will have to be delegated to others," a voice from behind me said.

"Phet! You made it back."

"Kishan found me and was kind enough to escort me to camp."

Ren shook Phet's hand and happily clapped his thin back. "We are happy to have you. Welcome."

Ren locked eyes with mine briefly. Kishan stepped between the two of us and faced his brother with a tight expression. Phet detected the tension between them the same time I did.

Patting both of them noisily on their cheeks, he said, "Come, tigers. It is time for two worthy sons of India to fulfill their life's calling."

"Teacher?" I heard a soft feminine voice query.

We stood aside as Phet moved forward. "Anamika, it is good to see you."

The future goddess cried out and ran to the little monk, wrapping him gently in her arms. "I never thought I'd see you again. You didn't tell us you were leaving. How did you come here after all these years have passed?"

I held up a hand, "Wait just a second. Teacher? Years have passed? Phet, would you mind telling us what's going on? I thought you were the humble servant of the goddess."

"And so I am. Come. We have much to discuss. Bring all the weapons and gifts of Durga. We will need them tonight."

The wiry shaman slowly shuffled off in the darkness.

Anamika nodded vigorously and left to retrieve the bag of weapons while Ren put a few men in charge of seeing that the remaining troops drank from the barrel that Anamika spiked with the mermaid's elixir.

Then the five of us—two tigers, a goddess, a dubious old monk, and a very confused and out of place girl from Oregon—headed off in search of our destiny.

We walked west, away from Mount Kailash and the devastation that happened there. None of us spoke. The sounds of my feet moving seemed loud, especially because no nocturnal animals were rustling in the brush. It felt unnatural. Strange.

Finally, Phet stopped at a trickling stream and scooped some water into his mouth. "My, that's cold."

Anamika stepped forward. "Forgive me, teacher." She took the Divine Scarf from the bag and held it in her open hands. "Scarf, create a warm cloak and protection for his feet and hands."

Wisps of thread flew into the air like silken cobwebs and streamed toward Phet as they wove their magic. In the space of a few seconds he was encased in a warm coat, thick gloves, and boots.

"I am so sorry I didn't think of your comfort sooner." The goddess genuflected humbly.

"Think nothing of it, my dear. The small irritations of the flesh are for but a passing moment. Still," he pulled his coat closer, "it's nice to feel warm too. Kahl-see, perhaps you could—"

"Oh, of course," I sputtered.

Soon the air around us was warm and balmy as I radiated heat in a circle.

"Ah, that's better." Phet found a smooth stone to sit on. Anamika immediately positioned herself at his feet like a young acolyte. Ren touched my arm and pointed to a place where we could rest. Kishan quickly positioned himself on my other side and took my hand while frowning at his brother.

"I know you're all wondering why I am here," Phet began. "Anamika is correct that I was her teacher when she and her brother were young."

"And what did you teach?" I asked.

Anamika glared at me. "It would be better to show a respectful attitude."

"Hey, he's the one who lied to *me*. He's going to have to earn back my respect."

"Kahl-see is quite right. I deserve her suspicion. I am not who I led her to believe. In fact, I am not who I led any of you to believe."

"What do you mean?" Ren asked.

"Perhaps it would be best for you to think of me as the Spirit of India. I serve as a protector or guardian. By ensuring Durga's place in history, I secure the future. In doing this I have assumed many roles, including that of teacher to a young girl who happened to have a brilliant mind for strategy." He smiled at Anamika.

"Thank you, wise one."

"Hold on a second," I said. "This is all backward. You told me that you served the goddess."

"Yes, I do."

"But—"

"Be patient, Kahl-see. I will explain all." He made himself a bit more comfortable and continued. "I was Anamika's teacher. When she was a young lady I spent several hours a day with her so I could prepare her for what lay ahead. I taught her about war and peace, famine and plenty, wealth and poverty. I tutored her in many languages including English because I knew that one day she would meet the three of you."

"Was this before or after you met me?" I asked.

"There is no before or after. There is only finished and unfinished." He smiled at my puzzled expression and held out his hands. "Some of my work I have finished and some remains to be done. But when the work is completed, what was undone will cease to exist and all that will remain is what is."

My mouth dropped open, and I said, "Phet, you're killing me."

With a twinkle in his eye, he confessed. "Sometimes I get confused myself."

"But why the ruse? Why make me believe you're one thing when you are actually some kind of supreme all-knowing spirit?"

"It was necessary for me to be the person you saw so that you could become the person I see."

While I puzzled that out, Kishan suggested, "You mentioned you were here to help us defeat Mahishasur. Perhaps if we could focus on the concrete, the complexities of eternity might seem less taxing."

"Spoken like a true warrior," Phet said and rubbed his hands together. "I have always admired your ability to remain steadfastly focused. Very well. We will start with the weapons. May I?"

Anamika offered him the bag, and he removed the *gada*.

"Ah, a finely crafted instrument. Has this weapon been of benefit to you in your travels?"

Ren answered, "I used the *gada* in Kishkindha against the needle trees. It wounded them so they left us alone."

"Hmm," Phet grunted. "Anything else?"

"I used it against the column in Durga's temple," I volunteered.

"I . . . I have a temple?" the fledgling goddess asked.

"Yep. Several of them."

"We also used it in battle as a weapon," Kishan added.

"Yes, but you," Phet said looking at me, "have not wielded it as it was meant to be used."

He selected the golden bow and arrows next and asked the same questions. I told him about infusing the arrows with my fire and he seemed pleased by that, but indicated that the arrows had even more power that had yet to be tapped.

One by one he showed us our other weapons—the *chakram*, the trident, the brooches, and the swords. Then he picked up Fanindra and she came alive. He stroked her golden head.

"She is perhaps the most underutilized gift of all," Phet accused gently.

"But Fanindra only helps when *she* wants to," I said.

Phet peered at me, and Fanindra turned her green-eyed gaze on me. "Did you ask her for help?" he prompted kindly.

"No," I admitted, "I didn't."

As he ran his fingers over her gleaming coils, he said, "Fanindra's bite can heal. She has influence over other natural creatures, more so over reptiles with close ties to her, but she can even calm large predators. If they look into her eyes, they will be caught in her spell. Supernatural creatures such as those created by Lokesh naturally fear her. She lights the darkness, but she can also discern darkness in others. Were you at all aware of this?"

All of us shook our heads, and I felt regret for not truly appreciating what an incredible gift Fanindra was.

"All of these golden weapons will display their true powers when properly wielded by a goddess."

I raised my hand in the air like a student in a classroom. "About that—"

"All will come to light soon, Kahl-see. First, I must teach you the proper way to use the Gifts of Durga."

He dug through the bag and found the Golden Fruit, the Rope of Fire, and my Pearl Necklace. Then he politely asked Anamika to hand him the Divine Scarf.

"When used alone, these gifts have great power, but when they are combined they can become something more. For example . . ."

He took the Necklace and the Scarf, one in each hand, and touched them together. When they connected, the Scarf wound quickly around the Necklace and shifted colors until it displayed a rainbow. The fabric soared into the air and the length of it encircled Phet and then it whipped around and between each of us. As it did, we were freshly cleansed and clothed in new garments. I touched my face and found it slightly damp, as if I were covered with morning dew.

After the Scarf finished its work, it settled back into its original form, softly draping itself over Phet's hand.

Anamika marveled, "This power is truly amazing!"

"We've seen this before," I remarked. I glanced at Anamika. "Durga used this power on us in the temple before we met the dragons."

"Yes." Phet smiled. "That is right."

Anamika's gleeful expression changed to one of sobriety, and I felt sorry for her. *What must it feel like to have your entire life mapped out by unseen forces?* Actually, it seemed like all four of us suffered from something similar; we were just lucky that for at least a while we felt like we were in control and making our own decisions. As it turned out, Phet or the cosmos had orchestrated everything.

I looked at Ren and Kishan and wondered if destiny chose one of them to be with me—and for a moment I wondered if that was why I loved them. *No. My heart is my own. But, what if that is why they love me, because destiny told them to? Certainly if destiny was in charge it wouldn't have picked both of them*, I argued with myself. *There would be only one.*

Ren interrupted my thoughts when he asked Phet, "What happens when you combine the Rope with the Necklace? Will the fire and water cancel each other out?"

"Let's try them and see." Phet picked up the Rope of Fire and said, "Kahl-see, if you would."

I stepped forward and gripped the Rope's handle, infusing it with my flame. Phet wrapped the Necklace around the end and snapped the Rope into the air.

It produced a large crack and a boom in the night sky, and soon I saw what I thought were fireflies falling all around us. I held out a hand and caught one. It sizzled, burning briefly and then extinguished in my palm.

"What is it?" I asked.

"Fire-rain," Phet responded. With another snap, the fire shower ceased and the little fires that started in the grass disappeared. "When these two are put together, water will take on the properties of fire and vice versa. You can create a lake of fire or you can make fire flow like a river. You can also create a liquid that burns. The three of you would call this acid."

Ren nodded as if he understood all this.

"The other thing to keep in mind is that when wielded by a goddess, the Rope burns blue. This is a cleansing flame. It seeks out the dark places in men's hearts and scalds them, not physically, but it causes great inner turmoil for one who gives pain to others.

"You also know that you have been able to travel to the past using the Rope of Fire. This is because the Rope has the ability to open a cosmic string. When you asked the Rope to take you to meet your destiny, it found a crack in the fabric of the universe and opened a doorway, allowing you to follow the string to this place."

"I do not understand such things," Anamika said. She turned to us and asked, "Are the three of you not from this world then? Are you gods who travel on strings?"

Kishan answered, "We are not gods, Anamika. We are from this world like you, but we were born many years in the future."

"Such power is beyond my comprehension."

Phet put his hand on her shoulder. "You must try to learn these things. I know this is overwhelming for you. Perhaps I can explain it another way." He lifted the golden sword and held it toward her. "How do you know when a sword is made inadequately?"

"The hilt is loose or poorly wrapped, it vibrates too much when used on a target, its balance is off, and if it was not fired properly, it will become brittle and fracture."

"That is correct." Phet smiled warmly at his former student. "Think of the world as a sword. The steel is folded in on itself over and over again. Earth has many such folds or layers. This folding makes a blade stronger and more beautiful. When a sword is forged, the steel is heated to a very high temperature then is rapidly cooled. If it's done properly you will have a strong, solid weapon. If not, microscopic fractures or cracks form where the crystalline structure is weak.

"Our world is much like this. There are fissures and splits in space and time. The fabric of the universe is constantly moving and shifting as it expands and contracts like metal that is heated and then cooled over and over again, and as matter rips apart and reforms, it creates threads. Threads that lead to what once was, what is now, and what will be. Everything is connected. This is what I mean by cosmic strings. This is how these three have traveled to you."

Anamika nodded. "Then we will reforge the world and heal what is weak."

"That is your birthright, Anamika," Phet affirmed.

Phet proceeded to show us one amazing power after another. He used the *gada* and the Necklace to open a fissure in the earth, and a geyser shot up into the air higher than anything at Yellowstone. He dipped the tip of a golden arrow into the *kamandal* and shocked us all when he fired the arrow into Ren's leg. The arrow disappeared quickly, and the cut on his scalp healed. When Ren examined his leg, it was as if nothing had hit him.

"Are Ren and Kishan no longer able to self-heal?" I asked Phet.

Phet rolled the *kamandal* between his hands and replied, "No. Sadly, they are not."

"Why? What did we do?"

"You did nothing. It is simply time for them to fulfill their destiny. Their bodies were kept young and preserved so they could fight here."

"And what will become of us when the fight is over?" Ren asked.

Phet set the *kamandal* down and said quietly, "It is perhaps better to think of the future after we have taken care of the present, hmm?"

Phet wrapped the Rope of Fire around his waist, where it locked together like a belt. When he touched any weapon to it, the weapon lit on fire. He touched an arrow to the Necklace and sunk the projectile into a tree trunk. The entire tree turned into water, held the shape of what it once was for a few seconds, and then fell, flooding the undergrowth.

It seemed that the possibilities were endless, and the only limit was our own creativity. All of us were eager to try out the weapons, and Kishan was the first on his feet. But Phet caught his arm as he reached for the *chakram* and shook his head. Kishan backed up a step.

"I must caution you regarding two things. The first is that when you use the Rope of Fire, you must be very specific with your instructions. If you ask it to take you to a safe haven you may end up in another time and place. I cannot emphasize enough the importance of each of you in this battle. You must stay here. You can, however, use it to move quickly around the battlefield, but you must tell it exactly where you wish to go."

Kishan nodded and asked, "What is the other warning you must give?"

Phet said nothing for a moment but looked at Anamika. "Is there a reason you didn't fight as the goddess today or lead out in battle as you wished to, young one?"

Her head dropped, and Kishan and I turned to look at her. Ren put his hand on her arm to offer her support.

"I am ashamed to confess it but—" she glanced at Phet, who was patiently waiting for her to finish.

She pulled a knife from her boot and stabbed the ground a few times. "I was under the thrall of the demon."

Phet pressed, "You felt this overtake you the nearer you were to the mountain. Am I correct?"

"Yes," she admitted.

Ren added, "I had to pull her away when she got too close. I took the weapons from her because she turned them on her own troops. The further she was from the battle, the more control she had over herself."

"I suspected as much," Phet said. He knelt in front of Anamika and lifted her chin so he could see her face. "This is not your fault. This has happened to Ren and Kishan as well."

"What?" Kishan took a step forward.

"I was not under the thrall of Lokesh even when he tortured me," Ren declared.

Phet took hold of Kishan's arm and explained, "You were under this same power before the tiger saved you."

Ren stood up. "You're speaking of the talisman. Yes . . . it affected both Kishan and me because we have the same blood."

"He uses it now combined with the amulet to create his demon army, and Anamika's twin brother is the head of it. Because he is under its influence, the sway Lokesh has over Sunil overpowers her control when she gets too close."

Durga gasped, and tears formed in her eyes. I reached out to hold her hands. "We'll just have to destroy the talisman then."

"You must make this your priority." Phet gave me a telling look, and I dipped my head slightly to acknowledge that I understood. "The four of you will ride into battle in the morning. Now you must use these few remaining hours to rest. I will return to camp and prepare your troops to accompany you. Stay here until my return."

Clutching his newly made cloak, Phet wandered off into the darkness, leaving us and our weapons behind. Anamika still seemed to be overwhelmed by everything. I used the Scarf to make her a comfortable tent and guided her inside. When I was satisfied that the tent was warm enough and saw that she'd rolled onto her side, obviously not wanting to talk, I left her alone.

I found Kishan waiting for me outside.

Wrapping his arms around me, he asked, "Are you still angry with me?"

"I was never angry with you. I was angry with Ren and Anamika, and I was confused."

Kishan sighed deeply. "I understand. It must have been hard for you to see them together. You still have feelings for him."

I couldn't respond. I couldn't share the knowledge that the Phoenix had burned into my soul. There was a part of me that loved Kishan and desperately wanted to return the love he deserved. But I was still in love with Ren, and that feeling couldn't be pushed aside or denied.

Kishan gently cupped my chin, and I looked into his warm golden eyes. Eyes full of patience, love, and acceptance.

I wrapped my arms around his waist, buried my head against his shoulder, and wept. He stroked my back and said, "Don't cry, *bilauta*. You can always tell me how you feel. You can talk to me about anything, even if you think it will hurt me. I love you, Kelsey Hayes. I want to marry you, have a dozen kids, and grow old with you. You've made me a whole man again, and you've given me more than I could wish for, more than I deserve by agreeing to be my wife. I know that Ren is a part of your life. He's a part of my life too. We'll worry about the future after we take care of the past. Agreed?"

"Agreed," I said and blew my nose.

I stood on my tiptoes to kiss him briefly, but he pressed me close and kissed me with a fervent passion that I couldn't help responding to. My arms snuck around his neck and held onto him. He ran his hands down my back and gripped my waist, pulling me closer. When our lips parted, he smiled and dipped his head to kiss my cheek.

I whispered, "I love you too, Kishan," and his happiness at hearing my words warmed my heart.

Phet returned a few hours later. It was dawn, and the clouds looked like pink cotton candy. It reminded me of the fateful day I first met Ren back at the circus in Oregon. The sight made me think of happier times, happier places. Somehow the clouds seemed out of place on the morn of a battle.

Phet had gathered our weapons, which lay in a gleaming pile at our feet. I rubbed my eyes to clear away the layers of sleepiness. Anamika stood beside me, nervously wringing her hands. Kishan and Ren seemed ill at ease as well.

Phet picked up the Divine Scarf and held it in his palms. "To truly become the goddess, you must touch all the gifts as you change."

He handed Anamika the Golden Fruit, fixed the clasp of the Pearl Necklace around her neck, and wrapped the Rope of Fire around her waist.

"Now wind the Divine Scarf around your body and wish to appear as the goddess Durga."

A brief moment passed and the cold breeze played with the edge of the Scarf. I'd just used the amulet's power to warm the air around us when she lifted the Scarf away.

I'd seen her as Durga before with all eight arms, but she seemed different this time. Her skin was glowing as if it was lit from within. Her long, black hair seemed to have a life of its own as it moved softly in the breeze. She was beautiful and fierce. Power seemed to radiate from her in waves.

Gently, Phet took the Scarf, the Fruit, and the other items from her. Her arms flexed and twitched as if ready for battle. She turned toward me and moved as fluidly with eight arms as she did with two.

"And now, Kahl-see, it's your turn."

"What?" I gasped in shock.

Ren and Kishan both reacted instantly.

"What are you doing?" Kishan asked.

"Isn't there a way to leave her behind?" Ren protested.

Phet replied to both of them. "It has always been Kahl-see's destiny to fight in this battle. This is why she is, was, and always has been the chosen one. Without her," he looked at Ren, "you will lose everything."

The wiry monk handed me the Fruit, but Kishan took the Necklace and affixed it at my neck. Ren settled the Rope of Fire around my waist. After kissing my forehead, he stepped away.

"What do I wish to be?" I asked.

"You are to be Durga as well."

Setting aside my confusion, I wrapped the Scarf around my body. I grimaced beneath it, thinking about all the arms soon to be waving at my side but obeyed the instructions and told the Divine Scarf I wanted to be Durga. What happened next was amazing.

At first, I didn't feel any different, but as the Scarf did its work, I felt my clothes shift. Little electric fingers ran through my hair, giving me goose bumps, and then I realized I had goose bumps on more than one set of arms. The Scarf tickled, and I pulled it off with a hand I'd never used before. Blood surged through my body, and I clenched my fists, all of them, as I felt power move through me.

I looked at the new goddess Durga standing across from me with several sets of arms folded and she smiled. I grinned back and felt full of confidence and control. It wasn't until I looked at Ren and Kishan that I felt self-conscious. They both stared.

"What?" I asked them. "What is it? Is one of my arms doing something wrong?"

"It's you . . . you're—" Kishan began and swallowed.

"Breathtaking," Ren finished.

He offered his hand, and I placed one of mine in his. He brought it up to his lips and kissed it warmly then rubbed his fingers over the ring on my finger and smiled. I drew my hand up to look at the ring and saw it was Ren's.

Automatically, I rubbed eight thumbs over thirty-two fingers and found another ring on my right hand. I looked at it and let out a pent-up breath seeing Kishan's ruby ring safe on my finger. Kishan stepped forward and took my hand, boldly placing my palm against his cheek. He kissed it and stood to the side.

Phet announced, "Now use your power to draw your weapons to you."

Both of us lifted our arms, and the golden weapons rose into the air. We opened our hands, and weapons flew into them. The *chakram*, a brooch, the *kamandal*, and, to my dismay, Fanindra, flew to Durga's outstretched hands, as did the Golden Fruit and the Divine Scarf.

The Pearl Necklace and the Rope of Fire stayed with me, and I also got a brooch, the *gada*, the trident, and my bow and arrows. The golden sword rose into the air and split into two. One sword flew to Durga and the other to me. I caught it in my topmost right hand. As I caught the weapons in my grip they shifted color from gold to silver while Durga's weapons still gleamed in the familiar gold.

"Now, you are ready for battle." Phet clapped Ren on the shoulder and continued, "Dhiren and Kishan will enter battle with the goddesses and will fight alongside them in the way destiny has chosen for you. Ladies, if you would activate your brooches."

I touched the trinket and said, "Armor and shield."

Thin plates of silver encased my limbs and a shield grew in one of my left hands. The armor traveled down my torso, over my hips, and down my legs, and I was surprised how easily I could move in it.

I turned to look at Anamika and saw that golden armor had encased her upper body like a corset, leaving her neck bare, but then rounded out over her shoulders. Golden cuffs protected her forearms.

She wore a black cloth skirt lined with golden plates and black boots covered in strips of golden metal. A golden crown took shape over her head.

I snickered at the sight of Durga's golden tiara, but then I reached *down* with one of my upper arms and patted the top of my head. Sure enough, I wore a silver crown too.

To my dismay, I looked down and found I also had a breastplate and that my outfit was identical to Anamika's, except for the coloring. My skin almost sparkled with inner light. My brown hair was golden and was as thick and as long as Anamika's. My dress was similar in shape to Anamika's but was white. Ren stood there gaping, and my face turned red under his scrutiny.

When the process was completed, Ren and Kishan doubled over and groaned painfully. Alarmed, I took a step toward Ren just as he shifted into tiger form. He roared loudly and shook himself. Kishan changed into the black tiger.

"What's happening?" I asked Phet.

"The time has come, Kahl-see. They are fulfilling their purpose," he said.

I touched Ren, and silver plates covered his muzzle and made their way over his head. Soon his body was encased in silver armor. A double-rigged cinch circled his torso and formed a white saddle on his back, complete with two metal handgrips by his shoulder blades. Kishan was outfitted identically in golden armor and a black saddle.

Anamika-as-Durga stepped between Ren and Kishan. She patted Kishan's head.

"Interesting," she said.

Kishan growled lightly in response and walked over to me, putting his head under my hand. I folded two sets of arms, resting a hand on Kishan.

"You're kidding, right, Phet? This isn't what I think it is."

"It's exactly that, Kahl-see. The goddess Durga is supposed to ride her tiger into battle."

29

defeating mahishasur

f you are hesitant, then stay here, little sister," Anamika teased.

"This is my war even more than it is yours, *big* sister."

She frowned, which made me just the tiniest bit happy, and attempted to swing her leg over Ren's back. Surprisingly, the new goddess fell over in an awkward flurry of arms. Irritated, she got up and gave it another go, but try as she might, she was not able to take her place atop Ren.

She took hold of the handgrip over his shoulder blades, but trying to mount him required a monumental effort on her part. When Ren leaned toward her to make it easier, he was violently shoved by an unseen force. He danced away from Durga, leaving only his paw prints behind in the soft ground.

"Why is this happening?" she demanded of her teacher.

Phet shrugged his shoulders. "Kismet, my dear."

"Kismet?" I whispered. Curious, I took hold of Kishan's saddle and felt an immediate force pressing against me. I let go and stepped away. "Um, I sort of have the same problem."

Phet took his former pupil's hand and placed it on Kishan's back. "You must ride the tiger chosen for you."

Kishan huffed, and as he and Durga stood evaluating each other, Ren moved around them and rubbed his head against my leg. I patted his armor-plated shoulder, took hold of the handgrip, and swung my leg easily across his back. I felt a pull and a snap as my silver armor touched his.

"It's like we're magnetized," I exclaimed.

"You are correct," Phet said. "There is a similar power that connects you to your tiger as at the ends of a magnet. This bond will help you in battle. The metal will hold you together to prevent you from falling. In theory, you could even stand on his back and your boots will lock in place like an astronaut standing on a space ship."

I nodded and snapped my feet onto the metal plate on either side of Ren's body. Satisfied, Phet headed over to Kishan and my Durga twin.

The awkwardness of the past few weeks dissolved the second I felt the bond between Ren and me thrum through my body. Energy poured from my limbs into him and then back into me, and I realized that I could hear his thoughts.

Ren was . . . proud to carry me into battle, but I also sensed he was desperately afraid. He did not want me to face Lokesh, and he was prepared to sacrifice himself to save me. He also didn't want to be a tiger in battle. My fists tightened involuntarily as he attempted to switch back into a man. Ren's efforts were fruitless though, and he soon resigned himself to his tiger form.

Even though I had ridden the Qilin and was starting to get pretty good with the mare, I wasn't all that sure how complicated riding *and* fighting at the same time would be. I raised the sword and swung it back and forth, trying to decide which hand worked best. I switched a few weapons around, rotating them from hand to hand quickly and then adjusted one of my eight forearm guards.

I must weight a ton, I thought. *Poor Ren.*

You're not heavy at all. Ren's intoxicating voice slid into my consciousness, startling me. The sensation was like rich, velvety chocolate pouring into my soul. It completely filled and warmed me, making every square inch of my skin tingle with delight. My breath caught, and my heart raced. The feeling was intensely intimate.

You're making me blush, priyatama.

Hesitantly, I discovered that he was just as aware of me as I was of him. In his mind I was like liquid sunlight with the taste of ripe peaches. I felt heat warm my cheeks, and Ren guided me to a secret place deep within his mind where he opened himself to me completely. I swiftly became aware of everything: his isolation in captivity, his joy when I chose him over Li in Oregon, his self-recrimination when he broke up with me, and his utter despair when I became engaged to Kishan. The layers of loneliness almost smothered me. But woven through all of his thoughts was a constant hope coupled with waves of love. It tickled my toes and lapped gently at the edges of my heart.

Ren, I—

Unable to form a coherent thought in response, I wiped a tear from my cheek and stroked the white fur of his neck where it peeked through the armor.

His reaction to my touch was overwhelming. I felt his need for me. It twisted inside him like a tornado. Raw emotion swept through him, triggering my own. Memories circulated inside the storm, one after another.

Some of them I recognized, like the image of me snuggling on his lap after our Valentine's dance, but some of them were new: Ren clenching his fists, ready to rip our diving instructor, Wes, to pieces when we danced on the beach; Ren holding other women in his arms and still feeling empty; Ren seeing me cry and knowing he was the reason.

Then Ren showed me how he felt when I touched him for the first time as a tiger, his memories of us kissing in the kitchen while cookies baked, of how perfectly my hand fit into his, and the utter abandon and wild joy he felt when he took me into his arms. This part of him had been locked away, restrained. His heart was indeed caged, and like in the poem, it paced, waiting to be set free.

You hold the key, he told me.

Then that wonderful, beautiful, amazing man put his heart into my hands at that moment and waited to see what I would do with it.

I sucked in a breath and sensed his expectant tension. He didn't care what happened in the war. Durga and the prophecy and all that pertained to it meant nothing to him. As far as he was concerned, this was the battle he was fighting. He was on a crusade, not to gain glory, secure a kingdom, or fight for a goddess. His campaign was to win *me*.

I crossed a set of arms over my heart and closed my eyes. Leaning down, I pressed my cheek to his soft ear and wrapped a couple sets of arms around his neck.

Ren.

At that mental whisper, a dam broke inside me and all of my feelings and thoughts poured out. I felt the impact of them hit Ren like a tidal wave. He stood quietly and absorbed everything. I let him experience all of it: the confusion, the heartbreak, the anguish, and now the happiness. I held nothing back—not even my feelings for Kishan. I sensed his acceptance and his understanding about my relationship with his brother. There was no feeling of vindictiveness or judgment, only a deep heartfelt regret, and I felt his surprise in at last understanding why I had kept him at a distance for so long.

Finally, I showed him the depth of what I felt for him and how desperate I had been without him.

Ren, I love you more than anything in this world, and I don't know how I can possibly live without you.

You'll never have to, iadala.

His thoughts were hushed for a few seconds, and then our souls twisted together like clinging vines and both of us rested, our thoughts content, peaceful, and calm. Tingling bubbles of power coursed lazily between us. At that moment, all was right with the world. The one I loved was woven tightly into my soul, and I hoped we would never let go of each other again.

A loud voice interrupted our thoughts.

"I apologize. I didn't mean to treat you like a pack animal," Anamika said, bringing both me and Ren back to the battle looming before us.

It was time to go. Time to end this thing, once and for all.

She kicked Kishan in the ribs lightly, and Kishan moved forward grumpily. A thoughtful expression crossed her face, and then Kishan picked up speed and began running. We followed suit, and I felt Ren's exhilaration as he stretched his tiger legs, traversing the countryside, eating up the distance in great leaps and bounds.

Ren was all muscle and endless energy, and as I clung to his sides, I found the rhythm of his gait. We moved together as one. His tiger lungs worked like powerful bellows, and I realized that we were breathing in concert. When I looked behind us, Phet was nowhere in sight.

We arrived back at the center of camp. Men of five different nations knelt all around us, touching their heads to the ground in deference. They were awed by the presence of not one but two goddesses in their midst. My twin took the lead and asked the generals to approach. She told them of a new plan, one that did not involve animals that the demons could turn against us. This battle would be waged on foot.

She then turned to me and indicated that I should say something inspiring. Ren's thoughts flowed through my mind.

They need a symbol to look to on the battlefield.

In the loudest voice I could muster, I shouted, "As of this moment, you are no longer the armies of China, Macedonia, Myanmar, Tibet, or India. You are now the warriors of Durga! We have already fought and overcome many fierce creatures. Now we give you the symbol of their power."

I borrowed the Scarf and touched it to my Pearl Necklace. The silken material sped through the air, fragmenting and spinning off, touching down on each and every solder to cloak them in the most brilliant red, blue, green, gold, and white. Even the flag bearers were not left out and now held banners depicting Durga riding her tiger into battle.

"Red for the heart of a Phoenix that sees through falsehood!" I cheered and raised the trident. "Blue for the Monsters of the Deep that rip apart those who dare to cross their domain! Gold for Metal Birds that cut their enemies with razor beaks! Green for the Horde of Hanuman that comes alive to protect that which is most precious! And White for the Dragons of the Five Oceans, whose cunning and power has no equal!"

Ren reared up on his hind legs briefly and roared. The men all marveled at the power we displayed.

I handed the Scarf back to Durga, who pledged, "This battle and your valiant service will be remembered for generations. As you honor us this day, we will honor you in the days to come."

Soldiers were sent to prepare, and they hurried off to obey the instructions of their goddesses. Everyone's spirits had lifted. Men who had despaired the day before now looked confident that we could accomplish the impossible. I knew we looked like we could handle a lot, but there was a part of me that was still very afraid. It was only Ren's conviction that gave me courage.

A devoted heart can overcome any obstacle, rajkumari. *Believe that I will keep you safe.*

I gulped, wondering if I had it in me to do what must be done. I would need every bit of my training and every drop of courage in me to come out on top today.

When everything was ready, Durga smiled benevolently at our troops and called out, "I vow to you that if you fight alongside me, I will protect you with every power at my disposal, and together, we will win. We *will* defeat the demon. Warriors red, blue, green, gold, and white, will you follow us into battle?"

A resounding cheer echoed through the camp, and we all headed toward Mt. Kailash.

Mr. Kadam once shared with me the story of the three hundred Spartans who held the vast Persian army at bay for seven days in the Battle of Thermopylae. He told me that this story had been remembered for centuries not only because it was a lesson in bravely standing your ground but also because it showed that even a small number of men who were well trained and who had a sound plan could thwart an enemy who was much more powerful.

These men were like the Spartans. They'd come here to fight the demon, and they would complete their mission or die trying. I'd have to do my best to be worthy of their faith in me.

When a bugle-like horn sounded and the wispy fog rolled in, hordes of demon soldiers materialized and began banging, stomping, and howling, waiting for their leader to release them. Durga's men remained brave and steady, unflinching in the face of the enemy.

Durga struck first.

Three catapults whipped large barrels into the cold air. They hit the mountain with a bang. The barrels burst, spilling their contents over the demon army. The demons shook their arms and heads and watched as more barrels were launched. The wooden bang was accompanied by a heavy *thwap* of canvas as the payload whistled through the air and broke, showering oil over the heads of the enemy.

In retaliation, bird-men took to the sky, heading straight for the catapults. Every man who could string a bow launched arrows at the flying demons. Durga raised her arms and sent thousands of threads into the air that wove thick nets and captured the remaining demon birds. The creatures dropped heavily through the air.

The sounds of battle were replaced with cheers from Durga's army, filling us with hope. It was a small victory but a victory nonetheless, and my men stirred impatiently, waiting for our turn to enter the fray. The demons doubled their speed and thundered across the field. When the bulk of them passed us, I gave the signal to torch the oil field that we had had created.

The demon army shrieked horribly before falling to the ground, succumbing to a final death. Those that passed through in safety were set upon by Durga and our men who sent up a volley of arrows that I lit with fire power. As the enemy fell, one by one, and the souls of the men and beasts were released, I murmured a last wish, "I hope you find peace."

When the battle was too close for arrows, my men raised their swords and ran forward. I stayed behind using my fire power and was able to take out a large pack of canine-demons. I cremated them in large groups, but when my men got in the way I had to switch to weapons. Ren sped forward and leapt into the fray with me on his back. My tiger pounced, ripping demons apart with teeth and claws.

He stood on hind legs and raked a paw across a demon's head. My armor held me tightly to Ren's body, but I could no longer see our opponent. When Ren sunk to all fours again, the demon had wicked slashes that went from the back of his neck to over the top of his head and ended between his eyes. I finished him off while Ren lashed out at a second foe on the left.

Ren, this is horrible.

It's how a tiger fights, Kells. Try to distance yourself. Read my thoughts.

I sunk arrows into creatures' legs, pinning them to the ground while

Ren ripped their chests apart. I targeted a demon with a raised ax and hit it with darts from the trident. When one attacked me, I blocked its claws on my forearm cuff, smacked its face with my shield, and then ran it through with my sword. Another came at me with a studded mace. It hit me hard, but my armor withstood the blow and my magnetized connection to Ren kept me upright. Ren swept its feet, and when the demon fell, Ren tore at its neck and crushed its windpipe.

Becoming Durga had somehow turned me into a superhuman fighting machine. Ren and I worked in a deadly symmetry, and nothing could stop us. I was able to borrow from Ren's battle experience and shut off the part of myself that reacted in horror. Our minds came together as one, and I realized that when I fought with a sword or used the trident, it was as much Ren wielding the weapon as me. Likewise, every time Ren swiped the enemy with a paw or spotted a charging demon, it was as if I were also his claws and eyes.

When a new group headed toward us, I touched the trident to the Rope of Fire and shot jolts of electricity at the demons. The sound it made was like the crack of thunder or a hammer hitting sheet metal. The group exploded. Before one of the enemy died, it had managed to get off a poisoned dart. With preternatural speed, I caught the dart between two fingers and flipped it around, jamming it into the tough hide of a nearby cat-demon.

Others headed our way and when Ren jumped on top of one, I leaned over almost upside down. My boots locked onto the saddle, and I was able to zap two demons with fire power underneath Ren's chest. Then as Ren landed, I flipped up and spun backward, slashing a demon with a sword in one hand and swinging the *gada* with another.

Ten came at us at once and instinctively I kicked away from Ren and cartwheeled off of the saddle. My arms seemed to almost function independently. I knocked one attacker over with my shield, cut off the head of another with a sword, and while the hand with the henna tattoo glowed red, I hit others with flame. As I continued to flip, I stabbed an opponent through the heart with the trident, shot an enemy through the neck using my golden bow and a flaming arrow, and blasted two away with a wave of water that I shot from my hand using the Pearl Necklace.

Pushing off the ground as though I had jumped on a trampoline, I flipped into the air. Twisting my body up, I saw Ren tear apart a few of the cat-demons to my right. Below us, a big bear-demon growled viciously and swept the air with sharp claws, waiting for me to fall. Thinking quickly, I unwound the Rope of Fire from my waist, lit it with a blue flame, and snapped the Rope around the demon's belly with a sizzling crack.

The momentum yanked me sideways, and I whipped around Ren's body just as he leapt. I managed to grab Ren's torso with one of my arms. As he shot forward, I slid into place on his back just in time. With another flick of my wrist, the Rope of Fire was once again settled at my waist. The bear-demon's body fell, sliced into two. Ren leapt cleanly over the body and landed lightly on his front paws.

Don't do that again, he growled in my mind.

Smiling, I thought. *You have to admit it was cool.*

Cool? You are a devastatingly beautiful angel of death. If death came for me and it looked like you, I'd go willingly.

Realizing they were no match for us, the demons switched course and headed toward my men.

Ren, our soldiers.

He whipped around and raced back to the small group of our men who were still alive. He rounded their flank and leapt toward the largest of the demons: an elephantman that stood on two powerful legs. It raised a weapon to defend itself but Ren was too fast. With a swipe, the weapon was gone. Then he leapt up, grabbed the beast in his jaws, and with a powerful clench and a twist of his body, threw the creature onto its back. I burned it and a dozen others.

Be careful, I admonished. *You don't heal any longer.*

Don't worry about me, sundari. *Today I can do anything.*

To prove his point, he used his teeth to crush the bones of one evil demon and leapt upon another, pinning it to the ground so I could finish it off.

When the last of the stragglers were taken care of, we retreated and regrouped with our remaining soldiers. We'd overcome several hundred demons with only a handful of men, but only a few dozen of our troops had survived. I told them they had served me well and told them to circle round the fire and rest.

Ren and I had a mission of our own.

Together we raced back to the grassy field. Smoke from burning bodies drifted into the air. I twisted to see the catapults still standing and cocked my head when I thought I smelled burned sugar. I heard the noise of fighting coming from beyond the fire and the roar of a distant tiger: Kishan.

It's time to go, Kelsey.

Ren began running, gathered speed, and leapt over lines of fire. We raced toward the mountain, which was guarded by a long line of demons. They stood firm, completely unafraid.

I recognized Sunil standing on a rock jutting out from the cliff.

Raising my arm, I used fire power to take out every demon in my line of sight. Ren never broke his stride.

I glanced up at the overhang, but Sunil was gone.

"Lokesh!" I shouted. "We've come for you! Show yourself, you coward!"

Ren paced back and forth as we sought the devil we'd come to fight.

A laugh echoed deeply through the purple mountains. Wind whipped around my body, carrying sinister words in its cold breath.

"At last we will be joined. The amulet will be mine. You will be mine."

"I'd rather go with another option if it's all the same to you!"

Ren's eyes scanned the barren terrain. Neither of us could tell where the voice was coming from.

Then a swirling dark cloud descended from high above. Cold air moved as fast as a cyclone, and at its core stood the creature Lokesh. Dust and leaves whipped around us. He jumped, and the ground shook. Just as quickly as it swept in, the torrent blew away.

Lokesh looked like an Asian version of a Minotaur, but he was much bigger. He wore a long black robe with a Mandarin collar. His eyes narrowed, and he panted heavily with excitement, sending bursts of steam from his wide nostrils.

"So," he said, "you've returned to me at last. You are even more beautiful than when last I saw you. The power of the goddess suits you, my dear." He took a step toward me, and Ren roared and swiped at his feet.

Lokesh hissed. "Still have a cat tripping at your heels, I see. We'll have to remedy that." He raised his eyes to the flames on the field. "I see you've brought more men to add to my ranks."

"That's not going to happen," I said fiercely. "The ones who have fallen have been burned. They will not rise again. I've released them from your spell."

Lokesh shrugged. "No matter. There are more, many more I can recruit. I can simply end the fight with a flick of my wrist. It would be so easy to destroy what's left of your pathetic army."

"You wouldn't do that. You'd harm your own soldiers too."

He studied me for a few seconds, and then said, "I wouldn't want my future bride to doubt my word."

He smiled evilly, clapped his hands together, and parted them.

The ground shook, and I gasped to see the catapults teeter and fall, collapsing into the hole Lokesh had created. Men and demons ran in every direction as those in the center fell into the chasm. Madly, I scanned the landscape for Durga but couldn't see her. I watched horror-struck as the hole began to close.

Kishan!

No. He's fine, Ren told me.

I saw a flash of gold as Kishan clawed his way out of the closing pit. Durga was clinging tightly to his back. I breathed a sigh of relief.

"Is that the younger prince I see?" Lokesh snorted. "His resilience is tiresome."

As Kishan and Durga ran, Lokesh opened new holes in the ground and laughed. Kishan leapt over them one after another until he and Durga finally disappeared into the trees.

"Leave them alone," I threatened.

"Or . . . what, my little love?"

I raised my bow and nocked an arrow, infusing it with lightning power. "Or I'll end your existence."

He bent at the waist with a flourish. "Please do try."

I let loose the arrow, and he twisted his fingers. A wind knocked the arrow wide, and it sunk into the side of the mountain. The explosion caused a shower of stone.

"I'm disappointed. I was rather hoping to see you put on a show."

"Don't return your ticket just yet." I smiled and narrowed my eyes.

Faster than thought, Ren dodged around Lokesh and jumped, hitting the side of the mountain. In great leaps and bounds he climbed and flipped over in a barrel roll with claws and teeth aimed at Lokesh. I stood on the saddle and cast myself into the air. All of my weapons were fixed on the demon. At once I fired darts with the trident, shot arrows, and swung the *gada*.

Lokesh deflected the projectiles with the wind and raised a wall of stone to block Ren, who hit it hard and fell to the ground, but the *gada* struck the evil sorcerer's shoulder. Lokesh staggered back, bellowing in pain.

"I'll make you pay for that."

"Promise?" I asked as I landed smoothly on my feet and raised my sword.

Lokesh came after me and just as he was about to wrap his arms around me, I closed my eyes and disappeared, reappearing on top of the stone wall.

"How did you do that?" he demanded.

"Give up and I'll tell you."

Ren crouched behind Lokesh, momentarily forgotten. His tail twitched back and forth, and he gathered himself to spring just as an arrow grazed his shoulder. Sunil had joined the fight and raced toward Ren.

Lokesh raised his hands, and a cyclone of air lifted him on top of the rock wall next to me. He attacked with a huge scimitar, but I blocked it with my sword. I advanced with a flurry of arms, dancing atop the thin rock wall, but Lokesh deflected each blow with shields of ice and stone. I realized he was playing with me and decided I needed to bring in the big guns. Gracefully, I backflipped off of the rock and landed lightly on my feet. I glanced at Ren, who was trying to overcome Sunil without killing him. One of his paws was bleeding.

Stay focused, Ren thought.

Lokesh brought his hands down and the rock wall sunk into the ground. I raised a hand to blast him with lightning power, but he combated it with ice. He sent a wave of water at me, which I turned to fog. Anamika must have finished off the remaining demons because some of our soldiers joined us in the fight. The plan had been that when the demon army was all cremated, she and Kishan would rally the others to help us.

The men fired arrows against Lokesh but he turned the arrows back on them using the power of the wind and killed many. The rest he turned to stone or ice statues, and I despaired knowing that our army—a half a million men—had been mostly wiped out in less than forty-eight hours. He tried to freeze me, but I gripped the Rope of Fire and moved myself to another location.

He raised a mist that crept over the entire battlefield, obscuring our position but still another small group of soldiers came upon us and threw spears at Lokesh. Once again, he reversed them in the air. In a flash I snapped the Rope of Fire and flicked the weapons away just before they hit our men. I shouted for them to go help Ren.

I felt a rumble in the ground. A boulder tore away, and heavy rocks lifted into the air. Trees were uprooted and then hurtled toward me, but I whipped the Rope of Fire in a circle beneath me and rose into the sky.

My foot touched an outstretched branch, and I leapt from treetop to rock to branch and rode a falling trunk until it crashed to the ground. Scraped but otherwise unharmed, I stood up atop the teetering mess and glared up at Lokesh. In an instant the Rope of Fire moved me to him, and my sword pressed against his throat.

"Impressive," Lokesh said.

I cut the ancient medallion of black magic from his neck and burned it instantly.

"Your zombie army days are over."

He shoved the sword away from his neck, grabbed one of my arms, and pressed me close. "*If* that had been the real medallion, but it's not. I learned the trick from you, my dear. Remember?"

I glanced down at Sunil. He was still fighting with Ren. An arm hung punctured and broken but he was obviously still under the power of Lokesh. Bitter disappointment washed through me but again I heard Ren's voice.

We'll get it.

I wiped Lokesh's spittle from my cheek and prepared to fight anew, but before I could lift a weapon a rider charged in through the mist below. He bowed before Lokesh and his raven cape billowed behind him.

"General Amphimachus!"

"I delivered your message," the traitor said to Lokesh.

Lokesh raised his head as if sniffing the wind. "Yes, she is close enough now, and he is not resisting."

"What did you do?" I asked Amphimachus.

The general whirled. "The other goddess is on her way to rescue you, but that will not come to pass. Mahishasur, the demon king you call Lokesh, is going to make me the leader of his army. All I need to do is pick an animal, and because you love them so much, I will choose . . . a tiger."

"You may not have this one," Lokesh said. "You can have the other."

"But she's the one I want," Amphimachus whined.

"Would you prefer having me remove your other leg?"

Amphimachus shook his head, and Lokesh waved him aside. "Go deal with the tiger," he commanded.

Lokesh stalked toward me, and a long forgotten story Mr. Kadam had shared flashed through my mind. Taking a few steps back, I held up a shaking hand, fell to my knees, and said, "Please, don't hurt me or my friends any longer. I . . . I give up. Spare me."

Lokesh grabbed a fistful of my golden hair and tugged. "Perhaps," he said lustily, "if you please me suffic—"

Before he could finish his gloating, I whipped my golden sword up to his throat. It cut deep into his thick neck, and he stumbled back, clutching at his wound and bellowing. For a moment I thought I had killed him, but Lokesh's wound began to heal. The gurgle of his breathing steadied. In that instant, I knew that it would take much more to destroy him.

Ren felt my dismay at my failure. He knocked Sunil over and raced back to my side. I leapt on his back and without breaking his stride we circled widely and headed back to confront Lokesh again.

It's okay. We'll get him, but we can't let Lokesh control Durga, Ren quietly insisted. *We have to stop whatever it is that he has planned for her.*

As we spoke, the goddess riding the black tiger appeared out of the mist. Amphimachus lifted a spear, ready to meet Kishan and Durga. Kishan fought him with heavy claws, but Durga seemed to be in a trance.

Ren headed toward them as I raised the Rope of Fire and whipped it around Amphimachus' leg. The blue flame did its work. He screamed in terrible pain, clutching his head. Kishan leapt at his throat and finished him off.

"That's unfortunate for him. He won't be able to fully appreciate his transformation. When they're dead it doesn't hurt," Lokesh sneered from behind me and yanked the real medallion from his pocket.

Suddenly, Durga came out of her trance. She touched the Scarf to her sword, gripped the blade with two hands, and formed a kite that lifted her into the air, away from Kishan. She dropped to her feet and drew her weapons, aiming them on me. I whipped my body to the side, barely hanging onto Ren as the *chakram* flew over our heads.

Kishan leapt toward us but he slid in a sudden pool of oil and fell hard as threads wound around his body, trapping him in a tight net. He kicked and struggled, trying to get loose while Sunil headed toward Kishan with a spear.

I raised my bow and arrow but threads shot toward me and ripped them from my hands. A rope tightened around my ankle while another slithered around my waist and I was yanked from Ren's back.

"Anamika! Stop!" I yelled as I raised my sword to her throat. "I don't want to hurt you!"

She knocked the sword from my hand and gracefully slipped the Rope of Fire from me and wrapped it around her own waist. She used the Scarf to tie me down. One by one, her eight arms grabbed mine and wrestled the other weapons from me. When she was done, she turned to Lokesh.

"What do I do now, Master?"

"Tell me, my girl," he cooed in her ear, "what is the secret of your power?"

"Our power lies in the weapons," she explained in a mesmerized voice.

"Does Kelsey have a power of her own?"

My eyes widened, and I gasped for air as she clutched my throat and squeezed.

"No more than I do," Durga replied.

"Ah, then perhaps . . ."

Lokesh screamed as Ren sunk his claws into his back. The evil sorcerer fell to the ground and rolled but not before Ren slashed at him with his claws and bit his shoulder. Violently, Lokesh twisted back and forth and used his horn to pierce through Ren's armor.

Ren got to his feet while blood dripped heavily from his side. His tiger limbs shook, but he gathered himself for another leap.

Lokesh rose and bellowed, "Today you meet your death, Prince Dhiren." He raised his arms, and spears lifted into the air, shooting toward Ren.

I yelled and summoned the only power I had left: fire. I raised my hand and shot a flame at Durga but she didn't even react when I burned her skin. Aiming my fire power at Lokesh didn't work either. He immediately created a shield of stone. Ren leapt toward Lokesh, claws extended and teeth bared. The dark demon twitched his fingers to redirect the spears to hit Ren mid-flight.

"Ren!" I shouted.

I could actually feel the sharp pointed tips enter his body. Some of the weapons glanced off his silver armor, but one sunk into his hip, another penetrated near his neck, and a third pierced his exposed underbelly. Ren cried out and fell heavily to the ground. Lokesh slammed his cloven hoof down on Ren's foreleg, and the bone snapped.

Pain flooded Ren's mind and I screamed. A few seconds passed and I felt him shutting me out until all I could sense of him was a weak mental voice. I felt a surge of power enter my body and knew that he'd given me all the remaining strength he had. He strained to push one final thought into my mind. *I love you, Kelsey.* And then his voice was cut off completely.

The threads from the Divine Scarf tightened around my limbs as Lokesh approached. He leaned over me and ripped the crown from my head. My hair fell in waves and he picked up a lock and rubbed it between his thick fingers. He touched my cheek with a jagged, filthy nail and trailed it down to my collarbone, leaving a wicked scratch.

"You've deceived me, my dear. I can't let that go unpunished."

With a rough snap the last piece of the amulet was ripped from my neck.

"I've waited a long time for this."

Tears slipped down my face. Anamika was under Lokesh's power, Ren was incapacitated if he was alive at all, and Kishan was tied up somewhere. I was all alone.

A glint of gold wrapped around Durga's upper arm caught my eye. Fanindra!

"Fanindra, help me," I begged, weeping openly.

Green eyes flashed, and the golden cobra came to life. She launched herself from Durga's arm and with jaws wide open sunk her fangs deep into Lokesh's hand. He screamed, but she managed to bite him again before he ripped her away. The golden snake disappeared in the grass.

Immediately, the dark sorcerer's hand began to swell and golden venom dribbled from the puncture wounds in his palm. He dropped my piece of the amulet onto the ground and clutched at the medallion controlling Durga. "Kill her," he ordered.

The goddess raised the *chakram* above my head. I closed my eyes . . . and then felt something hit us hard and push us over. Claws scratched my thigh. It was Kishan! Shaking the last remnants of the net from his body, he leapt onto Durga while Lokesh bellowed in frustration. He tried to use his magic on Kishan but he screamed in agony and clutched his hand.

I hoped it was a permanent situation, while acknowledging it was probably not the case.

Kishan and Durga struggled together, and she slashed him with the *chakram*. Lokesh called out for Sunil, who inched forward, a mangled leg slowing him down.

One of Durga's arms flailed near where I lay bound on the stony soil. I grasped the edge of the Scarf. Instantly the threads holding me captive melted away. I inched my fingers toward her and took hold of the Rope of Fire trying to move as little as possible. I clenched the Rope, knowing this was my last chance.

Sunil drew near and hollered in anger, but Lokesh tossed him like a rag doll.

"Never mind! I'll take care of the black thorn in my side myself!"

Manipulating his good hand, Lokesh grit his teeth and created a dozen shards of ice that he aimed at Kishan. I could see that using his power cost him. Lokesh moved back a step, almost tumbling over Ren. In retaliation, he kicked my white tiger brutally.

Ren lay quietly, spears sticking out of his body at every angle. I could no longer feel Ren's presence at all. Closing my eyes, I called out in my mind.

Ren?

Nothing. No warmth. No heartbeat. Not even a whisper of thought.

Blinking, I looked into his tiger eyes. Their glassy stare reminded me of the stuffed tiger I'd purchased so long ago. Tears ran down my face in rivulets, and I shook with grief. Ren was gone.

Anger shot through me, and I felt a wave of power flow through my frame. Using the only power I had left, I repositioned myself behind Lokesh, drew back the Rope, snapped my arm forward, and whispered, "For Ren." With a crack, the Rope of Fire wound around Lokesh's neck.

Lokesh screamed in agony. He lifted his hands to the Rope and tugged on it, trying to remove it but it only tightened. The zombie medallion was still clutched in his fingers. I channeled all of my remaining power into it. Light coursed through my body, and I felt Ren's spirit. I closed my eyes, and it was as if he were standing behind me, pressing his cheek against mine, one last time. Our combined life-force was greater than earth, wind, fire, water, or space. I knew this power was love.

Golden light poured from my hands and streamed along the Rope. Lokesh's medallion turned into ash. A wave of golden magic picked him up in the air. The light was so intense that it shot out in a blast and filled the sky with color. A sonic boom accompanied the flash, causing the mountains to shake and funnels of water to erupt from the nearby lakes.

With a final terrible scream, it was over. The lifeless body of Lokesh, the demon Mahishasur I'd been destined to defeat, dropped heavily to the ground.

My energy waned, and I felt ghostly hands slide away from my skin. My hot cheek became suddenly cool.

Ren? I begged. *Please don't leave me.*

You are in my heart. Always. His warm voice whispered softly and then faded away.

I collapsed to the ground, my body quaking with torrential sobs.

30

amulet united

A warm hand slid over my shoulder.

"Kelsey?" Kishan's loving voice trembled.

I shook my head back and forth wildly, not able to comprehend what had happened, not wanting the comfort of anyone but Ren.

Kishan stumbled to the body of the white tiger. Carefully, tenderly, he pulled out each spear.

"He's really gone, isn't he?" I asked.

Kishan looked at me, tears filling his golden eyes, and nodded. Swallowing, he stared at the lifeless body of his brother. Then he dashed the back of a hand against his eyes and let out a terrible roar. He yanked out the spear buried in Ren's chest, which jostled Ren's tiger body, and spun.

Running a few steps, toward the inert form that was once Lokesh, he lifted the spear and thrust it into the sorcerer's body. Weeping openly, Kishan sunk to his knees.

Durga crawled toward Ren and poured elixir from the *kamandal* into his mouth. But the liquid just dribbled out onto the ground. I knew there was no point. The elixir couldn't revive the dead. She shook him a few times and spoke in her native tongue. Tears filled her eyes as well. An emotion welled in me, and I shoved her arms away from Ren.

"Get your hands off him! You betrayed us. If it weren't for you he might still be alive."

"I tried to stay back," she explained, "Kishan—"

"Don't you dare blame Kishan for this!" I pointed to Ren then I jabbed my finger angrily into her direction to emphasize my point. "This happened because you were incompetent! I had to come here to this time and do your job. Some goddess you turned out to be. Well, I have news for you. I am *done* being your chosen one. Do you understand?" I spat.

She brokenly nodded then murmured quietly, "I loved him too, little sister."

"Love? *Love?* How *dare* you speak of love! You've known him for what . . . a month? He was mine long before you set your eyes on him, and he was mine when he died. The only thing that *ever* kept us apart in the past or the present was you. You stole his memories just like you stole him here. If it hadn't been for you, we would still be together. Ren was *never* meant for you."

Tears spilled over her lashes. "But I never . . ." she began and then stopped as I turned away, completely uninterested in anything she had to say.

I shook with a righteous tension, fists tightly clenched. In that moment I think I could have killed again. She sat back on her heels and gaped at me, but I ignored her. Instead I picked up one of Ren's paws and smoothed the fur with my hand, pressing my lips against it.

My many arms got in my way so I wrapped the Divine Scarf around me and asked it to make me Kelsey again. That's all I'd ever wanted to be—just a girl from Oregon who went to college and had dates with the boy I loved. But that would never happen now.

Tapping the brooch, I whispered instructions and my armor and the plates covering Ren shrank down. When it was done, I flung the shining piece of jewelry, hard, at the ground near Durga's feet. She seemed shaken, traumatized, but I didn't feel an ounce of sympathy for her. Without a word and with great effort, she picked up the brooch, pulled herself up, and slunk off into the brush.

I scooted closer to Ren and lifted his head onto my lap. Crying, I played with his soft ears and told him that I loved him over and over again. "Please come back," I sobbed. "I need you."

I was surrounded by death like in my long-ago dream. Dead soldiers lay scattered across the field. Ashes from the cremated demons stirred in the breeze. My parents, Mr. Kadam, Ren. They were all gone, and I wasn't sure what else I had to live for.

I held Ren tightly and rocked back and forth. Kishan crouched down next to me, hurt radiating from his eyes. I felt a twinge of guilt, but it was quickly enveloped in my overwhelming anguish. He pulled a strand of hair away from my sticky cheek and tucked it behind my ear.

A movement in the grass caught my eye and a golden head parted the blades, moving toward me. I smiled as I stretched out fingers to touch Fanindra's golden head. The fire amulet was wound around the snake's delicate body. I pulled it off, and Fanindra slid over Ren's back. Her tongue flicked several times as she looked into his glassy eyes.

"Can you heal him?" I asked.

She turned her head to me and left him, gliding over my arm and legs and then resting her head on my thigh.

"I guess that's a no."

I held out my left arm and she took the invitation, winding her body up the limb, circling until she was in her favorite position and then she hardened, becoming her jeweled version.

"We wouldn't have defeated him without you. Thank you," I said softly and her green eyes glowed for a moment before becoming hardened emeralds. Kishan stood silently at my side, waiting for me. I smoothed the fur on Ren's brow and pressed a lingering kiss on top on his head.

"I love you," I whispered.

"We need to leave, Kelsey."

My hands clenched in Ren's fur. "I won't leave him here."

"I'll carry him," he volunteered.

I nodded, tenderly set down Ren's head, and stood.

Dusting the amulet off and removing the broken chain, I handed it to Kishan.

He cupped it in his hand, touched it with a finger, and mused quietly, "This was the first gift I ever gave you." Closing his fingers over it, he looked at me and said faintly, "I don't think it can be fixed."

Something about the way he said it made my throat tighten, but I pushed that feeling aside and used the Scarf to make a ribbon. When the amulet was tied around my neck once again, I felt better.

"Get the rest of the amulet," I instructed Kishan.

Lokesh lay on the ground, his two sets of sharpened horns pointing skyward. Ren's blood still glistened on one of them. Kishan ripped open the top of Lokesh's robe and tugged the amulet loose. He placed it in my open hand. It was an almost complete circle with a carved tiger in the center.

I squeezed the disk tightly between my thumb and forefinger and said, "The blood of Captain Dixon, Mr. Kadam, Ren, and countless others has been spilled by this . . . demon. He needs to be destroyed utterly."

Without knowing exactly how or why, I knew what to do. Using the fire piece of the amulet, I cracked the Rope of Fire against the ground. A chasm opened, widened, and deepened to the molten core of Earth.

Terrible flames leapt from the fissure. Lifting my hands, I commanded a gust of air to pick up Lokesh's body, which rose and hovered in front of us.

I looked into the monster's eyes one last time. I could almost hear his derisive laughter, and I wondered if this creature would haunt me for the rest of my days.

Kishan touched my arm, breaking my trance. I stepped back and sent the demon king into the flames. Lokesh plummeted through the chasm. When he was nothing but ash, I cracked the whip once more, and the earth closed over him.

"I am glad he is gone," Durga said quietly as she walked slowly toward us, this time accompanied by her brother.

Sunil leaned heavily against his sister and watched us with a look of awe, but I wasn't in the mood for introductions.

I turned away from the pair. "Can we go now, Kishan?"

"Just a minute, Kells."

The goddess quickly handed Kishan the *kamandal*. It was then I saw the terrible wound in his side.

"Drink," she commanded.

He took hold of her wrist and her eyes darted up to his. "Drink," she said again, softer this time.

Kishan sipped the mermaid's elixir and then she brought it to me. I pushed her hand away.

"You need to heal, Kelsey," she said.

"The pain I feel isn't going away."

"Please, take some."

After glaring at her and seeing she wasn't going away, I took the *kamandal* and drank. Immediately the pain in my muscles started to diminish.

As I handed the shell back to her she asked, "Is there anything you can do . . . for them?" She indicated the troops that stood around us, frozen in stone and ice.

"I can try," I replied.

I rubbed the amulet between my fingers and sensed through the pad of my thumb which piece represented water. The power of rivers, streams, oceans, and rain filled me, and at that moment, I felt as if I could dissolve my body and sink through the ground I stood on.

Though I stood still I felt the movement of rocking water as it swirled through me. Stretching out with my mind, I found the men who were frozen and slowly breathed warmth into their bodies. Water molecules quickened, and the men began to move.

My thumb shifted and I found the Earth piece. My body suddenly became heavy, unbreakable. Earth's power grounded me, gave me a center. Earth does not despair or feel loss, I realized, for all living things come from it, and all living things return to it. Refocusing, I found the stone objects dotting the area around me and asked the stone to return life to these beings. The stone obeyed and melted back into the landscape. The men took a breath and lived.

Durga wove between each man and bid them drink from the *kamandal*. She was full of compassion, and they each dropped to their knees and gazed upon her with worshipful, trusting eyes. I folded my arms across my chest, determined not to be moved by her display.

When she had administered to every man, they gathered close and she turned to us. "These people need rest and food. We must lead them to camp and help them recover." Then the humble goddess turned to Sunil in deference. "If that is acceptable to you."

"No. You're right, Mika. We should take care of them," he replied, stepping back.

She nodded and gave instructions to return to the camp. Flanked by Durga and Sunil, the men set off immediately.

With a graceful sweep of his arms, Kishan lifted Ren's tiger body, and we solemnly followed our troops. Ren's white tail brushed the ground and his head lolled as it hung over Kishan's arm. My breath caught and I had to swallow several times.

Back at camp, I used the Pearl Necklace and the Scarf to create a bucket of warm water and cloths and cleaned the blood from Ren's fur. Kishan had left me alone for a time, saying he'd return to bury Ren after the camp was settled. There was something comforting about being alone with my tiger and preparing his body. It was a final act of service I could do for the man I loved and I spoke softly to him as I worked.

The light dimmed and I started when I heard a noise.

"How long have you been standing there?" I asked Kishan.

"Long enough," he answered with a tight expression.

He came into the tent and was followed by Durga and her brother. A moment later, the tent flap parted and a bald head poked through.

"May I come in?" Phet asked.

"Please!" Durga responded.

Phet caught sight of Ren at that moment and shook his head. "This is a most unfortunate turn of events," he said as he lowered himself on a cushion.

"You have a gift for understatement," I replied with fresh tears.

Phet took my hand into his wrinkled brown ones and said, "There is hope, my flower. Do you have all the pieces of the amulet?"

"Yes."

"May I see them?"

I took the fire piece from my neck and placed it in his hand then I picked up the one worn by Lokesh that I'd set down next to me and handed that to him too.

As he removed the fire piece from the ribbon and handed it back to me with Kishan's golden key, he explained. "The Damon Amulet is an Astra. An Astra is a cosmic weapon or a tool, if you will, that channels great power when properly invoked."

"Invoked?"

"Yes. A deity will respond to an incantation and endow a weapon with their gifts. For example, an Agniastra creates inextinguishable flames, a Suryastra generates brilliant light, and a Varunaastra produces vast quantities of water. The greater the god, the more power the Astra wields."

"Well, which one is this?" I asked. "And how do we invoke it?"

"You have already used many of the forces contained within these individual amulet pieces, but what you haven't had access to is the power of the combined amulet."

With a snap, Phet fit the fire wedge into the empty section of the amulet disk. The edges of each piece briefly glowed with a white light, and then the five pieces became whole. He held the Damon Amulet up, and firelight glinted off the stone.

He handed it to me, and I ran my finger over the carved tiger in the center. "We know that Lokesh had power over elements and even living creatures," I said. "Now that the amulet is whole, what do you want us to do with it?"

"Well, the first thing *I* would do is bring back your handsome prince," Phet said with a wink.

I gaped at him.

Softly, I asked, "Can I really do this?"

"*You* can't. The Damonastra can. But you must invoke the power of Damon."

"Damon as in Durga's tiger?"

The shaman hesitated and carefully chose his words. "The one and the same. Damon sacrificed himself, giving the tigers life in the very beginning," he explained gently. "He can grant the same gift again. All you have to do is read the incantation."

I squinted at the Sanskrit words circling the amulet. Nervously, I wet my lips and looked up. "Kishan? Could you read it?"

Kishan nodded, sat beside me, and gave me a quick but tender embrace.

Pursing his lips and tracing the words around the amulet with his forefinger, Kishan murmured, "*Damonasya Rakshasasya Mani-Bharatsysa Pita-Rajaramaasya Putra*. It says:

> The Amulet of Damon
> The Father of India
> The Son of . . .
> Rajaram."

31

trading places

t he word *Rajaram* had barely escaped his lips when the Damon Amulet began to glow. The Sanskrit lettering seemed to float up from the stone, and the outer section of the disk started to spin. The words circled faster and faster until they became a solid white line.

"Now, use the power of Damon to bring life back to your brother," Phet instructed.

"But how?" Kishan mumbled.

"The difficulty is not in the knowing; it's in the choosing."

Kishan closed his eyes and his body burned with a white energy. He gasped and trembled.

Alarmed, I asked desperately, "What's happening to him? Is he in pain?"

Phet replied, "Kishan must choose whether or not to accept the price in order to save his brother."

"A price? What price? Kishan, don't do this. I can pay whatever price is necessary."

Phet squeezed my arm. "This is something Kishan must choose, Kahl-see. This is *his* destiny."

Kishan panted. Sweat trickled down his face. His head and arms jerked back violently, and he cried out.

"Kishan!" I started toward him, but Phet held me back and shook his head.

As Kishan writhed in pain and agony, a small light rose from his chest and headed for the fallen white tiger. As the bright beam passed by me, I swore I could see the Sanskrit symbols twisting and swirling in an arc around Ren. A thin mist materialized and hovered over Ren like a silky funeral shroud.

Suddenly the blanket of light melted into Ren's body. Kishan stiffened and fell forward on his hands and knees, groaning, and breathing heavily. I threw my arms around Kishan's trembling shoulders. As his chest rose and fell, I became aware of another chest moving.

The white tiger inhaled deeply, and Phet said, "Anamika, hurry. He must drink from the *kamandal*."

She positioned herself at Ren's side and dribbled the elixir into his mouth. The spear wounds on Ren's body began to heal.

"Now, it's your turn, Kahl-see. Heal him with your golden flame."

"But . . ." I faltered. "I don't have the fire amulet anymore."

"The golden flame comes from inside you. It always has."

Leaving Kishan for the moment and cradling the body of my white tiger, I channeled what was left of my energy into him. I sent him my thoughts, whispering to him in my mind and heart, willing him to live. I felt the warmth of the golden fire run through me. Ren's body hummed in response.

Gaping wounds healed rapidly and within a few minutes he was able to roll toward me and sit up. As he huffed softly, I buried my face in the white fur of his neck and wrapped my arms around him. I cried with joy.

Ren shifted form and held me tightly against his body. Pressing his lips against my temple, he murmured words in Hindi as he stroked my back. Finally lifting his head, he asked, "How has this happened?"

Phet answered, "Your brother has made the necessary sacrifice," Phet said somberly, and we all turned our attention to Kishan.

"What does he mean?" I asked.

Kishan cleared his throat. "It's hard to explain. A life restored is no easy thing. To bring him back, I had to give up a part of myself."

"I still don't understand." Reluctantly, I slid away from Ren and knelt at Phet's feet.

"What did Kishan give up?" I asked.

Phet sighed, and said, "His immortality. Fortunately, he was strong enough to survive the process."

He patted my hand as a tear dripped onto my cheek. "Do not fret, Kahl-see, Kishan will still live for a long, long time—much longer than several human life spans."

I nodded and knelt by the man with the golden eyes, the man I had relied upon since leaving Oregon, the man who was in love with me. His elbows rested on his drawn up knees. Little tremors still shook his body and his breathing was shallow. When I touched his shoulder, he gave me a distracted smile.

"Thank you for saving Ren," I whispered and wrapped my arms around his neck.

Kishan stretched out his legs and took hold of my waist, shifting me onto his lap. He searched my face and with naked emotion said, "I'd do anything for you, Kelsey. You know that, don't you?"

Softly, I smiled and stroked his cheek. "I know that."

The brothers gave each other a long look. They didn't utter a word, but I could tell from their solemn faces that much more than gratitude was conveyed in their silence.

Kishan wrapped his arms around me and held me close. When I pulled away, Durga and her brother were gone and Ren was studying his hands as he rubbed them slowly together. Phet stood and announced, "You must eat and rest tonight. Tomorrow we will discuss the future."

Then he stepped outside the tent. Kishan took my hand and rose to follow. Ren stood too, and I was momentarily lost in his gaze as I passed him. Cobalt blue eyes captured mine, and my heart fluttered like a butterfly caught in a net. Ren ran his hand down my arm and our fingers brushed together briefly before Kishan led me outside the tent. Phet had disappeared.

The five of us regrouped to eat around the fire, but after giving Kishan and me the once over as we stood side by side, hands clasped, Durga narrowed her eyes, said she wasn't hungry, and stalked off into the darkness.

Kishan called out, "Ana, you need to eat something," but the Amazon warrior goddess with an attitude disappeared.

With raised eyebrows, Kishan gave me a peck on the cheek before leaving to retrieve the Golden Fruit. Ren readily took his spot next to me.

"I'm sorry I've acted . . . less than hospitable," I said to Sunil as we warmed ourselves by the flames. "Things have been . . ."

"Very strange," he admitted. "I have not felt slighted. In fact, I have much to thank you for. I apologize for my sister. She is not behaving much like the sister I know. When she remembers herself, she will return to thank you as well."

I laughed softly. "I won't hold my breath but thank you."

Kishan returned with the Fruit and paused when he saw Ren sitting with me. He shook his head as he approached, then, stubbornly sat on my other side, pressing his thigh and arm against mine. I suddenly felt like I was a very thin layer of chocolate separating two cookies fresh out of the oven.

Shoving entire pizza pies at Ren, Kishan, and a happily surprised Sunil distracted everyone a bit.

After Sunil was on his fifth slice of cheesy goodness, I asked, "How did Lokesh catch you anyway?"

"The irony is that if I'd listened to my sister, I wouldn't have been taken," Sunil explained. "We first heard of the demon a year ago. Rumors spread from trade caravans saying that he was gathering an army and that entire villages were disappearing. Anyone who ventured north near the Great Mountains were warned that they risked their lives if not their very souls.

"The people said that once the demon leader looked into your eyes, you'd live for an eternity enslaved by him, an evil spirit that would never let you go. The stories were terrible, and when one of the most treasure-laden caravans of our king went missing, we were finally sent with our armies to take care of the situation.

"It was during our second assault that I was taken. I'd been hit on the head and knocked unconscious. Anamika found me and brought me back to camp and I am sad to admit that I doubted her when she described the horrible fate of our dead. I couldn't comprehend such an evil. It was impossible. I'd always been the practical one, the skeptic, and I told her that magic such as that did not exist."

"But didn't you see the enemy soldiers?" I asked.

"We fought them in the swirling mists and during that fight many of them wore armor. How could I ask my men to fight magic? I simply refused to give in to the wild speculation and told them we fought clever men who used tricks to frighten their enemies."

Sunil bent his knees and wrapped his arms around them. "Anamika was the believer between the two of us. She worshipped the gods and always felt that something, or some . . . power, dwelt outside of our human existence. She showed great faith in everything our teacher told her, but I considered them to be just the fabricated stories of an imaginative monk.

"After my first defeat, she described terrors so indomitable that our only option was to turn our heads toward home in shame. My pride wouldn't allow that. A few days later I strapped on my armor and left only a small number of soldiers behind with my sister. She cried and pleaded for me not to go. A few men had to physically restrain her from jumping onto her horse to follow me. As I left, I heard her voice carrying in the wind, begging me to return and leave this place of death.

"When the battle started, my men were literally ripped apart. I'd just given the signal for retreat and turned my horse around when I heard a screech from above. Huge claws sunk into my shoulder and talons pierced my skin. I was carried through the sky and was dropped on a stone outcropping. Before me stood the demon himself. Somehow he pinned me to the side of the mountain using only his mind to freeze my body. I was still aware of what was happening, but there was nothing I could do about it.

"He took my knife and cut my palm, dribbling my blood onto a wooden talisman. He said, 'I have need of a commander for my army. This is why I have kept you alive, little warrior.' He began chanting, and the medallion glowed red and then white. Light shot toward me and entered my body. The pain was so intense that I would have sunk to my knees and begged for death if I could have. Everything went black and then my body was no longer mine to control."

"Do you remember what happened to you?"

"I can recall bits and pieces, but it was almost as if I was in a dark waking dream. The things I experienced happened in a place far away, outside of me. Does that make sense?"

Ren nodded.

"And your sister? Did she feel this pain?" I asked.

"Yes," Kishan said flatly, "she did."

"I'm sorry."

I put my hand on Kishan's arm as Sunil rose, saying he was going to find his sister.

"'Night, Sunil. Let's get some rest, Kells," Kishan said, and we ducked into my tent. He flashed a look at Ren and added, "Don't you have somewhere else to be, big brother?"

Ren shrugged and smiled shamelessly at Kishan. "Think of me as your chaperone. Are you regretting saving me now?"

Ren was so good natured about it that Kishan's lip twitched.

"Maybe," he grumbled and busied himself setting up a place to sleep.

I caught Ren's eye and he winked at me; then prepared his own place to rest.

Laying down, I tucked my arms beneath my head and asked the two men on either side of me, "Can you still become tigers?"

"Yes," they both answered simultaneously.

"Then the curse hasn't been broken. There's still something else we need to do, isn't there?"

Kishan grunted and Ren said, "I believe there is."

I turned to look at his blue eyes in the firelight. "That's what scares me," I said softly.

We were quiet after that, and I fell asleep listening to the pops of the crackling fire and the deep breathing of both of my tigers.

We found Durga busy with the remaining soldiers the next day. She was a natural leader, and even her brother stepped back and let her command the army. Scribes were brought forward to write dictated letters that would be sent by messenger to all the different tribes and kings that had a vested interest in the outcome of the battle.

I could tell as I listened that she downplayed her own achievements and noted that instead of writing about Kelsey, Durga, Ren, and Kishan, the letters only mentioned the two incarnations of the goddess.

As different men stepped forward to share their own interpretation of the battle, I thought back to my research on Durga, and I finally understood where all the references came from. Phet had been right. We had always been destined to take this road. The stories I'd read were *our* stories, and if we hadn't been willing to go through with our quests, history as we know it would have changed.

The soldiers talked of boiling lakes, battle drums, and the divine breath of the goddess that gave life to men encased in stone. Mountains shook, a goddess danced across the tops of uprooted trees, and the roar of tigers was heard around the world.

They also listed the powers they'd seen, and the words contained in the prophecies were finally clear. With the Golden Fruit, Durga could feed millions. The Divine Scarf would help her clothe the masses. The Pearl Necklace would be used to end drought, fill rivers, and provide drinking water, and the Rope of Fire surely fulfilled its purpose in bringing peace to the nations by helping me slay Mahishasur.

The goddess Durga was created in a time of great need to overcome a foe that no man could destroy. A woman *was* fated to fight the demon Mahishasur, but history got it wrong. Not one woman but two. Two avatars of the goddess overcame Lokesh.

Phet said that our future would soon be determined. I wondered if that meant we had to stay here. *Could I be happy living in the past?* As a goddess I'd be waited upon. Thousands would come to worship us. We'd have all the gifts and weapons at our disposal, and we'd have the Damon Amulet. The power we had was virtually limitless. We could help so many.

I sighed. I didn't crave ultimate power. I didn't want to lead an empire or make myself out to be the some kind of heroine for the masses. Living as a goddess was a noble sacrifice to make. I'd spend the rest of my days serving others, which was a great thing. But, deep down, a normal life was really what I craved. I wanted a chance to be a mom. To marry a wonderful guy—someone who would take me out to dinner once in a while and who I could nag about putting his socks into the hamper.

That was the life I'd planned on.

I didn't want to be magical.

I didn't want to be a goddess.

I just wanted to be . . . me.

Anamika and I spent the rest of the afternoon organizing the camp. It was good to be doing something useful, and it kept my mind off whatever the future would bring.

After a time of working together quietly, I said to Anamika, "I'm sorry."

"For what?"

"For blaming you for Ren's death."

She paused while folding a blanket, then set it softly on top of a pile. "You were right to blame me. If Lokesh had not killed Ren, I would have tried."

"You were under Lokesh's control. It's not your fault."

"I should have been strong enough to resist him."

"No one could."

"You did."

I sighed. "He didn't have my blood."

"He . . . he wanted you. I could feel it when he controlled me."

"Yes, he wanted a powerful son, and he thought I could provide one."

Anamika nodded. "You are very beautiful. I understand why he would desire one such as you as his mate."

"Me?" I almost choked with laughter. "Are you serious?"

"I do not jest, Kelsey. They all want you. Your tigers are devoted to you utterly. Their eyes never leave your face. You are as the sun to them. You are strong and powerful, and yet your skin is as soft as a flower and your hair smells of perfume. You are small, which makes a man puff out his chest and sweep you into his arms to carry you to safety.

"I am not like you. I am big and clumsy. My hair is always in knots and my skin is not creamy like goat's milk. I fight men and often overpower them, which makes them feel weak. They have no desire to be close to me, and any man who tries is soon scared away when I argue with him. My temper is too fiery."

"I have a temper, too. You should hear some of the fights I've had with Ren."

"But still, there is great love there."

"Yes," I admitted.

"When I was with Kishan in battle, our minds connected, and I knew his thoughts about you. He worried that you are still in love with his brother. You once loved Dhiren."

"Yes."

"But now you are betrothed to Kishan."

"Yes."

She considered me quietly for a moment then stood. Before she exited the tent, she said, "I am envious of the love both brothers have for you. Treat them well, litt . . . Kelsey."

Anamika left, and I stayed in the tent thinking about what she said for a long time.

The sunset that night was beautiful. The sky was full of puffy clouds that reflected gold, pink, and orange bands across the sky. The purple and blue mountains cast their shadows over the valley, but the white snow laden tips sparkled in the diminishing sunlight. The smell of pine and oak and campfires filled the air.

I sat between Ren and Kishan as we mingled with Anamika and Sunil's men, sharing an evening meal. I felt content and at peace until the air twinkled and Phet appeared.

Saying nothing, he headed through the forest to a secluded glen. The five of us followed, and when Phet turned to speak, my stomach fluttered nervously.

"Do you have the Rope of Fire?" Phet asked.

Anamika nodded, took it from her bag, and handed it to him.

He coiled the Rope in his hand and said, "I am proud of all of you. You have accomplished a great thing and have protected the world from the demon. The stage has been set, and the time has now come for you to take your places and act your parts."

The last rays of the sun hit Phet's back and shone on his bald head. It might have been an illusion, but his body looked like it was surrounded by light. A bird made a pecking noise on a tree.

This was it. The moment when Phet broke the tiger's curse and Ren and Kishan could be fully human. We'd worked so hard for this. Overcome so much. Would the universe give them what they deserved—a normal life—or would the two of them suddenly age and die before my eyes?

I didn't know what would happen, but I held their hands tightly and wished on the still invisible stars that Ren and Kishan would survive this. Breathing in the scent of the forest, I swallowed nervously and closed my eyes. When I opened them, Phet was smiling at me which I took to be a good sign.

"Kelsey," he said, "It is time for you to go home."

I clutched my tigers' hands. Uncertainly, I asked, "But what will happen to Anamika?"

"She will take on the role destiny created for her."

I looked over at the woman who would become a goddess. She shifted uncomfortably at the news.

"You must leave all Durga's weapons and gifts with her, for she will need them," Phet instructed.

Ren, Kishan, and I handed over everything to the leggy Amazon.

She stood stiffly. Her brother said something softly to her, but she refused to make eye contact with the three of us. Her expression was stony, and she seemed determined not to say good-bye.

Something in me softened, and I put my arms around her waist. I hugged her fiercely and said, "You're the bravest woman I know. You'll be a wonderful Durga."

She hesitated only a moment before hugging me back. Her rigid expression relaxed into one of sadness.

"Thank you for returning my brother to me. It is more than I deserve."

I slipped Fanindra from my arm and pressed the snake's nose to mine. "I never thought I'd get used to having a cobra for a pet. Thank you for saving all of our lives."

The cobra's golden body grew and she coiled herself around my hands. Her pink tongue shot out and tickled the tip of my nose, and her emerald eyes gleamed. I passed her to Durga who carefully readjusted Fanindra's coils over her arm.

"Take care of her," I whispered.

"We will keep one another company," the goddess replied. "Good-bye, Kelsey."

Sunil smiled and squeezed my arm.

As we parted, I saw Ren nod to her. She gave him a small smile in return, but when Kishan stepped toward her with his hand outstretched, she turned away and wrapped her arm around her brother's waist. He stubbornly waited for her to look at him, but she refused.

I took Ren's hand in my left and Kishan's in my right. I had only the clothes on my back. Durga would keep the Damon Amulet, the golden weapons, and all the gifts, and I would return to my time with only myself and my tigers and a crazy story. I was ready.

"There's still one last thing that must be done before I send you back, Kahl-see," Phet said.

He began speaking words in Hindi and then asked, "Do you remember the first piece of the prophecy that was translated?"

"'Seek Durga's prize. Four gifts, five sacrifices. One transformation. Beast becomes mortal.'"

"That is correct. You have found the four gifts of Durga."

"We've also given sacrifices at her temples," Kishan said.

"You have, but in this instance the five sacrifices spoken of are not worldly in nature. You have offered four of the five sacrifices. The first sacrifice was when Ren gave up his memory of Kahl-see to save her life."

Ren squeezed my hand as my breath caught.

"The second was when Mr. Kadam gave up his life to send Lokesh into the past."

I clutched Kishan's forearm. Tears welled in my eyes.

"The third sacrifice was when Kahl-see gave herself up to the Phoenix as a Sati wife. Her body burned so the tigers would be safe. The fourth sacrifice happened yesterday when Kishan gave up a piece of his own immortality to bring life back to his brother."

My mouth suddenly went dry. "Then the fifth sacrifice . . . ?"

"Must be made before you can return."

I couldn't control the trembling of my limbs. I suddenly felt like my entire body was made of water, and it was all I could do to remain upright.

"What else do we need to do?" I whispered.

Phet looked at me with deep regret. "Durga needs a tiger."

I sunk to my knees at Phet's feet. Tears spilled onto my cheeks. "No. No. No." I mumbled over and over again. This was it. I was so close to getting safely home and now one of the men I loved would remain behind.

Durga took a few steps toward me, but I held up my hand and stood of my own accord. She seemed sympathetic but also a bit hopeful.

"Stay away from me," I said. "I . . . I just can't look at you right now."

As she dropped her hands to her sides, my gaze flitted over to Ren and Kishan, who were talking quietly with Phet. Ren looked up and what I saw in his eyes frightened me. His gaze was full of regret and sorrow.

My hand shook as I cupped my mouth and breathed quickly.

"I am truly sorry for this, Kahl-see," Phet said when he approached me.

"Sorry doesn't fix it."

"No, it does not."

I paced back and forth, glancing from time to time at Ren and Kishan who were in deep discussion. This was what I'd always been afraid of. Ren was going to sacrifice himself. He couldn't help it. I knew him very well. If he could spend his whole life serving the world, he would do it. He'd give up what he wanted so his brother could be happy. He was going to stay behind with Durga. He'd be a king, a god, and I'd never, *ever* see him again.

I couldn't look at them anymore. I spun and headed into the trees and collapsed onto a fallen log, sobbing. My heart was breaking. Ren had been brought back from death only in time for me to lose him again.

After a while, Kishan crouched in front of me and pushed limp hair away from my stinging eyes.

"Shh, *bilauta*. Everything's going to be okay."

"How can you . . ." I snuffled loudly. "How can you say that? We're going to . . ." I hiccupped. "Going to lose him *forever*."

"Come on," he said as he pulled me to my feet. "Dry your eyes and try to smile. It's time to say good-bye."

"I can't, Kishan. I just can't."

"Please try." He kissed my forehead and used his thumbs to wipe the tears from my cheeks.

I nodded, but looking up at him and seeing his tender expression full of love and patience made my eyes fill again.

Softly, he said, "I wanted you from the first moment I saw you hiding in the bushes, Kells. The truth is I knew you were there the whole time. I laid my eyes on you that day, and I haven't ever been able to look away since. I tried to, but . . ." he smiled as he pressed his forehead against mine, ". . . there was something irresistible about you. You were so lost and yet such a spitfire—just like an angry little kitten. I wanted to tuck you into the crook of my arm and keep you."

"Kishan, I—"

"I know you love him, Kelsey. I've known since that day in the jungle when you confessed your true feelings to Saachi, not knowing it was me in disguise. If I was completely honest with myself I'd confess that I even knew before that."

He took a deep breath and his voice trembled. "I told myself that as long as you wore my ring, as long as you wanted me, needed me, that I would be there for you. That I'd try to become the kind of man you could love. There *is* love between us isn't there, Kells?" he asked almost desperately.

"There is," I answered as I smoothed his hair from his face. "I could no more give you up than I can him."

He laughed shakily and nodded. "That's really what I needed to hear." With a small smile, he kissed each of my hands in turn and said, "Then kiss me good-bye, *bilauta*."

"What? Good-bye? What do you—"

Kishan interrupted me with a kiss. Wrapping his arms around my body, he kissed me softly, sadly. My mind swam with questions, with worries, and with confusion; but all that suddenly became unimportant as I focused on the man who loved me so much he was willing to let me go.

I placed my arms around his neck and pulled him closer. Tears dripped down our cheeks. I could taste the saltiness of it. I poured all of my love and affection for this good man into the kiss. It blazed with heat and passion for a short time and then changed into something soft, something tender. When his lips left mine, they trailed over my cheeks and temple as Kishan held me close.

I pressed my hand over the heart of my black tiger and knew I'd never be the same without him.

"Why are you doing this?" I asked faintly as I sniffled.

"It's the right thing, Kelsey."

"I can't give you up, Kishan. How can we be asked to make this choice?"

He stroked my hair softly and said, "Once, a long time ago, you asked me to let you go. Do you remember?"

I nodded against his chest.

After a moment, he took my hands and turned them over. He pressed a gentle kiss on each of my palms and said, "Now I'm asking you, Kelsey, to let *me* go."

I trembled. "Is this what you truly want?"

He hesitated only briefly before answering. "It's what needs to happen."

I cried with renewed vigor while Kishan rubbed my shoulders and back and pressed kisses along my hairline. Finally, he sighed and asked, "Are you ready?"

"No," I dashed my hands across my cheeks. "I promised you a happy ending."

He smiled. "My ending hasn't been determined yet." He took my face in his hands and vowed, "I will always hold a piece of you in my heart, Kelsey Hayes."

"And I will keep a place for you in mine, Kishan Rajaram."

Taking my hand, he pressed a golden key into my palm and closed his fingers over mine decisively.

"But it belongs to you," I protested.

"Take it with you and build a home like the one we talked about."

"I will," I whispered.

He kissed my closed eyelids. "It's time, Kells."

Tucking my hand around his arm, we walked back toward the others. Just before we stepped through the trees, he paused. "You'll remember me?"

"How can you even ask?"

He grunted. "Promise me something."

I looked into haunted golden eyes full of heartbreak and sorrow and said, "Anything."

"Promise you'll be happy."

I nodded as he wiped some tears from my cheeks with his thumbs and then guided me out of the trees.

"We're ready," Kishan announced. He led me over to Ren and put my hand into his brother's. Ren's bright blue eyes were red rimmed and full of unshed tears, but they met mine unashamedly, and he squeezed my hand gently.

"Take care of her," Kishan said to his brother.

Ren clasped Kishan's arm in his and said with a quiver in his voice, "Yours in life, Kishan."

"Yours in death, Dhiren," Kishan finished.

"Thank you," Ren said softly.

"Strive your whole life to deserve her, brother."

When Ren nodded, Kishan stretched out his fingers to trail them briefly down my jaw before turning away. He stopped next to Durga and folded his arms across his chest. Neither of them looked at each other.

Phet stepped forward. "A sacrifice has been made. Kishan will henceforth be known as Damon, the tiger of Durga. He will keep his power to heal as well as his ability to shift into tiger form, though there is now no limit on how long he can remain human. As for Ren . . ."

Phet lifted the Damon Amulet and murmured a few words. A bright light circled around the amulet. It seemed to draw a white mist from Ren's body and pull it through the disk.

"The transformation is done. The beast is mortal." Phet stepped forward and clasped Ren's shoulder. His eyes were also full of tears. "Congratulations, son."

Ren put his hand on his chest and gasped. "It . . . he's . . . gone. The tiger is gone."

"You are a mortal once again," Phet said. "You will live a normal life span as if you were starting over again at twenty-one years of age."

Phet approached me and took my right hand. He pressed his over mine until the henna tattoo he'd given me glowed red and then faded. He patted my newly naked right hand. Turning away, he flicked the Rope. Fire shot down the length of it. He whipped it into a circle to open a vortex.

Phet announced, "Three of you came to the past, and three must return. Sunil?"

"No!" Durga gasped in shock. "You will *not* take my brother."

"One that they love for one that you love, Anamika. This is how the universe maintains balance."

"It is not fair! My burden is too heavy to bear!"

"Damon will help you," Phet counseled.

She narrowed her eyes at Kishan, who accepted her scrutiny with patience.

Turning to her brother, she took his hands. "I never asked for this," she said with a voice cracking with tears.

"Shh, Mika," Sunil said. "It will be alright. Phet told me about this last night, and I agreed." He gripped her arm and explained. "There is no longer a place for me here, dear sister. The armies look to you now. You are their leader. If I stayed by your side, I would only remind them that you were once human. Men will test you, question you, and use me as an excuse to try to strip the power from you. It must be made known that Anamika and Sunil Kalinga died in this battle. Durga survived, and it is Durga you must now become. Hold this power close. Guard it. The world is in your hands, my sister. It is not easy leaving you, but for you to take your true place in history, I must."

"How will I do this knowing my brother exists in another time, another place?"

"The same way I will. I will send my wishes to you in the stars. I'm so proud of you, Mika." He kissed his twin sister on both cheeks.

"I will miss you, Sunil."

"And I will think of you every day."

He clutched Kishan's arm. "Will you care for my sister?"

"I will protect her with my life," Kishan pledged.

The two men studied each other for a moment before Sunil nodded. We all took a final sip from the *kamandal* so the pressure of the universe would be less heavy to bear.

I turned to look into Kishan's golden eyes one last time. He smiled softly, and I whispered, "I love you."

Then Ren took my hand, and together we ran for the vortex, Sunil at our side.

As I jumped through, I heard Kishan say softly, "Good-bye, *bilauta*."

Thoughts dragged sharp claws across my heart, threatening to tear it open. I closed my eyes and whispered to the universe to please take care of Kishan and give him the life he deserved.

Pressing Kishan's ring to my lips, I gave myself up to the darkness.

promises

Kelsey. Miss Kelsey. Wake up!"

Someone shook my shoulder, and I groaned.

"Come on, Miss Kelsey. Please."

"Listen, bossy warrior Barbie, let me sleep," I grumbled and rolled over onto cold, smooth tile.

Placing my palm down on the hard surface and propping myself up, I cracked open a crusted eye. "Where am I?"

"You are home," a friendly voice answered.

"Home?"

I sat up and rubbed my eyes. *Nilima!*

I was sitting in a ray of sunshine in the foyer of Ren's house.

She hugged me lightly, and we both turned when we heard a grunt.

"Ren?"

I crawled over to Ren as he blinked and sat up.

"Are you okay?" he asked as he cupped my cheek.

I pressed my hand on top of his. His eyes searched mine, and I knew he was asking about more than my physical health.

"I will be," I answered softly.

We heard another moan and found Sunil sprawled on the thick

carpet of the music room. Nilima stepped around us, and her eyes widened at the stranger.

Trying to get his bearings, Sunil stood and gaped openly at the grand piano, Ren's guitars, and the giant stereo system gleaming before him.

"Welcome to our home," Ren said. "We'll put you in Kishan's room for the time being."

Sunil nodded distractedly as he stretched out his fingers to touch framed pictures and an antique lamp, but when Ren pulled Nilima into the room to make introductions, the stranger from centuries earlier ignored everything but the woman in front of him.

Sunil smiled disarmingly, and I was struck again by how handsome he was. His green eyes flashed as he took Nilima's palm. Bowing, he pressed his forehead against her hand and said, "It is an honor to greet one so beautiful. Thank you for your hospitality."

Nilima narrowed her eyes suspiciously and snatched her hand back. "You're welcome." Turning to Ren, she queried, "Who is he? And where is Kishan?"

"Kishan . . . won't be returning," Ren said softly.

Nilima turned questioning eyes to me. I swallowed and nodded as I felt the pain of leaving Kishan creep back up my throat.

"Tell me we haven't lost him too," she entreated.

"He has not passed on, dear lady," Sunil explained. "He has stayed in the past to take care of my sister."

"Who is your sister and why is she worthy enough to demand his attention?" Nilima asked hotly, tears in her eyes.

"My sister is the goddess Durga. Your brother Kishan has become the tiger Damon. He is to serve alongside her."

"I see," Nilima nodded and took a step backward, stumbling a bit.

Regret stole over Sunil's face. "Forgive me. I am sorry to bear news that causes you pain."

Ren put his arm around Nilima. "We have much to tell you."

She wiped her eyes and straightened her shoulders. "Perhaps you'd better tell me everything that has happened over the last six months. It's June already."

Ren and I couldn't believe so much time had passed. The four of us went to the Peacock room and spent all afternoon speaking of our travels. Sunil asked many questions about how we obtained the gifts for Durga and was fascinated by the Fire Realm. I sat next to Ren and didn't say much. I just listened to his warm voice as he patiently answered question after question.

Later that night I called my foster family. Nilima had been sending them cards from me, but it was good to hear their voices. Mike and Sarah had a thousand questions and stories to tell. They weren't my parents, but they too were part of what I'd come to call home and talking with them helped ease the ache of missing Kishan a little.

At sunset, Nilima brought in food, but I found I didn't have much of an appetite. Ren kept me close by wrapping his arm around me. I fell asleep cuddled on Ren's chest to the sound of the three of them quietly talking.

Waking abruptly in pitch darkness, I discovered I was lying in my bedroom upstairs. Automatically my hand shot out over the side of the mattress, searching for my tiger. He wasn't there. Sleepily, I stumbled to the sliding balcony door and opened it.

"Kishan?" I called softly. But there was no black tail hanging lazily over the swinging bench.

Reality crashed into my brain: I'd never see my black tiger again. Tears slipped down, tickling my cheeks like soft fairy wings. I closed the door and pressed my forehead against the glass. "Ren?" I whispered, but there was no response.

Staggering back to bed, I grabbed my grandmother's quilt and slid under the sheets. My hand hit fur, startling me, but I quickly realized that it was only the stuffed tiger I'd purchased in Oregon so long ago. I pulled him near, lay my head on his paws, and slept.

After a hot shower and putting on fresh clothes the next morning, I felt more human. I found Sunil at the kitchen counter, getting a lesson in how to use the microwave. A variety of breakfast items were spread across the counter.

I selected a plate of sliced fresh peaches over reheated waffles while I watched Sunil and Nilima, who was uncharacteristically flustered. She blushed often while he seemed not to mind a whit that he was in completely unfamiliar territory.

After the microwaving lesson, Sunil quickly picked up a glass and asked for another demonstration on how to get "icy cubes."

I smiled, thinking that Nilima had better watch out; Sunil was a wily one. As she showed him how to work the refrigerator, I could see he was paying more attention to her than her teaching. Stirring my mug of chocolate, I wondered how Anamika would feel about her brother courting Nilima.

After a hearty breakfast, I wandered the house and found Ren in Mr. Kadam's room, reading some notes.

Closing the book with a pop, he rose and took my hand. "Did you sleep well?" he asked.

I shrugged, not really knowing what to say. He frowned slightly and lowered his eyes.

"Do you," he swallowed, "do you want to go home? To Oregon?"

"I . . . I don't know. I'm not sure," I admitted truthfully. Ren, Kishan, and I had had such a focused goal for so long. Now that our task was completed, I felt a bit directionless.

Nodding, he kissed my cheek. "Please let me know what you decide," he said and then turned and left the room.

What was that about? I wondered.

On June twenty-fourth, one week after traveling through the vortex, I dressed with extra care and straightened my hair before heading downstairs. Nilima had left a note saying she was taking Sunil clothes shopping in town and that they were staying late to have dinner. I ate breakfast alone and then searched for Ren, but he wasn't around either.

With not much else to do, I read most of the afternoon, took a call from Mike and Sarah, and then watched a series of movies in the theater room. I made kettle corn and fondly remembered how Ren, Kishan, and I liked to watch movies eating great big bowls of the stuff.

After the film ended, I was surprised at how late it had gotten. The kitchen was dark, and Nilima and Sunil still hadn't returned.

"Well, happy birthday to me," I muttered and headed up to my room. Not even bothering to turn on the light, I slid open the glass door and stepped out onto the dark veranda. Stars twinkled in the sky, and the fountain glistened below.

It had been two years since my birthday party back at the circus. Two years since I'd met dear Mr. Kadam and had been pulled into the incredible world of the tiger's curse. I was twenty years old. *What was I supposed to do now?*

I'd fought kappa, dragons, and a kraken. I'd been bitten by a mega-shark, survived the burning of a Phoenix, dined with fairies, and killed a demon king intent on taking me for his own. I'd held limitless power, but that power was now stripped away. I rubbed my arms, but it didn't make the feeling of vulnerability lessen.

I was back in my world, a world that should be familiar, and yet it wasn't. For the first time in two years, I didn't know what to do next. The feeling was not unlike the day my parents died. That experience changed me forever, and the things I'd gone through these past two years left scars behind as well.

My throat tightened as I wondered again why Ren was avoiding me. *Does he blame me for his death? Does he wish he had been the one to stay behind? Does he feel obligated to take care of me?*

I briefly entertained the idea of heading back to Oregon without him, but I'd already done that once before. Ren and I needed to talk before I made any big decisions. We owed each other that much.

I wiped a tear from my eye and heard a door opening.

Ren stepped out onto the veranda and approached me but stopped a few feet away, leaning his elbows on the railing. He looked out at the pool and said quietly, "Happy Birthday, Kells."

"I thought you'd forgotten," I replied softly without looking at him.

"I remembered. I just wasn't sure if you wanted to celebrate."

I shrugged. "I guess not."

We stood there for a few silent moments. My pulse pounded as the seconds went by and the tension between us built. I waited for him to say something, but he wouldn't even look at me. Finally, I couldn't stand it any longer. I turned to him and asked fervently, "Why have you been avoiding me? Do you regret being the one who brought me home?"

He stood up straight and looked at me with confusion. "Is that what you think?"

"I don't know what to think. You've hardly spent more than two consecutive minutes with me since we arrived. If you don't want me here, just say so."

My eyes stung, and a fresh tear plopped onto my cheek.

Closing the gap between us, he nudged my jaw, tilting my face to look at him. His cobalt blue eyes were full of emotion. "You think that

I don't want you?" he asked, his face incredulous. "Kelsey, I want you more than I want to breathe. I just wanted to give you space. You loved Kishan. It tore you apart to leave him behind. Anyone could see that."

My fingers slid over his wrist, and I admitted, "I promised Kishan that a piece of my heart would always be his."

Ren lowered his eyes and nodded. "I understand." He stepped away from me as if to leave.

A righteous fury stole through my frame. "Alagan Dhiren Rajaram!" I yelled. "Don't you dare walk away from me!"

Taking two giant steps forward, I circled him jabbed my finger at his chest. "You don't understand anything!" I accused. "I have been in love with you for two years. If you haven't figured that out yet, then I don't know what else to tell you. I did love Kishan, but even *he* knew I was *in* love with you. Besides, you were the one who was willing to stay behind with Durga. If anyone should be feeling hesitant about our relationship, it should be me!"

Ren advanced toward me, and I swallowed, backing up until I hit the railing. Taking hold of my shoulders, he declared, "Let's get one thing straight, Miss Hayes. I was absolutely unwilling to leave you. I told Phet that I couldn't care less about protecting history or about Durga or her need for a tiger. All I wanted was to be with you. If that meant staying in the past, then I would stay in the past. If that meant coming home, then I'd come home. I would only serve Durga if you were with me. *Kelsey*, I *never* would have let you go."

"*Oh.*" My voice cracked.

Ren slid his hands up to my neck, cupping it. "Kelsey, my beautiful, stubborn girl, if you are telling me that you're ready to be with me, then you should know that I am damn sure ready to be with you."

He wiped a tear from my cheek with his thumb and studied me intently with his mesmerizing eyes, waiting for my answer.

I reached up, brushed his silky hair away from his forehead and said simply, "Ren, you're all I've ever wanted."

A smile softened his chiseled lips, and he ducked his head to kiss me. The sweet kiss sparked into a blaze that sizzled and devoured. It had been so long since we kissed that I suddenly couldn't get enough of him.

Running his hands down my back, he drew his palms slowly down my waist and over the curves of my hips, yanking me roughly against his chest. Our bodies were pressed close together but I wanted to be closer still. I wanted to be wrapped in him.

My hands gripped his waist and, growing braver, I slid them up the outside of his silk shirt. My fingers played along the length of his abdomen. Ren whispered my name, and I ran my palms up his broad chest and shoulders, around his neck, and into his hair. I wasn't sure if the groan was from him or me.

Ren slowly drew his hands up my bare arms, caressing me with his fingertips and tickling the sensitive places along my collarbone and neck. He trailed kisses along my jaw to my ear, causing goose bumps to shoot down my arms.

Moving as one, we leaned back onto the couch, and I cuddled against his chest. My hand had been captured, clutched in his, and pressed against his beating heart. His passionate kisses softened and became sweet and tender, slow, velvety, and incredibly seductive. In each gentle caress, I felt his love for me as clearly as if I could hear his thoughts. When his lips found my ear, he murmured warm endearments and promises, and I was lost in the heady experience until something that he said made me pause.

My breath caught. "What did you say?" I asked.

His expression was full of warmth and love. He smiled hesitantly. "I asked if you would be my wife," he said simply.

I looked into his cobalt blue eyes and grinned. "What would you do if I said, 'If you have to ask, then the answer is no?'"

His eyes narrowed playfully. "Then I suppose I would have to seduce a yes from you."

"In that case, my answer is definitely no."

With a determined gleam in his eyes, he trailed his lips along my jaw and murmured a few lines from my favorite play. "Now, Kells, I am a husband for your turn. Thou must be married to no man but me. I must and will have Kelsey to my wife."

Nuzzling his ear, I whispered enticingly, "Do you think me as stubborn as Katherine, Petruchio?"

He squeezed my waist. "I still haven't heard a yes from you yet. That proves you to be not only stubborn but also uncompromising," he said with a wry smile.

A few moments and some outstanding smoldering kisses later, he asked again, "Marry me, Kelsey. I want you . . ." I nodded and felt his lips smile against my neck. ". . . to be my bride."

Mm-hmm was the only sound I could produce.

"That doesn't count." Ren pulled away to take both of my hands in his.

"Kelsey Hayes, I love you. I belong with you. I have been yours, body and soul, for two years. My destiny has always been you. Be my home, *priya*. Be my wife."

He gazed at my face earnestly, and my heart stilled. The time for teasing was past. I raised his hands to my lips and kissed each of his palms.

"My heart belongs to you, Alagan Dhiren. I would be honored to be your wife."

He smiled triumphantly, and my heart leapt with joy as he scooped me into his arms. Ren's happiness swept through me until I laughed, delighting in the knowledge that I hadn't lost my tiger after all. Building a life with Ren would be an amazing journey, one perhaps even more magical than all of our quests. The future seemed at once bright and hopeful.

I twined my arms around his neck and between soft kisses he asked, "Would you . . . like . . . your birthday present now?"

"Can it wait until tomorrow?" I asked as I pressed my lips against his forehead.

He pulled me even closer, smiled, and said, "Definitely."

I laughed until he took hold of my face and brought my lips back to meet his.

33

futami rope

To say Nilima was thrilled about our engagement was an understatement, and she helped organize the wedding in her usual efficient and elegant manner.

Ren put me in charge of the guest list, which was very short, considering there weren't many people on either the bride's or groom's sides to invite.

Nilima was the one who suggested we have our wedding in Japan because the major headquarters of Rajaram Industries was located there. Mr. Kadam had made plans upon his death to bequeath the business to his young grandson, Dhiren Rajaram, with Nilima as the acting head until he finished school. Our wedding was the perfect time to introduce Ren as the new president of the company and, in a social setting, meet those who helped run the business.

Ren set the wedding date for August seventh. It was only six weeks away, but he romantically explained, "It's when the stars come together this year."

"Are you talking about the Star Festival?"

He stroked my hair and nodded. "The Sky King must have heard my wish last year."

"Which one?" I teased. "You put hundreds of wishes on that tree."

Leaning toward me, he cupped my cheek. "All of them," he said softly.

After a very thorough kiss, I commented, "If we can't arrange everything in time, how do you feel about eloping?"

Laughing, he hugged me close as Nilima bustled in, arms loaded with boxes, and leaned down to whisper in my ear, "Don't tempt me."

My foster family was flown to Japan a week before the wedding, and we both celebrated our happiness and mourned our losses together. We told them that Mr. Kadam and Kishan had died in a plane crash over the Andaman Islands a few months before. Sarah cried with me and expressed great sadness over Kishan especially, whose life had just begun. I nodded my head and felt the bitter pang in my heart whenever I thought of the golden-eyed prince.

Ren took my hand as I finished my story, and Sarah wiped her eyes and smiled at him. My brilliant diamond and sapphire ring sparkled in the light, catching her eye. Sarah gasped at its beauty. Smoothly exaggerating, Ren made up a story about negotiating with a private dealer, and I laughed as he described the gold dragon Jīnsèlóng's human form and character in great detail.

Nervously, I twisted my ring and rubbed the bare spot directly below it where Kishan's lotus shaped ruby used to sit. The night before, Ren had asked me for Kishan's ring, which I reluctantly gave to him.

Knowing what I was thinking, Ren kissed my fingers and winked as he smoothly answered Sarah's and Mike's questions.

August seventh approached quickly and late that afternoon I found myself standing in front of a full-length mirror. A beautiful woman looked back at me. My brown eyes sparkled, and I could have sworn my jeweled-slipper-covered feet weren't touching the ground.

Nilima had done an amazing job choosing my wedding dress. The tight beaded bodice cinched in my waist and was a perfect contrast to the dramatic and voluminous ball-gown skirt. I slid my hands over the ivory satin fabric and its intricate lace peek-a-boo underlay. The edges of the sweetheart neckline and dress's split were lined with cascading champagne silk roses, and floral appliqués spilled over my shoulders onto the cap sleeves. It was the most beautiful thing I'd ever seen.

Nilima fussed with my cathedral train and helped me to put on hair combs adorned with creamy pearls and champagne-colored diamonds. I slipped on a matching pair of dangling earrings next, followed by what Nilima called a traditional Indian slave bracelet. A chain of tiny pearls attached the thick, jeweled bracelet and ring set.

I'd convinced her that I didn't need the *maangtika*, a jeweled bindi hairpiece. Ren and I together had decided I would not get the traditional henna bridal tattooing because it reminded us too much of Phet's tattoo.

Nervously, I spun around and asked Sarah, "What do you think?"

She put her hand to her mouth and smiled widely. Waving her hands over her eyes so she wouldn't cry, Sarah said, "I think you look like a princess."

"That's very fitting, then," Nilima said with just a bit of smugness.

I clutched her hand and gazed at Nilima's and Sarah's satin gold-draped gowns. "You look beautiful too."

A soft knock on the door turned out to be Mike, who stepped into the room and offered his arm. Nilima handed me my bouquet. It was a gorgeous arrangement of cream and champagne roses, gardenias, sprigs of white jasmine, and buttermilk tiger lilies with little black streaks that reminded me of Ren's tiger form. The scent was heavenly. Sarah blew me a kiss as she and Nilima left to take their places.

Mike looked handsome in his father-of-the-bride garb, but he pulled at the high collar of his *sherwani* coat a bit. I patted his shoulder, flashed him a smile, and said, "Just be happy you're not wearing five hundred pounds of fabric like I am."

Grinning sheepishly, he quit fussing and pulled me into a hug. "Thank you for asking me to stand in for your father."

I felt emotion well behind my eyes and blinked rapidly. I had way too much mascara on my eyelashes to even think of crying. "You've been a great dad," I replied.

Without further ado, we stepped outside onto the smooth stone pavement of the Futami Okitama Jinja Shrine and began our long walk to the spirit gate overlooking the ocean. I hoped that somewhere my parents were able to see me marrying the man I loved.

I also thought of my other father, Mr. Kadam. I wished that he could have been with me. He would have been so proud to walk me down the aisle and give me away to Ren. As Mike walked soberly beside me, I was sure I felt Mr. Kadam's presence and joy for us.

The sunset was beautiful. Clouds had covered the sky for most of the day, but now the light hit the water, making the dark blue ocean glimmer like sparkling sapphire.

When we turned a corner, I saw the small gathering ahead: my family; Nilima, who was my bridesmaid; Sunil, who stood in as Ren's best man and whose eyes were fixed on Nilima; my old wushu partner Jennifer, who had been flown in as a surprise and who was already crying; and a handful of carefully selected employees of Rajaram Industries. I'd been sad to learn that Murphy had passed away in the six months we'd been gone.

I had sent invitations to Li and Wes, both of whom sent cards wishing me congratulations. Li still wanted a rematch with Ren when we returned to Oregon and was dating off and on but hadn't found anyone yet who appreciated game night.

Wes said he'd finally talked with his old girlfriend, and she forgave him for leaving her. She was happily married, and his mother began arranging blind dates for him with every eligible girl in Texas.

Li and Wes were good men, but they didn't make my heart pound out of control like the man waiting for me at the end of the aisle. Japanese drums beat in rhythm as I headed toward the man I was going to marry.

At that moment, Ren turned his head toward me, and my breath caught. He looked so handsome in a traditional, cream-colored silk *sherwani* coat and jeweled *mojari* slippers. His hair curled at the nape of his neck and hung appealingly over one of his eyes. As I came near, he brushed it back, away from his face, and held out his hands. His cobalt blue eyes locked onto mine, and he smiled his special lopsided smile. Everyone else seemed to disappear, and I felt as if I were in a dream.

My fingers tightened on my bouquet as I marveled that this gorgeous Indian prince, born centuries ago, would be my husband. The universe had given me an incredible gift, one more precious than fire power or the Divine Scarf. I had been given this extraordinary man to love.

I handed my bouquet to Nilima, slid my hands into Ren's, and gazed up into his eyes as we stood beneath the shrine's spirit gate. A thin Shinto priest stood on a simple wooden box next to us. He was bald and grinning, and he reminded me of Phet.

As we waited for him to begin, Ren smiled and I let out a nervous breath. The ocean breeze played with the fabric of my dress, which shifted softly, but at that moment, no power, natural or otherwise, was going to distract us from each other. His hands were warm, and I felt a slight hum of energy cycling between us.

Now I knew that our connection had always been cosmic. Ren and I had been destined to be together. He was always meant to be mine, and I was always meant to be his. Even though we no longer played the roles of the golden goddess and her tiger, our bond remained. I couldn't read Ren's thoughts, but I could sense his emotions—a twinge of nerves, sadness at the loss of his brother, and more than anything else, his overwhelming love for me and desire to make me happy.

The priest asked, "Who is responsible for this woman and gives her in marriage?"

Mike stepped forward. "I do."

"Do you accept this young man and believe he will be a proper husband to her?"

"He has given me his oath that he will care for her as we do."

The priest and Mike bowed to each other and then Mike stepped aside.

The priest began telling us about his shrine and the two rocks that jutted out of the ocean behind him. One of the rocks was much bigger than the other, and they were connected to each other by a type of rope.

"These rocks are called *Meoto Iwa*, the wedded rocks. In English, they are *Love* and *The One He Loves*. The larger rock is husband to the smaller one. He takes her to be his wife. They are joined by a *shimenawa*, an enclosed rope. This rope must be strengthened many times in the year.

"As you are entering a marriage you must also strengthen your bond to each other. When the tide is low, the rocks are not separated. But when the waves rise, only this rope attaches them. When troubles crash upon you, stand firm like these rocks and cling to each other through the bond you make this day."

Then it was time for our vows. I heard sniffling nearby, which was clearly identifiable as Jennifer, but I ignored it, hoping I'd be able to recall everything I wanted to say to Ren.

I began, "Shakespeare said that journeys end in lovers meeting. You once asked me if our story was a comedy or a tragedy. We've seen our share of tragedy, and there are empty places here today, but my heart is not empty. My heart overflows. It's warmed by your kindness, your patience, and most of all your love. You have been a steadfast companion, a supportive friend, a persistent wooer," he raised an eyebrow, and I smiled, "and you've been my warrior angel. Your love has saved me more times than I can number. I hope, in time, that I'll be able to return the favor.

"I know that each day I get to spend with you is a gift and one that I vow to treasure. I promise to always be yours. I belong with you and from this day forward I belong *to* you. If the universe had allowed me to fashion a man of my fondest desires, I would have created you."

When I was finished, Ren squeezed my hands and smiled softly.

"Is it my turn?" Ren asked the priest.

"Yes, young man, you may now speak."

In his warm voice, Ren promised, "My world was dark and bleak when you first came into my life, and at that time, you offered to me what I thought was the most precious of gifts—hope. It wasn't long before I realized I needed more from you. I asked you to love me. Not a moment has gone by in the last two years when I wasn't overwhelmed by my feelings for you.

He stretched out his hand and touched my cheek, stroking it with his thumb. "You are everything to me, Kelsey Hayes. Every moment with you shines brighter than the last."

I heard the hiss of the ocean as the sun began to sink below the horizon. The warm rays of the setting sun touched Ren's beautiful face as he softly sealed his vows with a poem.

I PROMISE

I promise to remain faithfully beside you.
I pledge to conquer faults; perfect my character.
I vow to deserve you.

I declare you're my dream, my fervent wish fulfilled.
I offer my past wealth and future promises.
I swear to keep your trust.

I commit my soul's fire and my body's force.
I profess I am forever bound to your heart.
I proclaim I am yours.

"My heart is caged no longer, *iadala*, for you have set me free. I walked a very long and lonely road to find you, and I want you to know I'd go through it all again a dozen times over as long as I knew you waited for me at the end."

My eyes filled with tears, and Ren caught one as it trickled down a lash. His warm smile filled me with happiness. I didn't think the wedding could have been more perfect. And then Ren cracked open a jewelry box.

Two strands of tiny beads wound around each other in gold and blue. Small diamond and sapphire flowers ran down the length of the chain and in the center hung a diamond lotus flower with a ruby center. I pressed trembling fingertips to my lips as I recognized Kishan's ring reworked into a new form.

Ren turned me around and then his warm fingers brushed my neck as he secured the clasp and explained, "This necklace is called a *Mangalsutra*. The tradition of a groom giving this token to his bride on their wedding day goes back centuries. In ancient times, it was a simple bracelet that indicated to invaders that this woman belonged to another and was, therefore, under a man's protection. Later, the necklace became a sign that a man and woman were committed to each other, much like an engagement ring. It's a sign of an inseparable bond between a man and his wife."

I turned back to him, and as he touched the beads along the edge, he spoke quietly, "Gold and blue tiger's eye to remember what was found." His finger trailed down to the lotus ruby in the center. "A diamond lotus and red ruby to remember what was lost." He slid two fingers up the length of the chain over the dozens of tiny blue flowers. "And sapphire flowers that symbolize what will be."

Ren took my hands and stepped closer. "Today, I give this precious token to the person most precious to me as a sign of my devotion and love. You are my *mere jaan*, my life, Kelsey Hayes."

A few thin tears trickled down my cheek, but Ren gently brushed them away, his touch as light as the breeze. Then he nodded to the priest, who said, "As these two young people have pledged their lives and love to each other, with all of you as witnesses, we will now make their union official."

He chanted in a singsong voice accompanied by the drums and pipes until the music abruptly stopped. With a toothy smile, he looked up at us and said, "This *torri* gate represents a crossing from the earthly plane into the spiritual. As you take your bride's hand and step through to the other side, you begin your new life together. Before you were two and now you will be one, forever connected with an unbreakable bond."

Confidently, Ren gripped my hands. "Are you ready?"

I leaned toward him with a smile and whispered, "What would you do if I said no?"

He ducked his head near my ear. "I have a remedy prepared should you prove to be a reluctant bride." With a playful glint in his eye, he quickly bent over and before I could mutter a word of protest, he swept me into his arms, five-hundred-pound dress and all.

Laughing softly, I brushed his hair from his eyes and wrapped my arms around his neck while our audience cheered.

"Can I kiss you now?" he asked.

"I think you'd better, tiger," I replied.

With a lingering kiss, Ren carried me through the torri gate and spun us in a circle to the accompaniment of enthusiastic Japanese musicians. He set me down and slid his hands down my arms. He was about to whisper something else when Sunil slapped him on the back, and well wishers surrounded us.

After animated congratulations from our family and friends and taking a few pictures before the sun was completely gone, Nilima bustled about, getting everyone moving along to the reception.

Ren kissed me thoroughly until I protested, "You're ruining my makeup."

He narrowed his eyes playfully. "That sounds like a challenge."

I lifted my voluminous skirt and darted toward the waiting limousine. Over my shoulder I called out, "You'll have to catch me first, tiger! Perhaps you'd rather be chasing monkeys."

I squealed when I heard a growl right behind me and was suddenly lifted off my feet. After he bundled me into the limo, Ren pressed his cheek to mine.

"I've caught your scent, Mrs. Rajaram, and you'll never escape my clutches again."

"I sincerely hope not." I giggled as Ren swept me into a passionate kiss that, despite my protests about my hair and makeup, didn't end until we were halfway to the reception.

"I started off with a tiger and ended up with a husband," I said as Ren wrapped me in his arms.

He kissed my nose. "And I started off with nothing and ended up with everything. I love you, Kelsey Hayes Rajaram."

I smiled, loving every syllable of those three little words.

rising generation

Ren drove the McLaren roadster, my birthday present from Mr. Kadam, along the tree-lined road to the pretty South Salem duplex we had lived in so many months ago. Ren had shipped the car and bought up a significant amount of property in the surrounding forested hills with the intention of building us a home on what we both thought of as our mountain. We were finally starting our new life together, and in some ways, returning to our old one in Oregon.

Hopping out of the car in the driveway, I smiled, enjoying the pine and rain scent I loved so much. I'd just pulled a bag from the backseat when Ren nudged it off my shoulder and scooped me into his arms.

"You weren't going to deny me the opportunity to carry you over the threshold, were you?" Ren said, kissing me softly.

I stroked the hair at the nape of his neck and grinned. "Despite what you think, I'm not in the habit of denying your requests."

"I think you may be in denial about your denials, Mrs. Rajaram."

As Ren strode to the front door of our duplex, he listed all the things I'd denied in the time we'd known each other, stopping only when I pressed my lips against his.

He murmured finally, "I like the way you change the subject. Feel free to stop all our disagreements in the same fashion."

I laughed and wrapped my arms around his neck. "I'll keep that in mind. You know, you really don't have to carry me. Your super-strength is gone now, and I don't want to be the cause of my husband's back problems."

He narrowed his eyes playfully. "There is nothing wrong with my back, *hridaya patni*, and though I may not have the strength of a tiger any longer, I still have the ability to seize willful women who cross my path."

"Is that a threat or a promise?"

"Yes."

Ren unlocked the door, stepped inside, and kicked it closed. Then he proceeded to make good on his promise. I protested briefly that our bags were still outside but his fingers had already unwound my braids and after another minute I no longer cared about our bags.

We broke apart when the doorbell rang. Outside on the front steps stood a mail carrier with a package.

"Can I help you?" Ren asked.

"Delivery for you, sir," the man said and handed off the package.

With a nod and a smile of farewell, Ren closed the door and tore open the mysterious package. Inside it lay a heavy, wooden box.

"What is it?" I asked.

"I'm not sure," Ren said as he clicked open the lock. He lifted the polished lid to reveal a scroll perfectly encased in glass.

"It's the Scroll of Wisdom," I whispered. "The ocean teacher said we weren't to read it until after the fifth sacrifice had been made. How did it get here?"

"I don't know. I thought it was in the safe."

I picked up the packaging. "Ren, there's no shipping label."

We made eye contact and I jumped up and ran to the front door, throwing it wide. The postal worker was walking slowly down the hill.

"Wait!" I shouted.

Ren and I ran outside, coming to an abrupt halt as the man stopped and turned. The courier smiled. Then he pressed his hands together and inclined his head. The air swirled around him, and his hat vanished to show a balding head and a crown of wiry gray hair. His blue uniform and boots transformed into a roughly woven wrap and sandals.

I gasped and took a step forward. "Phet?" I asked earnestly.

The man smiled. A tear slipped down his cheek, and the magic that swirled around him intensified, obscuring him from view.

"Phet!" I reached for him, but his body faded until he was gone completely.

Once again, my mind reeled. If that was Phet and he had come all this way to give us a message, I definitely wanted to know what was so important.

"I didn't imagine it, did I? That was Phet, wasn't it?" I asked, already walking back up the driveway to the house.

"Yes," Ren confirmed, trailing along behind me.

Even though he stopped by the car to retrieve my grandmother's quilt and our bags, he quickly caught up to me at the front door, and we both rushed back into the house, straight to the Scroll.

The glass tube seemed to have been blown around the document inside. There was no way to open it.

"I'll have to break it," Ren said. "Stand back a little."

I moved back a step or two as he gripped the cylinder. There was a snap and the tinkling of broken glass, and then Ren had the Scroll in his hand. A heavy wax insignia sealed it shut.

Ren trailed his fingers over the imprint. "It's my family seal—the house of Rajaram . . ." he said excitedly.

Carefully, Ren broke the seal and spread the ancient pages on the kitchen counter. The sheets of thick Sanskrit-covered parchment quickly began to yellow around the edges.

I smoothed the paper flat for Ren as he ran his fingertip lightly over the words.

"Kelsey, this is a letter from *Kishan*."

"What does it say?" I asked anxiously.

Ren and Kelsey,

I apologize for corresponding in such a dramatic fashion, but I couldn't risk either of you reading this before certain events had been set into motion, and I wanted to dispel any worries either of you might retain over my decision to stay in the past.

After you left, Anamika and I spent many years serving people of different countries. We built a home high in the clouds on the rocky slope of Mount Kailash and used the power of Durga's gifts to supply food, clothing, and healing all over the world.

Our home was considered sacred ground for many world religions, and pilgrimages were made to the mountain base to worship the goddess Durga. The peoples of Asia thrived under her hands. She inspired artists, poets, political reform, religion, and social harmony.

Anamika and I formed a bond of friendship and respect that led to love. I am proud to have served as her companion, and I am blessed that she agreed to be my wife. We have had a very long and happy life, and it would have been wrong for me to leave you thinking that I was miserable or disappointed with the choice I made. It took me some time to learn to live without you, Kelsey, and I'll admit that there were many times I cursed my decision to stay behind, but destiny treated me well, and I have a family and a life that has enriched me and made me a better man.

Kelsey, there is still a piece of my heart that belongs to you. I have cherished it all these centuries. You were the angel who saved me from a life squandered, and your influence has impacted me in more ways than you know. The warmth, kindness, and love you offered when you decided to save two lost tigers changed the course of my life. A happy ending was promised, and a happy ending was delivered. Every single day my heart swells with gratitude for you.

Ren, forgive me for my jealous, impetuous youth. Whatever good I have done in the world, whatever strides I have made as a man, it was because I was able to look to my brother for an example. For what it's worth, you would have made a great king.

If there is one regret that I have, it's that I wish

I could pass through the long centuries with you. I miss you both, but I know that your lives will be full and rich, for I have glimpsed what is to come. Forgive my interference, but it was something I needed to do. The question that has often plagued my mind have been answered.

He's yours, brother.

May your love for each other continue to grow, and may you find joy in the life you build together. Treasure your time with your family for the days pass quickly.

Perhaps in another time and another place we will meet again.

—Kishan

I dashed tears away from my eyes. "It was a letter from him all along. If only we'd opened it."

Ren covered my hand with his. "If we had, the course of all our lives would have changed. Destiny has been fulfilled the way it was supposed to have been."

I nodded, overcome with emotion. Ren wrapped his arms around me, and I buried my face in his chest and thought of the brother we'd left behind.

"Ren?" I mumbled against his shirt. "What did Kishan mean when he said, 'He's yours'?"

Hesitating briefly, Ren sighed and pressed a kiss in my hair. "When

Lokesh took you from the yacht, Kishan and I went looking for you. Do you remember?"

I nodded. "You were on your motorcycles."

"Yes. On our way to rescue you, Kishan told me that he'd had a vision of you with a little baby."

"It was his vision from the Grove of Dreams," I said softly.

"What he didn't tell you was that he lied to you about seeing the baby's eyes. In his vision, your son had golden eyes. He also heard you say his name. You called him Anik Kishan Rajaram."

I softly gasped. "Kishan . . . he must have thought that the baby was his."

"He did. When he agreed to stay behind, he believed the golden-eyed baby would never be born."

"So then his message—"

"His message means that the father of the golden-eyed baby, the man he saw with you in the Grove of Dreams, was me." Ren pressed his forehead against mine. "All this time I believed that I had stolen his rightful place. That his destiny was to be with you, when really the baby was always mine. *You* were always meant to be mine."

"He never told me," I whispered sadly. "Why didn't he tell me?"

Ren lifted his head. "He wanted you to choose, Kelsey. He wanted the decision to be yours."

After a pause, doubt filled Ren's eyes. "Do you regret it, Kelsey? Choosing me?"

I placed my palms on both sides of his face and willed him to looked at me. "Never. Alagan Dhiren Rajaram, I will never regret choosing you. But—"

"But?" he whispered.

"But every day I regret leaving Kishan behind. He's always in my thoughts."

"He's in mine too," Ren confessed. "Kishan sacrificed himself so I could have what I always wanted. At least now we know he found a measure of happiness."

We held each other for a long time until I asked, "And speaking of happiness, how long do you think it will take Sunil to catch Nilima?"

Ren smiled. "It could be a while."

"She is a bit stubborn," I conceded.

"Stubbornness runs in the family." Ren laughed when I punched him in the arm, and his eyes sparkled with a familiar gleam. With a squeal I took off running while Ren grabbed my quilt and wrapped it around me.

He kissed me thoroughly and with me on his lap, we sank into our favorite chair.

"You can't escape my clutches, Mrs. Rajaram," he said brusquely.

I put my arms around his neck and drew him closer, his lips right next to mine. "And I'll never want to," I whispered confident in my choice.

I knew then that my future had always been Ren.

Destiny chose me . . .

To *befriend* him . . .

To *save* him . . .

To *love* him.

And I would spend the rest of my life doing just that.

ACKNOWLEDGMENTS

Finishing a book is an exhilarating sensation. I imagine it's similar to the feeling of reaching a mountain peak or finishing a marathon—utter exhaustion meets a deep sense of satisfaction. Occasionally, I look back at my writing journey, marvel at just how far I've come, and wonder how on earth I did it.

But, I also remember that I didn't climb that mountain alone. I had companions in this marathon. My family has always been a source of strength. My brothers and sisters and their respective spouses are dauntless in their support and encouragement.

In creating *Tiger's Destiny*, I'd like to especially thank my youngest brother Jared for patiently going through all my battle scenes. He acts out each one which is so important in getting it just right and he makes me laugh when my life gets too tense.

I'm also deeply grateful for his wife, Suki, who manages all my give-aways and contests. She's always available and shows great patience with me when teaching me how to better my social media skills. Thanks to my sister, Tonnie, for taking on the juggernaut that is my fan mail so that I have more time to write.

Mom and Dad, you two are the best. This past year my mom has painted, glued, strung, sewed, glittered, and dyed more things than I could ever wear or give away. She is amazing and I'm always in awe of her talents. My dad organizes all my personal trips. It's so nice to be able to say, "Dad, I need a hotel in Timbuktu," and he's off and running.

Special thanks to Alex Glass, my agent who helped make my dream of being an author possible and to Raffi Kryszek who has made the optioning of my books a thrilling roller-coaster ride.

At the publishing house, Sterling, I'd like to thank Judi Powers, Katie Connors, Meaghan Finnerty, Katrina Damkoehler, Mary Hern, Fred Pagan, and especially my editor, Cindy Loh.

I believe I've been remiss in forgetting to thank Cliff Nielson who designed my brilliant covers. He does an amazing job!

Sudha Seshadri has been a wonderful guide and adviser on all things India. She's been with me through the whole series and is always ready to lend an expert hand when I need it.

I'd also like to express my appreciation for my fans. You guys are all amazing! You send me poetry, art, gifts, and special notes that make my day. You also tweet, blog, like, friend, and follow me everywhere with many of you interacting with me on a daily basis. You're all lovely and a delight to meet online and at my events. I send good wishes out to you every day and heart your homemade T-shirts. Your support means the world to me.

Lastly, I'd like to thank my husband, Brad, who sees the best and the worst of me. Tigers have pretty much taken over his life but he enjoys every minute. It's wonderful to have such a good man at my side—one that walks with me through this journey and helps me over the rough spots. I couldn't ask for a better companion.

the tiger saga

Find out how it all began . . .

book 1

book 2

book 3

Visit
www.tigerscursebook.com
www.hodder.co.uk
for the latest news, trailers and exclusive material.

HODDER

The best books live on in your head long after they are finished. As you read, you are turning the pages faster and faster to find out what happens next, only to feel bereft when you reach the end.

If that is how you feel now, you might like to join us at www.hodder.co.uk, or follow us on Twitter @hodderbooks, and be part of our community of people who love the very best of books and reading.

Whether you want to find out more about this book, or a particular author, watch trailers and interviews, have the chance to win early limited editions, or simply browse our expert readers' selection of the very best books, we think you'll find what you're looking for.

And if you don't, that's the place to tell us what's missing.

We love what we do, and we'd love you to be part of it.

www.hodder.co.uk

@hodderbooks

HodderBooks

HodderBooks